Phoenicia Rogerson has no discernible sense of direction so it's only natural that she'd get lost in books. When she's not reading, writing, or spinning in circles, she can be found knitting copious amounts of socks and throwing herself in freezing water. Originally from Cornwall, she now finds herself in London, where she's aiming for the highest possible bookshelf to floor space ratio.

Aphrodite is her second novel. She is a winner of the Somerset Maugham Award 2024 for her debut, *Herc*.

HQ

@HQStories

Hardback 9780008589905 £16.99 | Trade Paperback 9780008589899
eBook 9780008589912 | Audio 9780008589929
For publicity enquiries: HQPressOffice@harpercollins.co.uk
Australia: jo.munroe@harpercollins.com.au
New Zealand: sandra.noakes@harpercollins.co.nz

UNCORRECTED PROOF COPY NOT FOR SALE OR QUOTATION

'A rollicking ride through Greek mythology, *Herc* tells the story of the famous hero through his impact on the people around him. By turns quippy, hilarious, and shocking, *Herc* will make you want to hide in a jar like King Eurystheus, dodging all your responsibilities to read it from cover to cover.'
Luna McNamara, author of *Psyche and Eros*

'A brilliant, witty, and unique retelling of the myths that at times had me laughing out loud. Rogerson's impressive talent leaps from the pages.'
Carly Reagon, author of *The Toll House*

'A wonderfully layered piece of storytelling which manages to be earthy, haunting, and beautiful all at once.'
Stacey Thomas, author of *The Revels*

'Funny, action-packed, violent, tragic . . . this is the story of Hercules as you've never experienced it before! An eye-opening treat.'
A.J. Elwood, author of *The Cottingley Cuckoo*

APHRODITE

PHOENICIA ROGERSON

ONE PLACE. MANY STORIES

HQ
An imprint of HarperCollins*Publishers* Ltd
1 London Bridge Street
London SE1 9GF

www.harpercollins.co.uk

HarperCollins*Publishers*
Macken House, 39/40 Mayor Street Upper,
Dublin 1, D01 C9W8, Ireland

This edition 2025

1
First published in Great Britain by
HQ, an imprint of HarperCollins*Publishers* Ltd 2025

Hardback ISBN: 9780008589905
Trade Paperback ISBN: 9780008589899

This book is set in 10.6/15.5 pt. Caslon by Type-it AS, Norway

Printed and bound in the UK using 100% Renewable
Electricity by CPI Group (UK) Ltd

FSC
www.fsc.org
MIX
Paper
FSC™ C007454

For more information visit: www.harpercollins.co.uk/green

For Luke

Author's Note I

A quick note on names in this book: there are a lot of them.

There are lists of names. There are family trees. There is a chapter that is *only* names. (I'm not sorry.)

Maybe I'm out of control, like a particularly nerdy Godzilla on a rampage, but my publishers have been very obliging, and I love the names. They show where stories land in this massive world of Greek mythology I get to write in, how interconnected everything is, and how no hero, god, or anything in between existed in a vacuum.

What they're not is a test. I'm not going to pop out at you when you turn a page and start quizzing you on who's related to whom. You don't need to remember every name and passing mention in the book. You don't even need to remember most of them – even I have pages of references to go back to. The important characters will come back.

So my advice to you, before you get started, is that all reading is optional. If the trees and names delight you, then spend all the time you want on them, and if they don't, feel free to skim. Enjoy the book how you want to, not how you think I want you to.

But that's enough from me, it's time to meet someone even more opinionated.

Say hello to Aphrodite.

THE TIME BEFORE

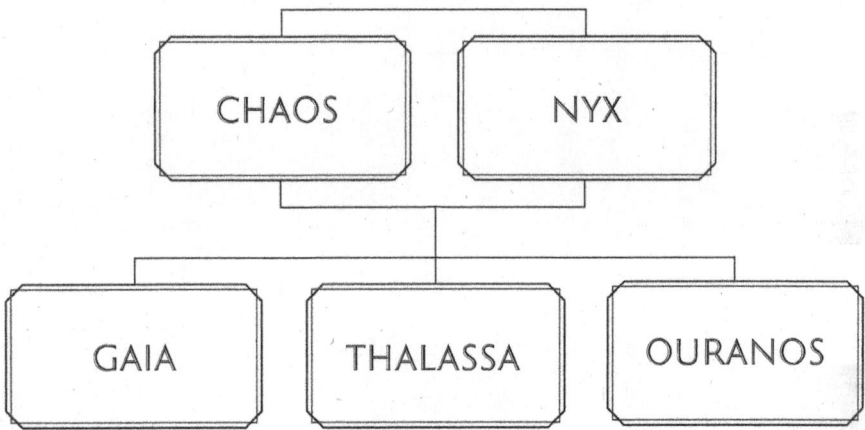

```
        ┌─────────────────────────┐
        │                         │
   ┌────────────┐         ┌────────────┐
   │   CHAOS    │         │    NYX     │
   └────────────┘         └────────────┘
        │                         │
        └────────────┬────────────┘
                     │
   ┌─────────────┬───┴────┬─────────────┐
┌────────┐   ┌────────────┐   ┌────────────┐
│  GAIA  │   │  THALASSA  │   │  OURANOS   │
└────────┘   └────────────┘   └────────────┘
```

Aphrodite I

I'm a liar, to begin with.

Well, if I'm being exceedingly honest with you – and I am *trying* – I was nothing at all, to begin with. Then I was my father's testicles. Then the weaver of Fate itself, which is when the lying started. After that, it all got a bit complicated.

I was the daughter of Ouranos. The daughter of Zeus. The daughter of no one at all. A winner, a loser, though never much in between. The world standard of beauty and a crone, both. Olympus' very own it-girl. Maybe the worst wife in all of history. A lover, a friend, a co-conspirator. A snitch. Selfless – once or twice. A bitch – more than twice. A monster, a villain, a victim – if you must. A good mother, a bad mother, a *really* bad mother. Lonely and famous and beloved and alone. Precious and worthless. A rival, a cheat. Afraid, often, and terrifying, also often. Oh, and I started a war. That's very important.

The goddess Aphrodite. I was that too. I don't think I am anymore.

Look, it's all very knotted. Maybe I should start from the beginning.

First, there was Chaos, which meant something different then to what it does now. The time of Chaos was empty. It was a blank canvas for the optimists and an endless sinkhole for the pessimists. It was a time of absolutely nothing. I suppose I was nothing then, but we all were, so I won't hold that against her.

Chaos was empty, until she met Nyx. I like to think that the two of them were in love, but I've never met my grandmothers, so I can't say for certain. The two of them created the earth and the seas and the sky, and they had three children to gift them to.

Their daughters received the sea and the earth, and they were happy with them.

Their son wasn't, as is the way of youngest children. He wanted to be the king of a world consisting of only five people, so they let him.

My father, given the world like a toy so he'd play nicely with his sisters. I suspect he was spoiled rotten, but then I quite like being spoiled, myself. And he did ask, before he took. He spoke with such conviction about the glittering future he would bring, the life he would spread across this world, that they believed him.

Ouranos became the first king of this world. He took his sister to be his wife and he made good on his promises. Together – let's not give him all the credit; he didn't carry their children – they filled the world with life. They brought forth the Titans, beings more powerful than even they were, who could control the elements around them more easily than breathing. And they brought forth the Cyclopes, and the Hecatonchires – the hundred-handed ones – who Gaia loved and who did not ask for power, only a life, which meant Ouranos did not respect them. He thought them irrelevant to the world, because they didn't demand to own it. They lived between the oceans and created beautiful wonders with all the energy they saved from fighting.

I don't know how many children they had together. It doesn't matter. All that really matters is it was one child too many.

It's always the youngest son who has the most to prove.

Their youngest was a Titan, Cronus. He wanted to be king too, only Ouranos wasn't like his mothers. He didn't want to give up what was his.

Cronus asked for power; his father said no. Cronus did not ask a second time.

So the world came to know a new word: war.

It didn't last long, that first war. It couldn't. All the Titans could be counted on fingers and toes.

Cronus armed himself. He went to the Cyclopes and asked for their support. He promised them positions in his new order, new lives beneath the sun instead of deep below the sea. He told them he would respect them as their father never did. And he let their conversation be heard just enough to build fear in his father.

It's a bold strategy, to tell your enemy that you're coming, but it works well with the men in my family. They're so afraid of it, it eats away at them, into their very bones, and they forget that they're anything other than the position they hold.

Ouranos ordered the Cyclopes sent to Tartarus, a prison in the underworld he'd had to create personally, because one had never been needed before.

(It's a problem when you're an immortal fighting other immortals. You have to be careful about who you piss off because there's no getting rid of them. They'll be there, hating you. Forever.)

How Cronus himself escaped being tied up in proto-damnation is beyond me, but he did. I suspect his mother helped. He promised her – how they promise! – he would free her sons, bring them to the power they deserved. When Cronus was king, everyone would live equally in a utopia, just below him.

He had his people behind him. He had his shining vision for the future. He had the weapons and the belief. It was only a matter of time.

He followed his father across the land, over the oceans, waited for the perfect storm to be whipping around them, for winds too loud for words – I know that for certain. I made my entrance soon enough.

I think it's unlikely they'd have had much to chat about, anyway. When you get to weapons at dawn, what do you say?

I want power!

No, me!

No, me!

They were both armed, but Cronus' reach was longer. That's been true of every new generation I've seen, that they're just a little bigger than their parents, trying to prove they're better in the most pointless of ways.

Cronus carried a sickle. I don't know what my father's weapon was. He lost.

There was no point in aiming to kill. There never has been, for us. Instead, Cronus thought of the worst shame he could possibly imagine, and he castrated his father.

Chopped his balls off.

De-testicled him.

I've heard every possible variation of the phrase, some with great solemnity and some with a snigger, and I've never been able to explain why I'm not laughing.

I can tell *you* now, though.

Those balls were me.

I grew from them. I was born from them. They were me and I am them and that will always be the truth. *That* is my beginning.

I made my debut at the end of the first great war, in a storm unlike any other, as the world turned itself upside down trying to find its way in the new order. All of this is true, yet my birth is reduced to a punchline.

I hid it for so long, not wanting my entire existence to be reduced to one man's shame, but I'm over that now. I'm much more famous than him, after all.

I've always wondered *how* Cronus managed to castrate him so neatly. It was *only* my father's testicles that made me – call my knowing that feminine intuition, if you want – but Cronus used a *sickle*.

How? Were they hanging so low? Was Ouranos' stance so wide because he needed the world to see his mighty balls? What possible physical arrangement leads to one man being able to castrate another with a weapon made for cutting wheat?

Cronus would have had to practise, but he can't have. Surely he had better things to do in the war, and I've *met* some of his generals. I can't imagine them offering themselves up for the chop.

That one is a mystery for the ages, I'm afraid, but it doesn't matter, because now I'm here. That's it. All of the relevant history before I arrived. Done.

Cronus lifted his arms in mighty victory and bellowed so that all around him could cheer and crown him the new king of everything. Like his father, he went home and married his sister, ready to fill the world with people who looked just like him.

Ouranos, newly ball-less, gave an anguished cry.

'You think yourself so smart, so powerful, but one day you will be just like me, dethroned by your own children.'

Cronus looked at his father's crotch. 'I will never be *just* like you, will I?'

He ordered Ouranos tied and bound in Tartarus, that prison of his own making, never to be seen again.[1]

So distracted were they by their respective shouting that the testicles fell into the ocean, instantly swallowed by the swells of the waves, pulled down into utter blackness, presumed lost.

Wrong.

---

[1] For a certain value of never. We are immortals, after all. —A

Chaos & Nyx I

Now that was a good hit.

That's our son you're talking about.

Hey, it was our grandson doing the hitting. Can't I be proud of him? He used to hit like a girl.

You're a girl.

I am Chaos personified.

Also a girl.

So are you.

I'm not cheering that our grandson castrated our son.

Things were getting a bit boring around here.

And you think castration is the answer?

You want Ouranos to win the war then? And everything will stay the same?

I didn't say that.
Wait.
Do you see that?

I don't see anything. How do you see anything? You're darkness itself.

I look properly.
Over there, see? The girl. She wasn't there before.

Isn't that where Cronus dropped Ouranos' balls?

She's drowning, Chaos.

We throw her a line, then.

Too obvious. We don't want the boys to know we're still here.

How about a thread?

. . .

. . .

. . .

You threw her the threads of Fate?

They're all I had to hand! What do you think?

Well, things aren't going to be boring around here anymore.

THE AGE OF THE TITANS

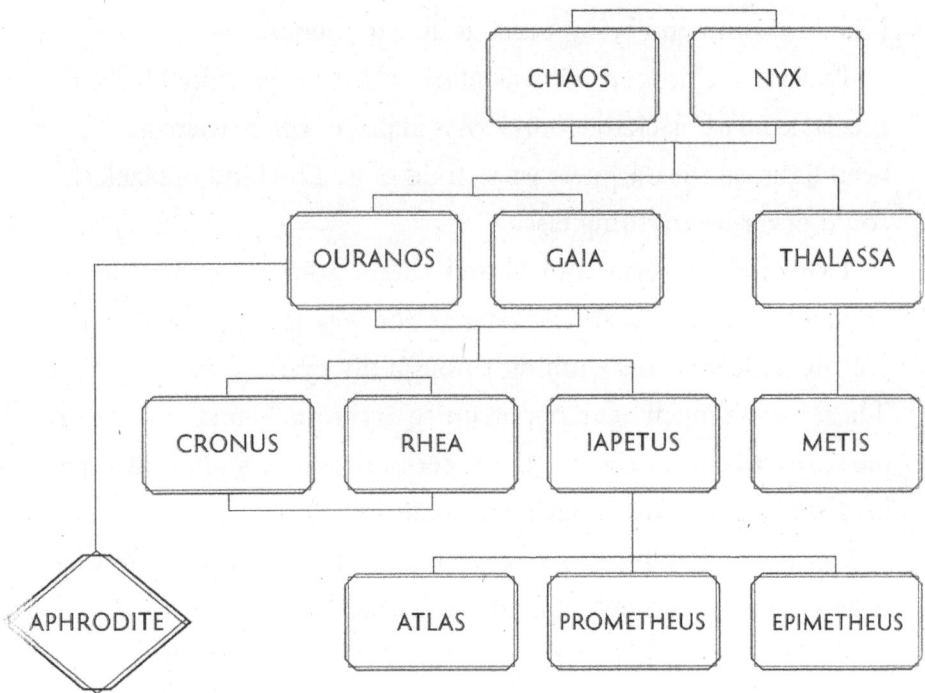

```
                    ┌─────────────┬─────────────┐
                    │    CHAOS    │     NYX     │
                    └─────────────┴─────────────┘
                           │
          ┌────────────────┴──────────────────────────┐
   ┌──────────┬──────────┐                    ┌─────────────┐
   │ OURANOS  │   GAIA   │                    │  THALASSA   │
   └──────────┴──────────┘                    └─────────────┘
        │                                            │
   ┌────┴─────────────────────┬──────────────┐       │
┌────────┬──────────┐  ┌──────────┐   ┌──────────┐
│ CRONUS │   RHEA   │  │ IAPETUS  │   │  METIS   │
└────────┴──────────┘  └──────────┘   └──────────┘
   │                        │
◇ APHRODITE ◇      ┌────────┼──────────────┐
              ┌────────┐ ┌────────────┐ ┌────────────┐
              │  ATLAS │ │ PROMETHEUS │ │ EPIMETHEUS │
              └────────┘ └────────────┘ └────────────┘
```

Aphrodite II

I don't recommend being born, as an experience.

Everything around me was black. Rich black, inky black, the special kind of black that only exists in places where there has *never* been light, so the darkness isn't afraid of it. The kind of black that could never be anything else.

I opened my eyes and closed them, something within me demanding that this should change the way things were. I could see the delicate veins running through my eyelids, and only that. There wasn't much of an opportunity to ruminate on the nature of darkness, eyelids, or veins, the sheer pointlessness of all of them, because I opened my mouth to scream.

Opening my mouth is where the real trouble began – and has been the cause of much of my trouble ever since.

The moment I parted my lips, water began to flood in. It came and it came, relentlessly battering me from every side, from *inside*. Even though my lungs are functionally useless – I'm immortal; I don't need to do anything so quotidian as *breathe* – they filled with water, and you don't need to know a lot about this world to know that is wrong.

I don't know why I, or the Titans, or the gods, have lungs or livers or kidneys or any of the above. They can't be doing anything vital, because nothing is vital for any of us. Maybe the lungs are there to let us talk, but no king, no creator, at any point in the process, has ever seemed happy that anyone was talking, so their existence remains a mystery. One I wasn't concerned with at the point of my *drowning*.

I learned what I was through the suffering of bringing myself into being. I had lungs, I knew, because they were screaming. I had eyes that stung from the salt in the water, as though they were some incurable wound in me to be sanitised over and over again, I had hair pulled by the seaweed already entangled in it, and a throat, already raw from crying out, which let more water in and brought me right back to my lungs again.

Arms. I had those, and they didn't hurt, not yet, and so I flailed them, trying to bring me closer to the surface or the bottom, I didn't mind which. I needed change. That was my first want: the incurable, unstoppable need for change. To be anywhere but here.

And then.

Magic.

A golden thread appeared in front of me. It glowed. Softly, in truth, but that far into the water that had never known any light at all? That thread was lightning, a crack ripping the world in two. I reached out and grabbed it, wrapped it round my wrists, though I barely needed to. It tangled around me, and I tangled around it, more and more and more, until I couldn't tell you where I ended and it began. Then – only then – I pulled. It pulled. *We* pulled.

I've never moved so fast. The threads were gathering more and more speed, ripping me through the oceans, through the waves that were cresting and crashing in the wake of that most terrible storm, tearing me out of the water too fast to see the sun or the stars or the sky, leaving me lying on the sand, the last of the water turning to air on my skin, suddenly so cold that I wrapped myself tighter into the threads to protect me. Even then, my threads felt *right*, like this was coming home.

So there you have it: my birth. Not some beautiful, organised, orchestrated thing where my modesty – as much modesty as I've ever possessed – was protected by hair artfully flowing in the wind, but an unceremonious dumping on the shore. There was sand trapped under my breasts and behind my testicles.

And I was blinking, blinking so much, as my eyes tried to establish what they were meant to do with all this *light*.

Not an auspicious start, I'll admit, but don't worry. My first birth wasn't my last. I got better at them.

That first day, week, month, I slept. I lay splayed across the ground, half tangled, half free, probably drooling given how unattractive the rest of it was. When I woke up, the threads weren't just wrapped around me anymore. They'd taken over the cave I was sheltering in, crisscrossing and interweaving until I could barely see the walls underneath them, so thick across the entrance it seemed impenetrable, like the very idea of a world outside was something I'd dreamed up. I did rather a lot of blinking that day too, as I tried to piece together what was true, and walking around, touching things. I like to touch.

It was big, as caves go, deep enough you couldn't see through the darkness if you stood at the front. There was a kink in it, not a full corner but enough to divide the place in half, to give the feel of more space than there was. And stalactites and stalagmites – there were thousands of those. Some were huge, wider than my waist, older than any other part of the world felt, but most were tiny. Brittle. Reaching desperately for their counterpart. I ran my fingers over each one, marvelling at them. I didn't break any, but I revelled in the knowledge that I could. From the beginning, this place was mine, and nothing could hurt me here.

But that only lasted me a day. I needed *more*.

The mouth of the cave was blocked by water, the sea that had so recently tried to *kill me*. For me, that water created a barrier stronger than even the gates of Tartarus.[2] It didn't even cross my mind that I might try to pass it – as far as I was concerned, this cave was my world. It was safe here, but safe has never been enough for me.

Those first few weeks, when everything hurt so much, I'd walk up to the threads and run my hand down the wall they had created, gently at first but growing bolder with every passing day. I wanted them to make a noise, to harmonise with the waves behind them or the sounds of my feet against sand in front, but they refused. They stayed perennially, maddeningly silent, and I grew bolder, treating them with less care and more anger every day as they refused to give me any of the answers I wanted.

Where was this? Why was I here? Who was I?

'What am I meant to do now?'

The threads still didn't respond, and my patience reached the end of its span. I pulled the threads in one sheath from the entrance to the cave. They resisted, but I am stubborn, and so both they and I went tumbling to the floor.

'How do you like that?'

They said nothing. Threads don't talk, not even to me.

That wasn't good enough. They were my only company, so they had to give me *something*. I made them my own. I've learned since

---

2   The underworld's underworld, where only the worst mortal souls can go, and in the centre of it is a prison where immortal kings stash their predecessors. The gates present a remarkably weak barrier, all things considered. —A

those days – in a lesson too painful to describe right here, involving my arch-nemesis and more wine than was strictly sensible – that what I did shouldn't be described as weaving.

I didn't have a loom or a needle or a comb, but I had two arms and ten fingers and more stalactites and stalagmites than a forest has trees, and I put them all to good use. I started slowly, with the worst offenders wrapped tight around my limbs, and I coaxed them from my skin, whispering, singing sometimes, to encourage them off without tearing into me.

I wasn't always successful at this, truth be told, and the sand of that cave dripped red with my blood more than once before I got the hang of this whole being alive situation.

I wrapped the threads around my arms at first, until they grew long enough to be looped around the rock formations. When they met each other and pulled together, I didn't fight them. I thought if I was nice to them, they might be nice to me.

It must have been months before I had anything but tangles and knots, as thread turned into cloth, and longer still before the change happened, but time is not a resource immortals struggle with, and I was in no rush back then. I'd been relaxed when I caught a glimpse of something forming in the gold, a snatch of the utter blackness that I'd only seen deep in the sea.

Naturally, I put my threads down that day and didn't touch them again for weeks, afraid the darkness would grow out of them and come back for me. Laugh all you want, but I've lived through a lot of things, and none were so terrifying as not understanding what was going on around me, being caught in a world where things happened *to* me and never *because of* me. So yes, I was afraid of water and the dark and even my own shadow. Even the threads that saved my life.

They didn't like that. The threads crept up on me in my sleep, wrapped themselves closer and closer, until I woke with a mouth full of them. I didn't get a choice in the matter.

I had to go back to weaving, darkness be damned.

I whispered that to myself so much the words lost all meaning, and I found myself giggling as I clutched onto the things that were binding me there. Whisper, giggle, whisper, giggle.

The darkness grew. It grew and grew and grew, and my fingers began to shake as I moved them, but the darkness was the lesser fear, smaller than drowning, choking on what I did not yet know was the future, and so I let the darkness grow beneath my fingers, grow and grow and grow, until it split apart, into something else entirely.

I saw the creation of our world in that fabric I made. I saw Chaos and Nyx come together, primordial forces without real form, but I *saw* them. The threads of Fate have never been so helpful as to make clear, moving pictures, but they gave impressions, and I could read their meaning as well as if it was being acted out in front of me.

After that, the threads didn't have to compel me to weave them. I was hooked.

I saw their children gain forms and kingdoms and powers. I saw Ouranos stand for what he wanted – only saw; there were no words to be found in the images I received, but I've always found body language to be much more honest – I saw his union with Gaia and their children. But I saw so much more than that.

I saw a time before the cave I sat in existed, before there was rock beneath my feet and a sky above my head. I saw the first swell of waters in our world, the mighty oceans swallowing it, taking vastly more than the land could hold on to.

I saw *life*. Not humans, not thinking mortals, not yet, but life all the same. Deer and bears and birds and *fish*. Magical things, fish, that can live under that water, that pressure all the time, and flash every colour I could dream off and then far more than that. I saw the plants grow and grow and grow without seasons yet to tame them. I saw the sun and the moon hang together in the sky, watching but unmoving without anyone to drive them. I saw the night before there were stars, because there was no one yet to mourn, no one who could only be explained by casting them bright enough for everyone to see.

Is it any wonder I became addicted to beauty? I was drenched in it, every moment of every day. I grew to resent sleep, resent night, resent the weakness of my own fingers, because I could not bear to stop weaving, to stop seeing all of this incredible wonder burst into life beneath my fingers like it was me – *me*, the wretched rag doll born already dying – creating all of it. For a while, I could believe that, that this cave *was* the world, and I was the god of it all, and once I could believe it, I had to have it. Power, if you like, or influence. Creation. That feeling you get as it all comes together under your fingertips, better than it was before. The first world I lived in was moulded by my hands and my hands only. Anything else would be a demotion.

That fantasy lasted me through all of history – a shorter story back then – without ever seeing myself. My shadow did not cast in that external world – I didn't belong *in* the threads, but in front of them – so I didn't realise these pictures that had me so enraptured were the tales of my own hated birth.

I saw only wonder, magic, endless possibility unfolding, and I didn't think I needed to be part of it, because what the world could show me was so much better than anything I could think to do with it.

So I held on to my fantasy. I left the world well enough alone.

The world did not extend me the same courtesy.

I'm irresistible.

LOST

Trophy of war, most likely appearing in the state of two testicles. Last seen above the oceans of Cyprus.

Infinitely aged and all-knowing, with a history of violent behaviour. Approach with care.

If sighted, contact Cronus immediately.

Atlas I

'What's this, then?' I said when I saw that message Cronus put out.

'Our esteemed leader is trying to recover his father's testicles,' Prometheus said.

He's my brother, but he's an annoying bloody know-it-all, is what Prometheus is. He can never answer a question without using the longest words he can think of.

'I got that. I can read, you know.'

'I didn't doubt it for a second. You did ask, however.'

'What does he want with someone's old balls, is what I meant.'

'They're a physical demonstration of his domination of his father.'

'Ain't all this that?' I meant Mount Othrys, where we were living. Best place on Earth, looking out over the mountains and plains and sea and all that. It had been barren and all, when we arrived, but now it was covered thick in plants. Rhea did most of that. It's the way it goes. Girls get the plants and the men go and fight.

'One might think.'

'Still gonna look though,' I said.

'Indubitably.'

See what I mean about the words? Indubitably. Who says that? Cronus was our king. I shouldn't've been going around questioning why he wanted what he wanted. Way I saw it, he could ask for whatever, as long as he kept passing the good stuff on, and I'd bet he had a prize in mind for this.

'Where're you going to look then?' I asked. Prometheus thought different to the rest of us. Right useful sometimes.

'I thought I might ask Cronus for his best recollection of the location of the event, then create a diagram of the tidal movements on the date it happened and follow those through to the most statistically likely location.'

'How're you doing that? You weren't even alive then.'

'I am going to use my words, Atlas.'

'I'm not fucking stupid.'

'I never said you were.'

Then he walked away before I could deck him. I decided right then and there I was going to beat him and be the one to find the balls.

I didn't need charts or diagrams or *words* to be better than him. I did ask Cronus where the fight was, though – that was a good shout, to be fair.

Decided not to bother with trawling the bottom of the sea or any of that. Figured if they were down there then one of them water people would get there first. Nah, I went to where the fight was and started hitting up all the land round that way. Problem was, I didn't know what I was looking for. Years-old balls and all that. They must've meant something, or Cronus wouldn't've been into finding them. They must've been something special.

Easy then. I'd look for special.

Not so easy, it turned out. First place I checked, nothing.

Second, nothing.

Third, nothing.

And fourth and fifth and sixth and all. I must've been looking for months, till way past everyone else was done with it and had moved on to other things, but the signs stayed up. Cronus still wanted them and that was good enough for me.

The way I figured, the balls'd be close to the water's edge – they float, but it's not like they can get up and walk off – so I'm checking out the caves, and I got to this cave. It looked like the usual, with the rocks and the damp, right up till someone chucked a rock at my head.

'What the *fuck*?' I said. *Then*, fucking *then*, it ignored me. 'Who are you?'

Nothing.

'How dare you throw a rock at me? Do you know who I am?'

Still nothing. That was enough nothing for me. I took my own rock – bigger – and went after it. I could take it. I was Cronus' general, after all.

I couldn't see it for shit, but I heard its feet go and that was enough. It was small, easy enough to knock down and hold it there.

'Who are you?'

'Fate.' Eventually. It said it like a whisper. Scared and all. Like it was some hard thing to say its name when a name is just a name.

'What the fuck does that mean?'

'It doesn't mean anything.'

'Then why didn't you want to tell me?'

It started to fight. Not strong, but squirmy, like some fish under me. It threw me off into some pile of string wrapped across the rocks.

'*Fuck*.' It shocked me. I hadn't felt nothing like that before. It ran right through from where it touched me all the way across to the other side of me. 'What was that?'

'Fate.' Quiet again, but louder this time.

'What does that even *mean*?' I shouted, and when the thing didn't answer, I went in properly. I don't like things I don't understand. I took it by the neck and held it against the wall of the cave, tight, until it answered me. 'What are those things? You can start with that.'

'They're threads.'

'I know that.'

'Then I don't know what you're asking of me.'

Fuck me, it sounded like Prometheus. 'Why did they shock me?'

'I don't know. They don't shock me.'

'Do you know anything?'

It was getting limper under my hand, not struggling so much, but that didn't mean anything. It waited before, but then it came back at me. That wasn't happening again. I kept my hold of it.

'I know—' Its voice broke off in bits and pieces, right up till the sound stopped coming out. Might've been a trap. 'I know you're looking for testicles.'

'How'd you know that?'

'It's in the threads.'

'Bullshit.' They were just strings. They might've been biting, angry strings, but they were just strings.

'The king wants them.'

'Everyone's talking about it on Othrys. You don't need some bloody magic strings to know that.'

It coughed. The cough sounded like *threads*. 'You're trying to beat your brother.'

'Everyone's trying to beat their brother. It's what brothers are for.'

'He's going to win.'

'No.'

And it pissed me off, all right? It pissed me off going and talking about things like that when it had no idea what I was talking about, and I hit its head against the rocks and then it stopped talking at all. Knocked right out. I went and dragged it out to the front so I could get a good look at it.

It looked like a woman, one of the Titanides, right up until I got to the crotch – then I had no clue. It had one of everything. The hair was gold and the eyes were blue. It didn't have any weapons I could see but I held it down anyway.

'What's the bloody point of you?' I shouted, but it didn't wake up. Useless.

I went back to Othrys. My brother was there.

'How goes the hunt?' he said, smiling. I hated that smile. He did it when he thought I was being thick. 'Did you find anything of interest today?'

'I found a woman.'

That stopped him.

'A woman? What happened?'

'Threatened her, didn't I?'

'For what cause?'

'See if she had anything useful to tell me.'

'And?'

'Useless. Talked some bullshit about magic threads but nothing good.'

'Where did this take place, exactly?'

Aphrodite III

As far as introductions to the world go, it wasn't everything a little Fate could dream of.

I was held down and asked questions that made no sense to me, and when my answers made no sense to him, he choked me. At the time I, idiotically, thought if I could have given him the answers he wanted, it would have protected me, and my neck would never have known the purples and greens it was mottled with after that first meeting.

There wasn't a lot I could do as a Fate, but answers I could handle.

I may have got a little obsessive about him after that.

I hadn't realised before that each thread corresponded to a single person, that it followed their tale. Before then, I didn't have much of a concept of other people as individuals. They were all parts of this grand story I was watching: characters, figures, moving parts, not *people*.

That realisation changed a lot.

Before, I'd only been keeping up with what had happened, trailing behind. It was sheer luck that I'd picked up on Cronus' great ball hunt. Realising I could pick and choose which threads to follow, which were truly necessary for this tapestry I was creating, gave me time and space to look around.

I had the whole world at my fingertips, and I used it to stalk the man who choked me. Heroic stuff, truly.

I followed him home and I saw him talk to his brother, his father. I saw him bow and worry and exclaim, and in *days*, I stopped being afraid of him. He was stronger than me, sure, but he wasn't the biggest or the strongest, and if I bothered being afraid of everything bigger and stronger than me, I'd hardly have a chance to breathe.

There are some benefits to seeing people who don't know you're looking.

And I learned that wouldn't be the end of it. If that idiot could find me, then others could too. I could prepare for that. I made my defences. More rocks, more threads, looping across the mouth of my cave, not enough to trip me, but enough to slow anyone who came my way.

If my threads shocked Atlas enough to get him off me, then I hoped they would work on everyone else. I was right about that, at least.

I waited in the darkness as my next visitor approached, his footsteps growing louder as they moved through the waves, and when he came too close, I grabbed the threads in my arms and threw them on top of him. They did just as I wanted. They knocked him out.

Not for too long. Just enough for me to tie his arms and legs together – over his clothes, I wanted answers, not pain – and stand over him with my biggest, sharpest stalagmite.

Fate binds us, after all.

'Who are you?' I said, the moment he opened his eyes. It was my turn to make demands. It's been my turn for a while now.

'I am Prometheus.'

26

'What does that mean?' My name was my title, was my being. I assumed that was the same for everyone else. *Prometheus*. I didn't know the word.

He frowned, just gently, the centre of his forehead creasing, but he banished it so fast it could have been a fleeting shadow. 'Forethought.'

'How can you be in charge of all forethought?'

'It is merely a name.'

'Explain.'

'My parents chose it for me shortly after my birth. They thought it might suit and encourage me. Did your parents not choose your name the same way?'

I had options here. Options are good, but options are hard. Especially when you have someone waiting in front of you and you're only just learning how quickly time can move.

Unusually for me, I went for the honest answer. I had much to learn.

'I don't have parents.'

'Do you have a name?'

'I'm asking the questions.' I raised my big stalagmite at him again. Splinters came off it and into my hands, smearing red down my arms. 'What are you doing here?'

'I hoped to meet you.'

I looked down. He looked down. 'Why?'

'My brother said some strange things about you.'

'Your brother?'

'Atlas. He said he met you.'

My neck was still bruised. It stared at me from my reflection in the water, mocking that others could override my decisions about *my* body. I could see the entire world, but I didn't have control over myself, which is not to excuse what I did next. In truth, I didn't think before I drove the stalagmite into Prometheus' shoulder.

'Ow,' he said. Just like that. Flat. Bemused. No shouting, no threats. I didn't know what to do with that. 'He hurt you then?' he asked.

'No.'

'Those bruises are reminiscent of his handiwork.'

'Are you here to hurt me too?'

'*No.*'

'Then why?'

'I've met all the Titans. We don't get on very well. I was hoping you would be different.' On later meetings, Prometheus would describe this approach to my nascent insanity as *radical honesty*. I've never found honesty to be much use, but it worked for him. 'How about I sit on this side of the trap, and you can stay where you are, and we just talk?'

'I don't understand.'

'Aren't you bored in here?'

If I were to hate him for only one thing, and really I hate him for half as many reasons as I loved him, it would be for introducing me to the concept. Boredom. From then on, just from knowing it could afflict me, it drove into me like a splinter, growing and breaking off until it felt like daggers spreading through my blood.

I wasn't the only one.

'You are. Bored,' I said.

He tilted his head. I interested him. That was good. Interesting is good. 'That's right.'

'You want something only I can give you. I want something in return.'

'Only a fool would agree before hearing the terms.'

'Your brother. He doesn't come back. You stop him, and I'll talk to you.'

'Atlas is a hard man to stop.'

I turned my back on him. I didn't need him – I really believed that. I'd lived alone my entire life, and I began my retreat into the shadows.

'Fine,' he said. 'I'll find a way to stop him.'

'Now. Do it now.'

He never told me what he did to his brother, what promises or threats were exchanged to keep me safe, and I didn't really care. Atlas never came back, and Prometheus did. We talked. *He* talked mostly, at the beginning, telling me about the creation of the world – which I knew, but I didn't tell him that – and his life among the Titans. About his other brother, Epimetheus,[3] who spoke without thinking.

'Whereas you think without speaking?' I asked.

'Something like that.'

He was trying to impress me; I know that now. He brought me food: roasted meats, and sweets and wine, as if he were the host and this weren't my home. It wasn't a seduction in the way people think about it now, but it was a seduction nonetheless.

Prometheus moved slowly. He was careful in all things, and I was no different. In the end, I started talking too.

'How do you do it?' I asked.

'Do what?'

'Get here. Conquer the sea.'

'I don't conquer the sea; I move through it.'

---

[3]   Meaning "afterthought", which feels like a fuck you from his parents from the out. —A

'No, *the sea*. It wouldn't let you move through it. It's out there to kill you. You must dominate it. How?'

'I don't—'

'I need you to destroy the sea, Prometheus.'

He laughed, then, a true laugh, where he threw his head back and left his neck bare so that someone could easily grab it. I could see all his teeth, even the wonky one at the back. He was acting without thinking. It was beautiful, and I hated it.

'You're laughing at me.'

'I'm sorry,' he said, and just like that, the laugh dropped and the serious expression was back, layered thick across his face, until I wondered if I'd really been seeing him at all. 'What did the sea do to you?'

'It tried to kill me.'

'The sea isn't a thinking being. It cannot *try* to do anything.'

My eyes widened. I scuttled back without thinking, ducking behind the rocks and holding tight to them. 'That's *worse*. If I can't talk to it, then there's no reasoning. It could come for me at any time.'

'It won't.'

He was so confident it annoyed me, so out came the entire story of my birth, of drowning, of pain, of being cold and ugly and afraid.

'You are beautiful,' he said, the first of many times. 'And strong. And *immortal*. The sea will not hurt you.'

'You can't know that.'

'No,' he said, still carefully. 'But no one can know the future.'

I could, I realised. I was different from him. I couldn't control the elements or the animals or perform any of the magic the Titans could do, but I could always *look*. I might not understand *now* all that well, but I could see *then*.

'Please leave.' He looked bemused, upset almost. I was always forgetting how fragile real people and their feelings were. I was still learning how to manipulate people, but I was learning, so I softened myself. For him. 'I need to think.'

He bowed to me. Success. 'I will see you next week, then, if you are amenable?'

'Wait, before you go.' He'd given me a gift whether he meant to or not. I wanted to return the favour.

He wasn't allowed into the back, where I kept the real threads. Just because he was nice to me didn't mean I'd immediately give up the only bargaining chip I had, aside from being *interesting*. I found his thread – I knew his thread, returned to it near as often as I checked where his brother was – and I pulled it, not just using the trails that already lay before me, but pulled, dragging it through my hands, out of wherever it came from, until I had more than *now*, I had *later*.

It wasn't as clear as everything that had already happened; the images blurred around the edges, some of the figures unsure. If I took the time, I thought, wove it properly, I could improve that, but I found enough to give him his gift.

I went back to him.

'The king is giving up on anyone finding his trophy. He'll be angry when he does. You should avoid him that day.'

'I know what I'm doing.'

'You're not going to find it.'

'I think I already have,' he said, and then that *dick*, that absolute *shit*, used my own move against me and turned and walked away, straight into the water so I could see him slowly sink under the surface – toes, knees, shoulders, head – where he knew I couldn't follow.

'What does that *mean*?' I shouted.

31

He knew how to be interesting too, how to keep me on a cliff-hanger so I'd want to speak to him again, and it worked. On the days I knew he was coming, I loosened my traps. I let him in.

It was a long week that I waited for him. I spent most of it with my threads – not something new for me, but this was more frantic than it had been, trying to find myself in the tapestry, as though I'd just been *hiding* from Fate all along. I thought if I could find myself, I could know I was safe; I could know that I mattered, to him, the world, to anyone, but it was all for nothing. I didn't have a thread. As far as the future was concerned, I didn't exist. All I have ever wanted is to exist.

As far as Prometheus considered it, I'd cheated.

'How did you do that?' he demanded. It must have really got to him too, because his hair was fluffy and ruffled, like he'd been dragging his hands back and forth through it. I hadn't realised I knew him well enough to notice that.

'Do what?'

'About Cronus. How did you know?'

'I saw it.'

'You live in a cave. Did he come here?'

'No, I *saw* it.'

'That is impossible.' He said it kindly, the same way he tried to explain to me that the sea wasn't out to kill me, like it was me and not him who was misinformed but it was okay, because I couldn't be expected to know any better.

'Let me show you.'

And so I took him to see my threads, not because I trusted him, but because he was being patronising and I wanted to be right. Which I was, though he couldn't see that. For him, there was no past, present, or future in the threads. There were just threads, which led him to think I was getting confused and seeing things that weren't there and I'd just come to a lucky guess before.

'Perhaps you have a good read on people, and you extrapolated it from my stories,' he mused.

'Or perhaps I can see the future.'

'That would imply the future is set in stone, that we cannot mould or bend our own fates. It is *impossible*.'

'What do you mean *your* fate? Fate doesn't belong to you.'

'Who does it belong to, then?' Back to being patient, like a teacher, coaxing me to the right answer on my own, though he should have known by then that the two of us were never going to reach the same conclusion, even with the same information.

'Me.'

'That doesn't make any sense.'

'Why not? Because I don't deserve any of it? Because I wasn't born from the earth like the rest of you?'

'Because it's the damned *future* . . . And, on that note, you very much need a name.'

'So you can tell me off with it?'

'Yes! How can I efficiently argue with you without a name?'

'By accepting that I'm right?'

It was a good diversion, choosing a name. It took us the rest of the day, what with my wanting something that sounded nice and him wanting something with some profound meaning, in case it should ever become relevant to me, proving that nominative determinism does at least apply in the case of people called *Prometheus*.

'Weren't you the one on about not limiting your options?' I said.

'I was.'

'So why do you want to limit mine?'

You probably know what we decided on. I am very famous, after all. A name so old that the language was already being forgotten. I liked that.

'Aphrodite,' he said. 'It suits you.'

And, because being right suits me too, I told him to keep an eye on Cronus. He was looking for a wife.

'I do not believe I'm his type.'

'Do you trust him, Prometheus?'

I have no idea when or how we crossed the barrier from being strangers who were deeply, deeply suspicious of one another to being friends who were deeply, deeply suspicious of one another. There was no stand-out moment. Every day where Atlas didn't show up to choke me helped. Every story Prometheus told me about life on Othrys helped. My perilously low bar for friendship helped. Every joke and smile helped, or maybe none of it helped and the whole thing came from stubbornness on both our parts, but something shifted, and then I was there, asking who he trusted.

'Why?'

'That's a no, then.'

'Aphrodite—' said like he was testing it.

I grinned. I was a *person* now. I was more than just *Fate*. 'Cronus won't be the king forever—' I said.

'Nothing is forever.'

'Let me finish, Prometheus. He's not going to be king forever, but he's going to do some monstrous things to hold on to his power.'

'Such as?'

I would have told him earlier. I meant to, but it was so ridiculous I assumed I'd read something wrong. I went back to it, over and over, but the answer never changed.

'I think he's going to eat his children.'

Metis I

There were fewer than twenty people living on Mount Othrys, and more than three thousand in the oceans, which implies osmosis brought me to the mountain, where I manoeuvred directly to the king and kneeled before him, kissing his hand as he held it out to me.

'My king, my uncle—' I said.

'Yes, yes, thank you, my niece,' Cronus said. 'I am marvellous.'

'I have come to serve, if you will have me.'

'One of Oceanus'[4] lot, are you?' he said, pulling me up to get a good look at me. There was nothing so obvious about my siblings and myself that we could be so easily attributed to our parents with just a glance, but the numbers were in Cronus' favour.

'I am indeed.'

'Thought you all preferred the water?'

'Not all Oceanides are the same as each other.'

'Quite right,' he said. 'Now, if you want to help, that's all well and jolly, but what are you good at?'

'What am I *good* at?'

'Yes. Running, fighting? Swimming, I suppose.'

---

[4]   One of Cronus' brothers. Lived in the oceans. Never did much of note, apart from siring an improbable number of children. —A

Swimming has never been my greatest strength, in truth. Compared to my siblings, I moved through the water slowly, more octopus than dolphin. I *could* change my shape, become something other: a bird, a beast, a bug, but I did not share that with the king of the Titans. It did not seem prudent.

'I give good advice,' I told him.

'Do you now? Well, that might just be the handiest thing of all.'

'Might it be?'

Cronus became the king during wartime. All of his councillors, his right-hand men – how many men can be fit on someone's right-hand side, honestly – were his generals. They were loyal fighters, but you merely had to take one glance at Atlas to know that giving *wise counsel* was not his greatest strength.

He did have Prometheus, but he did not like Prometheus. They did not mesh as personalities. On Othrys, there was space for me to be more than another Oceanide.

'I wish to marry,' he told me, quite cheerfully.

'Oh, I—'

'Not you.' He was harsher then, a burr found in the ointment. 'One of the earth-born.' That's what they called themselves, those who are now known as the Titans. Earth-born, therefore entitled to lead the planet that was two-thirds water.

'Rhea could be a good choice,' I suggested.

'Why is that?'

1. Rhea was a lot like their mother, who had supported him through the war.
2. Rhea had no interest in fighting because she preferred the ground itself to the conversations above it.
3. Rhea was not a threat to him.

'Because you have already decided on it and you only ask me as a test to see if I am here to procure more power for myself or to actually help you.'

He gave a great laugh and patted me on the back. 'Right you are again. You will make a fine addition to my council.'

He married Rhea shortly after, which was the beginning of the end for him.

He did not struggle to impregnate her, a fact that was vaunted as some extraordinary demonstration of his own good leadership. Perhaps to be expected from a man who seized power through the means of castration.

It was only while she was pregnant that Cronus realised he was the one to depose his father, and that perhaps filling the world with smaller versions of himself would not be the wisest course of action.

'You let me do this,' he said to me. 'Why did you let me do this?'

'If I recall correctly,' I said carefully, 'you were already set on this plan before I arrived. I assumed you had considered it then.'

'Well, yes, obviously I *considered* it.'

'These things do not *have* to follow the same cycles,[5] if you are willing to distribute power evenly among your children—'

'What? No. It's mine.'

'Cronus—'

'It doesn't matter what I do. They're going to overthrow me. My father laid a curse upon me to that effect.'

I am unconvinced that curses are real, any more than the bias they create that causes a person to re-evaluate their version of events until it fits within the parameters of the aforementioned unreliable

---

[5]   My experience of both history and Fate implies they do. I'm working on it. —A

source. That said, I was convinced that *Cronus* believed it, and it does not do to call kings paranoid, even when they are so.

'Such things can be unreliable. We know the future is not set in stone.'

He harrumphed at that, but did not bother to argue further with me about the matter. He had committed himself to the terrible idea that the future is a thing that happens to us, not because of us, and – in the same process of thought – he had decided to change it.

He did not discuss this with his wife.

He waited until the child was born. The Titans celebrated the new generation with great enthusiasm. They clapped and cheered as he led his wife, newborn in arms, into the centre of events.

'Hello, one and all,' he announced. 'I am your king.'

More applause.

'This is our child. Rhea, hold up the child—' This was duly done, to yet more applause. 'You might think that the child is our future.' Pause for effect. 'You are wrong. My wife carries a traitor.'

The gasps broke out immediately.

'But do not worry, my dear citizens, I will do everything I must to keep us safe from the traitor. Rhea, pass me the baby.'

'Her name is Hestia,' she muttered.

'The baby, Rhea. Pass me the baby.'

She may have been crying – it was unclear to me – but Rhea passed him the baby. If I had to wager, I would say that she was no longer *entirely* loyal to her husband.

This was confirmed when Cronus dislocated his jaw, placed the baby in his mouth and, with a gulp of wine to encourage movement, swallowed her whole.

It was horrible. Everyone saw. It was assumed that that would be the end of it.

The king rediscovered his joy in life after that. He had a solution to his only problem. There was no reason for him to stop impregnating his wife.

It happened four more times.

The whispers began on the second child.

(Rhea named her Demeter.)

The questions began on the third.

(Hera.)

The fourth child made him wonder.

(Hades.)

For lack of a better word, siring a son without fathering him made Cronus *broody*.

He brought animals into Othrys and began to train them. He ordered towers and palaces built. He asked Rhea to plant a garden with him, and he was honestly perplexed when the plants died. He wanted his name carved on all things, and he wanted his own hands to be part of creating them.

He called Prometheus and me to see him.

'I want more,' he said. Gone was the jovial king I had first met, who happily took counsel from any who walked into his realm. His arms were crossed in front of him. His leg bounced on the floor in an uneven but unrelenting pace. His stomach was distended, his face drawn and tired.

The king had become grotesque in his suffering, but he wanted more.

'More?' Prometheus and I enquired, together. We looked at one another, uncomfortable with the similarity.

'More. I want to make something.'

'The palace is well underway—' Prometheus said.

'And the gardens,' I added. We had asked his mother to work

on the gardens, rather than his unhappy wife. It was progressing better for that.

'No. Not plants. Not buildings. I want a legacy. People.'

'More Titans?' I asked, with the minimum suspicion I could manage.

'No. Don't be stupid. Something lesser. Something that can appreciate our wonder.'

Thus, because the king could not bear to let his children love him, the first race of man was born. They did not bear so much resemblance to the later stages. He bade Prometheus make them from only the finest materials, and so the first men were made of gold.

'Only men?' I questioned.

'Cronus does not want them reproducing,' Prometheus said. He too fought to keep the suspicion out of his voice. I did it better.

'And that is all women are good for.' I'd had such hope, when I arrived on Othrys, about all this space there was for me, but the longer I stayed, the smaller that space became. Soon I would be reduced to only the threat of what might come from my womb.

Yet, Prometheus could be trusted when *he* was able to breathe life into gold.

'In Cronus' mind,' he said, the barest edge of future betrayal in his voice. I looked to him. 'But all things change.'

'As they should.'

'Indeed.'

We were some way off becoming co-conspirators, but that was the beginning.

The men of gold did help. They lived among us, happy and healthy and well-fed, with all of the luxuries that we ourselves experienced. They did not lack for anything. Even our attentions were lavished upon them with the wonder that is novelty.

Those men did not grow old. They did not fight or war. When their time had come – for all things, even gold, must decay – they simply lay down to sleep, so Prometheus could take back the gold and breathe new life into it.[6]

'They're a template,' I realised. 'For how you think the Titans should behave.'

'I have said no such thing.' Prometheus replied.

It lengthened the time between the fourth and fifth children of Cronus and Rhea, created a long tail on the timeline, but the men were too happy, too quiet, to distract Cronus forever, and soon enough, their fifth child came.

With him, we spoke of rebellion.

(Poseidon.)

All too soon, their sixth child was born. When he arrived, we spoke no longer. It was time to act.

(Zeus.)

---

[6] Oddly enough, he couldn't reuse all parts of them. When the men of gold died, an ethereal version of their form would sink from their body, through the ground, all the way to the underworld. Because of that, the Titans expanded the underworld past the prison at its core and declared it the resting place for mortal souls. —A

Aphrodite IV

There was a time when I knew *everything*, about everyone, and it didn't matter whether I could hear the words they were saying or not, because I saw everything they did and that matters so much more.

When it was just the Titans, I could handle it. I could follow everything and still make time to look ahead. Prometheus gave me the context I didn't have already, and everything was so interconnected that to understand one part of it, I had to know it all.

The creation of the first age of man put an end to that.

Mankind then wasn't like mankind now. They were made of gold, and while I'll argue until the end of the next great civilisation that you don't have to be what you were born to be, gold *is* special. Not because it shines and glistens or any of that – anything will shine under the right circumstances – but because it resists. The men of gold were brilliant. They resisted. They were honest.

They didn't have time to be anything but honest. They were the first introduction we had to time, really, let alone the idea that it might run out, that there might come a day where someone we loved wasn't there anymore, or, in the more hopeful variant of the same thought, that there might come a time when someone we hated wasn't there anymore.

I dreamed happily of Atlas' death.

I had nightmares about Prometheus'. I weaved their threads regardless.

I didn't have scissors. I don't know who introduced scissors to Fate – it feels like it must have been Zeus, but I've got no good reason for this other than my general dislike of the man, and you don't have to be Athena to know that's a bad reason to blame someone for anything – but they weren't there for me. I didn't have to cut anything.

Fate, for those first mortal men, was gold too, like the lines of the Titans, of Ouranos and Gaia and Chaos and Nyx before them. Their threads looked the same and so I thought they were the same, even as they eroded in my hands, right up until one of them whittled down to nothing and I choked, thinking I had, with my own clumsy fingers – stupid thought; I have *very* talented fingers – destroyed the balance of this entire world.

Inevitably, this was how Prometheus found me.

'Has Atlas been back?'

'No.'

'You're crying.'

'I cry a lot.' True. Over the sea and the nightmares and the threads and the world that refused to let me be part of it.

'You cry for a reason. What is this one?'

I didn't want to tell him it was the threads, since his belief in what they could do was fictional, at best, but he was there and there was no logical explanation for *why* I was crying that wouldn't cause him undue panic, so I held the thread out to him.

'It broke.'

'I may need additional explanation.'

'They've never broken before.'

'Never?'

'Never.'

'What does that signify to you?' He was trying. Bless him, he was trying to understand me the same way I was trying to understand him, and the both of us were trying, trying, trying, all the time, even though we got on best when neither of us was trying at all.

'Each thread is a being.'

'The threads are being?'

'No. They represent someone. Show their life.'

'How?'

'It'll be easier if I show you,' I said, pulling up his thread. 'Look, this is yours.'

He must have believed me at least a little; he jerked away from me as though I was on fire. You don't do that when you think it's all make-believe.

'I don't understand,' I said. 'You told me it doesn't make any sense.'

'It doesn't. The future can't be set in stone.'

'It's not, it's in the threads – look!' I waved them at him; he moved further from me, until he was half-hidden by a rock.

'I don't want to.'

'Why not?'

'Because what if it is true, Frodi?' A new name for me, shorter, to show he cared, though in that moment it felt like he was using it to manage me, to stop me from getting irrational and overemotional. 'What if it is true, and nothing any of us does will have any impact? I cannot live that way; it will only bring misery.'

I looked at the threads in my hands and at the walls of the cave behind me.

'This is my life.'

'You're more than this.' It was an incredible compliment in the words of it, one of the better ones I've received, but not said that way, with one corner of his lip turned down and the other one up, and the furrow not in the cute place in his brow like when he laughed, but sinking lower towards his nose, closing around his eyes like he couldn't bear the sight of me.

'You think I only bring misery.'

'I did *not* say that.'

'But you do. Either you don't believe me or you think I'll make you miserable. Which is it?'

'You were telling me what happens when the thread finds its end.'

'You're trying to distract me. Don't do that. Tell me.'

'I don't think this conversation will be productive,' he said, and he left.

If you're looking for a reason, for me, for all of this, if anything anyone does can be boiled down to a single reason, a single moment, then this is mine. That was the moment I decided to leave.

I wouldn't wait forever for my friend. I wouldn't have conversations on his terms and *only* his terms. I wouldn't be left behind feeling useless and disgusting at the same time. I wouldn't see the world without being able to touch it.

I didn't believe anyone's choices could change anything, but I needed to make them anyway.

When he came back, he apologised. Not particularly effusively – my Prom didn't *do* effusive – but he apologised and he told me I was right. I liked that better.

'You were right about him eating his children. I believe you, about what you can do, but it feels so wrong that it should be possible. All this power you have, it scares me.'

'I'm stuck here. No one needs to be scared of me.'

'How do I go about talking to you when you can always inform me that my predictions are wrong?'

'I won't do that.'

'I tell other people that they're incorrect all the time.'

'Prometheus – Prom.' I leaned over and took his hand in mine, and I stood on the very tips of my toes so I could reach up and kiss him on the top of his head. His hair smelled like the sea. 'That sounds like a you problem.'

He laughed, then, so hard I worried I'd broken something. There was panting and wheezing and folding in half and standing up again and then going right on back to folding in half.

'And you'll just have to get over yourself because I'm not willing to lose you.' I was lying, with all that confidence, but it felt amazing to make him laugh, see him change his mind because I was strong enough to make him.

'I suppose that's that, then.'

'You suppose right. Now, will you stop being such a scaredy-cat and come see how great this can be?'

The best way to tell a lie, as any good liar knows, is to convince yourself of it, and I'd needed that, after his last visit. I'd spent hours and hours with the threads, not weaving so much as looking, until I could convince myself they were no terrible thing, that the end of a life didn't negate everything that happened before.

In convincing myself that their end wasn't my end, I accidentally fell in love with all of humanity, in their very earliest edition. For them, everything was new. Even as they got towards the ends of their lives, their threads growing weaker and duller, the sky remained a miracle, the plants a wonder, let alone each other. They didn't have to worry or want for anything, that golden generation of man, so they revelled in this world.

46

I thought it was beautiful when I was discovering it, but it was nothing compared to what happened through their eyes.

They flirted and they danced and they swam in all the water they could see. Prometheus thought he could cure my fear of the oceans with logic and reasoning, but nothing did quite as much as seeing these frail mortals throw themselves in for nothing but a joke.

They could do no wrong, to me, not even when they lied and cheated – how soon they developed dice, so they could play better games among themselves – their stories wove together in more ways than I or the Titans ever could have imagined, and I was transfixed.

I got lucky. My best friend was too.

Prometheus found them ingenious. He saw them develop, create new technologies, out-think what we'd ascribed to them, and so our conversations became more. Neither of us appreciated what the other did, but it didn't matter because we loved exactly the same thing.

'See how they dance—'

'They have designed rope!'

'And inventing their own stories—'

'And a pulley system!'

Hours and hours, I watched; days and days, Prometheus came to me with new tales of what they'd been up to, until I thought he must spend more time with me than he did with the rest of the world, until one day we lay side by side on the floor of my cave and Prometheus let out one deep breath, as though that were the stopper of all the thoughts he was afraid of having.

'What do you think of Cronus?'

'He made the best thing in the world,' I said.

'He ate his children.'

'That sounds like what *you* think of Cronus.'

'You didn't see it.'

'I did.' And I wouldn't waver on this, not when he adamantly refused to let me view his Fate so I might guide him to the best side of it.

'Not in person, not the way that I did.'

He described it in his best attempt at vivid language, trying to impress the horrors of the act on me, even though I'd watched it live. I saw Rhea cry. I saw the way she held herself after she and Cronus lay together, as though she wanted a child more desperately than anything else in the world, even though that scared her more than anything else too. I saw the way she brought herself close to her husband's stomach while she slept and whispered into it, quietly, lest she wake him up.

I saw more than Prometheus ever did.

'Cronus did a terrible thing,' I said.

'Is doing.'

'Sorry?'

'You stated that he *did* a terrible thing, implying that it is over. It is not over. He has done it five times and he will do it again if we are not careful.'

'He's created so much life.'

'This tyranny is just the beginning of it. Metis says—'

'Metis?'

'A friend.'

'A friend you're conspiring with?'

'A *friend*, Frodi. And a wise one. She says this indicates worse behaviour in the future.'

'And you listen to her more than you listen to your friend who can tell the actual future? You, who value logic above all things, prefer vague predictions to surety?'

'I prefer someone who's *there*. Someone who understands what is happening, who knows what it is to fear the very real threat of being cast out by the king instead of spending her days questioning whether the ocean is coming for her tonight.'

'You haven't drowned.'

'Nor have you.'

'Nearly.'

'Nearly drowning is not the same as actually drowning.'

'It feels like it.'

'Nobody is threatening to *eat* you.'

I knew how ridiculous I was being; I could feel it all the way to my bones, and if I could feel it then Prometheus could too. If I tried, I could probably pull out of it, be reasonable, but I didn't want to be reasonable. My heart was beating too fast for that.

'You stay here then. If your life is so hard, I'll take it,' I said.

'So that you can support the *dictator*?'

'So I can live, Prom. So I can love the life you hate.'

'So you can leave the world in the exact disastrous state it's in? No thank you.'

'You're going to fight him, then?'

'Don't look at my future, Aphrodite.'

A Domestic Scene Among Swallowed Siblings in their Father's Stomach

Hestia: Isn't it exciting? Our new sibling should be here any time now.

Demeter: There's not enough space.

Hestia: We'll make space, won't we? They'll only be little.

Demeter: Do you think it'll be a girl? I want a girl to be my friend.

Poseidon: It's going to be a boy and he's going to be *my* friend.

Hera: It has to be a boy. He's going to be my husband.

Hades: He's going to be *my* friend and we'll go on adventures and he'll teach me—

Hestia: No matter what they are, they'll be one of us, and we'll all love them, and—

[Enter a rock, pursued by wine.[7]]

---

[7] Rhea's way of avoiding handing her sixth child over to be eaten. She swaddled a rock in blankets and waited until her husband was very drunk to hand it over, leaving her safe to hide baby Zeus in a cave as he grew up. —A

Hades: Has the old man gone mad?

Hera: Like eating rocks is less mad than eating *us*?

Hestia: Maybe Mum's lonely, so she kept the baby to keep her company.

Demeter: Why him and not the rest of us?

Poseidon: I wish I was lonely.

Hera: Hey, no leaning. That's my space.

Hestia: Guys, guys, calm down. I'm sure he'll be here soon. And we want to look our best for him, don't we?

Hera: I'm not a guy.

Poseidon: What's wrong with being a guy?

[The five siblings devolve into a shouting match.]

Zeus I

Dad ate all my siblings after they were born so it was just me and Mum growing up. But she was away so much, sometimes it felt like it was just me.

'Where have you been? You said you'd be here in the afternoon and it's dusk—'

'I know what I said. I got caught up talking to your father.'

'Why were you talking to him? You should have told him you're busy.'

'You know I can't do that yet.' She put her hand on my shoulder like that would make it better. She crouched to look me in the eye but she went too low. She didn't see how tall I'd got. 'You just have to be patient a little while longer.'

'But I don't *want* to be patient.'

'You're whining, Zeus. I didn't raise you to whine.'

'You didn't raise me *at all*. You're too busy spending all your time with *him*.'

She always did this: showed up late and didn't have enough time and then said it was *my* fault when it was *her* fault for giving all her time to my stupid dad. She said I was the most important thing in the world. She didn't act like it.

She acted like it was so easy to wait and be patient. It was for her. She got to go and be the queen of the Titans and have everyone do stuff for her, and I had to hide in a cave because she hadn't told my stupid dad I was still alive because he was so stupid he mistook a rock for me.

'If you're going to act like a spoiled child, I'll go. I don't have the energy for this today.'

'Wait,' I said. My voice came out higher than I wanted. It meant I was growing. I was going to be big and strong someday. I knew it. 'Stay.'

'What do you want from me, Zeus?'

That was easy.

I wanted to go outside.

I wanted to be king already.

I wanted to see my brothers and my sisters.

I wanted the biggest spear anyone had.

I wanted to practise my throwing.

I wanted to play sports.

I wanted to try ambrosia and nectar.

I wanted to go swimming.

I wanted friends and soldiers and my own humans to play with.

I wanted all the things she promised me. I wanted the world and the sky and the gods. I wanted all of it and if it was going to be mine sooner or later, they should just give it to me now.

We'd been through all that a million times though. Mum just said it was hard for her too.

'I want you to stay.'

'Oh, Zeusie. You need to be tougher than this. Kings have to be able to stand on their own, and you want to be a good king, don't you?'

'Tell me a story,' I said. There. That wasn't talking about my feelings. Stories didn't make me weak or a bad king.

When she was in a good mood, she told the best stories all about how I'd be the best king ever and everyone would respect me and ask my opinions and do what I said. She told me my brothers and sisters were so excited to meet me and we'd be best friends and conquer the world together. She told me how great it would all be, when it was mine.

Then she told me not yet.

'When?'

'Soon.'

'That's not a proper answer.'

'No one can know the future, son.'

'But you said the reason we had to hide from Dad is because someone told him in the future we were going to hurt him, which means *someone* can do it and if someone can do it then I want to be able to do it.'

'Sweet pea, that was a prophecy, not the future.'

'What's the difference?'

'Prophecies are vague.' She paused and scrunched up her face like there was something bad stuck in her teeth. 'And florid.'

'You like plants.'

'Florid, not flora. The language in prophecies isn't very precise, so it could mean anything, and somehow the oracles can only clarify what they meant *after* all the events have transpired.'

'Does that mean I'm not definitely going to be king?' I didn't cry. Brave kings don't cry. They have to be strong.

'No—'

'No?!'

'Of course you're going to be the king. You just need to wait a little while longer.' The sky flashed outside. 'Your father is calling. I should return before he gets suspicious. I'll be back tomorrow afternoon.'

She wasn't. It got all the way till dusk again and she still wasn't there for me, so I stopped waiting. I snuck out. If she wouldn't take me to see the amazing world she promised me, I'd find it myself.

She was lying about that too. The world was *terrible*. No one came rushing out to see me and it was cold *and* wet *and* I slipped on a rock and cut my arm. That wasn't allowed. I stomped on the rock so hard it broke into two.

'How do you like it?'

I turned into an eagle. I can do that because I'm special. The sky was better than the land anyway. The sea was fun too – I could fly with my toes still in the water – but I liked the sky the best. It was so empty; sometimes I was the only thing going through it. I flew higher and better than any of the normal boring birds. It was *mine*.

But the sky's just one part of the world and I was going to be king of all of it. I had to know what I was going to be king of, so I explored everything. My favourite was when there were monsters. I swooped in close to them, then flew off as fast as I could when they started chasing me. I laughed when they tripped. They were so slow and I was so fast. They'd never catch up to me: Zeus.

It took me ages to get to the caves though. I thought they'd all be boring like my cave. Most of the time they were. They were all full of rocks. Seeing if I could break them was fun for a bit, but it got old fast.

Caves are only really fun when there's something hiding in the back, like there was that day.

'Who are you?' I said. It didn't say anything, like I'd get bored and walk away. *As if.* 'Are you a monster? I'll kill you if you are.' There were bits of string all over the place. Maybe it shed them. 'Tell me.'

Nothing. Rude.

'If you're not a monster, we can be friends,' I said. 'Look, I have nuts.' Mum gave them to me whenever she was late so I had loads of them.

'Who are you?' the maybe-monster said, still in the dark.

'I asked first.'

'But you came barging into my home,' it said.

'That's no way to talk to the future king!'

'How do you want to be talked to, little Zeus?' It sounded like a girl, but I couldn't see it to know. It was hiding in the back and there were all these stupid strings in my way. It sounded like it was laughing at me.

'Hey! I didn't tell you my name.'

'Did you not?'

'No, I didn't, because Mum said I shouldn't go round giving my name to just anyone, and you still haven't told me who *you* are. It's not fair.'

'Maybe I don't go giving my name out to just anyone either.'

'I'll trade it for a nut.'

'Three.'

'One.'

'Three.'

'Two.'

'Fine, little king—'

'Don't call me little.' I threw the nuts at it.

'—I am Fate.'

'What's that?'

'I didn't trade that to you.' It was definitely laughing at me now.

'Five nuts.'

'I need a bit more than that.'

'I don't have anything else. I could give you something when I'm king though? Do you want to be a god? I could make you a god.'

'I thought we could trade questions and answers,' it said.

Stupid choice. Being a god is better than anything else. Or it was going to be. But if it wanted to trade for answers instead, then—

'Fine.'

She – it was a she. I asked and she told me for free – asked how I was born so I told her about Mum, and Dad eating my siblings, and how he wanted to eat me too but Mum gave him a rock so he couldn't because I was special and I was going to be the king one day. Then I asked her how she was born and she said she didn't know. She came out of the ocean and landed here.

'That's it?'

'You asked me how I was born; that's all I know.'

'But I told you so much! That's not fair.'

'I'm told that life isn't.'

'You should tell me what Fate is. Then we'll be even.'

She stopped for a second. 'Okay.' And she held something out to me. She was still in the back but I saw her hand. It looked like a normal hand. Boring. '*This* is Fate.'

'I thought you were Fate. This is just string.'

'It's not just string to me.'

'Explain. I want to see what you see.'

She had me run my fingers up and down it, and she kept on going about how it felt different and what these little lumps and whorls were, but I couldn't feel any of them.

'Do you see?'

No. It was stupid. She was probably stupid. She was probably making it up.

'There's nothing there. You're lying.'

'I am not.'

'What do you see, then?' I demanded. Then, when she didn't say anything, 'See, you don't see anything. I knew it.'

She raised an eyebrow. 'I see an eagle smashing rocks.'

What? I only did that when no one was looking. Mum would be mad if she knew. She'd say I was breaking my cover but I wasn't. I was just breaking rocks.

This woman did see something. She was special. I wanted to be special too.

'I see it now!'

'What do you see?' She didn't sound convinced.

'Other places. And times. But it's all vague and florid.'

'Is it?'

'Don't laugh at me.'

'I'm not laughing. You're amazing, Zeus. You know that?'

Mum told me it was rude to say I know.

'I know.'

She laughed. I liked it. 'What do you see in your future?'

'I'm going to free my siblings. Then they're going to help me fight Cronus and then I'm going to be the king and then I'm going to make mankind better and then everyone will be allowed to go where they want and then it will all be great.'

'I see that too.'

It was getting late. I didn't want to go back on time because Mum was always making me wait so it served her right if I made her wait back, but I didn't want her knowing I'd been sneaking out.

'I should go.'

'You could come back,' she said. 'I'd like that.'

'Okay!'

Mum was on time for once. She was mad.

'Where were you? You're not meant to leave.'

'Explor—'

'What if someone caught you? What if they found you and told Cronus, Zeus? Then all of this would have been for nothing. What then?'

'It's—'

'Everything is too risky now. You have to be patient.'

I didn't fight her. I didn't need to. I had a friend now.

Aphrodite V

We were fighting, Prom and I. He thought I was being illogical, talking to the boy-king, and I didn't think he had a leg to stand on, logically. He was the one signing up to fight a war on someone else's behalf. That's what it always came down to. He was leaving me, not just for a day or a week, but forever, to create his brave new world. He was leaving, because his actions mattered, and I was staying, because mine didn't. I didn't want any of that to be true, but I didn't know how to change the world. Not yet.

'I am merely saying, his conversation is a risk you do not need to take, and one that is not worth your time,' Prom said.

'If he's so worthless then why are you fighting on his side of the war?'

'Because *you* swear he is certain to win.'

'Prom, are you *jealous*?'

'No!'

I wanted him to be, I realised. I was, when he talked about Metis. Stupid, clever, logical Metis, who lived in the real world with him and experienced the same dictator as him and swore to fight in the same war as him. Metis, who got to know him in a thousand contexts I never would. Metis, who was his friend and not a project.

I wanted him to be jealous so he would realise how little of me he knew, so he would want more of me.

He sat down from where he'd been pacing, too tall for where we sat at the back, really, the top of his curls tangling where they brushed the ceiling. 'If I bring you a veil, will you wear it when he visits? Stop him seeing the real you?'

Stop protecting me, I wanted to shout. He doesn't need to see me. I want you to see me. I want you to love me.

'Fine. I'll wear it. I'll sit here and cover my face and not have any friends while you go and save the world. Is that what you want?'

'You're being ridiculous.'

'You're the one worrying about my safety when you're the one fighting.'

'Yes, Aphrodite, because your safety is something I can control. Not mine.'

'You can control yours.'

Don't fight.

Stay.

Take me with you.

'Or I can look at the threads, tell you—'

'How many times must we go through this? Are you stupid? I don't want to see my future.'

'No, you just want to control it.'

We were shouting. Of course we were shouting. I loved him and he loved me, but we never loved each other in quite the same way. Our tapestry wouldn't weave, not smoothly. There would always be lumps and tears in the fabric. Fuck the lumps. Fuck the tears. I loved him.

'What other choice is there?' he asked, really asked, hands up, eyes up, as though the walls of my cave would hold an answer his own brilliant mind couldn't find, almost begging me to ask, begging me to beg him to stay. 'What do I do, Aphrodite?'

I couldn't do it. Not in words. I couldn't ask and be told no, not by him, for him to stutter some version of the fact that he loved me, but actually that my life was too miserable to consider and he'd rather fight a war than be alone with me all the time, that I just wasn't enough.

I couldn't hear it, and I couldn't let him walk away from me. What other choice was there?

I was scared, and there was no time for that, so I moved faster than I could think. I reached up and I grabbed his head, my fingers lost between his curls, and I pulled him to me, closer and closer until my lips were on his.

He froze, and I stopped, the two of us held there for a perpetual moment of stillness where the fear could catch up to me, envelop me, throw me a thousand questions about exactly how much I'd fucked everything up.

And then he kissed me back.

He wasn't a comfortable man, my Prometheus. His hands were a bit bigger than they should have been, his arms a bit longer, which wouldn't have been a problem, except his mind seemed to tell his body that everything was the exact length it should have been, so he was forever bumping and scraping and not quite fitting into the spaces he put himself into.

All that melted away.

He scooped an arm beneath my legs and lifted me, pulled my chest into his, so I could wrap my arms around his neck, his shoulders, so I could pull him so close to me I couldn't see anything else. Not the world, not the threads, not the cave or the shadows or the water, just him. And for those seconds it meant all he could see was me.

His pupils grew wider and wider, until he looked hungry. Until my clever, thinking Prometheus looked more animal than man.

A noise came from my throat, unlike any I'd made before, and I opened my mouth to apologise, but he met it with the same, so I adjusted: I grabbed the front of his clothes and I pulled the both of us down to the floor. I put my hands everywhere I wanted, and he followed and matched until both of us were a mess and still I didn't stop. I took and I took and I took.

I was real. I was alive.

Eventually the pace slowed, both of us gluttons finally full of the greatest joy my life had to offer. He slung an arm around me and I laid my head on his chest so, once more, he was all I could see.

'I love you,' he said.

There you have it: my first time. The goddess of love's first time – only I wasn't, not yet; it was just me, and him, and it didn't feel the way I thought it would.

'Your plan is good,' I told him.

'Pardon.'

'For the war, your plan's a good one. You shouldn't be afraid.'

'Aren't you going to ask me to stay?' That felt like a victory. He might not stay, but he was thinking about it now. He asked. I didn't.

'You wouldn't.'

'Do you know that?' he asked, sharply, pulling as far away from me as his arm would allow. 'I don't want to know my future. I need to live in a world where my decisions matter.'

'I didn't look.' I pulled away completely, untangling myself from him. He didn't get to hold on to me, and to hold me away, not at the same time. One or the other. 'I just know you.'

'I will miss you, you are aware?'

'What do you mean?'

'I won't have time to come out here, when the war starts—'

'I could—' *Just say it, Aphrodite, say it fast before the fear can catch up with you.* 'I could go with you. Fight with you.'

'Oh, Aphrodite, that's a . . . an interesting thought, but you're—'

Something worse. Something lesser. Something you drop and pick up when it's convenient for you. A project and a hobby and a secret. Not a fighter. Not a lover. Not a friend.

'I get it. Go and fight your war then.'

'Aphrodite—'

'Go, Prometheus.'

'Frodi—'

'Leave.'

And he did. He left and he started a war. Without me.

Emetic Solution

Zeus,

This should do the trick!

Metis

Potion to ~~empty~~ soothe the stomach after
ingestion of foreign objects. Single use only.

Take three gulps ~~after~~ before food. Results
visible within thirty minutes.

Side effects may include:
Headaches
Dizziness
Loss of balance
Tremors
Vomiting
Irritability
Uprisings
Impulsivity
Paranoia
Hiccoughs
Death

Metis II

In an ideal world, we would have brought about the war between the gods and the Titans sooner, but our plan relied on the good temper of the youngest of the gods, and that took some years to develop. To this end, we let the future king have his outings. We permitted them; we simply did not inform him of the permission. It was *deception* practice.

Prometheus, Rhea, and I all tested him, all baited him into the lies and pressed when they were obvious, rewarding him when he held his nerve. As he grew older, we lost the opportunity to test him so often. Not only had he become quite the accomplished liar, but he was better at hiding the signs of his misbehaviour. He was ready.

We told him so during a storm, so he might celebrate his readiness and not be heard. By that juncture we had learned some things would never be trained out of him.

'*WOOO. Who's the king? Who's the king?*' he chanted until Prometheus and I were forced to admit that he was, in fact, the king.

'How are we doing this then?' he asked.

He had grown into an attractive young man; it was undeniable. He did not look like his mother or father, or any of us Titans. His skin was lighter, less clearly a product of the earth, and he shone like precious metals. He was taller than all of us too, but proportional.

You could see him at a distance and believe he was immediately in front of you.

He smiled more brightly than any other. He hadn't lived through a war, yet.

'Our first priority is to extract your siblings,' Prometheus said.

'Yeah, obviously. So what do I do? Do I cut Dad open and see them all come spilling out?' He mimed this action, first by stabbing his hand into the air, then by inflating his cheeks and releasing spittle ahead of him.

'You are to serve as his cupbearer, little one,' Rhea said.

'Serve? I'm the king. I don't want to serve.'

'Only for the moment.'

'When he trusts you, we will poison his wine, make him ill. He will . . . release your siblings that way,' I said.

'Okay. I'll do it. I will!'

We faced the small matter of convincing the king of the Titans to trust some previously unknown youth with his drinks. We accomplished this by passing him off as my son—

'I didn't know you had it in you,' Cronus interrupted.

'Thank you?'

'You're welcome.'

'He's grown beyond my handling. You'd be doing me a great service if you could find some work for him.'

'He doesn't look like much of a fighter.'

Zeus opened his mouth beside me. I stamped on his foot. The inevitable complaint about how good he was at fighting was *not* a part of the plan.

'*Please*, Cronus,' I said. I have no issue begging if it serves a greater purpose. 'Surely he could do something small. Hold your cup perhaps?'

Cronus looked at his cup, resting on the table beside him. It did not beg for further holding.

'I suppose.'

'Thank you.'

I bowed and left Zeus there, where he would hopefully be friendly, quiet, and observant. He could listen in to find where the one-eyed Cyclopes and hundred-handed Hecatonchires had been buried. He could even make friends who could be convinced to support him.

Instead of returning with such observations, Zeus returned with a list of complaints.

'He's the worst. He doesn't see me as a real Titan. He didn't let me take any breaks all day. And he complained his wine was too *temperate*. What even *is* that?'

'Cronus likes his wine to warm him in the afternoons,' Prometheus said.

'Why do *you* know *that*?'

'It's a matter of paying attention.'

'You hold his bloody cup then!'

'Little one,' Rhea said. 'This is just the first step to you becoming king. You do want to be the king, don't you?'

Zeus stormed out, and we worried that might be the end of our grand plan, but he returned mere hours later, refuelled and refocused. After that day, he did everything we asked of him and more. He smiled and made friends, flirted even. Held his tongue when necessary. He supported Cronus in all things and did not tap his feet when he was bored. He waited until he knew the locations of our future allies and until Cronus was unprotected. Then, he poisoned the wine.

I did not suffer the misfortune of seeing the return of Zeus' siblings. I am informed it was grotesque, and that Cronus' jaw was able to dislocate.

Zeus attempted to behead his father while he was distracted with the regurgitation, using the same sickle that had castrated his grandfather. I assume Prometheus advised him on this tactic. Prometheus likes symbols, and the implications of Zeus overthrowing his father with the same weapon his father had overthrown his grandfather with were too strong to ignore. Cronus was king, after all. Regardless, he failed, and it became official. We were at war.

Zeus' siblings banded with him and his mother, as we knew they would. Not many Titans followed us, but more remained neutral than we had expected. It was something.

We were outnumbered at the outset, which we had always expected, but it's rather different to know something and to be faced down by a horde of raging Titans.

It took ten years, the war between the gods and the Titans, and it is a miracle it did not drag further. With the numbers as they were, it seemed we were bound to ignominious failure and the consequences that come with it. Zeus did not agree.

'I'll find recruits.'

'We have already asked—'

'I will find them,' he insisted.

I should not have doubted him. He did precisely that, digging the Cyclopes from the ground with his own hands, converting them with sweet words of freedom.

With dirt on his face and under his nails, and shoulders too tired to move more than a light sway, he smiled at me. 'I did it.'

'That you did. Well done, Zeus.'

The Cyclopes released their brothers, the Hecatonchires, and between them, the tide began to turn in our favour. The Cyclopes built forges, and from those forges they made weapons, lightning and thunder for Zeus, a trident and a helmet for his brothers. The three of them travelled through air, water, and shadows, striking whenever an opportunity could be made.

The Titans largely ascribed to classic thoughts of honour. They had to; they invented them. They believed that a war should be fought face to face, between only those involved. The gods couldn't afford such lofty ideals. If they did, they would lose.

They sneaked and cheated and stole when they needed to. They banded together and broke when they needed to. Zeus bade the Hecatonchires shower Othrys with rocks, making it uninhabitable, as he moved himself and his siblings to Olympus. It was the highest mountain in our world, covered with the richest mixture of plants and animals, and endlessly battered with winds so strong you had to be divine to withstand them. Divine, however, does not entail godliness, no matter what Zeus seemed to think. The other Titans and I could handle it perfectly well.

Olympus began as a fortress, a temporary camp in the middle of the war, but it grew from that. For the gods, it was the only home they'd ever known.

Prometheus sighed as he watched the destruction of our home. 'I will miss Othrys.'

'We signed up for this. No use complaining now.'

'It will be over soon.'

'Why do you say that?'

'There was another prophecy.'

I harrumphed, and waited for him to do the same. We had long agreed the ridiculousness of such things. 'You believe in prophecies now?'

'They do continue to come to pass,' he said.

'Because they're so vague, remember?'

'The final fight is coming.'

After the war and all the damage therein, the final fight was not one to be shouted about. This prophecy suggested that whoever sacrificed a particular magical sea cow would win. Ten years we fought, and countless more were spent planning, but one word from their *mothers*, and Zeus and Cronus lost any sense they had to begin with. They stopped their battles immediately, and rushed to the ocean to hunt a *sea cow*.

If I sound judgemental, then that is an accurate summation of my feelings on the matter.

Cronus was the first to capture the cow, but that was no problem for us. Prometheus still had significant spies among the Titans and was able to ascertain the time and location of the intended sacrifice. From then it was a straightforward enough matter for Zeus to transform into an eagle and fly down to retrieve the entrails.

Zeus burned them immediately, in the name of the gods. The clauses of the "prophecy" were complete, and the world did not end. Othrys did not crumble. Cronus did not clutch his chest and fall to the floor because the sea cow had been taken by another.

Some days later, the Olympians – as they had begun calling themselves, cementing their ties to a place that was still not much more than a tent on a hill – successfully bypassed Cronus' defences, trapping him where Atlas wouldn't be able to hear his calls for help. Zeus' siblings each took one of their father's limbs in their hands and held him as far apart as his body would stretch.

Using the blade of Cronus' sickle, Zeus slowly removed his male appendages. He did not strike to kill, did not attempt what the prophecy had dictated was impossible. He passed the pieces to a waiting Hera, who wrapped them carefully in wool, each tied with a dainty bow.

They talked, the Olympians. Of the weather, of the day's fights, of their attempts to build palaces on Olympus and how each wished to decorate. They chattered, as though this were merely another day at work.

Bile rose in my throat as I realised it *was*. We had allowed these children to grow up in the middle of a war. They had known only this. No wonder they took no horror from the horrible.

Smiling and laughing together, they lifted their father and carried him to Tartarus. He had his own pit there, deeper than any others. They draped it with chains, set fires in the perimeter, invited the Cyclopes to do the same. Cronus did not scream as it was happening. It was only as his youngest son turned to leave him, that he leaned forwards and whispered something with a wicked grin.

Zeus was shaking afterwards, but he did not share the missive. He stood before his siblings and made his first pronouncement as king.

'He did not fight alone. We must find the others and punish them equally.'

His siblings cheered. Together, they hunted and rounded up the Titans loyal to Cronus, to be cast into Tartarus alongside their master. Zeus took particular dislike to Atlas and singled him out for a unique torture. He was to stand and bear the weight of the world upon his shoulders.

'So that he can know what he has done,' Zeus said formally – he hadn't complained that something was *unfair*, or that he wanted it *now*, for years. We'd broken him.

Atlas, as the rest of us, did not age. Now, he seemed to wither and decay in front of us, but he could not, would never die.

Zeus destroyed Cronus' men of gold, demanding they be melted down and cast for decor for his new utopia.

Finally, he approached the Cyclopes and Hecatonchires, his faithful allies. He thanked them for their painstaking work on his behalf. Now, he said, they would receive their promised freedom; they needed only to follow him.

He led them merrily back to Tartarus, and he locked the door behind them.

All hail Zeus, the new king.

Aphrodite VI

I wasn't meant to be involved in the war, but there was no avoiding it. It pulled in all the threads, knotted them together, and sparked off in colours so ugly I couldn't tear myself away, but that's just an excuse.

Prom and I might have fought about it, I might have thought he was stupid for going, and he definitely thought I was stupid for not understanding, but my best friend was fighting in that war. I couldn't ignore it. I couldn't bury myself in the sand and pretend the pictures in the threads were nothing but an amusement.

Prom didn't come to visit me often while they were fighting, though he did drop off a veil the day after we slept together, almost adding insult to injury. Practicality over emotion. He told me it wasn't safe, and I believed him. I hated that I believed him, but I did.

If you must talk to the boy, stay hidden. —P

Like I hadn't been doing that the whole time anyway. Zeus had never seen more of me than my hands. The veil gave me that freedom, at least, to move forwards and talk to him in the light. He gasped the first time he saw me.

'You *are* a woman.'

74

'Yes, Zeus.' I smiled. He was funny.

'You're not hiding anymore?'

'Well.' I gestured to the veil. Prometheus had done a good job. It totally covered my face. 'I am a bit.'

'Why do you hide?'

This was precisely the kind of thing I was trying to hide, more than my face. 'Not everyone is pleased to see me.'

'Why?'

'Sometimes they want things I can't give them. The first time someone came here, he did, and he attacked me.'

'Who? I'll destroy them.'

It was charming, having a child – an adolescent now. I was born an adult, and how strange it was to watch something grow – stand earnestly in front of me and promise destruction. It shouldn't have been, but it was. And, you know, that child was going to be the king of fucking everything someday, so I thought, no harm in sharing.

'Atlas.'

'That *fuck*.'

Zeus visited me most often just before the war started, complaining about being his father's cupbearer, lowering himself to some lesser position to get what he wanted.

'But you're not lowering yourself, are you?'

'I am.' He frowned. 'I told you. Aren't you listening to me?'

'No, you're lowering them. They're so stupid they can't see how wonderful you are, no matter what position you're in.' I really thought I was helping. Prom was fighting on his side, and I knew it was the winning one. It might not have been obvious in the world, but it was clear in the threads. It was clear to me.

'Everyone should see, if I'm so great.'

'You are great.'

He was so powerful, even then. The air thickened and cleared with his moods, grew heavy enough to spark with his tempers. He could start fires with nothing but a feeling.

I liked him, then, and I got it, in a way Prom never could. I understood this boy who'd grown up alone in a cave, unable to tell anyone who he really was. I loved Prometheus and all that he brought me, our conversations and the different perspectives and the jokes that just belonged to us, but sometimes it was easier to talk to someone who got me too, someone I could roll my eyes with, and complain about the state of the world with, not because I wanted to change it, but because it sucked.

I could do that with Zeus.

'I am great,' he said. 'And these idiots don't know it.'

'So you go back to them, and when they're rude to you, you'll know it's because they're too stupid to realise who you really are. And then you beat them, because you're a winner.'

'Okay. Yes. You're the best.'

'I know—'

'I have to go laugh at the stupid people now, though.'

He ran off, feet bouncing against the surface of the water for ten long bounds, until his legs pulled into him and he took off, a mighty eagle in full flight, not realising for a second quite how much power he had.

The war started, and I was alone again. I didn't have enough to do. Not with everyone busy fighting. Not alone with only the visions of the future to taunt me. There were no distractions, only my fears.

I tried to do what Prometheus had asked of me. I tried to keep his future blocked from both of us.

I lasted ten years.

Ten bloody years on the word of someone who couldn't find the time to come and see me. Ten years of fighting and of war and of fear without end. Ten years of relentless worry. I lasted. I endured. But those ten years will be forgotten, because I did not last eleven.

There was no reason, on that day. There hadn't been some particular glamorous fight; I can't pretend that all looked hopeless. I didn't believe Fate was making a difference to anything but my own mind. It was just one day too many of being afraid. One moment too long alone in my own head.

One moment was all it took.

One lie to convince myself it wouldn't change anything to know Prom's future.

I only had to touch his thread for it to hit me like a wave, a storm, a cascade of rocks burying me in the truth of it.

pain pain pain pain pain pain pain pain pain pain pain pain pain
pain pain pain pain pain pain pain pain pain pain pain pain pain
pain pain pain pain pain pain pain pain pain pain pain pain pain
pain pain pain pain pain pain pain pain pain pain pain pain pain
pain pain pain pain pain pain pain pain pain pain pain pain pain
pain pain pain pain pain pain pain pain pain pain pain pain pain
pain pain pain pain pain pain pain pain pain pain pain pain pain
pain pain pain pain pain pain pain pain pain pain pain pain pain
pain pain pain pain pain pain pain pain pain pain pain pain pain
pain pain pain pain pain pain pain pain pain pain pain pain pain
pain pain pain pain pain pain pain pain pain pain pain pain pain
pain pain pain pain pain pain pain pain pain pain pain pain pain
pain pain pain pain pain pain pain pain pain pain pain pain pain
pain pain pain pain pain pain pain pain pain pain pain pain pain
pain pain pain pain pain pain pain pain pain pain pain pain pain
pain pain pain pain pain pain pain pain pain pain pain pain pain
pain pain pain pain pain pain pain pain pain pain pain pain pain
pain pain pain pain pain pain pain pain pain pain pain pain pain

pain pain pain pain pain pain pain pain pain pain pain pain pain
pain pain pain pain pain pain pain pain pain pain pain pain pain
pain pain pain pain pain pain pain pain pain pain pain pain pain
pain pain pain pain pain pain pain pain pain pain pain pain pain
pain pain pain pain pain pain pain pain pain pain pain pain pain
pain pain pain pain pain pain pain pain pain pain pain pain pain
pain pain pain pain pain pain pain pain pain pain pain pain pain
pain pain pain pain pain pain pain pain pain pain pain pain pain
pain pain pain pain pain pain pain pain pain pain pain pain pain
pain pain pain pain pain pain pain pain pain pain pain pain pain
pain pain pain pain pain pain pain pain pain pain pain pain pain
pain pain pain pain pain pain pain pain pain pain pain pain pain
pain pain pain pain pain pain pain pain pain pain pain pain pain
pain pain pain pain pain pain pain pain pain pain pain pain pain
pain pain pain pain pain pain pain pain pain pain pain pain pain
pain pain pain pain pain pain pain pain pain pain pain pain pain
pain pain pain pain pain pain pain pain pain pain pain pain pain
pain pain pain pain pain pain pain pain pain pain pain pain pain
pain pain pain pain pain pain pain pain pain pain pain pain pain
pain pain pain pain pain pain pain pain pain pain pain pain pain
pain pain pain pain pain pain pain pain pain pain pain pain pain
pain pain pain pain pain pain pain pain pain pain pain pain pain
pain pain pain pain pain pain pain pain pain pain pain pain pain

That couldn't be it. That couldn't be all of it.

I kept running my hands down the thread, hoping this too must pass – it had to pass – but the thread kept going, running and running and never changing. He was going to survive the war, and it didn't matter, because his reward was an eternity of pain.

My tears fell. My hands bled. They mixed together, staining that long-off future, bending it in ways I couldn't possibly predict.

That was it.

I held the future. In my hands, I held it. There was no one to tell me I couldn't nudge the threads, have them behave better, have them give Prometheus the life he deserved. Why not?

'We're friends, right?' I whispered to them. They tensed away from me. It was slight, but we spent our entire lives entwined around one another. To me, it was noticeable. 'Come on, I need you.'

They didn't relax; they didn't hang as they usually did, nearly weightless in my hands. They hardened, unyielding. They wouldn't bend for me. But I wasn't asking.

I forced them to my will.

They shocked me, then, but I wasn't going to let go just because it hurt. They kept pushing against me, pulsing those shocks into my hands. I gripped even tighter, pushing them into any part of the fabric I could, anywhere they'd stick.

I wasn't gentle. I couldn't be. I could only hold on so long, and I could already see the veins in my arm starkly rising beneath the skin. I had to move faster.

I pulled knots until they gave, and if they wouldn't then I wove them in as they were, creating mountains and crevices and holes in the fabric that had been so smooth before, forcing untold damage in the landscape. I let our beautiful new world get ugly, and I didn't even question it. That could not be Prom's fate. I would not allow it.

'I won't. Do you hear me?' I yelled.

I didn't get to be part of the fabric, didn't get to be seen, but I would make it feel me. I had to.

I was getting close. A strand of my hair had fallen while I was working and that had gone in too, but it didn't matter. The whole thing was painful and messy, but I just had to change one more thing, I thought, one last fight, and I would be done.

I have *never* got to be done.

The thread broke in my hands, right in the centre of all that suffering. It twanged louder and brighter and more fearsome than any thunder from Zeus' tantrums could wish. It shook the cave so hard the stalactites came crashing down in a single movement.

I didn't think to dodge them. I was only looking at the broken string in my hand. I didn't notice the rock drop straight across my face, cutting it bloody. I didn't care.

I'd severed his future.

In trying to save him, I'd done something that no one has successfully done before or since.

I'd killed an immortal.

Not now. Not yet. But it was coming.

I tried reversing it, but it's so much harder to fix broken things. All attempts to hold it back together, to knot it in place, failed as fast as they started. His future crumbled into the sand, indistinguishable from the rest of the dirt.

'I thought we were friends,' I told them. 'You were meant to be there for me.'

The threads didn't say anything. They were threads.

I pulled them from me, ripping as hard as I needed. I threw them on the floor and turned towards the ocean. It was stupid. I didn't have a plan. But I was sick of being here where I was scared and weak and invisible, and the only thing I had was incapable of caring about me. I was sick of all of it. I didn't want to be the arbiter of who lived and who died. I just wanted to be.

I threw myself into the water, not stopping to breathe, not stopping to think, not stopping to anything. If I drowned, then so be it.

Nerites I

I have fifty sisters, but there's only one of me. Why make more when you've got perfection, right? When a hot woman – woman, man, both, doesn't matter so long as you're hot – came crashing into the oceans like she'd had too much to drink and then some, it only made sense that she grabbed a hold of me. I have that kind of face. You love it because it's so gorgeous or hate it because you want to be me so damned much. She was the first kind.

She didn't have to say it. We both knew she wanted me. She pulled my face in and started kissing me like I was the only source of air in the whole freaking ocean. She jumped up and wrapped her legs around me.

'Take me somewhere quiet and fuck me so hard I can't think.'

'I can do that.'

I did that. Then some. A nereid doesn't kiss and tell, right? That's not classy. But if I did then I could write a whole damned *epic* about the things we did together. We were wildfire. Electric.

'Who are you?' I asked.

She kissed me again and again and again – we went again and again and again – until the sun went down and came up and went down. I've got no clue how many times it was. I fucked her until we both passed out in a heap.

She still smelled like sex when we woke up. Sex with me. If you could bottle that smell the whole world would buy it, then starve 'cause they were so caught up in the things they wanted to do to each other.

'Do it again,' she said. Demanding, pushy. I liked that. Confidence is hot, right? It meant I could demand back.

Hands here, and here, and here. Like that. More. Faster. *More.*

I made her fucking scream when she came. Loud enough for everyone to hear.

Then she blinked.

'This was fun,' she said, easy, like it had been some business meeting or something. Like, the second we stopped touching she wasn't thinking about me anymore. She should have been. No way she'd had sex like that before. 'Tomorrow?'

'What are you doing now? You could stay.'

If I had my way, the two of us would never leave my bed, world be damned. Forever, with her, like that? Absolutely. Sign me up.

'I need to—' She looked at her wrists and blinked. Was she *sad*? There was no way, not after I made her sound like that. Blink again. Headshake. 'Be somewhere else for a bit. I might come back later.'

I didn't push. Didn't matter to me what she was doing in the days, did it? I wanted her nights. Plus, the war was finished and everyone was all over the place with what would happen next, and I was sick of hearing about it. Everyone talking about their feelings all the time. If she wanted sex and nothing but, we could do that. Didn't expect her to start crying in the middle of the next night, did I?

'I don't know what's happening,' she said.

'What are you on about?'

'What's coming?'

'*You* are.'

And I made her, 'cause I could. 'Cause I didn't sign up to sit there and listen to some girl cry about her feelings when she wouldn't even tell me her name. It was never meant to be a *thing*, you know? When a girl comes through town smelling of mystery and getting all cagey whenever anyone asks her questions, you don't think she's in it for some forever romance.

And, like, some nights she didn't want to see me, couldn't stand the sight of me, it felt like, but other nights it would have taken Zeus' own freaking lightning to pry her off of me. She'd wrap herself round my arm or my leg and ask me a million questions about the oceans and my sisters and who was fighting—

'My youngest sister stole one of the other's—'

'No. In the war. What's happening?'

'The war's been over for months.'

She blinked. 'Where was I?'

How was I meant to know? Not being normal. That much was obvious. She got stranger by the freaking day. One time she walked through my house, touching everything, almost freaking *drooling* at the textures, until she hit some snag in the fabric and it pissed her off and she jumped back swearing. *Or* she'd start drumming her hands against my stuff, getting louder and louder, until it got loud enough she scared herself? Like she had no idea what she was doing.

She was always touching my hair, but that's fair play. I have great hair. Oh, then there was the time she stared at my walls all day, tracing her finger across the veins of crystals that ran through the stones.

'Are you crystal or water?' she asked.

'Why don't we go back to bed?'

She was fun in bed. Shame she was a nightmare everywhere else.

'Are you crystal or water?' She got louder with every word. 'I think I'm water sometimes, but then I fall down and I'm crystal and—' She threw herself down on the floor. 'Shatter.'

'Okay, maybe I should take that off you.' I grabbed for her drink – she always had a drink – but she swung it out of my way, spilling it through the water around us.[8]

'Come down here.' She laughed. 'I want you.'

She didn't wait. She pulled at me, until I was as naked as she was. The sex was great. The sex was always great. She was smoking hot and she knew it. When it was done, when I almost couldn't breathe for how much I wanted her, she laughed again.

'Now you're shattering too.'

She looked different sleeping. Prettier, but not so hot. More like everyone else. Boring. Then she woke up and she was dancing round my house. She'd already poured herself a drink, and she was singing.

'I was waiting for you, sleepyhead. We're going out!'

My head hurt. I'd been asleep for ten minutes, it felt like, but I couldn't tell *her* that. 'Where are we going?'

'Digging!'

'Digging?'

'I want to see Tartarus.'

'Why?' There's literally no worse place in our world.

'Maybe we'll see my dad!'

'What?'

---

[8]   Don't ask me how drinks worked in the oceans; no one knew, and they weren't questioning it as long as they had them. —A

'Daddy? Can you hear me down there? I'm coming!' She was shouting at the floor. Not even a hole in the floor. Just the floor.

I grabbed her by the shoulders and turned her to look at me. 'You can't say that.'

'Why not?' Her eyes were all wide like this was really news. Shiiiiiit. I'd been fucking a moron.

'If your father is in Tartarus, and *you want to see him*, that would make you a traitor to the new king.'

'I didn't choose who my father is.'

'But you can choose whether you see him.'

'I want to.'

'We can't always have we want.' Who was I? What had this girl turned me into? I'm not built to be the voice of freaking reason.

'I want you.'

So it went on. I assumed she knew it was a casual thing. It's not like *she* was forever material, the way she was, but it could be fun while it lasted. And it was fun, when it was fun, but she was a *lot*, and I was exhausted, okay? She was *on* all the time, and I never signed up for being her babysitter.

Maybe I was relieved when the call came from Poseidon. He wanted me to serve as his cupbearer, and we all know what that means. He was married already, but that didn't matter.

I tried to let the girl down gently.

'I have to go.'

'No,' she said.

'We don't have a choice.'

'I want you.'

'He's an Olympian. He gets what he wants.' I was already half out the door.

'I'll make myself an Olympian, then. We can have what we want. Come with me. We can be together forever.'

Hmmm. Unstable girl who wouldn't tell me her name, or the king of the oceans?

'I'm leaving.'

It wasn't clean. She wasn't happy. She yelled and I yelled. We both threw things. Called each other names. It didn't matter. Poseidon wanted me so he got me. I was a nereid, and he was the king. You can't just decide to be something else, I thought.

She proved me wrong, to be fair.

She went up to Olympus and she made herself one of them. I didn't see her for years – water people versus land people, you know? – and when I did, she'd got so big nobody believed what I had to say. They didn't believe my stories about the goddess Aphrodite.[9]

---

[9] Would you tell your friends you slept with this guy? —A

Aphrodite VII

I wasn't very good at the present, when I arrived in the oceans. I'd spent most of my life in the past, dabbled in the future, but I rarely had to deal with right now, and when I did, it was too much. It took me a while to get used to all that stimulus pounding from every direction.

The physical helped. When you're in a bed – or on the sand or up against a wall, wherever makes you happy – with someone, and they're good at what they're doing, your body takes over, shuts up the rest of the world for a bit.

I didn't love Nerites. That's why I went for him. He was pretty, sure, but he wasn't *mine*. He didn't share all this history with me; he hadn't planned a war right beside me. He hadn't laughed at the past and future kings with his hand dangling right next to mine so I could grab it if I needed to. He wasn't always thinking about what would come.[10]

He wasn't Prometheus, not by any stretch of the imagination. And so he was safe. I could go ahead and like him and not love him and, with him, I could be someone different to the

---

[10] Well, he was, but as long as the answer was him, he was okay with that. —A

person I'd always been, even if I didn't know who I wanted to be yet.

I knew I didn't want to be alone though, so I let him think that I loved him. I thought it would make him stay.

Love, real or fake, has never been enough for that. Nerites was no exception. Poseidon took him, which made it clear there were people in the world who *had* and I wasn't one of them. I could have stayed with the nereids, become just another nymph, but they didn't *have* either.

Do you know what *nymph* means?

Young girl; bride.

As far as I was thinking about anything, when I was there in the complicated midst of a grief that hadn't yet come to pass, I was thinking that I needed to be something else. I couldn't be happy as a Fate without Prometheus – I wasn't even particularly happy as a Fate *with* Prometheus – and I couldn't be a nereid or a nymph, and always know that everything I had could be taken away, even me.

I didn't want to be traded or bartered or demanded. It doesn't seem like very much to ask for, but it was everything. I had to be so much to get that little.

So, Nerites left to go carry Poseidon's wine – I can only assume Amphitrite[11] demanded he got a title other than "my husband's live-in boyfriend" – and I began to plot, but not like my best friend once had. Prometheus wanted out. I wanted *in*.

I stayed in Nerites' house, after he left. Maybe that was strange. Maybe I should have been haunted by the remains of him, how he permeated everything, but I'd lived so long in the shadows of what

---

[11]   Poseidon's wife. Did a lot in the oceans but not much anywhere else, so unless you're planning a trip down there, you can ignore. —A

everyone else was doing that it didn't occur to me to be bothered by it.

Besides, I had a new life to plan.

I began to watch again. I couldn't go back to my threads – if I re-entered that cave, if I even got too close, I thought they'd reach out to me, wrap themselves around my limbs and pull me back in, glue themselves to me so I could never escape again. Fortunately, there's more than one way to gut a fish, and I've always been good with my mouth.

I made myself another veil and played the part of a naiad – the freshwater equivalent of a nereid – so I had an excuse not to be recognised, and I listened. I learned what I needed to learn.

The Olympians had won the war, which I knew. The brothers had divided the world between them: Zeus taking the heavens, Poseidon the sea, and Hades the underworld.[12] Apparently they drew lots. I don't know if they all cheated or Fate itself intervened, but from what I saw of them *before* that, it was pretty damned clear who was going to get which.

Zeus sparked lightning between his fingers and turned into an eagle when he was bored. Are we going to pretend there was a real chance of him becoming the king of the *sea*?

Zeus restarted his father's old project with mankind, having destroyed the old lot as part of his glorious victory. He made the next batch out of silver. People seemed to think this was because he was bored.

His men of silver didn't have his energy. He'd tried for contrast, something to calm him in a world that had never been kind, but he went too far. One night, they lay down to sleep, and they never woke up.

---

[12] Including, but not limited to, Tartarus. He named the whole lot Hades. Not the most imaginative deity in the pantheon. —A

He ordered them covered with dirt and had another go, with bronze this time.

They were more like him, too much like him. They fought among themselves and tore one another to death in days.

And so Zeus made the men of clay. By value, the weakest of the lot. They were only mud and dirt, these new men, and I loved them from the moment I saw them. They were not afraid, not even when they should have been. They were so fragile, the men of clay, but they didn't seem to know it, or maybe they didn't have the luxury of caring. They spent every minute of every day surviving.

The base materials weren't the only difference, though, between them and their predecessors. The old generations looked like the Titans: two arms, two legs, one body, one soul. In his infinite wisdom, when he created the men of clay, Zeus decided to double everything but the number of bodies. These new men were fused down the back, with four arms and four legs pointing outwards, meaning they no longer resembled the Titans so much as they resembled crabs. It didn't seem convenient until I realised that everyone was born with their soulmate by their side.

Basically, the king of the gods created a generation of mankind who would always have a friend. From birth to death, they could never be lonely. And people thought he did it because he was *bored*. Did they not look at him? Did they not see this boy who was still so alone, who couldn't admit a single moment of weakness? Who wanted more than anything else to have someone he could trust? Did they not feel it too?

There's a reason they stayed nymphs and I became a goddess.

I kept a low profile when I was with them. I saw what happened to nymphs who stood out for their beauty. I sneered and rubbed sand into my hair and wore unflattering clothes when needed, kept my face low when I spent time with the relevant people. I didn't want to find myself in demand.

I watched and I waited and I learned.

Zeus didn't trust many people. He didn't trust anyone, really, but he could at least paste on a veneer of it for his family.

So. I knew where to start.

I couldn't be his sibling, the circumstances of their birth were well known enough, or any of his parents' generation, given all the overthrowing. There was only one thing for it. I had to be his child.

I stalked every single person the king of the gods slept with. For months. It was exactly as weird as it sounds. I didn't really know what I was looking for – some combination of disgruntlement and a lack of ambition and the ability to bear children. Some magical X-factor of saying fuck you, but only passively.

I found it in Dione.

She was a Titan and, I think, technically my great-niece – it's not good for the sanity to track these things too closely. She was a daughter of the oceans and danced as the moon danced on the waves.

She hadn't fought in the war. That was important.

He slept with her the night Poseidon's first son was born, which didn't feel like an accident. Dione wasn't unwilling. She wasn't chasing him, but when she met an attractive young king at a wedding, he didn't have to do much pursuing. I didn't have to sneak around to see who Zeus was romancing that day. They were both in human form, which was far from a certainty with Zeus.

He kept telling her he'd marry her.

'That'll show Poseidon,' Zeus said, more than once. I didn't have siblings, so I couldn't say for sure, but it's not something I'd say during sex. 'Marry one of his nymphs.'

(Zeus lacked volume control.)

'In Olympus?'

'Where else?'

'No. I belong here, Zeus, and you belong there.'

He didn't give up. He loved her, he said. He sent her message after message, and she withdrew further and further into the waters until not even the most determined of messengers could find her.

She knew as well as the rest of us that Olympians get what they want. She did what she had to to stay, even though that was never leaving again.

Sad for her, but perfect for me.

I had my "mother". Next, I made my plan, researched how I was different, how they were different, how I could cover the gaps between me and them.

I learned that the gods and the Titans weren't very different at all. They were both born of the earth, both immortal, powerful, taller than me. The biggest difference, aside from who was in power at any given moment, was that the gods were *obsessive*. It wasn't enough to simply be one of the ruling class; they had to be the very best at something, to embody that more than anything else. You could not simply be a god: you had to be the god *of.*

I needed my *of.* It had to be something new – I didn't want to go straight in starting fights over territory – and it had to be powerful. I wasn't going to waste my time being the goddess of dainty feet or something.

I ask a lot of the world, as a whole. That was one of my bigger demands, but I didn't rush it. I watched and I waited – I was much better at being patient then, when the present and the future were still so intertwined in my mind. I waited and I waited and I waited, and I got my reward for that when one day, Zeus walked down to the mortals, calmly put a hand on each of their shoulders, and tore them in half.

They were no longer two souls in a single body, no longer forever bound to have a best friend. One body, one soul, and one space between the two of them.

A space for me.

It was time.

I didn't go straight to Olympus. If I was going to inform the world I was the most beautiful thing since leavened bread, I owed it to them to at least make an *effort*. I visited Lemnos, where the waters are said to purify and cleanse, though as I stood there and tried not to shiver, I realised I had no idea what I was meant to be cleansing myself of.

There were frogs playing in the waters by the pool. Their skin shined so brightly with the reflections on the sun I couldn't help but stare. I took inspiration from them, anointing myself with oils until I too glistened like I was some ethereal thing, both real and not real.

I watched them for longer than I meant to, how they jumped and interacted with one another. How they shouted *brekekekex koax koax*. I wondered if the gods would be the same. Shouting and pulling at each other.

I'd been working on my voice since I decided to do this. It was lower in those days, and it harmonised with something mystical deeper in the world, which scared people, but most of all, Zeus knew it. Too many people knew it. I brought it up, higher than was comfortable to begin with. I practised my laugh too. Everyone liked the nereids with laughs like pools of water and tinkling bells. It wasn't enough for it to be beautiful: it had to sound *easy*, like I hadn't tried at all.

When I giggled, it was delicate, like fine metals gently meeting. Perfect.

My hair dried while I was watching the frogs, and I curled it around my crown, looping over and over itself. The weakest form of armour, but armour nonetheless.

I didn't own anything in those days – why would a newly born goddess have earthly possessions, after all? – so I made do with what I could find. I created perfumes from the flowers around me, running my fingers across my skin to disperse them, pausing at my wrists, my neck, my ears. I took the flowers I hadn't crushed, and I wove them into wreaths, draping them across my shoulders.

At a certain point, preparing becomes procrastination, and I could feel the balance tipping. I closed my eyes and took one final moment to breathe.

You are Aphrodite. You can do this.

Then, before I could talk myself out of it and return to the life I hated, I marched right up to Olympus. I was nervous, sure, but it was the best sort of nervous, where the excitement bubbles over and leaks into your other emotions. I was proud of who I was that day. I'd done so much to get there.

I made my entrance.

The Plan

What can they do that I can't do?
  - *Change their shape:*
    - *Solution: Make my shape the best – then why change?*
  - *Change other people's shapes:*
    - *Solution: Avoid. Say I don't want to.*
  - *Create life from random materials:*
    - *Solution: Zeus seems possessive over this one so should be okay.*
  - *Bleed gold blood:*
    - *Solution: Don't get in any fights!*
  - *Control their own domains as gods:*
    - *Solution: Hard to test for. Insist that I am and pay attention, Frodi!*

What can I do that they can't do?
  - *Read the threads of Fate.*
  - *Remember the Titans.*
  - *Be me.*

THE AGE OF THE GODS

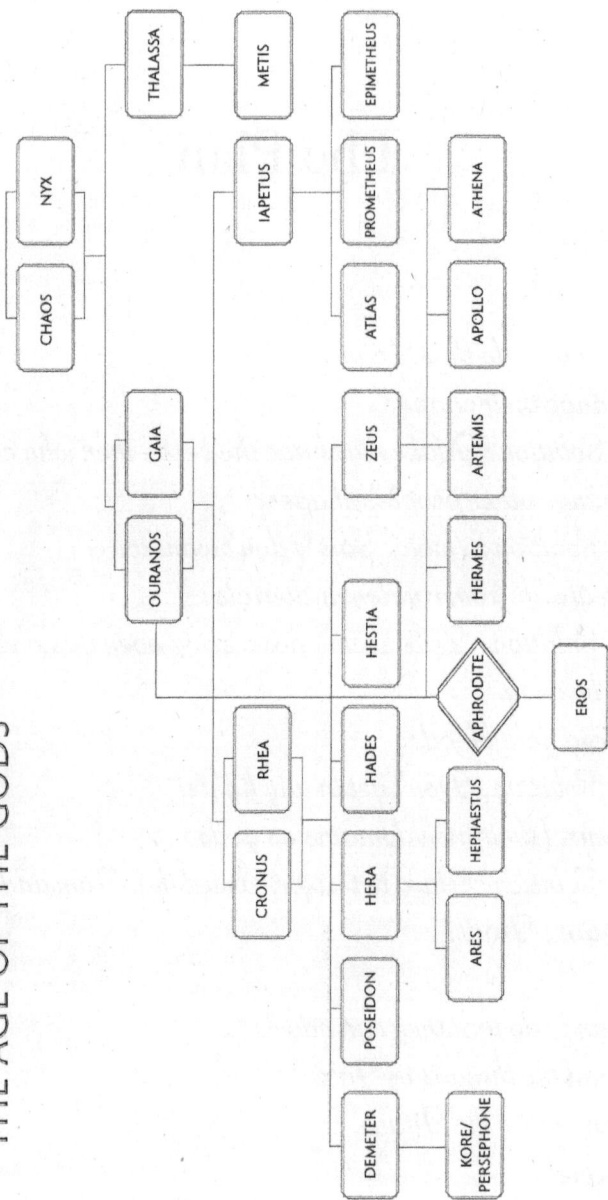

Aphirmations

I am beautiful.

I am a goddess.

I can overcome any obstacle.

I deserve to be happy.

I am Zeus' daughter.

I am not afraid of moving forwards.

I am not afraid of not knowing.

I am not afraid.

I am beautiful.

I will move confidently through today.

I will be loved.

I am worthy of love.

I am beautiful.

I create my own destin—

I create my own—

I create—

I—

I am beautiful.

Hestia I

The boys were fighting that day. The boys were always fighting. The silly bears were embarrassed that they cared about one another, so they showed it through fighting. They bickered about who got which kingdom, who got which weapon, whether the sun was shining or glimmering that day, who got to sit at the head of the table.

'We could get a round table?' I suggested. 'Then everyone can be happy!'

'Shut up, Hestia.'

I just wanted everyone to get on, like family, so I invited them round to dinner and I made sure we had everyone's favourite foods and more ambrosia than we could possibly eat. That way no one could fight over who got the most.

'Why do you always take your portion first?' Poseidon, god and king of the oceans, said to Zeus, god of the sky and king of Olympus.

'Because I'm the king.'

'We're all kings,' Hades, god and king of the underworld, muttered.

'If any of us eat in *your* kingdom then we can't escape it, so I think that shows some kingdoms are better than others,' Zeus said, quaffing wine dramatically from his goblet.

More spoons next time, I thought, then everyone could take their pieces together and they wouldn't be able to fight about it.

'How are the renovations going in the underworld?' I asked Hades. I tried to make them feel seen that way. It's a nasty thing, not feeling seen by your own family. They didn't always have time to answer when I asked them questions, but I know they appreciated it. Our sisters too. I stoked the fire and made sure there was someone waiting at home for all of them. It's not much of a home without other people in it, after all.

'It's dark.'

'Don't be rude to Hestia,' Poseidon snapped.

'You told her to shut up!'

'Well, *I* had the best day,' Zeus said. 'Not that anyone is going to ask.'

He was our fault. Not that our baby brother isn't perfect just the way he is – we all love him *so* much – but he's always been an eensy bit worried he's being left out, and we didn't know how to help him. We'd spent so long waiting for our Zeusie, that everyone built up these pictures in our heads of what he was going to be like. He was going to be Hera's husband. He was going to be Poseidon's best friend. He was going to teach Hades how to fly. He was going to be Demeter's protector.

Me, I just wanted to meet my brother. I knew I was going to love him.

But he didn't feel like my brother, or Hera's husband, or Poseidon's friend, or any of those other things, because he wasn't, not really. He didn't grow up with the rest of us. He came from a totally different place, which I know wasn't his fault, but it still hurt to look at him and know how much we missed out on.

He wasn't very good at talking to us, and we weren't very good at talking to him. I tried to make him feel included, but then someone would say something about when we were growing up, and everyone would chime in talking about it, and it would be such a lovely chat, until all of a sudden Zeusie would be standing with his arms crossed and the cutest little pout on his face.

So, when he sat there saying *not that anyone cares, not that anyone is going to ask*, it was a beacon declaring that dinner was about to be ruined, and I didn't want that at all.

'What did you do today?' I asked him. I tried to grab his hand and squeeze it so he knew I was feeling what he was feeling, so he knew I was in tune with his world, but he snatched it away. He didn't know how to let me love him.

'I tore humanity in half.'

I half choked on my wine. Demeter spat hers out.

'You did what now?' Hades said.

'I tore humanity in half.'

Zeusie had been working on humanity for ages. It was his big special project – you know, something just for him. He'd tried making them out of different things: silver, bronze, but there had always been some fatal flaw in them, some hamartia. This latest batch was made of clay – it was always on Zeusie's hands, leaving trails across his skin whenever he wiped his hair away from his face or covered his mouth because he didn't like showing his lovely smile. Our grubby baby brother.

'*Why?*' Poseidon said.

'They weren't progressing. They weren't quite right.'

I think my brother got bored with these humans.

'So you tore them in half?' Hades shouted. He was the biggest yeller of all of us, bar Zeusie.

'I didn't kill them.' Zeusie shrugged.

'How would you feel if I ripped your arms off?' Poseidon said. He was exaggerating, obviously, but Zeusie worried. His eyes got all hard, and just like that he seemed so much older than the rest of us. He came from a different place, and we couldn't always reach him there.

'Is that a threat?'

Lightning crackled as he said it. I'm really not sure why Poseidon and Hades were yelling. The humans weren't their toys, *their* big exciting project. They'd been grumbling about how boring they were every time Zeusie brought them up, but I made sure I told him they were *really* interesting.

'No,' Poseidon said. 'No, I'm not threatening you, Brother. I was just saying—'

'You think you're right about *my* people and I'm wrong?'

'You're not wrong,' Hades said. 'Just—' Wildly out of control.

Don't tell him, but the five of us met up every once in a while, maybe three times a week, when Zeusie was busy with his humans, and it came up. Zeusie was struggling. I didn't want our baby brother to crack under the pressure.

'Learning,' I insisted. 'Everyone's learning. Right, Zeusie?'

'Don't call me that.' He liked it, really. Silly bear. 'They're my people, and I'll do what I want with them.'

'Who died and made you king?' Poseidon grumbled.

'Cronus.'

'Technically dying and being cast into the depths of Tartarus for eternal damnation are different things,' Hades said.

I thought they were going to fight, right then and there. I couldn't always stop them, when they were being like this. I gripped my poker tighter in my hands. I normally used it to stir the flames of the hearth but, well, I'd fought in a war too.

The air was heavy around them, and the fighting only made it thicker, until there were sparks crackling against every surface. Soon, there'd be full-on lightning, if I knew my family. We'd probably have to find new chairs, after.

But then, a miracle arrived.

She shouldn't have got in without me noticing. I tried to welcome every new arrival in Olympus, so they could be part of the family, but the timing was what it was. I'd catch her later and tell her all about us.

She was beautiful. Her hair didn't have any particular colour, but it caught every speck of light, until she almost had rainbows shattering off her. She was taller than I was, but most people are, since I take the body of a young girl. She was shorter than my brothers and sisters, and she moved so smoothly. Still and in motion, her body was like silk. I could tell she was one of us right away, just from that.

She was wreathed in flowers, sharing that lovely smell with all of us. She didn't wear much else.

I gave her an extra big smile, but she wasn't looking at me. She was going straight for Zeusie.

She was so *so* lovely, and I just wanted her to fit in, but she made me think of a doe, a little bit. You know, natural and beautiful and elegant, but also a bit scared. Big eyes. Ready to run away, that kind of thing.

It must have just been nerves about meeting all of us, the poor dear. I'd make her some barley water later. It's good for calming restless minds.

She was quiet as she walked, and the boys were distracted. They didn't notice her until she'd found her way between them, jumping slightly to land on the table and push herself across it.

'Hi,' she said. She smiled. She was beautiful before, but her smile was *everything*. 'Is one of you Zeus?'

Zeusie's hand went up right away, and it took a tick for his eyes to catch up. He slapped it down. 'That's me. Zeus, king of the gods.'

She smiled, even wider this time, then bit her lip and looked down, like we had got to such a terrible place we were embarrassed about being *happy*.

'Hi Zeus. I'm Aphrodite.'

'Hello.'

'I'm your daughter.'

Aphrodite VIII

I was hoping for more of a response, with my grand entrance. Some drink-spitting, chair-falling, light shouting, and just a little bit of general chaos. Instead, I was met with a sigh.

'Another one?'

'Who with this time?'

'Out of wedlock?'

'More family!'

Hestia immediately tried to hug me, which was awkward, because I'd positioned myself right in the middle of the table, where they had no choice but to notice me, so she had to lean across what was far too much food. Also, because I was naked, she started overthinking it halfway to the hug and she couldn't work out which were the safe places to put her hands, and she ended up patting my shoulders for far too long.

Zeus was the only one who hadn't said anything, and that scared me. All of this hinged on him not recognising my voice, on the hope that he'd never seen my face. If I was wrong about those things, if he was going to notice them, I needed him to do it now, when I could still pretend this was a tremendously unfunny joke and I was his old friend from the cave popping up for a visit.

Everyone was talking, but all I could hear was my heart. I'd spent my entire life afraid. I refused to go back to that, so I pushed.

'Dad?'

'Who?'

I'd already given him my name, so he must have wanted my mother's. 'Dione.'

'The Titan?' The word sounded like a shit in his mouth.

I was jealous, I'll admit it. I'd spent hours upon hours training my voice so I could be everything I needed to be, and he could cram those two words with more hate than I had in my entire body without even thinking about it.

'Your mother is a Titan too.' Some questions were easier to prepare for than others.

'Don't say a word about my mother,' Zeus said.

His siblings – my aunts and uncles, I reminded myself, my family – shared a look. It spoke multitudes, but mostly it said *mama's boy*.

'Mum said Rhea was one of a kind – I should be glad to have her for a grandmother.'

'Damn right.' He leaned back and flicked sparks of lightning between his fingers. Such a petty way of showing your power, and I don't even think it was intentional. Zeus isn't so subtle when he's trying. 'What is Dione doing now?'

'She has withdrawn from politics and retired peacefully to the depths of the oceans.'

'And what are *you* doing here?' Hera said. She'd shuffled closer and closer to Zeus while all this was going on. She wanted him. Message received.

'I don't know,' I said. I raised a hand to my hair so I could twirl it, but it was too tightly wrapped for that. Dammit. I needed to play the part. I ran a thumb across my lip. Was that laying it on too thick? I didn't know. Only Hestia was looking that high up, anyway. 'Something just drew me here.'

I could see his eyes begin to shutter then. I was boring him.

'It's like two things have been pulled apart and I'm meant to bring them back together. I can just *feel* it, you know?'

Zeus' eyes lit up. 'My daughter! The humans have brought you here!'

I tilted my head questioningly.

'I split the humans in two so they'd have something to yearn and fight for. You're the spirit of that yearning.'

Yearning, not fighting. Even then, I didn't look to him like I could fight.

'I am?' I bit my lip now and clutched my hands to my chest. If only I could blush on command. 'Surely, if they were attached at their very souls, you've created more than *yearning* between them?' I kept the lilt, the question, in my voice. He'd never responded well to demands.

'Of course. Of course! I couldn't create a bond so weak. It is . . . love. Love! And you shall preside over it. Everyone,' he called, and suddenly the room was full of nymphs and spirits. 'Presenting my daughter, Aphrodite – the goddess of love.'

I twirled and bowed to everyone around me, letting the biggest, cheesiest grin settle on my face. It was real too, as the weight of all the worry evaporated from me.

I was a goddess. It was that easy. Zeus said so, and Zeus could say those things.

'Now,' Zeus said. 'Will someone get my daughter a seat?'

Hestia rushed to pull one out for me – next to her, she cooed – and she asked me many, many questions about my past. They were all perfectly polite, the kinds of things it's easy to answer when your past isn't a blatant fabrication.

'Oh just a normal childhood, you know,' I said.

'How come we've never heard of you?'

'My mother wanted me to have a quiet life, until I was ready.'

'Oh, that's so sweet. And did you like that? The quiet? Were you and your mum close? Do you have any brothers and sisters?'

'I think Olympus might be more my speed.' I smiled, conveniently forgetting to answer the other two questions. 'What was your childhood like?'

She went through the whole rigmarole, which I knew because I'd watched it unfold in real time. I was trying to work out the socially acceptable way to peel myself from her when Zeus interrupted.

Thank you, Zeus.

'Everyone, raise a glass to our newest Olympian!'

They dutifully chanted it back, in a more-or-less monotone, but so it goes. Zeus called for a real party, and the hangers-on flooded back in. I could feel it, even then: the *in* and the *out*.

I'd done it. I was *in*. They saw me.

The nectar flowed. The *wine* flowed. Gods have to drink enthusiastically before they reach the point of falling over, but they managed. It was the most amazing chaos, everyone introducing themselves and welcoming me and promising they loved me already. It was so loud my mind couldn't drag me anywhere else.

And there was Zeus. How to explain Zeus as he was back then? He smiled, all the time, and he liked throwing his hands about. It was his world and it was full of his things and he was so excited to show you around.

He never stopped moving. He flitted from person to person, nymph to nymph, and sure, sometimes he was chatting them up, but sometimes he was talking about what was going on in Olympus, and how they could make it better, but he was most alive when he talked about the mortals, what they were doing and where they were going, telling this and that funny story about what they had done this week. He was so in love with the whole world and he wanted to share it. It was a beautiful, beautiful thing.

I remembered him, of course, the little boy who'd come to visit me so often. There was enough of that still in him that it felt *bizarre* to claim he was my father. But there was no changing it now. And it was a good thing, really. He was the king, and I was a goddess. We'd made it, and now we could finally change things. I liked being part of a *we*, even if he didn't know it.

He took me around and introduced me to the stragglers who hadn't already come up and offered their wishes. The whole evening was wonderful, amazing, more than even I had dreamed of.

Until I saw the man in the corner of the room. He wasn't smiling, he wasn't drinking, he wasn't dancing. He almost seemed made of stone.

I stumbled at the sight of him.

'Too much wine, Daughter?' Zeus said, lifting me back up. 'I suppose you deserve it on a night like this!'

'Is that Prometheus—' I nodded in the direction.

'Oh, the Titan? Unpleasant to have around, I know, but he did fight on our side of the war!' Zeus sounded different when he talked about the war. His voice dropped an octave, his face grew older, and he puffed his chest out. I couldn't work out if that was because he was remembering everything he'd been through, or if he was trying to match up to what a king looked like in his head.

I nodded. I didn't care if he was a Titan. I thought I'd *killed* him.

I tried to glue my eyes to Zeus, focus on every single word he said, not let them drift, linger.

I failed.

Frequently.

Every time I glanced over, *he* was still there, refusing to look in my direction, but I knew his game. When I found something else to occupy me, and he became nothing more than another figure in my peripheries, *then* he looked. Fine. If he didn't want to talk to me then I wasn't going to talk to him. No skin off my nose.

I turned back to Zeus. I made it through the night.

And it's not as if I didn't have anything to distract me. Over the next few days, I was busy settling into life on Olympus. Zeus gave me a house, right in the centre, where only the most important of the gods lived.

'It's beautiful,' I breathed. It was white and gold, half open to the elements, but the weather didn't get much of a say up there anymore. Thanks to Zeus we could choose beauty over practicality.

'You will want to decorate.'

'I—'

'Just tell people what my daughter wants, and they'll give you what you're owed.'

'Thank you, Dad. This is all so amazing.'

I could get used to this.

By the end of the week, I had more jewels than I could carry. I didn't even have to ask. People brought them unbidden, and Zeus commissioned more for me – only the best, he said, for his newest daughter. Golds and silver and gems, twisted together to be interesting to my fingers, jewels that could hide what I wanted to hide and highlight what I wanted to highlight. I loved it all. Beauty for the sake of beauty, the freedom to just enjoy.

'You are radiant, my daughter. More stunning with every passing day.'

'By your grace,' I said, and I *meant* it. You couldn't live in Olympus and not know how much of it was controlled by Zeus, how much of it was shaped by his whims. One morning, he pulled the clouds from the sky and moulded their shape to match my form, just to say, *see how beautiful you are.*

He got me a chariot. It was smaller than some of the others on Olympus, but more intricate than anything I'd ever seen. It was encrusted with jewels and constructed of filigree so fluid your eyes could lose hours being drawn across the pattern.

'How does it fly?' I asked. There was nothing attached to draw it.

'Find something that will resonate with your powers, and it can be yoked.'

I knew my powers. With millennia at my disposal, I could never make that chariot fly. I wasn't going to lose everything I'd worked for over a *chariot*, but I couldn't panic, couldn't let that show on my face. Maybe I could feign a terrible fear of heights. Or maybe—

'I have always felt an affinity with birds,' I said. Birds can fly.

'Birds?'

'Birds.'

'Then let us look at birds!'

He took me out in his own chariot, which was drawn by horses, though not of any mortal kind. Zeus' horses, like everything else of his, were special. We travelled the world, examining every passing bird, so I might make a choice worthy of Zeus' daughter.

Symbols are important. Whatever I chose would be mine for as long as I was Aphrodite.

Eagles, obviously, were unavailable, being a symbol of Zeus. Ravens brought bad fortune. Crows were similarly inauspicious.

Owls always seemed judgemental to me. Seabirds were too noisy, always begging for attention.

It was Zeus who observed the dove in the distance.

'They are quite beautiful,' he said, and they were. Pure white, they stood out in the sky around them.

'They are, at that, though possibly a little small to pull my chariot?'

'You are a goddess, Daughter. Anything you wish for can pull your chariot.' He smiled indulgently. He found it cute when I didn't understand what was easily understood.

'Of course.' I mimed bashing my head with my palm. 'How silly of me. The doves are perfect.'

(I made up for their size with volume. I had hundreds of them, all living in the gardens at my house on Olympus. When the gods commented on the menagerie, I told them I just loved the little creatures too much to resist, even though it took twelve hundred to make the chariot fly – more if I had a big lunch.)

We were on our return when I spotted another bird. It squawked once, and that was enough for everything around it to scatter.

'What is that?' I said, pointing.

'A goose. Noisy, violent things.'

'It has rather a fine neck, does it not?'

'Do you like it?'

'I do.'

'Then take the goose too. Only the best for my daughter.'

Which is how I came to have two sacred birds. They didn't get along particularly well, my doves and my geese, but that's a small price to pay for getting literally everything I wanted, the moment I wanted it.

I had one goose to begin with, and I let it live freely in the house. I liked to see it waddling around, as if it owned the place.

I hugged Zeus, thanked him profusely.

'I love it! Now, what about you? What do you want to do?' I think I was the only person who ever asked him that. He demanded, and he got, but he was never asked.

I thought this was terribly cruel, until I heard his answers.

'I'm thinking I'll seduce Leto,' he said. I racked my brain. *Leto, Leto, Leto.* She can't have been very important either way[13] because I had all the main players down by then. I'd made notes.

'Leto . . . She's a Titan?'

'Yes.'

'How come? What's drawing you to her?' There had to be something, given how he spat the word *Titan*.

'Beauty.'

'We're already talking, you don't need to call my name,' I joked, and he actually laughed, more than it deserved, I thought. 'Would it make you happy?'

'I think so.'

'You should do it then. You deserve to be happy, Dad.'

I was getting better at calling him *Dad* without flinching.

'The others—' The sentence didn't need finishing. The other gods would judge him for enjoying sex in a multitude of odd ways, ranging from Hera's *obvious* desire for him to marry *her* – yes, they're siblings, but both their father and their grandfather married their sisters, so they had previous, and it never made much odds to gods – to Poseidon's growing unease about how many little allies Zeus was spawning.

'Fuck them,' I said. 'Say the goddess of love made you do it.' It was such a small thing, getting involved in Zeus' love life, convincing

---

[13] She's not important. Forget her at your own leisure. —A

him to seduce her, but it was something.[14] It was a change in the world that I caused. I was real, I could change things, and it was intoxicating.

He smiled and wrapped an arm around me and, for the first time since I'd come to Olympus, the king relaxed. *I* did that, and I was proud of it.

---

[14] Or so I thought. Encouraging seductions is all well and good, but they so often create children, and there's no telling what they're going to do. —A

Zeus II

I had everything. It was perfect. I was finally the king. I'd done what I was meant to. The gods bowed to me. The humans prayed to me. The nymphs— *The nymphs.*

Sounds great. Should have been. Wasn't.

Everyone was watching. All the time. Noticing. Judging. I gave them more jobs. Sent them to watch the humans – but not touch; they were *mine* – filled their hours so they didn't have time to question me.

With Leto, I fathered Artemis and Apollo. Hera sent a python after their mother while she was giving birth. Big snake, a python. Dislike. I didn't get why Hera did it. She said it was character-building.

'And if they're too weak to survive it, then do you want them as children anyway?'

Valid point.

With Maia, I had Hermes, and I thought he'd be easier. He wasn't twins. Hera didn't send a snake this time. But Hermes made his own trouble. Stole his brother's cows then traded his way out of trouble with an instrument he made out of a dead turtle? Made no sense to me, but Apollo was happy and they didn't bug me. Good enough.

'You're spawning criminals now?' Hera asked. I ignored her.

Gave Hermes many jobs to keep him distracted.

With Demeter, I had Kore. Lovely child. Bright. Did not do any crimes. Her mother knew it. Demeter hid her away from Olympus. No one cared. They thought I had enough kids. *Another one, Zeus? Really?*

Still watching. Judging. Hated it. Could feel it on my skin.

'It's because of Aphrodite,' I explained. 'She's been making me fall in love. Don't you feel it?'

Glared at them. They agreed. Yes, yes. Sex good. Aphrodite powerful. She agreed. Good girl. They didn't complain for a whole day after. I threw a feast. Why not? We're gods. What's the point being a god if you don't bloody enjoy it? Didn't think anyone would like it if I said it was to celebrate them shutting up for once. Said it was for my favourite daughter's birthday.

Everyone came. Muses[15] sang for her. I gave her a girdle. I let the Cyclopes out of Tartarus to make it. Mum was on at me to let them out so it worked for that too. Told them they couldn't leave the oceans.

'It will make you irresistible,' I said.

'Am I not already?' Aphrodite blew me a kiss. 'Thank you, Dad.' She bowed. Good girl.

Should have been a great night. Could have been. All the right things were there. But they didn't let me enjoy it. Every time, I say, the vultures never let up. Always pecking. Zeus Zeus Zeus Zeus Zeus. Always asking for things. Artemis wanted more names than her brother. Hestia wanted more family time. Demeter wanted less family time. Prometheus wanted more for

---

[15] Nymphs of music and the arts. Daughters of Zeus, but they mostly work with Apollo. —A

the mortals. Why should they get more? They were mortals. We were gods.

Always. All of them. Scraping at me. Wanting all of me. Pecking pecking pecking. If I let them have their way, there'd be none of *me* left. A puppet. That's all. A king nodding and giving himself away. That's not a real king.

My father told me that. When I overthrew him. When I showed I was bigger. Stronger. Better. Said no matter how much I gave them, I wouldn't be enough. They'd get rid of me.

That's how it goes. Sons overthrow their fathers. No matter how many you have, you'll always have one too many. They're coming for you.

He was wrong. I was bigger than him. Stronger. Better. My children wouldn't.

They'll destroy you, but they love their mothers.

I wouldn't let them. I kept them busy. Aphrodite kept them busy. All that love. Pointing them to irrelevant things. Not me. A good distraction.

'Zeusie?' Hestia. Coming my way. 'I'd like a little chatty-poo, if you have a moment.'

Never. Sisters don't overthrow their brothers. That's not the rule.

Hid behind a pillar. Half-worked. Avoided Hestia.

Demeter got me.

'My daughter is missing,' she whined.

'*Our* daughter.'

'Find her.'

'Let the girl have some fun.'

Someone should, and it wasn't going to be me.

Hades' Note

Zeus & Poseidon
The council of Olympus
Olympus

Hello brothers,

Since I am not invited to your ever-so-interesting council meetings, there has not been good opportunity for me to bring you the wonderful news: I have married. It has been seven years now, and my blushing bride is known as Persephone, though she was once named Kore.

As any competent king, as the two of you are, will know, there has been a recent swelling of the population in my realm. I'm sure you wish for me to continue to manage this, just as I am sure you will support my and my bride's happy future together. We have even acquired a dog. He is called Cerberus and he has three heads.

If you have any questions about my realm, please direct any missives directly into the Phlegethon,[16] where they will be promptly addressed in the most appropriate manner.

Most sincerely,
Hades

---

[16] River of fire in the underworld. Hades has good rivers. —A

Demeter I

Frankly, I don't think my actions need defending. I've been fighting for my daughter since before she was born, and I'll be fighting for her until the end of our world.

Zeus never felt like a brother to me. He grew up in his cave and we grew up in Cronus' stomach, and by the time we were freed and the war was done, I was happy to finally have my own space, rather than force a relationship that never existed. I could do my thing in the fields and let him do his in the skies.

Like a child picking a scab, Zeus could not let it go. He came to me when I was working. Frequently.

'You want me,' he said, without preamble.

'Does that often work for you?'

'You don't seem like a woman who would like flattery.'

Who doesn't like hearing nice things? Just because I didn't have the shiny hair, the long arms, the cow-eyes, it didn't mean I didn't care.

'Why are you here, Zeus?'

'Can't I just stop by and see you?'

'You're bored then?'

'You sound like Mum,' he said.

'Not the strongest line, as far as seduction goes.'

'Come onnnnnn.'

'Hera wants to marry you. Go pester her.'

He blanched at the thought. 'I'm not here to marry you.'

'What then?'

'We'd make a beautiful baby.'

I couldn't deny it. All his babies were beautiful, all of them healthy, glowing bundles of joy parcelled out to people who might or might not want them. But I did want one, very much.

'Okay,' I said. I began pulling my clothes off.

'Now?'

'No time like the present.'

We lay there, in the middle of my fields, in the middle of all the plants I brought to life, and it felt right. It felt inevitable that any child of mine would be conceived here, but it wasn't.

It was supposed to be easy. That was the trade-off everyone handed me. You won't be the object of desire. You won't be the centre of anyone's attention. You will be sturdy and solid and reliable, but you will be a mother.

It was supposed to be fucking *easy*.

And it wasn't.

It couldn't have been Zeus. Zeus only needed to look at a nymph to impregnate her. It had to be me. I'd committed to this, though. There was a baby in my head, a son, and I wanted him. Zeus obviously didn't care about the picture in my head – he had pretty nymphs to woo – but he wasn't getting what he wanted without giving me mine.

'Again.'

'Demeter, I'm busy.'

I undressed. 'Again.'

So we went: again and again and again. In the fields, in our beds, during a feast once. I washed in the water at Lemnos to cleanse myself. After years of mocking the boys for lauding carrots for virility, I ate them until my skin was tinged with yellow. Worst of all, I went to the women of Olympus for conception advice.

Hestia: That's really gross, sis.

Hera: I'm not telling you how to get my future husband to impregnate you.

And from Artemis, goddess of *childbirth*: I have no interest in the whole business. Your fruits do it better.

The only goddess who was any help at all was Aphrodite. She gave me oils. And tips.

It didn't work. I told her that.

'But did you have fun?'

'The point isn't to have fun.'

She looked confused. 'That's always the point. Maybe you can try—' There were more *tips*. None of them worked.

There was nothing for it. I went to see my mother, who also had no good advice because she couldn't *stop* having kids with the man who kept eating them. But she held me and she stroked my hair and whispered all those useless things about giving it time, it will come.

'You can make the fruits grow,' I said. 'You must be able to do something.'

'You, my love, are not a fruit.'

Entirely unhelpful, but I let her hold me anyway. I went back to Zeus.

'Again.'

'Demeter, I have a headache.'

There was no magical combination of words in the end, no special factors I could see. It was, as my mother said, all about time. Hera helped me with the labour, on the condition I stopped sleeping with her future husband. I had no problem agreeing to that. I had what I wanted.

'It's a girl,' she said.

She wasn't the baby in my head. Not the boy with the strong forearms and the big smile who loved the sky and the earth. Not the boy with my dark skin and his father's green eyes.

Hera handed me my daughter and none of that mattered anymore.

'You are beautiful,' I whispered to her. I said it every day, took every opportunity to remind her. She would grow up knowing all the value that she had. 'Kore.'

Zeus came to see her sporadically in her childhood. He brought gifts and played games and shot tiny sparks between his fingers so she could watch.

She grew up more like him than I expected. She liked the outdoors, the time spent under the sun and in the fields – she got that from me – but she loved beautiful things too. She was more of a fan of the flowers than the fruits, endlessly prodding them to feel the petals.

'Be gentler, dear,' I warned her. 'That could hurt them.'

'No! I will protect them.' She stood sentry in front of them the rest of the day, standing at attention and staring down any passing bird or animal. She can't have been very old then – she wasn't past my hips, for certain – but she already knew what she wanted.

Maybe she got that from both of us.

I thought my child would love me unconditionally. Instead, my little fighter quite often told me she hated me when I tried to protect her. That didn't stop me. I loved her so much.

I didn't trust my brothers with her. She'd already decided she wished to follow Artemis' path of eternal girlhood, and I supported her in that. I tried to ensure she got the choice. For that, I couldn't trust *any* man with her. I got by on my own because I was powerful and I was old and I was not beautiful. She was the opposite, in all things. Her power came from sheer force of will rather than anything innate. She was young and pretty and the daughter of Zeus, and she thought it made her invulnerable when it made her the opposite.

She took liberties. She flirted with the rules and she flirted with flirting. There was no intention. She said it was fun. She wasn't interested in anything further.

She pushed the boundaries of where young women were meant to go and what they were meant to wear. She wouldn't let me protect her.

'Mum! Stop following me. You're being weird.'

She went missing two weeks later, when the other gods were distracted by some party for Aphrodite on Olympus. I hadn't let her go. It wasn't safe.

She went out playing instead. She still played. She was so young, when she was taken. When she screamed, it wasn't the scream of a woman. It was the scream of my little girl, still afraid of the dark.

It feels wrong to complain about how young she was when she was taken, though, instead of the fact that *she was taken*. There's no special age she could have reached where it would have been acceptable to me.

I went straight to Zeus. He was no help at all.

'Kore is missing.'

'Let the girl have some fun.' He grinned, like this was one of his stupid games.

'She is my *daughter*.'

'*Our* daughter,' he corrected smugly. Wrong. Increasingly sparse visits with a cake she hasn't liked for years doesn't make you a father – not like arguing about her name *again* does. 'When you were her age, you were following me around taking your clothes off.'

I tore up Olympus looking for her and, when that bore no fruit, I tore up the world. I did not permit a plant to grow in my absence: no crop, no vegetable, nothing to feed or shelter his little projects. If I would suffer the loss of what I loved most, then so would he.

After a week or so, Zeus noticed a certain amount of wilting from his people and sent Apollo and Artemis after them. They found nothing, so the famine continued.

I didn't want to starve people, but I did what I had to. I have no regrets about that.

It took us *seven* years to find her. In that time, I did a great many horrible things. The mortal population was decimated. They started wars over people breathing too loudly, someone looking at them funny. A king invited us to dinner, but, when there was no real dinner to be had, he butchered one of his own sons and served us him instead. The other gods noticed and refused. I did not.

'Demeter, this is your wake-up call,' Zeus said. He was looking me in the eye for once. He was holding my shoulder. He didn't sound smug at all. 'You have to stop this.'

I didn't. Not when Zeus begged, nor Hera. I was done being sturdy and dependable and reliable. If they wanted their people back, they could get me my fucking daughter.

It was Hades who took her. We found out because he had the audacity to send a note, letting all of Olympus know about his new bride, *Persephone*.

He'd changed her name. It wasn't good enough to take her away from me; he had to entirely change who she was.

I tried to break my way into the land of the dead, to get her back, but I couldn't. My domain is about bringing life, so Hades rejected me. I stood at the border and heckled until someone brought her to me.

I hadn't done my hair. My face was a mess. I wasn't going to stop and fix those things, not when there was a chance they'd delay me seeing my daughter, even by a moment. When she appeared, I lunged towards her, ready to pull her into my arms, but she was on his side of the border, and I was on mine.

'It's cold here, Ma.'

'You can come home now.'

One tear rolled down her cheek. She was still beautiful, my daughter, even like this, and, for the first time, I regretted that.

'I can't. I ate the food of the dead. I have to stay.'

'Who says?'

'Zeus.'

I tried to lean over again, to cross that line and kiss her on the cheek, hug her, remind her it was okay, but it held firm. 'You just wait here, okay? I've got you. I can fix this.'

I went to Zeus. I threatened and demanded and said things that are never acceptable to say to your king, and he let me say all of them before he shrugged.

'Unfortunately, those are the rules,' Zeus said. 'She will have to stay with Hades. He wants her. And, as you promised, now she's been found, you will stop starving humanity.'

'No.'

'You swore on the Styx.'

Did I? It was a blur. By destroying the very thing I was in charge of, I'd undercut my own power while we were looking for her. It was . . . patchy.

'I don't care. This is stupid. Some technicality. I want my daughter back.'

'Then it is up to you to convince Hades.'

That was an exercise in impossibility and Zeus knew it. He rarely left his own realm and that was blocked to me. But I'd promised Kore. So I went to Aphrodite.

'Zeus is refusing to make Hades release her, and I cannot go to Hades directly to convince him. Please, Aphrodite, force him out of whatever infatuation he has with my daughter so she can come home. Please.' I didn't like begging, but I needed her help.

'You are aware that I'm the goddess of *love*, right? That kind of goes against what I do.'

'What you can make, you can unmake. Like I did with the harvest.'

She went silent after that. She twitched her nose, rocked her head from side to side, rubbed her wrists. And then—

'No.'

'No?'

'I can't break up love. I'm sorry, Demeter.'

'You have to.'

'I don't want to.'

'You don't *want* to? What's wrong with you?'

'There are a few too many virgins in Olympus, don't you think? I'd hate for your Persephone to go the same way.'

'Her name is Kore.' I accompanied this with a swinging punch to Aphrodite's jaw. She screamed, not like a girl but a monster, and raised a hand blindingly fast to cover her mouth.

'I deserved that!' she said. 'I deserved that, but don't you think you're taking this out on the wrong person?'

'You could help her. And you won't. That makes you an entirely punchable person.'

'You're right. I could. And I'm not going to. I'm a bitch!' It came out muffled, dragged across her mouth, still covered with her hand.

'What's wrong with you?' I shouted. 'Zeus, I can understand, but you? Are you so desperate for him to fuck you? Is he really worth it?'

'You have no idea how much you have.'

She was beautiful. Not like my daughter was, not even like my sisters. She transcended every boundary of beauty, redefined symmetry in her form.

I've never hated anything more than I hated beauty in that moment.

'Fuck you, Aphrodite. Fuck you and everything you do.'

'I understand.'[17]

---

[17] Demeter was an enemy I could have lived without, in the long term, but back then I was just trying to survive the day. —A

A Note From Zeus

LISTEN UP, YOU LOT. I KNOW YOU'RE ALL DYING TO
MARRY MY DAUGHTER, BUT YOU'VE MADE IT CLEAR
THAT IF SHE MARRIES ONE OF YOU, THE REST OF
YOU ARE GOING TO FIGHT OVER IT. SO, I SAY NO. THE
GODDESS OF LOVE IS MEANT TO BE FREE. IT'S HER
CHOICE. STOP SLIDING BIDS UNDER MY DOOR. I DON'T
CARE HOW MANY COWS YOU HAVE, APOLLO.

AND NO MORE KIDNAPPING, EITHER.

— ZEUS,

THE BEST AND THE GREATEST, KING OF OLYMPUS,
LORD OF THE SKIES

Eros I

Mummy made me out of a seashell and a strand of her hair.[18] She blew and out I came. It was such fun, being born. I came flying out of the end of the shell and across the waters, so I pointed and straightened up to get as far as I could, till I knew I was going down. Then I balled up to make the biggest splash.

'Hello?' she shouted. 'Are you still there?'

I waited low, keeping my whole body dead still below the water, without even a ripple, waiting for her to come in after me.

When she did, I sat bolt upright and spat all the water I'd been holding in my mouth into the sky.

'Look, Mummy, I'm a fountain!'

My jokes have gotten better since then. You have to joke, you know, because this whole life is a joke. If you don't see the fun in it, where does that leave you?

Don't believe me? Well, how's this for you then?

I'm the god of sex, and no sex went into my creation.[19] If it had,

---

[18]   Lies. I have male and female genitalia. I impregnated myself and hid it from the other gods. I had to get more doves to pull my chariot. I couldn't imagine Zeus being happy with the idea that a woman could make a child alone and, anyway, they could all make children from sunlight and sideways glances. I had to look like I could too. —A

[19]   Depends on your definition, I suppose. —A

then Mummy would have had to share me with someone, and she didn't want that. Even on the first day when I splashed her with water twice in the first three minutes and low-level faked my own death, she stared at me with the widest eyes and told me I was a miracle.

'It worked. I can't believe it actually worked. You're perfect.'

That's how it should be. Sex is for sex, and having babies is so you can love them.

She hugged me, wrapping her arms tight, tight, tight around me. I wanted to explore, but I know love when I feel it. I could wait one second while she had this. She rested her head on mine and breathed deep in.

'Mummy, are you smelling my hair?'

'No?'

'You are! Mummy, that's so weird.' So I picked her up and threw her into the water and splashed her more, and finally she splashed me back and we played, and that was the end of my first day.

She hid me away at first. We didn't like that.

'This isn't forever,' Mummy said. 'I'll get you out before long, I promise.'

We still hung out all the time. Every moment we both could. She was mine and I was hers, and that was all that mattered. Then we began on everything I was going to *get*.

We liked that.

'You're going to be a god, Eros.' That was my name. Eros. Sexual love. *My* kind of love. Mummy said I'd know which kind of love was right for me, so I pretended for a day it was the love you have for sports teams, until she buried her head in her hands and threatened to make me a brother who was less of a shit. But we were smiling.

'I'll bring you up to Olympus and introduce you as my son, and no one will be able to question it.'

'Yeah, obviously, we look just like each other.' Same hair, same eyes, same hands, even. Minus a couple of bits of equipment, we could have been twins.

'You do, don't you? Now, let's see what you can do.'

She'd brought toys for us to play with. A sword, a boat, a bow. Wine and food and birds and bees. Metals and clay. We sat in a cave and she handed me each one.

'Mummy, you take this one!'

'They're your toys, Eros.'

'No, I want you to play too. It's boring by yourself.'

'You're definitely my son.'

'Duh, who else would I be?'

But I did as she asked and took the clay from her hands, and I made little versions of both of us.

'They're beautiful, Eros. Shall I put them on the side, here?'

'No, you have to twist their heads off!'

'*Our* heads?'

'They're not real, Mummy. Do it.' She did. Bees came flying out. She made a funny noise at first, but then we were both laughing together. 'Again, again.'

'Why don't you try something else?'

The metal she gave me didn't bend in my hands, but it was shiny, at least. When it caught the sun, I could see our reflection together, all the ways we looked just the same all at once. And I could start fires! That was fun.

The sword was heavy. The birds I liked. They cooed and sang for me, and the bees danced around my head, a language in their bodies I didn't understand. All the animals had one, but the bees I liked the best. I could have fun with bees.

'Eros, my love, I know you're enjoying yourself—'

'It's *so* much fun.'

'But why don't you put the bees down for a bit? There are more things to try.'

'But I don't even know what we're looking for.'

She mumbled something. It sounded like *experimental method*. Then she scowled. 'There will be something that resonates for you, and you'll be able to channel your power through it.'

'What's yours?'

'What?'

'What do you control love through? I bet we have the same.'

'Oh, lovely, no. We're not the same for this. You'll have one because you're so special.'

'But you're special too.'

'A different kind of special, Ro-Ro.'

'I don't want to be different. You said we were just the same.'

'But think how cool it could be. Like how Zeus channels his power through his thunderbolts?' She'd told me about Zeus, how we were going to be friends but I shouldn't play any of my tricks on him – *really, Eros* – because he had a short temper. He was the king. He was powerful so I had to listen, like Mummy.

'Okay, we'll keep trying.'

We tried spears and food and music, and none of it did anything. We spent so long there it got boring. I wanted to sleep, but I could see Mummy wanted this so badly. I tried for her, playing with all these empty things, until we got to the bow. It was perfect. It tingled with possibilities. My hands felt empty when I put it down.

'This is it, isn't it?' Mummy said.

'It's it.'

We ran to each other and hugged and jumped and spun around,

and it was so much fun the rest of the day. Then she went home, and when she came back, it was time for us to work again.

She took me to the water and told me to try being everything I ever wanted to be.

'I want to be here, with you.'

She beamed and we hugged again. 'Of course you do, sweetheart, but why not try being something else, just for a minute? Like being a fish. Try being a fish.'

'How?'

Her eyes went all wide again. 'You'll know it when you feel it,' she said.

'That's not very helpful, Mummy.'

'What does love feel like, Eros?' Suddenly stern with the full name. Not a pet name or a nickname. Sometimes she called me Ro-Ro.

'You know it when you feel it,' I grumbled.

'So *feel* it – be the fish.'

It took ages, but the sun was nice and the water felt good on my ankles, and I imagined what it would be like to feel the water come all over me, to have no weight at all and be one with it, but that didn't work, not until I thought about how fun it would be to swim around with Mummy and all the games we could play in the water, and I wanted that more than anything. And I could have anything I wanted, so it did what I wanted, rising up and up and up, until I looked at Mummy and saw her *waaaaay* up above me and I realised the water hadn't grown, I'd shrunk. I was a fish.

Exciting!

I could swim and dart in and out of the waves; I could toss and turn. Every bit of my body felt right where I was, like it was doing what it was meant to, and I didn't have to think about anything at all.

'Come join me,' I tried to say, only I wasn't a boy anymore, I was a fish, so it came out as a dance. 'Swim with me, Mummy!' She didn't do anything. Just watched me through the water. 'Swim with me!'

'Ro-Ro, if you're trying to talk to me, I can't understand what you're saying. You have to be a boy again for that.'

And I wanted to tell her, convince her to come with me, let her know how great it felt, so I turned back into a boy, and I did.

'So, come on. Turn into a fish and we can swim together!'

'Oh, honey, no. Mummy doesn't change her shape.'

'Why not?'

'Because the body I have is already perfect. Why would I trade it down?'[20]

'Well, I want to stay with you. I won't change. I'll just be a boy.'

'Ro-Ro, the only way you could ever disappoint me is if you decide you're *just* anything. We need you to be so much more than that when you come up to Olympus with me.'

That's when she really told me about how Zeus was filling Olympus with his children because they'd be the most loyal to him, and Mummy needed someone who would be totally loyal to her instead.

'But the king is your friend?'

'He is, but family sticks around, even more than friends.'

'Didn't you say he was your daddy too?'[21]

She stopped. 'Can I tell you a secret, Ro-Ro? I love you the best

---

[20] Yes, if you're wondering, that is me lying to my son. Since I'm not a goddess, I can't change my shape, and I could hardly go around admitting that. —A

[21] That's the peril of lying to your children. They have an uncanny ability to remember things. —A

133

of everyone.' She booped me on the nose. I giggled. 'Now, how do you want to make your grand entrance? You could come in on a horse? Or a cloud?'

'I want to jump out and surprise everyone!'

'Of course you do.'

'So can I?'

'I think we can make that happen.'

She smuggled me into Olympus as a bee, then I hid in the fountain. The big one. I giggled. I was a fountain again.

I had to wait till they were having one of their special parties, but they had one all the time, so she said it wouldn't be too hard, just a little patience. I still made a face.

'None of that. Patience is important.'

It wasn't the *worst* waiting but it was bad. It took *days*. But she came and whispered to me so I'd know what was happening, and if anyone talked to her, Mummy lied to them! She told them she was talking to herself.

Then it was time. She made our signal. I jumped out of the water.

'My son is born,' she shouted. She only got to *son* before her eyes landed on Zeus. 'I shall call him Eros! Title forthcoming—' She bit her lip. 'Hopefully, Dad?'

'He shall serve as the finest of your retinue,' the king said. I looked at Mummy. That's not what she said would happen. She said I would be on the main council, be a proper god.

She turned and hugged me. It wasn't a real hug. It was so she could whisper in my ear.

'You promised—'

'I know, sweetheart, I know, and I shouldn't have because we can never know what's going to happen, but this is better, can't you see? This means you can work with me all the time.'

She was looking over at the other side of the room. At someone, I thought, but I couldn't tell who with all those people milling around.

'We'll stay together?'

'Always, Ro-Ro. Now, do you want to come meet Mummy's friends?'

I nodded. She was different around them. Not so fun. Always nodding and agreeing and wearing her serious face. I didn't like that, but I didn't know anyone else so I followed her.

I moved in with her, at the beginning, and every day she came home and asked me what I'd learned. I showed her myself as a bird, a bee, a tree, all the different things I could turn into. But I was most excited to show her what I could do with my bow.

'Mummy, *look*,' I said. I shot one of her doves with an arrow – don't worry, I made them specially; I didn't want to *hurt* the dove – and then another. They flew right to each other and one jumped on the other's back. 'I can make them love each other.'

'That's one word for it.'

'Eros! Like my name. You were right. I *knew*.'

'Does it work on everyone, Ro-Ro?'

'I haven't tried it with any people yet. I wanted to show you first.'

'Good, that's – that's really great. You should always tell me first. You're such an amazing boy – you know that?'

'Yup!'

'Don't tell anyone for now – we'll save it as a really great surprise, yeah?'

'Okay!'

'Now, be a good boy and show me what else you can do.'

Aphrodite IX

How would Prom have phrased it? Eros was a bold strategy. I knew I ran the risk of upsetting Zeus by introducing someone who'd be loyal to me over him, but my son was worth it. I refused to end up in the position I did with Demeter again, where I had to rub salt into the still-gaping wound of a still-grieving mother to keep my position. I don't *regret* the 'too many virgins in Olympus' comment – it's better to be a powerful bitch than a kindly weakling – but it's better still to have that power in the first place.

Hence Eros. I made him because I needed him. He was a god from birth, and he knew that unquestioningly. He would have the powers I didn't, and he would be only my son. He would be loyal to me. He would help, and he would lie for me, if I needed him to.

At the beginning, I used him for the most pointless things, just to show that I could, that I had that strength, and to rub it in everyone's faces. When a sculptor[22] fell desperately in love with his own statue,[23] I had Eros breathe life into the stone so they could live their happily-ever-after. When Poseidon and

---

[22] Pygmalion. —A
[23] Galataea. —A

Zeus started bickering over the same mortal boy,[24] Eros made sure he chose Zeus over his brother, and I made sure Zeus knew we did that for him.

And it wasn't so entirely cold-hearted as that. I was lonely. Demeter had a lot of friends. After I pissed her off, I found that I didn't. Hera wouldn't talk to me out of loyalty to Demeter. Artemis wouldn't talk to me because she thought I'd try to make her get married and, on the flip side, most of the men wouldn't talk to me because I refused to marry them.

I couldn't talk to Prometheus because Zeus made it *very* obvious what his feelings about trusting a Titan were, and I couldn't talk to Zeus because he liked the idea of people needing him much more than the reality of people needing him. I spent most of my days alone, and I couldn't live like that again. I wanted someone to love me. Eros would be my friend, attendant, confidant.

I still caught Prometheus looking at me sometimes, waiting for me to look his way too. I ignored it. Looking leads to eye contact, to a moment, to the reignition of a centuries-long friendship, and that was too dangerous, for both of us.

Especially then. I felt like Zeus was being cool with me. I'd stopped receiving so many gifts and invitations. He hung back from meetings so we wouldn't end up walking together and instead wrapped himself up talking to Metis, of all people. Clever, boring, stupidly perfect Metis, who used to hang out with Prometheus way back when. Titan Metis.

All in all, I was surprised when he had Hermes summon me to Earth, to a cave in a mountain far from where I grew up.

---

[24] Ganymede. —A

I didn't like it. It felt unstable. Too dry, with cracks webbing out from invisible faults.

'Aphrodite,' Zeus boomed. 'I have a project for you.'

'Oooh? And what does the king need his oldest daughter for?'

'You are to make a woman in your own image, give her every gift you can think of.'

'I love that. Where's she going, when she's done.'

Once upon a time, Zeus might have told me there couldn't be too much of me in the world, that he wanted more beauty, more love, more *Aphrodite*. I wanted that more than I'm proud of.

'It is to be presented as a reward for someone's loyalty.'

'I see. I do have to say, I'm not much of a sculptor. You might try asking Pygmalion.'

'Who?' So much for being noticed for my new power. 'No, you will be working with Prometheus on this.' On cue, Prometheus entered the cave. He looked at me. I looked at him.

'You.'

'You.'

'You two have met?' Zeus asked.

'Only in the usual way,' I said.

'Around and about on Olympus, and so on and so forth. You know how it is.'

'Do I?' Zeus said.

I revised my opinion. Zeus hadn't been cool with me at all. If his behaviour around Prometheus was any kind of baseline then he'd been flaming hot before, practically declaring his undying love with every passing sentence.

'I'm sure we'll do great work together!' I said, before anyone was actually set alight.

'Don't disappoint me. This woman must be perfect.'

'Like me?'

'If you want.'

He walked out and off the side of the mountain, transforming into an eagle as he fell, arms spread wide, turning into wings as he swooped across the bottom of the valley. Show-off.

'Well, that was dramatic,' Prometheus said. He looked at me significantly. 'I believe we're alone.'

'Why would it matter whether we're alone or not? This is how we behave together because we don't know each other.'

'Don't be like this.'

'How am I being any particular way? You don't know me.'

'Understood.'

I tried. I want it to be known that I tried. I tried to keep a straight face, maintain everything I'd strived for. I *tried* not to fall back in love with my best friend. The only problem is, I failed.

We worked together for weeks to make Pandora. Alone. And for weeks, when I arrived, he nodded respectfully and the conniving shit didn't say anything.

'I know what you're doing,' I said.

'I'm not doing anything.'

'You're trying to make me talk to you.'

'Why would a nice young goddess want to talk to a Titan like me?'

And so it went, hours of driving each other around in circles, pretending we didn't know each other's weak points, and pretending even harder that we weren't poking them, because admitting would be losing, and neither of us wanted to lose.

'Did you *see* what he has Ganymede wearing today?' Prometheus said.

'I am a goddess. I do not indulge in such petty comments.'

'Is that so?'

'And if I did, I certainly wouldn't be worrying about his clothes, with that awful *earring*.' Shit. I bit my tongue and turned away from him. It was too easy to slip back into old habits. Too easy to feel secure when we were easily monitored and eavesdropped on.

Yet, every day, I wanted more. It's so much easier to avoid completely than it is to have in moderation.

'It's a shame I'm stuck in here with an untrustworthy Titan,' I said. 'Otherwise I would have some incredible gossip to share.'

He hummed to himself, continued sculpting.

'Gossip about Zeus.'

He hummed louder.

'Zeus and a Titan.'

He might have been the one making the body, but he was clay in my hands. 'Frodi, you're killing me – are we friends or not?'

'All I'm saying is I wouldn't tell just anyone that Zeus is in love with Metis.'

'He is *not*.'

'Is too.'

By the end of the day, there was a line of clay across my shoulders where he had slung an arm across them, and my face hurt from smiling so much. It was so easy to talk to him, to be honest. To be around someone who had known me for as long as there was someone to know. To be around someone who wasn't looking for obedience or answers or any kind of perfection, someone who knew me and loved me at the same time.

I could just have this one thing, I justified, and it would be okay. As long as I could have him, then I could be who I needed to be for the rest of them.

'What if someone sees?' Prometheus asked, after he walked in and I summarily threw myself into his arms.

'Poseidon started sleeping with one of his nymphs, and his wife found out. All the gossips are focusing on that right now.' I was suspicious Eros had done that one on his own.

'I hadn't heard that. How do you know that? Are you—' Messing about with primordial forces again, he didn't say, but we both felt the question.

'I *am* all of the gossips.'

'Clever.'

'Thank you.'

'I missed you,' he said. 'You've done so well.'

'I have, haven't I?' And it was so wonderful, even just for a moment, to acknowledge I'd done something. I worked for this, and I succeeded. 'She's going to be so gorgeous.'

She was nearly done. She had a face and lips and hair and legs. We'd hand-crafted each and every one of her teeth, which involved no small amount of running my tongue across my own teeth to work out how many people had. Prometheus just *knew* the number.

'You do know Zeus is trying to trick us, don't you?'

'What?'

'Zeus wouldn't just ask us to *make a woman* out of the goodness of his heart.'

'It's a gift, he said. He gets me gifts all the time.'

'That's because he wants to sleep with you.'

'He doesn't! He thinks I'm his daughter.' Prom levelled me a particularly old-fashioned look. 'He wouldn't do that to me.'

I know. I know. But back then, Zeus had never done anything to hurt me. He gave me a home and a title and riches beyond anything I could have dreamed. He was my friend. He shared his world with me. He loved me, and all I had to do was love him back.

'He would do that to me,' Prom said. He'd got better at arguing, less focused on what was true and more on what made sense.

'I don't know why you think he's so out to get you.'

'Because he is out to get me. He thinks Titans are inherently untrustworthy.'

'He goes to Metis for advice all the time.'

'He wishes to copulate with Metis.' Sleep with me but copulate with Metis. Strange double standard. To be considered later.

Zeus' sex drive. It shouldn't be so much of the story. It shouldn't be so much of *him*, but it was, and I can't even complain about it, because if he was less of a pest, then what I did – what I *said* I did – wouldn't be half as important as it was.

'No, there's something else, isn't there? Something you're not telling me.'

'For whatever reason, he's your friend, Frodi. You don't want to know.'

'Stop trying to protect me,' I shouted, surprising myself with the sound of my own voice, the timbre of it changing, dropping back to what it had been so long ago. 'I'm a goddess now. I don't need that anymore.' He smiled, wryly. 'And stop that too, thinking you know better than me.'

'I cannot control what I think.'

'If anyone could, it would be you.'

He smiled, at that. Flattery will get you everything.

'I tricked him,' he said.

'What?'

'He was demanding too much sacrifice from the mortals, so I made up two plates of meat and disguised the bad cuts as the good, and vice versa, then proceeded to ask the king of the gods to choose.'

'And he chose the bad meat by accident?'

'I immediately announced that he had done it out of the benevolence of his spirit, so he could not go back on it. He was very angry.'

'No shit, Prom. Why?' For the Titan of forethought, Prometheus could be awfully impulsive.

'They were starving, Aphrodite. I remember when you cared about that.'

'Well, Zeus might be trying to hurt you then, but I still know he wouldn't do that to me.'

We both left the thought there, as pregnant as if Zeus had got to it.

Prom didn't bring up his suspicions for days after that. I took the body – we hadn't breathed life into her yet – around to the gods, asking for their blessings, as Zeus had demanded. Demeter spat half-masticated grain in my hair. It hurt. I didn't plan to be hated.

Prometheus noticed. 'Are you okay?'

'I don't have any friends.'

'You'll always have me,' he said. It was, objectively, the right thing to say in the situation, but since I ended his chance at *always*, it was absolutely the worst thing he could have said to me.

I burst into tears.

'Frodi? What's wrong? Is Demeter bullying you?'

I snorted. I couldn't help it any more than he could help being so ridiculously, obnoxiously *him*. 'I'm an immortal goddess, and you're worried about me being bullied?'

'Yes.'

'It's fine. It's just been a long day, is all.'

He leaned down and kissed me on the forehead. 'I don't believe

143

you, but I love you anyway.' He took a seat on the floor beside me – just like in the old days – and I let my head drop to his shoulder.

'I'm sorry, Prom.'

'Whatever for?'

'Let's get to work.'

By the end, both of us were dragging our feet. We didn't want to finish, because then what reason would we have to speak? But Zeus demanded, and there were only so many times we could claim a clay shortage, or a search for more gifts, or that the moon wasn't shining quite right. The day came when we had to admit she was ready, and pass her over to Zeus.

He had us dress her for a wedding. He didn't tell us who the groom was, but it wasn't like Prometheus wouldn't recognise his older brother. The one he loved, not the one who choked me.

'Epimetheus?' Prometheus said. 'What are you doing here?'

'Zeus said he'd found me a—' He didn't finish his thought. His eyes had found Pandora. I don't think they ever lost her again.

The two of them, they were perfect. Perfect in a way that should be entirely impossible if you weren't one soul in the first place. They locked arms around one another. She spoke faster than a horse galloped, and he smiled and listened and answered even faster. I couldn't understand what either of them were saying, but they could. All either of them needed was someone who moved at the same pace.

When they kissed, it was so tender I could feel it in my chest. It was all I could do not to reach a hand out and grab Prometheus', squeeze it.

'Good job, you two,' Zeus said. 'You can go now.' He waved us off.

'But—' Prometheus said.

'Do you not want your brother to be happy with his bride?'

'Of course I do.'

'Then be off. And you two.' Zeus turned to the happy couple. 'I have brought gifts for you, from all of us gods.'

He didn't ask me for gifts. He probably thought my making her counted, but I couldn't know that. I worried about it for months.

The other presents were of the usual sort, jewels and meats and finery that belonged on Olympus, not in mortal hands. They joked that they had a one-room house, but they had four hundred plates.

What? We made the girl. Of course Prom and I sneaked off to see how they were doing.

They made their way through their giant stack of gifts, laughing and sharing and smiling, right up until they reached the last of them. It was a large jar, with a note.

Do not open this jar.

And they didn't. For months.

They talked about it, a lot, but they didn't open it. They alternated by the day who was more intrigued by the jar. They hid it under their bed. They tied clothes around it, made a physical and optical barrier.

They lasted *months*.

This girl I'd made, this girl I poured myself into, she worked

145

so hard to do as she was told, and she did a far better job at it than I ever would have. She did as Zeus asked; she was obedient. But Zeus didn't want obedience. He can't have, or he wouldn't have gone to visit her.

'Have you been, ahem, *enjoying* all your gifts?' He was uncomfortable there, playing the part of the almighty king, in a house without fire. The mortals weren't allowed it, lest they become too strong, and Pandora was one of them, not one of us.

'Oh yes!'

'*All* of them?'

He didn't need to push it further than that.

She opened the jar. You probably knew that already. And when she did, she discovered that, to celebrate her marriage, the king of the gods had gifted her a collection of communicable diseases.

She didn't have to be a god to take one look at the contents and know devastation was coming.

'I'm sorry,' she told her husband.

'Don't be.' Epimetheus smiled, then. He wrapped her tight in his arms and lifted her clear from the floor. 'I would have opened it the first day.'

Their love was never clearer than it was that night when Pandora inadvertently ended the world as they knew it. They closed the shutters from the consequences, and for just one more night, they could be happy.

The jar didn't introduce mortality to the mortals – that's an exaggeration – but the plagues therein hurt humanity profoundly. They were still recovering from Demeter's famine; the loss of so many people was just one more blow they couldn't take.

I could have forgiven Zeus. I could have believed some flimsy justification about it being a test of their loyalty because Epimetheus hadn't really been on any side during the war against the Titans. I could have folded myself in half to believe the right thing, if it weren't for that last visit. As it was, he told me to make a woman in my own image, to fall in love with her, to make her obedient, and I did all that. But it wasn't enough. He poked her until she disobeyed, and then he told the entire world it was her fault – that women should not be too curious, too thoughtful – and why? Because Prometheus had tricked him? Because I'd made Eros and dared to love someone other than him?

Whatever made him do it, humanity was ravaged by disease. It got better after some years; they seemed to build up a tolerance, as amazingly resilient as ever, but those early days were horrifying.

It was difficult to watch, but it was impossible to turn away. I'd tied my fortune to mankind – the goddess of love cannot exist without people who love one another – and, for a time, it looked like Pandora's jar was going to destroy the whole project.

I couldn't let it stand. I went to Prometheus. He was right – I couldn't watch them suffer.

'We need to help them. Distract him.'

'Agreed. We could—'

I cut him off. 'Do you trust me?'

'I do.'

'Then leave this to me.'

The Metis Letters

Zeus,
~~I loved you.~~
~~You were my best friend. I didn't t h i n k you were my best friend. You w e r e my best friend. You overtook someone I've known since long before you were alive, and I didn't notice it happening, because I was so excited it was happening.~~

I nearly told you who I was, that I'd already known you for years and years and years, that you were my one spot of hope when I was younger, of a future when I was not alone in a cave. I nearly told you we watched the same civilisation live and die when there was no one else to cherish or curse it. I nearly told you everything, because you were my best friend.

~~You hurt me. With Pandora, you hurt me.~~ I wasn't the point. You weren't aiming my way, you were punishing Prometheus for being an annoying little prick, and I get it. I do. He's very smug and he loves being the smartest person in the room, and he never really took to you. I love him, and I accept he's a prick to you, but did you really need

~~to catch me in the middle of it? Did I really h a v e to make Pandora in my own image?~~

~~But you didn't ask me about any of that. You want advice for seducing Metis.~~

~~Zeus, you don't n e e d my advice for seducing Metis, or anyone. You're charismatic when you want to be, and you're t h e k i n g. People say yes to you.~~

~~The advice you do need, what I would tell you, if you felt like my friend right now, is this: DON'T MARRY METIS. Any s o n y o u h a v e w i t h h e r will o v e r t h r o w y o u. Non-negotiable.~~

~~But I don't know what we are anymore.~~
~~I miss you.~~
~~I love you.~~

~~Hugs and kisses,~~
~~Aphrodite~~
~~XOXO~~

Dad,

You should defo marry Metis. You're such a great match! I can just feel it, you know?

Hugs and kisses,
Your daughter,
Aphrodite
XOXO

Zeus III

Everyone was getting married. Before me. First Poseidon. One of his nereids. That was all right. I guess. He kept it in-house. No one yelled at me about it. But Hera heard. Went off on one about what a nice couple they made. How happy they looked. How happy everyone else would be if they got married.

'But Hera, *you're* not married,' Hermes said. Hermes used honesty like a shield. When it didn't work, he dodged.

Hera looked at me. 'I'm waiting for the right match.'

I knew she wanted to marry me. I didn't want to marry her. She was always getting in everyone's business. If my siblings didn't want me to be part of their little slumber parties where they reminisced about growing up in Dad's stomach then she didn't get to decide to be part of my life later on. That's not fair.

Poseidon got so *old* after he got married. He had a son. Named him his second-in-command, like he needed one. It was the sea. What was it going to do – dry up? Then when he did go out, he never wanted to hang out with me. It was all Nerites this, Apollo that.

Then Hades got a dog. A dog! This from the guy who used to— Actually, I don't know what Hades did. He was a killjoy. I didn't invite him to Olympus much. But that wasn't enough. He had to get married too. To *my* daughter. Made all these threats about releasing everyone from the oaths they'd made upon the Styx if I didn't go with it. Couldn't have that. Which got Demeter all mad at me. There was no winning with these people.

Hermes had stolen Apollo's cows. Artemis wanted Hera to stop yelling at her to grow up. Hera wanted Artemis to grow up. Hestia wanted everyone to *get along, please*. And they didn't get mad at *each other*. They got mad at *me* for not fixing their problems. Not fast enough. Not enough.

I was the king, dammit. I *am* the king. If anyone should get what they wanted, it was me. And I wanted. Something.

Maybe I wanted to get married. There must have been something good about it if they were all doing it. Had to find the best wife though. For the king. Someone powerful. Who respected me. And gorgeous. Who loved me most of all.

Aphrodite would have been the easy choice. *Aphrodite*, right? But I told everyone they couldn't marry her. Meant I couldn't either. They'd all riot – would they? They said so. I never saw any riots. Didn't want to risk it. Looked at the others.

Demeter was a bore, and mad at me.

Artemis and Hestia both virgins.

Nymphs and naiads and nereids all weak.

Persephone married to my brother.

Hera too keen. No thanks.

Metis. Perfect.

Not on the council – Titan, so she couldn't be – but wise. Calm. Even when the rest were loud. On my side for longer than anyone.

Aphrodite agreed. 'Opposites attract.'

'What does that mean?' I said. 'She's smart and beautiful. Are you saying I'm not?'

'No, I mean, yes, Zeus. You're very smart. You'd go well together.'

'Metis is a Titan.'

'And you're the king.'

Good point. I could do what I wanted. I proposed to Metis. She said no.

'It's not you,' she said. 'But I've survived this far without getting involved. It's the better strategy.'

'Who cares about strategy when you could be the queen?'

She smiled. Patted me on the hand. 'I'm sure you'll find your queen.'

No. I wanted her. Got her a gift. Not jewellery. Metis wasn't the type. I got her a shield.

'Pretty. Like you,' I told Metis.

She turned away from me. That wasn't allowed. Can't ignore the king. I was the king. Threw the shield after her. I didn't want to see it. Not without her.

Claaaaaang.

Metis turned back. 'Are you following me?'

'No.' Lie.

She turned the corner. I followed. Couldn't see her. There was a bird though. Flying up. Followed that. Became it. Bird dove into the sea. Became a fish. I followed.

Change. Follow. Change. Follow.

Woman to bird to fish to coral to fish to rat to dog to flea to bird to bird to bird.

'You helped me,' I shouted. 'Why won't you love me?'

The bird became air. I couldn't find it anymore. I changed everything about myself. She still didn't want me.

Back to Aphrodite. Told her about the running away. Goddess of love had to do something. Told her that too.

'Okay, leave it to me.'

Done the next day. Love achieved.[25] Good girl. Metis asked me that time.

Our wedding: best wedding. Apollo brought the sun. Had Artemis hang the moon too. Matching. Everyone cheered. Think Eris[26] was taking bets. That turned into a fight. Didn't matter. We were married.

Metis had big plans. I don't know what. Town layouts. Foot flow. Organisation. Not my problem. She listened to the stupid fights and gave the stupid answers, and I was free. Finally.

Should have been perfect. She was loyal. I had time.

It wasn't perfect.

They were watching me. Everyone. Longer pauses. Second looks. Mutters. I heard them. They didn't talk to my face, but I knew. I could see them thinking it.

Zeus, the king, really?

I was popular. Wife. Siblings. Children. Mortals. But no friends. I missed my friend. Hadn't seen her since the war. Too long.

Went looking for her. Cave was the same. Felt smaller. Too small for me. Now. Shoulders scraped the walls. Crushing. Dislike. And thread. Still. Not string. She didn't like that. Still gold though. Like my blood. Like the gods had fought and died there. My friend said it was different. Older. Its own magic.

'Fate,' I shouted.

'You don't belong here.' A new voice. A second. A third.

'You—'

'—Don't—'

'—*Belong.*'

Three of them. All speaking together. Creepy.

---

[25] Thanks Ro-Ro. —A

[26] Goddess of discord and ruiner of weddings. —A

'I'm looking for my friend. She used to live here.'

'It has always been us.'

'No,' I shouted. Good at that. Only ever give one warning. I can make anything I want. Break it too. What I say is all that matters. 'My friend was here.'

'We have seen no other bear the threads.'

'You must be blind then. Shall I pluck out your eyes to match?'

My friend lived there. She told me I would be the king. Listened to me rant. Didn't like caves either. She was there. She existed. She wasn't some invention. She was my friend.

'We can't know what came before us.' They said it weird. Emphasis crammed on *before*.

'You're like her.'

'We can't know what came before us.' Same thing. Same stress.

'Where's she gone?'

'The cave was empty.'

'What have you done with her?'

'We only watch.'

'Did you hurt her? Tell me.' Shouted. Again. Louder. Lightning came. It followed me. They ducked. Didn't matter. Lightning got them. Still nothing.

'We have never hurt anyone.'

Believed it. They were ugly. Skinny. Winced, looking at light. Couldn't win in a fight.

'Where is she?'

'We cannot tell you that. But—' Looks passed between them. Like I didn't know what that meant. That this was the future. They saw it and they were hiding it from me. 'We can tell you the future.'

Didn't want the future. Wanted my friend.

Wasn't going to get her. Took the future instead.

'Your son by Metis will usurp you.'

'No,' I said.

'Yes.'

'No. I'm the king. I will always be the king.'

'Everything ends. Everything changes.' Always together. Always speaking like that. Fucking shits.

'Where? Which thread?' I demanded.

They pointed. Good. Grabbed it. Tried to. Thought I'd tear it. Change things. It burned me. Fuck. Didn't do that before.

Got out my lightning bolts. Set that thread on fire. Did the trick. Lots of shouting while they put it out. Barely any damage. Just a little hole.

'Did that change it?'

Shriek. Shriek.

'Am I still having a son?'

My father's voice in my head. Sons overthrow their fathers. Always one too many.

'Will I stay the king?'

Crones didn't say anything. Too busy shrieking. Useless creatures. Left them to it – went back when they were calmer – and went home. Metis was pregnant.

'Congratulations,' she said.

Useless Fates.

Only one way to get rid of an immortal. It worked on my siblings.

Opened wide. Swallowed Metis. Sorry Metis. Until she started kicking me. Flailing. My power was bigger. Crushed hers. Enveloped it. She got smaller and smaller till I could barely feel the kicking.

The baby grew though. My son who would overthrow me. He

155

could try. See what he could do inside me. He did try. Kicked too. Kept kicking. On repeat. For years.

Painful. Annoying. Especially without Metis. Had to arbitrate again. Hated it.

Apollo and Artemis came in. Something about being twins. Something about her stealing his nymphs.

'She didn't even keep her,' Apollo whined.

'I don't give a shit, you two. You're twins. You're meant to like each other.'

Shut them up for about two seconds. Then one said *but*. Right back to fighting. Intolerable. Threw a bolt – warning only – between them. Stopped the fight. More whining.

Endless stupid questions. Endless whining. Endless headache. Told them go away. Get a job. Fix their own problems. Get out of my face.

Head still hurt. Fucking save me.

Aphrodite X

Have you ever broken up with someone? Not the kind of break up where it's been two weeks and you've maybe or maybe not slept together, but the kind where you were so far down the rabbit hole you were both putting in everything you had, even though it was never getting better, because you didn't know how you'd survive the end?

And when the end came, when that *one* unforgivable thing came, or the weight of all the tiny, forgivable things became too much to fight through, did you do it cleanly?

Tell me honestly. Was it clean? Did you leave and never look back?

And if you're reading all of this and thinking yes, I did, it was easy. Stop going on about it. Then, can you tell me *how*?

I've never managed it. No matter how swift the end was, how much of their stuff I returned immediately, how strongly I guarded my tongue to stop that traitorous promise slipping out, that we could be friends after everything, it's never been clean. I can't give back a memory, not without a trip to the Lethe,[27] can't forget the time when I did love them, truly.

---

[27] River in the underworld for forgetting. —A

Love doesn't just belong to people.

For all I hated the home I grew up in, I loved it too. I was born and made there. It was the only place I'd ever known and it will forever be the only place I know so well. Every crack and divot belonged to me. Olympus might have belonged to the gods, been the heartland of their souls in a way it never would be for me, but if every one of the Olympians crammed themselves into my cave, then I'd get the best seat, because I was the only one who knew how the rocks felt beneath me.

When I buried my feet in the sand there, my toes became roots and my body a tree. I was permanent. I belonged. I wasn't *happy*, but I belonged. I never wanted to go back, but I missed that more than I can say.

So no, when I left Fate, it wasn't a clean break.

I did my best. I made no lingering glances at my once-home, refused to stop in and see what it had become. I moved on, but it wasn't clean. The threads didn't stay where I left them.

They came with me.

Not all of them, not even most. Not enough to notice, I hoped, but when I was stressed or afraid, or sometimes for the sheer fun of it, one brave string would appear on my wrist, around my ankle, even wrapping my neck, and I'd rip it off before anyone saw and questioned this power that does not belong to the gods.

It wasn't enough to know everything, but it was enough to know that Zeus and Metis' son would depose his father.

I didn't want to hurt Zeus, but I wanted him to hurt. For Pandora and Prometheus, and for me. So I kept quiet. I didn't condemn him, but I let it happen. His eating Metis was a surprise. It must have been on another thread, I told myself. I was working with incomplete information.

It was a complicated time.

Prometheus didn't think so. 'He's not to be trusted.'

'I know he hurt your brother—'

'And *you*, Frodi. He hurt *you*.'

'He's just scared.'

'We're all scared. That cannot be his excuse for everything.'

'He was right to be scared. The child was going to take his life from him,' I said. 'I saw it. Does that make it different, do you think? Imagined threat versus the real one?'

'You still read Fate?'

I waved him off. 'Sometimes they follow me.'

'Frodi, this is enormous. You could manipulate them, follow them, take affirmative action, as it were. She who controls the knowledge—'

'Controls the world, yes, I know. But it's not about me—' A shameless avoidance, on my part. I didn't want to control the future because the last time I did that I *killed* the very friend I was talking to, even if it hadn't happened *yet*. 'How did *he* know that?'

This time it was Prom's turn to tap and sigh and avoid, but I chased him down. I could afford to be annoying. He loved me. He would never, ever leave me by choice, and I didn't need Fate to tell me that.

'Fate hasn't been alone since you left,' he said slowly, drawing every word out and pausing, as if the order and the way he said them would make it any better.

'What do you mean?'

'There are new Fates. Zeus has been visiting them.'

'Fate*s*? Plural?'

'Three.'

'Why didn't you tell me?'

'You wanted to leave that behind.'

'There's a difference between leaving the past behind and there being new Fates giving out the future like it's anyone's business. Taking away every advantage I have.'

'I don't know what you want me to tell you, Frodi.'

'The truth!'

'Like you always tell me the truth?' he said. That sat there, as heavily as words can.

'That's not fair, Prom. You asked me not to look at your future.' And I did anyway, and I broke it, and those echoed endlessly around my head, no matter what I did to try and stop them.

'Do you want to see them, your sisters?'

'No.' Enough threads had followed me out. If I went back there, who knew how many would grip me, if I'd ever escape again.

'You can fight knowledge with more knowledge,' he said. 'Use your influence to make everyone's lives better.'

After all those years, he still didn't get it. I didn't want to be a Fate pretending to be a goddess; I wanted to *be* a goddess.

'Prom—'

It was a bad time to be in Zeus' court.

He was in constant pain from eating his wife,
    which he didn't love,
        and it made him incapable of doing as much as he'd done
        before,
            which he hated,
                and it was all his fault,
                    which he truly despised.

He snapped at *me*, and I was his favourite.

It was worse to be a man, worse still to be anything but family. To be a *male Titan* around him was to court the threat of Tartarus every day, but Prometheus took the blows, the hate, because it was the best option he saw, and he thought that one day, we could make it better, and I couldn't bring myself to tell him otherwise.

I hated it with every fibre of my being, but there was nothing to be done. Fate, quite literally, was the way it was.

'What about the mortals? What can we do for them?' I said.

'How about . . .' I can't remember what we gave them that day. We did it as often as we could, taking them small advancements, ideas to make their lives easier, even songs sometimes. Always when Zeus was distracted, though. He didn't want anyone else playing with his toys. The smallest form of rebellion, but it was something.

We weren't the only ones.

'Sunset has changed,' Prom told me, one day.

'Pardon?'

'It's subtle, but where the sun used to meet the horizon there' – he nodded forcefully in that direction – 'it has been meeting it there.' He nodded again, an infinitesimally small change of location from the first one, but I believed him. It was quantifiable. Prom liked quantifiable.

'How do you even notice these things?'

'Zeus' speeches have a tendency to drag.' Right, and if you're bored during a speech the only solution is to *measure the geometry of the sunset.* 'Have you noticed anything on the council?' he asked.

'Apollo was late to the last meeting?'

'Is that unusual?'

'No, but normally it's because he's pursuing someone, and Eros hasn't mentioned anything to me. Not since the last one got turned into a tree.'[28]

---

[28] Daphne. —A

'I was hoping there might be something a little more solid than that.'

'I could start following him,' I said. 'Find something solid.'

'Please don't.'

'I'm going to start following him.'

'Of course you are. You might try Poseidon, also. It is possible they are using Apollo's orbit to arrange clandestine meetings at the perigee.'

Off I went to stalk the gods of the sun and the sea. I took Eros with me. He needed more to do. I'd been sending him to keep watch on all the mortals rumoured to be more beautiful than I was so he'd have something to do when I was visiting Prom, but he was running out of those. And I missed him. I wasn't used to juggling so many people.

He'd grown wings recently, so he flew and I rode my goose – less messy than the doves – and, while we weren't *stealthy*, we were so unstealthy people assumed the best of us. Mother and son having a gossip in the open sky.

It turned out I didn't *need* to follow them. When you report treachery to the king of the gods, no proof is required.

I went to Zeus and kneeled respectfully in front of him, careful in my every word.

'I don't want to cause strife at home, Father, but I worry that Apollo and Poseidon may be plotting against you.'

He took me by the hand and pulled me up again.

'None of that for my favourite daughter,' he said. 'I will handle this. Thank you.'

There it was, my status as number-one daughter and bona fide, trustworthy Olympian was assured. Job well done.

Apollo I

We *were* plotting to overthrow dear old dad, I shan't deny it. No one should watch their king start swallowing people whole without being a *tad* concerned, but it was about more than that.

There were so many people now, with more born every day. Olympus was beginning to feel crowded. Dad's remedy to this was to make it more exclusive, a club for his children and no one else.

Good enough for me, as his son, but not for any of my kids. Nor my loves. All the beauty and wonder in the world, and I couldn't share it. No splendour is quite so sweet without someone to share it with.

For me, the rebellion was about a boy.

I first saw him when I was visiting my oracle at Delphi. Reading the future is a vague art, but my lovely prophetesses did wonderful work with it, and we were revered around the world for our talents. I was admiring the view. And what a view he was.

Hyacinth.[29]

His hair fell in curls so gentle they appeared a little squashed, like flowers hanging from the vine. It was so dark it looked near purple in the sun. When he smiled, he caught the light of every—

What was I talking about? He was a mortal boy, not the

---

[29] Irrelevant, unless you're Apollo. —A

reincarnation of Aphrodite herself. He was a pretty lad, but I couldn't be so enraptured by a single glance at a *mortal*.[30]

I must have been hit by Aphrodite's arrows of love. They were the only logical explanation.

Truth be told, I didn't much care *why* I was in love with the boy, as long as I was. I scooped up the young prince – he was a *prince* – and taught him what I knew: the bow and arrow, poetry, the art of prophecy, even quoits.

It was the quoits that was our undoing.

It's a simple game in which you throw a ring to encircle one of a number of pegs. It can only *possibly* get complicated when the *king of the gods* has a hissy fit because his head hurts and decides we should live in *hurricane-force winds all the time*.

It didn't make for good games of throwing. Or hair.

But I refused to let it ruin my day – what a sad little life that would have been. I told Hyacinth that he would be quite the player if he could master the game in these conditions, and no other would be able to contend with him.

'Like this—' I said, my arms wrapped around his so I might guide him. Together, we threw the hoop.

The wind caught it.

Directly, and with malice, the hoop was carried backwards, straight into Hyacinth's head.

My sweet boy fell and did not get up. How I cried for him! How I yelled and pleaded and begged! But still, he did not rise.

I lifted him in my arms and carried him straight to the king.

'Zeus, my royal father, please.'

'I'm busy, Apollo.'

---

[30] He was. Frequently. Eros' involvement not required. —A

'I know, and I'm so sorry for interrupting your—' I looked. He was sitting in a chair staring into the middle distance, Ganymede[31] carrying a cup of wine to his side. What was he busy with? '. . . afternoon. But this is urgent. My love – he is dead.'

'A dead mortal does not sound urgent. A dead mortal sounds precisely like the natural order of things.'

It was all I could do, then, not to fall on the floor and howl at the unfairness of it all.

'Save him, please. He could be my cupbearer, my great love. He could be anything as long as you let him live.'

Zeus' own cupbearer did not twitch a muscle during this plea.

'Put the toy down, Apollo. Go do something useful.'

He was the king and my father, and his word was law. I did just as he asked.

I laid Hyacinth in a bed of flowers and called forth many new blooms, in the shape of his hair that I'd loved so much. By hand, I inscribed each petal by hand with a single word. *Alas.* It was all I could do to share the pain I was feeling so the entire world would know that this boy was more than some forgotten mortal. He was wanted, he was loved, and I was not allowed to keep him.

I mentioned my dangerous thoughts to Art[32] first. She's my twin sister, after all, and she'd never do anything to betray me in the grand scheme of things, even if she's a cheating cheater who cheats in the day-to-day.

'Artie—'

'Don't call me that.'

---

[31] After Zeus had won him from his brother, he made Ganymede immortal and moved him to Olympus, where their love could shine forevermore. Apollo knew this. —A

[32] Artemis for the rest of us. The goddess of the hunt doesn't appreciate nicknames. —A

'Is there something off about the king, do you think?'

'I like him well enough. *He* lets me hunt.' No idea who she was talking about. I wasn't stopping her hunting, merely following her on the trail so we could talk.

'Don't you think it's a bit sus?'

'*Sus*, Brother?'

'If he's already swallowing people, then who's next?'

'*Ooooh*. Well, the solution to that is perfectly clear,' she said. 'Don't be the slowest.' Just like that, my sister was off, sprinting like a doe, a lion, some wild thing, into the woods, and I had to leg it to keep up with her.

Without an official finish line, we both claimed victory, and while we were panting and recovering, Art *finally* gave me a real answer.

'These are dangerous questions to be asking, Apollo. Whether I agree with you or not' – she obviously agreed with me – 'leave me out of it. Do you understand?'

'Yes, Sister,' I intoned, deep as I could go, since she was being so weird about it.

'Did you know one of Poseidon's nereids joined my retinue recently? She says they're having a simply awful time in the oceans, what with the storms.' In other words: go talk to Poseidon, you muppet.

She was right. Poseidon agreed with me. We needed change.

We didn't get it. Our plans at rebellion were cut off almost before they started. We were still working out *how* we'd tie him down and make him promise to be a better king when someone tattled. I suspected Nerites. Poseidon suspected Artemis.

It didn't matter either way, even if it definitely wasn't my sister. We were called to an audience with one pissed-off king.

'You think *you* can overthrow *me*?' The words didn't matter, nor was it the way he said them – loath as I am to admit it, being the god of poetry – it was the rest of him. He was hovering off the ground, and between his fingers he held the sky. He might be the god of the sky, but it's not as though I can go holding *poetry*. I certainly can't take it and rip it apart at the seams. He could shred the cosmos without even looking, and fill the spaces with his anger, static thickening the air, crawling across our skin.

He wasn't even out of breath.

He was showing his power, and he was showing *this was not all of it*.

'Do you understand?' He hadn't said anything additional in between, but he didn't need to. He'd made his point. '*I* am the king. Not any of you.'

Poseidon and I were the only other people in the room. We nodded.

'I should send you to Tartarus for this.'

I fell to the floor. 'No, Father, please. It was just one moment of idiocy. Any other punishment, I will accept it gratefully, but don't send me there—'

I didn't want to debase myself, but I *really* didn't want to be sent to Tartarus, a prison from which there was no escape. Your boy knows when to pick the lesser evil.

'What you two need, is to learn to obey,' he said. 'Learn what it is to *truly* be at the bottom.'

Some might make a joke about my sexual proclivities in such a situation. They've clearly never seen my father truly angry. We had. We nodded.

Yes, sir, we will, sir, so sorry, sir.

'I have selected a mortal king. You will serve him for the next seven years.'

I looked at Poseidon. He looked at me.

That was it? Seven years of serving a mortal for rebellion? I could do that any day of the week.

I didn't say it. He didn't say it. I tried not to think it too loudly. But of course, I was wrong. We all were, when it came to Troy.

They'll tell you Troy was just a city. They never met Laomedon.

He had a wife, of course, but all kinds of men have wives. Even if he was interested in her, it didn't preclude him being interested in me. And he was interested in me.

He met the two of us, me and Poseidon, together, us both dressed in what passed as rags for Olympians, so more finely than any fabric he'd ever touched.

'I'm meant to tell the two of you what to do?'

Poseidon had no time for this.

'I will build you walls,' he said, and it was so certain, the conversation went no further. Laomedon nodded and let him go. I could have followed, and the world we live in would look entirely different now.

I've never thought of myself as a follower, though.

'What of you, Apollo? Will you build for me?'

'If you wish.'

'I think you know your skills better than I.'

And these things, these words, they feel stilted when I recount them, but they were not, because words are never *just* words. You don't have to be a poet to know that. Every word holds everything that came before it, cloaked in their context, and Laomedon knew how to dress his. He held his hair just so. His hip just so. His foot turned towards me.

'What can you do for me?' he said.

Laomedon might have been a good king, but he was a better lover. I sang for him. Poems and prose and sounds that held no meaning except in that moment. I sang them all, and the city sprang up around us. A city made of my words, my love, my care, all baked into its very stones.

So, I fell in love with more than the man. I fell in love with Troy. Made for me and around me and by me, separate from my family and Olympus and my oracle and my sister, even. Troy and I. Intertwined.

I loved Troy more than I loved Hyacinth. I loved it more than I loved *Artemis*. I loved Troy because of everything it could become. It would be a home for my poets, my archers, my kings. They could grow there, and it would be so much more than one life.

Do you know what it looks like for your father to be the king of everything?

He was unimpeachable. Not perfect, but unimpeachable, which obviously I know, because I failed to impeach him. In Olympus, I would always be a part of that, a chip off the old block, a level of the family legacy. And I am. I'm proud of where I came from. But I tried so hard to be more than Zeus' son, more than Artemis' younger brother.

In Troy, I found imperfection, and in Troy, I found something that was truly mine.

So why did my lovely oracle have to go and ruin that?

I went to visit her, and the priestesses there, often, of course, check on welfare, check the prophecies were good, that our fame was growing, our reputation pristine. I didn't ask about Troy – there are some things you're better off not knowing – but that didn't stop her.

'Listen, Apollo—' I knew that voice. I knew that meter – the first foot and the first step on the road to Hades.

'No.'

'Listen, Apollo, we're sorry—'

'I don't want to hear it.' Pathetic, the god of prophecy running away from his own oracle. But one can always get more pathetic. I clamped my hands over my ears. 'La la la.'

'It's true. The city is falling—'

'LA LA LA LA LA.'

I grew loud and she grew louder. I do not choose my prophetesses on the meekness of their spirit.

'Apollo, it's going. You have to accept it—'

'I can't hear you.'

'Destruction is coming. It won't go alone.'

'What?'

'Olympus falls too.'

'No.' The thing about prophecies, for the poor uninitiated souls out there, is that they're set before the oracle even opens her mouth, and once she starts going, it's like a boulder rolling down the hill. Not even Sisyphus[33] could stop it. It didn't stop me covering her mouth. 'No no no.'

Not just my city, not merely the only thing I have ever loved as much as my sister – that wasn't enough for Zeus. My punishment would not be complete with losing that love. I had to lose my home too. Olympus was the only place I had ever known. It was the gods' whole world, woven into the very fabric of our being, into our names themselves. We were Olympians, we were Olympus, and Olympus was us.

If our world was destroyed, there was no telling who we'd become.

'We love you, Apollo,' my oracle finished quietly.

I slid to the floor and cried for all the things I couldn't change.

Even then, I plotted how I'd try.

---

[33] Man endlessly rolling a boulder up a hill as punishment for his past sins. Otherwise forgettable. —A

Aphrodite XI

Zeus' pain only got worse as the years passed, and it took his mood down with it. He claimed we were breathing too loudly, so we, collectively, stopped breathing. Then he complained that no one was breathing and it was weird and we should just be normal.

Excuses were rustled up, all round, to get us out of his eyeline. Poseidon and Hades found emergencies to keep them in their own realms. Apollo disappeared into Troy and took Artemis with him. If anyone asked what they were doing, they'd explode into an argument that was so precisely the kind that only twins can have that I was absolutely convinced it was invented.

I skulked around with Prometheus, supporting humanity when Zeus' back was turned. With the gods hiding from him, they were his only source of entertainment and, his rage being what it was, the only thing that made him happy was hurting them.

He demanded more and more tribute from them, until they grew thin enough that their bones jutted out at odd angles, and they had no time for anything but gathering supplies. Not war or wisdom or the arts. Not poetry or mischief. Not love.

Zeus demanded so much of them that he became their totality, and the rest of the gods suffered with them. Not being a real god, I don't know the details exactly, but they derived a certain amount of their power from whatever it was they represented. So, if the oceans dried up, not only would the entire planet cease to function, but Poseidon might just evaporate too.

When Zeus stopped the mortals practising their specialties, the gods themselves began to weaken, until I was painting my face, not for beauty, but so I'd look gaunt enough to fit in.

'Revolution is imminent,' Prom noted.

'It'd be nice to go just one year without worrying about revolution.'

'Would it be such a bad thing to get rid of him?'

'I've put all my eggs in this basket,' I said. I didn't have a lot of friends. Lovers, sure, but the only thing a lover will do with you if they become the king is *keep* you. I didn't want to be kept. Zeus let me *live*. 'As have *you*.'

'I do not like seeing them suffer,' Prometheus said, waving vaguely in the direction of mankind.

'We could take them something? It's been a while.' It was harder to sneak them things, with Zeus down there so often, and with his mood so bad it was a high-stakes game. We still thought it was a game. 'What do they need?'

'More time.' This is doable, if you're a god. Specifically if you're Artemis and Apollo, with control of the sun and the moon. They could have brought more hours for the humans to till their fields and hunt their meat and do everything they needed to be happy on top of what they needed to live. Neither of us could, though, and this conversation was already too close to treason to share.

But I was sick of being pessimistic all the time, being careful and scared. So I offered a solution or two.

'We are not kidnapping the goddess Artemis,' Prom said.

'I'm just saying, it's an option. No moon means perpetual day.'

'I cannot imagine it would be good for the mental state of the people. What would be most useful, instead of more time, might be if we made their lives easier.'

'Prom, that's treason.' Not merely light rebellion. Full treason, accept no substitutes.

'You cannot know what I am about to suggest.'

'You're going to suggest we give them technology, and I'm telling you no; that's treason.'

It was one of Zeus' first laws. The nice explanation is that he wanted mankind to live without the stressors he had upon him. The cynical explanation is that he wanted mankind as a toy to play with, not to worry about their increasing strength.

'We have given them aid before.'

'We gave them food, and we sang to them – it's on something of a different level to *treason*.'

'Hmm.'

'Prometheus, no! What's got into you? You're meant to be the careful one.'

'I have spent the majority of my life fighting for Zeus in the hope that it would make for a better world, and all I have succeeded in is trading one child-eating tyrant for another. I do not wish to *see what happens*. I wish to act.'

'And we will—'

'Truly act. Make a difference.'

I couldn't deny him that, could I? With all my talk about being seen, about being real only when I left my footprints across the world.

'Okay, I'll think of something, Prom. Just, don't be all *me* about this, please?'

I didn't *know* he was planning something impulsive. I'd learned my lesson well enough about getting involved with his future, but I knew him well enough to be just as sure as if I'd looked. Finding a cure to the mortals' suffering was all I thought about for days, and I didn't do it for them; I did it for him. I couldn't approach it from the usual angles – Prom has those covered well enough – so I unpicked the problem from the inside out.

We didn't need to make their mortal lives better. We didn't need to lengthen their days. We didn't need to commit treason. I picked and picked away at it, until I found what I thought was the real problem. We had to take away the pressure.

We had to get Metis out of Zeus' head.

And I had an *amazing* idea for that. I ran – actually ran – to Prometheus to tell him, but when I arrived, he was looking sheepish and he was wearing gloves.

'You were all *me* about it, weren't you?'

'Frodi—'

'What did you do?' I'd got so good at controlling my temper, controlling myself, hiding everything I was, but I didn't need to hide from Prom. I didn't want to. I was pissed at him for doing something fucking stupid and putting himself at risk, and I was pissed at myself for not telling him he was at risk in the first place. '*Prometheus.*'

'I gave them fire.'

'Oh, Prom.'

I could see it then with all the details that had been missing from the threads and the gap between the man who *made* the king and how he ended up cursed and I should have known when he started talking about treason and I should have refused to leave his side and I should have made sure he was safe and he wasn't doing anything stupid and impulsive and *me* but I didn't and now my heart had fallen so far through me I couldn't feel it anymore and I was trying with everything I had not to start crying and it was kind of working but it had frozen me in place.

I still hadn't told him I'd looked.

What use would there be now?

'Frodi, it will be fine. I was very careful.'

'Zeus is going to be furious.'

'He is always furious. This will pass, like anything else.'

'I don't know, Prom.'

But I did know. I'd seen Zeus' fury. It was coming, the first of his rages that would truly ring down in legends, an anger that would outlast us all.

I had to decide, then, to tell or not to tell.

'Is there something I should be aware of, Frodi?'

'No, you're right: it'll be fine. I just really liked my idea.'

I was too late. No point bringing the pain forwards with anticipation.

'What was your idea? Could we do both?'

'Hitting Zeus on the head with a big rock.'

'We c—'

'Sorry, Prom, I just remembered, there's this thing with Eros. I have to go—'

I couldn't keep my best friend safe, but I could protect myself.

Athena I

There was no reason that my father should have eaten my mother. There was no reason I should have survived the ordeal when she did not. There was no reason I should emerge from my father's head clad in full armour, armour I was later informed resembled that worn by my mother.

There is *absolutely* no reason that someone should attempt to cure the headache of the king of the gods by hitting him on the head with a boulder. Yet, here we are.

I remember every part of my birth. Zeus' head opened around me and the sun shone through. It did not spill or any such melodramatic nonsense; the beam simply widened until it was large enough to envelop me. When it did, I took one dignified step from my father into the world, where a great many onlookers had gathered to shout incomprehensible things.

'What is going on here?' I demanded. The crowd looked at one another gormlessly. The chain of staring, of palming off the responsibility, finally made its way to my father.

'You are my daughter,' he said. There was a sigh in the background. I looked to the culprit. She was on Zeus' left. She tapped her foot, as if to say *get on with it*. Another daughter, then. Perhaps not used to sharing her things.

'Why has any of this happened?'

'We are gods,' my father said, as though that should answer anything at all.

I voiced that thought. It was he who sighed this time. 'You clearly have a great mind, my daughter. I hereby name you the goddess of strategy in wartime.' His other daughter whispered something in his ear. He nodded. 'And of women's arts. Weaving and the like.'

She gazed smugly at me. I refused to dignify her with a response. I would have loved to stick a tongue out at her, but I was not born a child, so I did not have even the opportunity to put away childish things. She seemed disappointed by my maturity.

Good.

Zeus demanded that we go somewhere private so he could explain to me the ways of the gods. I never did get a coherent explanation for why he ate my mother, though he assured me he was glad he had done it, for it gave him me. It did not reassure me. It told me that all people were disposable if there was a greater prize to be found. Or perhaps only women.

My father did not have a problem with women, per se. He loved women. He loved men too, in that way, but he generally preferred the female form. What he respected, however, was power. Strength. The kind that he had, which he believed to be quite masculine.

In a world where nothing made sense, I could see it would be helpful to have his respect, so I shed as much femininity as necessary to achieve it. In return, he named me his right-hand man, no mention of my womanhood at all.

I became his favourite of his immortal children, which was logical for the simple reason I no longer had a mother. My filial loyalty could not be divided. It belonged only to Zeus, and that reassured him.

This displeased his other daughter. Aphrodite did not like me.

She had been his favourite prior to my arrival, but *no mother* supersedes *long-disappeared mother*. She flaunted her femininity at me, her buttocks often bare and her breasts *always* bare. Zeus tolerated it. He laughed at her antics, but he did not respect her.

As much as it pains me to admit it, they held a great deal of affection for one another. To use the colloquialism, they *got* each other. They sniggered during important meetings, and played a game that consisted of one of them pointing at two people for the other to gauge whether they would make a good couple: a thumb raised for the positive, down for the negative, and a finger in the mouth to represent gagging, which may have been either bad or good, depending on the context.

In contrast, he came to me for advice about things that mattered. I did not have time for the trifles of the heart – what a farce that the immense power of the heart has been reduced to merely "love", when it supplies blood to all parts of the body, not merely the genitals. That said, even by my limited reckoning of matters of infatuation, the dalliances Aphrodite encouraged our father into were wretched. It did not make any sense at all that the goddess of love would support them. I attempted to flag this to my father.

'You are sounding jealous, Athena. We can find you a husband if you want one.'

'No! I—'

'Aphrodite knows what she's doing.'

That Aphrodite knew what she was doing was precisely my concern. I did not trust her, nor that meddling son of hers, but Zeus was not to be swayed. His marriage did not affect me in any particular way, so I left it. Best not to hurt a functioning working relationship, after all.

I did, however, endeavour to keep a closer eye on Aphrodite.

I did not have to wait long for this to bear fruit.

My father was unfathomably interested in humanity. I understand that he created them, so he was emotionally invested in their outcomes, but they were, fundamentally, a strategic error. He was not, at that juncture, overly concerned about attacks from within his own house – his defeat of Poseidon and Apollo's plot ensured that – but one should never be so comfortable in their position that they create *new* threats.

He believed he'd mitigated the risks with his edicts: do not bring technology to the mortals. Do not help them advance.

These, of course, were rapidly broken.

Someone gave mankind *fire*. Perhaps, for the uninitiated, this seems a trifle. After all, we are gods; we can have everything we want faster than we could ask for it. What does fire matter in comparison to that form of power?

Fire is, and do forgive me for this turn of phrase, a spark. It is the catalyst upon which all future developments in technology can be based. It represented potential and, in their potential, lay our danger.

'Who would *dare*?' my father said. He was pacing. I found that reassuring. It was when he was still that trouble was truly on the horizon.

'It is possible that mankind discovered fire on their own,' I said.

'No. Impossible. Someone has gone against my *direct* orders. Defied me for no reason other than defiance.'

I did not ask if he was sure. He did not like it when people asked him such things. It made him feel stupid, and there was nothing worse than my father when he felt stupid.

'So we find them.'

'Yes. How?'

'I assume you have spoken to Apollo and Artemis?' I said. As the

179

drivers of celestial objects, the two of them saw everything there was to see. Even a lack of evidence from them would be exemplary evidence, implying a culprit familiar with their strategies.

'I cannot trust them.'

'Do you have any suspects?'

'I have many enemies.'

'True, though it would not grant any of them a strategic advantage to support mankind like that. We seek someone overly emotional.'

'You think everyone overly emotional, Athena.'

Correct. 'Emotions often cause people to react irrationally. Who has an emotional attachment to humanity?'

My father's eyes narrowed. They seemed to have his lightning flashing behind them, though I knew that to be impossible.

'Do you know who it is?' I asked. 'It could be Aphrodite. She often professes to love—'

He roared. 'Do not question her, Athena. I trust her. Don't take that from me.'

'Trust is an error.'

'She has an alibi.' Odd that he should know that, given the aforementioned trust. 'She was with her son. Eros has confirmed it.'

There are many ways to fake an alibi, but it would not exactly have helped the situation if I were to have pointed this out.

'Who else, then?' I asked.

'I don't bloody know, do I?'

He stormed off. I often think those words were invented for my father specifically. He disappeared for a day and a night before he gathered all of Olympus around him and gave a grand speech about the importance of loyalty. He did not gaze around to see who reacted, whose face cracked, but I did, as he knew I would.

It was not a helpful exercise. Everyone has a tell, and during that speech, it was as though the crowd was shouting. Hair was brushed back, feet tapped, teeth clenched. Even Hera sucked her lips against her teeth.

'But the real villain . . .' Zeus began, 'is . . .'

He left both pauses longer than natural conversation would abide. In the first, the room remained silent, everyone looking at one another. In the second, he glared significantly at Apollo, who understood some unspoken message and turned to his Muses. With a wave of his hands, they began a drumroll.

I refrained from the urge to roll my eyes. What was the point of these theatrics? If he knew the culprit so well, then he would have been better off stealing them away in the night, ascertaining their guilt, and only then punishing them publicly. I did not roll my eyes, however. That would have been telling, and *I* know how to whisper.

Aphrodite stood on the other side of him once more, dancing along with the drums. It felt artificial to me, but the whole event reeked of artificiality. It threw me off. Hera had taken position directly behind him.

'Is—' Zeus said. He waved his hands. Thunder rumbled. His words were punctuated by lightning. It would have been impressive, had it not felt so childish, our king begging for our attention. 'Prometheus. He is the traitor. Apollo, Hermes, capture him.'

The square stayed silent. The Titan did not move; he did not run.

'I would not dare, my king—'

'And yet you did. We both know it to be true.'

'I suppose you are right.'

That was the end of his grand defence. He knew he had been caught, that his actions were not defensible, so he went calmly with Apollo and Hermes to wherever it was that prisoners were kept. He was notable in his dignity – a pointless thing. If he had so much composure within him, then he should have held on to it sooner, moderated his behaviour and prevented any part of this.

When he was taken away, most of the crowd looked relieved. Most of them calmed their tells, stood still. Some even smiled, applauded.

He was walked past my father, so that Zeus could spit on him or perform some other suitably grotesque display of dominance, I assumed, but he did no such thing. Instead, the traitor leaned in.

'I'd bet you're glad to have a girl. One of those sons of yours is going to overthrow you one day.'

Only then did my father spit. 'Finally, the Titan Prometheus has allowed us to see his true, untrustworthy nature,' he declared. 'And for his crimes, he will be punished.'

He had us follow them to Mount Elbrus, where civilisation met barbarism, the natural ending of our world. He chained Prometheus there, where he would be able to see his beloved mankind develop but he could never again interfere in their progress.

Alone, that would have been a clever punishment, but my father has never known when to stop.

'To ensure he remembers what is done to those who betray me,' Zeus continued, 'my sharpest-beaked eagle shall visit him daily, and enjoy the delicacy of fresh liver.'

It was a torture of the mind as much as the body. An eternity of suffering, for all of us: our daily reminder of what happens to those who go against Zeus. Every single god showed their unease at this, though one more than any other.

Aphrodite took something from her wrist – I could not see what; she had turned her shoulders away from the crowd – and pulled it with great fury. Her body moved, but the pain did not register on her face. She maintained a smile, a bow to our father, every inch the dedicated daughter, but I had seen it.

Aphrodite was silent, but she was screaming.

I told the world, afterwards, that I chose to forsake love because it does not make sense. It is strategically a poor decision. I stand behind that. However, it was not the entire truth. I eschewed love because the goddess in charge of it was lying about *something*. She was not who she said she was. I would find out the truth and, until that was established, I would not grant her a modicum of power over me. I took my suspicions to our father.

'Aphrodite is hiding something.'

'Jealousy is unbecoming,' he said. He had been spending more time with Hera recently. It showed.

'She was involved in gifting fire to mankind; I am convinced of it.'

'Prometheus has confessed to the entire crime.'

'Was his punishment to be different whether he committed the whole crime or only half of it?' I asked.

'Of course not. He betrayed me. He deserved to suffer.'

'Then why would he not protect his co-conspirator?'

He looked confused by the thought. 'Because they deserve to suffer alongside him?' It must have been lonely to be my father. He had no one worth suffering for. 'She has never been anything but loyal to me. I trust her.'

'You shouldn't.'

'Athena—' It was obvious that he was nearing the end of his patience with me, which left me in a difficult strategic position. I did not wish to undermine my own relationship with him, but he had to be wary. 'I questioned her. She had an alibi. *Leave it.*'

There is no use questioning what you cannot change, and so I did.

Aphrodite XII

When people talk to me about love, they normally want to talk about the beginning, about falling. The creation of jokes. The side looks. The uncertainty, even. No one actually wants me to tell them whether someone is going to love them. That's not the point. Falling in love is *exciting*. It's skipping and singing and hoping they pick up the same tune.

I love the beginning. I always will.

And Prometheus was worth more than all the beginnings. It wasn't romantic. It didn't need to be. I loved him when we were talking, gossiping, guessing what the world would bring us. I loved him when I was having the worst days and I could unload all of it onto him and he'd sit there and listen, and a week later he'd come back, having found me a solution. I loved him because he knew the old me as well as the new.

I didn't love his overthinking because it was inherently lovable. It wasn't. It annoyed me, but I loved it anyway because it was *his*. He made his foibles lovable, not the other way round.

Our love was the kind that feels like coming home. With him, I didn't have to choose between the beginning and the middle.

Leading up to it, I hadn't had a whole lot of either. Zeus was pulling away from me, his other daughter, his *real* daughter whispering in his ear, telling him I didn't belong. He wasn't safe anymore. Otherwise, well. I annoyed Demeter, and I didn't like Apollo because he claimed to be the god of prophecy, which we all know is just watered-down Fate, and Artemis didn't like me because she thought I was going to make her fall in love, even though I wasn't, because that obviously meant something different to her and I'm not an idiot. And I couldn't stand Hestia because Hestia felt like someone shoving a pillow in your face and shouting: *Are you comfortable yet? Are you warm?*

I was there when Zeus announced his brilliant torture plan. All of us were. *You're wrong,* I'd prayed. *You have to be wrong.*

I knew, of course, that no one was listening to my prayers, that anyone who might be was standing next to me in that moment, and they didn't care, but I prayed anyway. It was better than talking to myself.

And I *knew* it was coming, all of that pain. I'd known for longer than should have been possible. I was the one who had *looked*. Prom was right – of course he was; the bastard was always right – sometimes it's better not to know.

It was never a question that I was going to visit him. It wasn't safe, but I didn't care. I wore a veil and travelled at dusk to avoid Artemis and Apollo, and that would have to be enough.

'Do you want to see me?' I asked him. I wouldn't have wanted to, if it was the other way around. I would have been angry he left me to take the blame alone. I would have raged and spat and fought it.

We're not all me. The world is probably better for that.

'Irrelevant. I cannot exactly make you leave.' He— He was in so much pain. He reminded me of my best friend, but only reminded, like an uncanny stranger in the square, until you get up close and realise the resemblance is not so strong after all. The fluff of his hair, the vaguely intellectual sense of him, the gentle teasing – it was all lost between the grunts and the deep breathing and the faint smell of sweat I could catch from where I stood. He was the person I'd always known, but so much of it was gone, just like that.

'I can leave?'

'No. Stay.'

'Okay.' I sat for a while, facing the opposite direction, like that would stop me from hearing what he was going through. I didn't know what to say.

'What have I missed?' he asked.

'Nothing much.'

'Who has Zeus been after this week?'

'You don't want to hear about that.'

'Frodi,' he said. 'If it is not centred on the fact that there is an eagle currently eating my liver, then I absolutely wish to hear about it.'

'I challenged Athena to a weaving contest,' I said.

'What possessed you to do that?'

'She was being rude about love again, said I couldn't do anything worthwhile with my time.'

'So you challenged the goddess of weaving to a weaving contest?'

'Hey, have some faith, Prom. I did weave all of Fate together, back in the olden days.'

'Did you win?'

'That's not the point.'

'Was it bad?'

It was terrible. Normal thread doesn't behave the way the threads of Fate do. It doesn't have its own personality. It doesn't stay where you leave it. It seems to obey these unwritten rules about when it will stay and when it will drop, and Athena knew *all* of them.

I had my attendants – I had attendants now! – hold the thread, but they didn't know how to unspool it properly, and it unravelled and unravelled until I was standing in a pile of loose fibres and many, many mortal weddings were ruined. Athena was very smug about the whole situation.

Usually I wouldn't volunteer this information, it's not a good look on a goddess, but it made Prometheus laugh, so I gave him all of it, every ounce of my pain and embarrassment, every fumble and worry and faux pas, I gave to him. I drowned him in the ordinary.

And so it became our normal. I visited and told him all the day-to-day of Olympus, how Apollo had started some sporting competition to honour the python he killed, how all the gods competed in the first one.

'I won a zither,' I said.

'Can you even play a zither?'

'Not before I owned one, I couldn't.' And he nearly smiled, and he talked about what the sun and the stars and the clouds were doing until we both ran out of our ordinary. I didn't like it. When the world is quiet, my head gets very loud.

In Olympus, I made stupid choices, dragged the younger gods into escapades, just so I could go back to him with more stories to tell.

'So, Zeus and Hera were arguing,' I said.

'Something new and different for them.'

'I think it's her idea of flirting.' Prom made a face like that actually wasn't the worst kind of flirting he could imagine. Very Prom. 'And they were arguing about whether men or women enjoy sex more.'

(They were having this argument because I goaded them into it, but that's neither here nor there.)

'Naturally.' He winced as the eagle gave a particularly vicious peck.

'So they've turned a mortal man[34] into a woman so he can tell them.'

He cocked his head at me. 'Aphrodite.'

'Yes.'

'Were you standing right there?'

'I was.'

'And they didn't think to ask *you* whether the male or female genitals enjoyed sex more?'

'Not even for a moment,' I said, and we were both laughing, then, really laughing, even with all the pain.

(If you're wondering, Zeus and Hera kept the mortal as a woman for ten years, then turned them back into a man, who said women enjoy sex nine times more than men do, which made Hera very cross, so she blinded him, and Zeus gave him the "gift" of prophecy to make up for it.)

His laugh fuelled me to greater stupidity, to more meddling.

It fuelled me to help Hera seduce the king of the gods.

In retrospect, I could defend my actions by saying I was hoping to make another friend on Olympus, that hopefully Hera would no longer think of me as her competition if I helped her marry Zeus, and that a king *and* a queen who both supported me was the kind of security I hadn't even dared to dream of.

In reality, I was pissed at Zeus. He might not have meant to hurt me by hurting Prometheus, but he did.

So, I helped Hera seduce him.

If nothing else, it'd be a good distraction while I visited Prom.

---

[34] Tiresias, if you're interested. —A

Hesperides Holidays

Travel fit for a king! (And his new queen . . .)

Introducing the new and improved **HESPERIDES HOLIDAYS**. Featuring never-before-seen perks. Enjoy your honeymoon with:

- Immortality-granting fruits!
- Our resident dragon!
- Nymphs! Nymphs! Nymphs!

All this and more, at the holiday destination of the century – or three, if you're feeling frisky. Book now for our lowest ever prices and out eternal-wedded-bliss money-back guarantee.*

*Terms and conditions apply. Marry at your own risk.

Aphrodite XIII

Zeus and Hera got married. I refuse to feel bad about that.

He actually did love her, ridiculous as it might seem. She wanted him, and only him, and that's a really hot feature in a partner if you're ninety per cent insecurities and ten per cent raw power like Zeus was. She didn't love him, but he hadn't worked that out yet, so the beginning of their marriage was great. Zeus gifted Hera the Gardens of the Hesperides and the immortality-granting apple[35] tree that lay within it.

They went there for their honeymoon, and they stayed for three hundred years.

That was their gift to the rest of us. While Zeus was gone, we got to live.

Apollo found boyfriends and girlfriends, and boyfriends again. Without his brother to fight with, Poseidon let the sea grow calm and navigable. Athena invented all sorts of arts and crafts and had a city founded in her name, though Poseidon did sulk about that one later. Poor sailors.

The humans took their fire and ran with it, developed more

---

[35] They didn't resemble any other apples, mortal or otherwise, but with all the magical benefits they granted, people were pretty forgiving of that idiosyncrasy. —A

than any of us could have imagined. They smelted metals and grew kingdoms and fought over their kingdoms. They started to look much more like us.

And I visited Prometheus.

Every day. Normally in the early morning, when the sun and the moon were off duty and the pain was not so bad for him, his liver newly grown.

'The worst part,' he told me once, 'is the anticipation. To know that I will have to go through all of this again tomorrow.'

I couldn't help the pain. Anticipation, though, I could do something about.

I went to him with all my stories, harvested so carefully from the world and the gods and the mortals. Who's who and who's doing who. He pretended not to be interested in the latter, but I'd known him for long enough that he couldn't bullshit me.

Until one day, we were sitting there, and I was prattling on about Eros' newest hobby—

'Crab racing? Is your son riding the crab or does it run independently?'

'He stands on it; otherwise his legs would drag.'

Prom was quiet for a moment. '. . . And does he win at this crab racing?'

'He does.' I'd only been to one race, to see him, and I'd got a little caught in the moment when I did, cheering and supporting him and potentially shouting rude things at the other competitors.

Eros said I was embarrassing him. Probably. But that was my job.

'I do not understand sports,' Prometheus said. The eagle cawed in the distance. 'He agrees.'

'The eagle can talk?'

'There's a strong possibility that I've gone mad.'

'The threads used to talk to me,' I said reassuringly.

He looked at me like maybe I'd gone mad too and that was not, in fact, reassuring.

I didn't think much of the eagle cawing, its presence so early in the morning when it normally came closer to noon. It had been *three hundred years* of calm, of happiness – as much as could pass for happiness in this new normal of ours – three hundred years of lying to myself about Prom's Fate until I just about believed it.

Zeus and Hera returned from their honeymoon the next day, and a wave of emotions swept across the Olympians' faces before we all closed them down in some manner or another. I had three centuries of confidence instilled in me, though, so I didn't stop visiting Prometheus.

We watched the happy couple together. Watched as they argued, and their shouts echoed across the mountain. Watched when Hera announced she was pregnant and it became mandatory to tell her she was glowing at least three times a day.

Watched the baby fall off the mountain.

'Is that—' Prom began. We both knew what it was, and we both knew it couldn't have come from anywhere but Olympus.

'Should I catch it?' I said.

'Can you fly?'

'No.'

'Then I wouldn't recommend it.'

The baby hit the water.

'The Cyclopes will take care of it,' I said. 'Hopefully.'

'I thought Zeus reburied the Cyclopes?'

'Nah. It's the giants he's still got buried. He let the Cyclopes out and gave them forges so they could make his thunderbolts for him.

Plus, Poseidon offered to house them so Z couldn't even complain about overcrowding on Olympus.'

'He does that?'

'Frequently.'

'Take care, Frodi. He may start looking to remove people soon.'

That old conversation. 'He loves me.'

'He loved me once too.'

'Did he now?' I said, wiggling my eyebrows.

'Not in that way!' Then he paused and looked at me, half the way to aghast but not fully there. 'Aphrodite, you have not . . . with him?'

'You're an immortal Titan, a notorious spy, my ex-lover, and a war veteran, and you can't say *fucked*?'

'You don't have to be crude. I am merely concerned.'

'I'll tell you if you say it.'

'You are being immature.'

'Yup! I am just a young goddess.'

'You are older than the oldest of the gods.'

'Baby goddess!'

'Are you attempting to distract me from the question?'

'What question?' I had, honestly, half forgotten. I blame the threads, but object permanence is not my finest skill.

'The question of whether you and the king of the gods have,' – he worked his jaw as if warming up for one of Apollo's sporting contests – 'fucked.'

'Oh, that. No. Of course we haven't. Zeus doesn't respect the women he sleeps with; it would ruin the plan.'

His nostrils flared. 'You could have told me from the beginning.'

'But what would be the fun in that?' I stood up and kissed him on the cheek. It felt right, getting closer to him. Reminding him that there could be physical touch that wasn't more pain. 'Now, I'm going to see some Cyclopes about a baby.'

Don't worry, I wasn't going to kidnap him or anything, I just wanted to meet him, see what was going on. I got Eros to help me track the new arrival down – a son who races crabs has to be good for something.

The Cyclopes did have him. They'd taken him into their forges and handed him a hammer which he was happily using to bash away at something or other. He had some deformity of the foot by the looks of it, but other than that he looked just like any other baby in that he was screamy, squishy, and his face was mostly jowls.

Boring.

The real gossip was on Olympus, then.

'You coming?' I asked Eros.

'Nah, I want to ask the Cyclopes about something.' His eyes were transfixed on the metal they were making. My son always loved shiny things.

Olympus was agog. I wasn't the only person to see a baby come hurtling through the sky, and I definitely wasn't the only one to notice the previously pregnant queen of the gods was no longer, well, pregnant.

When it became clear that we were waiting for something, Zeus sighed and called everyone around and made his grand, sulky pronouncement: 'The baby fell.'

The head of every single Olympian turned to Hera for confirmation. Surely the goddess of family, of mothers, would be weeping at such a tragedy, but she wasn't. Her eyes were cold. Her hands were still.

She looked beautiful, no track marks from tears running down her face or anything of the like.

She nodded. 'The baby fell.'

That unison between the happy couple lasted maybe an hour, maybe two drinks, before Hera was whispering to Demeter and I was eavesdropping while Hestia told me about . . . something. Maybe the healing properties of barley water. She really liked barley water. No matter. She didn't expect a lot of responses, which meant I was free to hear Hera tell Demeter, her closest confidant – who had been rather cold with her that evening due to not understanding *why* anyone would let go of their baby – in a hushed whisper: 'It wasn't an accident of course. Zeus threw him off for not being worthy of us.'

The whisper ran rampant around Olympus, but neither parent made any comment on it ever again. Questions were met with glares and statements that *really, I thought we were done talking about this.*

Ares I

What? Not going to mention me then?

I'm Ares. Zeus and Hera's *other* son. The one they didn't throw off the fucking mountain. Sure, I didn't go and have a bloody uprising like Heph did, but you still need to know my name.

Ares. God of war. Remember me.

Hera I

Honestly, everyone was making a fuss out of nothing. When our eldest came back, it wasn't some war; he wasn't declaring enmity with our family forevermore or any of the nonsense you people like to spout. He was simply being overdramatic. So like his father that way.

It was a tantrum, throwing his toys around. It only *seemed* dramatic because we are the best and most powerful of the Olympians, so he had some rather large toys to throw around. His winged chair, for one, his father's lightning bolts for another, and his little Cyclopes friends for a third. I thought he could have done better, but he said they made him happy, and sometimes you have to let your children make their own mistakes.

When he arrived, taking the door down with him, I rushed to him. I know we shouldn't reward this behaviour, but he was my first baby, and I hadn't seen him for so long. I couldn't resist. When I saw the door on the ground, I couldn't help but roll my eyes.

'You could have *knocked*,' I said. 'We would have let you in.'

'How was I supposed to know that?' He looked sulky but well. His beard had grown out nicely, and he'd taken on a number of his father's features. I daresay he'd be quite handsome if he'd just let someone take care of him a bit. Trim his hair, neaten his clothes. Then any nymph would be happy to have him.

'You're so tall now,' I said.

'Dad threw me off a mountain.'

I regretted that rumour as soon as I started it, but I couldn't take it, the pitying looks, the scepticism when I talked about child-rearing when, in their eyes, I'd so clearly failed to guard my own. I told the world my husband did it, because it was better than saying I let my baby go.

'Well, you're here now. Why don't you send your little friends away and you can come in for lunch.'

'I don't want lunch.'

'A drink, then.'

'I want answers, Hera.'

'Mum.'

'I'm not calling you that.'

I began to cry. It is a funny thing, when your children can make you cry. Ares hadn't managed it in years of hair-pulling and punch-throwing and foot-stabbing. Hephaestus was more precocious; it only took him five minutes.

'I'm not going to call you Mum because you're crying.'

I couldn't stop. I'm ashamed to say my wails grew louder and more dramatic until tears were rolling down my face in a quite unattractive way. He dismissed his friends, pulled a piece of fabric from his bags, and handed it to me.

'You carry a handkerchief?' All these different ways our children can surprise us.

'I use it for polishing.'

It left a great greasy mark across my face. That would have upset me any other time, but for now it meant my son did care for me. That was enough to be getting on with.

I invited him in and called for his father. Our home was not well laid out for that flying chair of Hephaestus', so I rearranged the chairs in the garden where there was more space.

'This way we may admire the flowers,' I said.

'I've never been much for flowers.'

After some encouragement, Zeus emerged to speak with us. I wished for luck. My husband isn't prone to calm conversations to begin with, and our son seemed determined to bring chaos to proceedings.

'Who drops their baby off a mountain?' he asked without preamble. I have always hated that question for how it made people look at *me*. I always fought it, because I didn't drop him.

I let him go.

There is a difference, one I will never quite forgive myself for. That was the first I saw of how lost it made *Hephaestus* look.

'It's in the past,' Zeus said.

'Not for me.' Hephaestus looked at his legs. Zeus looked at his legs. I looked at his legs. We didn't talk about his legs.

'Now you're back, we can make it better,' I offered.

He looked above my head. He wasn't a great one for eye contact, but it was closer than the floor, which is where he'd been focusing before. 'I don't need to be fixed.'

'No, no, that's not what I meant,' I said. How are you supposed to talk to an adult child when they grew up without you? 'Tell us, how can we welcome you? What do you want?'

'I don't want anything from you anymore.'

I wanted to scream. There was no changing the past, only what we could do to make it better. 'There must be something we can give you, or you wouldn't have come back.'

'I want to know why.'

'It was an accident.'

'I don't think so.'

'You want love?' I said, desperate. He had to let me give him something. Sitting before me, he was guilt personified. He was my every regret, my every failure, all coalescing into someone who looked a little bit like me. 'I can give you love.'

'It's a bit late for you to love me.' Hephaestus scowled. He shouldn't do that – he'd look so much more handsome if he just smiled.

'Not from me – of course *I* love you – but I can give you love itself.'

'What do you mean?'

'A wife.'

My husband tried to stand, not realising I had the nymphs tie his legs to those of his seat – *encouragement* for him to sit through this conversation. He half toppled the chair before he managed to right himself. He didn't mention it.

'A grand idea,' he said. 'How do you feel about marrying the goddess Aphrodite?'

My son paused, his mouth open so wide he could catch flies. I'd have reprimanded him but I was doing much the same.

Many people had tried to marry Aphrodite over the years, but Zeus always said no. Leave her her freedom.

But why *not* set her up with our Hephaestus? She was unmarried – not because she found the concept of sex unnecessary (like Artemis) or because she found the concept of femininity unnecessary (like Athena) or because she found the concept of adulthood unnecessary (like Hestia) – and an Olympian, and attractive enough. She would be suitable for our son.

'Aphrodite?' Hephaestus said.

'Was I not clear?' Zeus said.

'Well . . .'

'Wonderful, it will be done,' Zeus said.

Hephaestus left soon after. He didn't want to talk, he didn't want to stay for dinner, he didn't want us to set up a room for him, but he agreed to love. Organising his wedding was enough to be getting on with.

The only issue was the bride herself, who was altogether too recalcitrant about the matter when I went to speak with her, as if *she* were too good for *my* son. She didn't say so exactly, but I could tell from her tone. It was like Demeter said: she was only out for herself and she didn't care about the rest of us.

Aphrodite said no and no and no, no matter how many times I asked, and it was all very frustrating, until I complained to my husband about it.

'I will meet with her, my love. I will sort it.'

He did just that. It was so good to see him use all his power for good. I would have happily conceived a third that night.

I planned the wedding. Neither bride nor groom made any real contribution to events, though I did ask them. The celebration was very beautiful, I thought, even if my son required a little convincing.

'Hephaestus, *smile*. She won't think you're handsome if you don't smile.'

'She won't think I'm handsome either way. You told everyone I was too ugly to be your son and that's why Dad threw me off a mountain, remember?'

The grudges we keep in this family, honestly. I said that *once*. I'd had a lot to drink. It was just after Hephaestus was born and I was missing, not him exactly, but the idea of him, the child that proved I was a wonderful wife and mother and, even then, when things were so difficult for me, my husband was out fucking nymphs and having perfect, beautiful, powerful babies with them the first time, every time. I shouldn't have said it, but the lies didn't come from nowhere.

'You fell,' Zeus said. 'Now. Do as your mother tells you. Smile.'

Hephaestus smiled. He did look more handsome, and the rest of the wedding went swimmingly.

Of course, the newly-born Eris did manage to "accidentally" spill a cup of wine on the bride – Eris has never managed to let a wedding pass unmolested – but, as far as her mischief-making went, it didn't cause much issue. Aphrodite simply removed her clothes and continued like that.

'Are you sure you want her married off?' the very married Poseidon whispered to my husband.

Zeus didn't respond. His eyes were wide and unmoving, trained solely upon her. And he wondered why we didn't copulate more often.

Other than that small fly in the wonderful ointment, everyone behaved remarkably well, promising their care and support for the couple, handing them gifts. And still the two of them looked miserable.

'Smile,' I urged, once more. 'It's your wedding. You're happy.'

'Yes, happy,' Hephaestus said flatly.

'Very happy,' Aphrodite agreed, just as flatly. He looked down at her then, the beginning of something more in his eye, a twinkle, maybe, and I knew in that moment that this whole thing could work.

Aphrodite XIV

Of course it didn't work. I didn't want to marry him, and I wouldn't have, if what I wanted ever came into it, but it didn't. Hera wanted me to marry him, which meant *Zeus* wanted me to marry him, and that I couldn't say no to.

He summoned me to his office one day. It was a nice room, smaller than you'd imagine, but it didn't feel claustrophobic – probably since it didn't have a roof, an implicit threat about the lightning Zeus could bring crashing down unto you.

'Hey, Dad, you asked for me?'

He sat with his legs spread as far as they would go. It was meant to make him look powerful. All it really did was show he wasn't enough to fill the space he'd been given.

'Don't call me that,' he said calmly, before belying that calm by throwing a vase at the wall. His hands moved so fast I didn't even see him pick it up, didn't know what was happening until I heard the crash, saw the shards fall to the floor. 'Nothing is too beautiful to be broken.'

'What do you mean?'

'You know what I mean.'

'No, Dad – my king. I don't.' That was true enough. There were so many things it could be, but I'd watched enough liars to not give myself away with guesses, with a blind confessional to the man who tortured my best friend. I should have given him *something*, but I had no small secrets. They were all tangled together in a lie too large to unpick.

'My son, Hephaestus, has returned. You will marry him.'

'As the goddess of love—'

'You are the goddess of *nothing*,' he bellowed, and with it, bile rose in my throat.

He knew. He knew I was nothing. He knew I was a liar. He knew I was never anything more than someone he used to love.

'Without me, you are the goddess of nothing. And you have chosen to betray me.'

Oh. Hyperbole. I'd never been so relieved. I could lie around hyperbole.

'I would never—'

'Why have you been sneaking off to talk to that Titan, Aphrodite? Why would you do that to me?'

I tried not to let the relief show on my face. Relief was a wholly inappropriate emotion for the situation, but visiting Prom was one of my smaller secrets. I could survive this. It would hurt, but I could survive it.

'What? You hate me? Is that it? You're planning a rebellion?'

'No,[36] it's not like that—' I filled, as I scrambled for a better lie, a forgivable one.

'Don't lie to me.'

'I won't,' I lied. 'We met when we were creating Pandora, on your orders.'

'I remember what I ordered.'

---

[36] I wasn't, yet. —A

I spoke slowly. Carefully. There was a stampeding beast in front of me. There were only lies behind. I had to be the barrier.

'I loved him,' I said. 'It was foolish, I know, it was wrong, but the heart can be a fickle thing. Our affair was brief. I was telling him that it was over, that I was ashamed to have ever been seen with him.'

'You met more than once.'

'He is . . . persuasive.'

'I thought you were loyal.'

'I am loyal.'

'How could someone loyal to me ever love one of them?'

'You loved a Titan too, once.'

'You lied to me.'

'I'm sorry.'

'You will marry my son. Keep that fickle heart of yours from wandering.'

'I can—'

'And it will prove your loyalty to the family.'

There was no argument to that. The family was Zeus, and Zeus was the family. I'd loved him once, and he'd loved me twice, and that wasn't enough, so I agreed to marrying this man I'd never even spoken to, who I knew quite profoundly I didn't want to marry, because I didn't have any other choice I could see. I traded all my loves for the power I already had. It was the best I could do.

People thought less of me after that. They assumed Zeus had that much control over me, that he could say anything he wanted and I would do it, the ever-faithful daughter giving up everything she held dear because Daddy said so, and that was still better than the truth.

We didn't bother telling people the marriage was because I loved

Hephaestus. Don't get me wrong, it was said that he loved me and his love was more important than mine, superseded the wishes of the goddess of love herself.[37] He loved me and I did what Zeus told me, and those things were sufficient.

I stopped visiting Prometheus immediately, without even explaining what had happened. He was smart enough to work it out; he had to be. Any more misbehaviour would get me thrown out of Olympus and my name scrubbed from history faster than you could say *love*.

I missed him, but I'd missed him before. I knew how to do it.

Anyway, I had a wedding to contend with.

The whole event was extravagant, from the music to the flowers to the guest list. It was showier than Poseidon, Hades, and Zeus' weddings combined and that, I think, was the point.

It was all anyone spoke about for months. Years, even. *The goddess of love is married.* That slut[38] is finally tied down to one man. Zeus made sure that everyone knew, that everyone remembered. There would be no fading away and pretending it didn't happen, not for me. My shiny new husband could end things whenever he wanted.

Still, Hephaestus and I tried, at the start. There was no point making myself miserable in this marriage just because I didn't have a choice in it. I made friends with his Cyclopes. He found my favourite flowers – bellflowers – and cast them into metal for me, their petals seeming impossibly delicate for something that would never yield.

'Strong,' he said. 'Like you.'

It wasn't often that someone found a novel compliment for me.

---

[37] Blah blah blah. I'm not a goddess and I'm full of shit, but *they* didn't know that. —A

[38] I like sex. Fight me. —A

I enjoyed that, but that moment was the highest point we ever reached.

He wanted to live together, since that's what married couples do, but he refused to move in with me and I refused to move in with him. I had too many secrets to share a home. And an Eros. I couldn't just kick *my son* out.

I told Hephaestus the second reason, so he gave me another house, near to where his forges were. He said it was mine, but we both knew that was a lie.

'It is well built,' he said, in a failed effort to convince me to move there. 'See the designs. The foundations are deeply dug.'

'That's not the point, Hephaestus. I like my home.'

'This can be a new home.'

'I like my current location.'

'And *I* like this one.' He didn't actually say it, that we should live where he wanted because this was his marriage that I happened to play a part in, but his tone gave it away. He was humouring me by having this argument and he was growing bored with it.

'Then we'll each stay in the houses that make us happy, Husband. You do want us both to be happy?'

He had no answer to that.

He came to visit me, sometimes. He brought me gifts – trinkets, jewellery – all so clearly made by him that no god could fail to recognise it. He wanted to drape me in markers with his name on them, announce to the world who I really belonged to.

So I thanked him for the jewellery, told him honestly that it was beautiful – he is incredibly skilled – and ensconced it in boxes where I could look at it if the urge so took me.

I think I still have those boxes locked up somewhere.

Once, he brought wine too. My attendants made dinner. We ate and we talked, and there were brief moments when it felt like the conversation was flowing, until one of us stumbled, offended. We were cordial enough, but it was always, *always*, work.

I took him to bed. I thought it might help.

It wasn't bad. He was attentive, and he followed instructions well, which meant it could never be terrible, but I didn't want to think all the time when I was having sex; I didn't want to map out my body one night only to be told off when I reacted differently the next.

'You *said* this was good.'

'It *was* yesterday.'

'How can it be different?'

'I'm not a machine, Hephaestus! You can't just pull a lever and . . . turn me on.'

We both sighed when I said that, the ridiculousness of the statement unheeded in the tragedy of the situation.

He took to reaching a hand out to me. Not in a grabby way, not insisting, just touching. It could have been wonderful, full of love and reassurance, but like our conversations, it never became more than awkward.

It's not much having your leg stroked *awkwardly*.

No matter, I was trying – as Hera said, it behoved me to try – so I didn't sleep with anyone else in those early days. Not even when I wanted to.

Eros II

Mummy was bad at being a wife. That was a secret, but one of the ones everyone knew. I wanted to make a game of it, guess how many people were going to say it that day, but Mummy said no, Zeus would be mad if we did that.

She wasn't much fun when she was worried about Zeus.

'I'll just have to live through it,' she said. 'We can survive this, Ro-Ro.'

'You could try loving him.'

'You know I'm not built for any of this.'

Marriage, she meant, and monogamy. We didn't believe in that. Why have one love when you can have many? But I still thought I'd be right and she'd be wrong. I knew Hephaestus better than her. Saw him round about in the waters. He was nice. Busy, but nice.

I think he did love her, you know.

He was bad at saying it. He was bad at talking at all, but he could say things without words. When he saw Mummy at the wedding it was like the rest of the world had been ripped away beneath him and she was the only thing keeping him there.

Mummy wanted to be adored? Worshipped? Seen before or else?

Hephaestus would have given her that. She said she wanted a home and he built her one, but when they opened their mouths they bashed against each other like waves hitting the cliffs. She was too fluid. He was too solid, and the words didn't make sense, even if they were talking the same language.

So Mummy came to me for help. I thought she wanted me to shoot them with my arrows, make them love each other, but she looked sick when I offered.

(Mummy thinks she's really good at lying, but she's not.)

'No, honey, not that.'

'Don't you want to love him?' It'd be so much easier if we loved him.

'Yes. But—'

'But what?'

'Eros, your kind of love—'

Want to hear what Mummy told me about my kind of love when I was growing up?

1. It was special.
2. It was magical.
3. It was natural.
4. It was what we were made for.
5. It was the future of the world.
6. It was older than the gods.
7. It would outlast the gods.
8. It was her favourite thing in the world.

She said it all the time. I was special and I was a god and I should be proud, and I thought she meant it.

'You're frowning, Mummy.'

'I just want us to get there on our own.'

'Why? You could be happy now. Don't you want to be happy?'

'Of course I want to be happy, sweet pea, but—'

'Is there something wrong with me?'

'No, no, Ro-Ro, you're perfect – that's what I was going to say. I need your help in another way.'

'How?'

'You know Hephaestus better than me. Can you come with me? Translate?'

Which is how I got to see Mummy really fall in love. Just not with her husband.

We went down to the forges, which was where Hephaestus spent most of his time. It was dull, Mummy said to me, and she didn't like that, but it didn't seem boring to me. There was so much going on with all the fires and the bashing and the work. I like things steamy.

'Honey, I'm here,' Mummy shouted. She was only halfway through the first word when Hephaestus appeared in front of her, his chair rising off the ground until their faces were about level.

'You have elected to visit.' He smiled under his beard, but it didn't come through in his voice. 'Finally.'

'I wanted to introduce you to my son, Eros.' She gestured at me, like I should step forwards or flap my wings and announce myself, but that's not the way it's meant to work. After my name, Mummy was meant to say that I was her favourite child and the most important person in her retinue, but she didn't. She just left it hanging there.

'Mummy!'

'*Eros.*'

'Where's the rest of it?'

She whispered something in her husband's ear. I didn't like it. It was about me. I should have known what it was about, and I didn't want them laughing at me, but he didn't laugh. He scowled.

'Parents should be kind to their children,' he said.

Take that, Mummy.

'That's what I came about actually,' she said quickly. 'I wanted us to make a gift for Eros. Together, as a family.'

'I have jewels,' Hephaestus said.

'I was thinking more like . . .' She leaned into him, until her breasts were on his shoulders and her lips were touching his ears. '*Arrows*.'

'Zeus wouldn't like that.'

'What Daddy doesn't know won't kill him.'

I'd never seen Mummy like that before, her smile curving hard into her cheek so I could just see the glint of her teeth at the edges. She looked mean. But Hephaestus liked it. He started forging my arrows, my special new arrows that would work on *everyone*, even though my old ones already worked on everyone I tried, so I didn't know who we were going to aim for next. But I like getting new things.

Mummy dipped them in honey to make the love all the sweeter, and she handed them off to me to add that something extra only I could bring to the world.

I made them invisible. Sneaky. You never know when love is going to hit you.

Mummy started humming and I joined in, and we both looked at Hephaestus like he would come in too and the whole thing would be perfect, but he was too focused on his work to see us waiting for him.

It wasn't just him who missed things though. He tried putting a hand on Mummy's leg, and she didn't notice because she was talking to me. The two of them were always out of time, out of sync. And I could have helped. I had the arrows right there, the special ones. I could make them happy.

Only Mummy said no.

So there we were making my arrows that I wasn't allowed to use, when the door fell down in front of us.

'Brother,' the intruder boomed. 'I am glorious in battle once more.'

'Is there any particular glory in conquering those weaker than you?' Hephaestus said.

'But I am glorious,' he insisted. 'Look at my mighty weapon.'

He was sexy, this man,[39] in that dangerous kind of way. The way you want for a night but will burn you if you hold on any longer. A man for the people who want to hold on so tight they don't feel the bruises till after.

Sexy, but not the sharpest. The way he was standing made the size of his *other* mighty weapon quite clear to everyone in the room, not least his own brother.

Mummy blushed and snorted through her nose.

'Very mighty, Brother,' Hephaestus said. 'And we are working.'

'What, on these puny things?' He gestured to my arrows.

Mummy stopped smiling. 'You think yourself strong enough to bear the weight of love?' she said.

'If love is so weak I could snap it between my toes, then yeah, *love*, I think I can hold it.'

'Eros, sweetheart, please let the nice man hold your arrows. Let him see your might.'

I knew that instruction. That's what she'd been telling me my whole life. Show off what I can do. Refuse to be anything less than everything I was and demand more if they let me, *make them* let me. I put every ounce of power and impudence I had into that

---

[39] Ares. God of war. Very important. Eros is being a little shit not introducing him properly. —A

arrow, every lost lover and broken heart. Every secret look and forbidden rendezvous. Every moonlight walk and sweet talk and dirty word. I let all of it run through my fingers into the arrow until I was sure I'd snap it myself and only then, still dripping in honey, I handed it to Ares.

His grin fell nearly as fast as his arms, but he didn't drop it. 'Fuck me, what did you put in this?'

Mummy smiled, sweet as honey. 'Love.'

'Take it back.'

'No.'

'It's fucking heavy – take it back.'

'I think you could use a little love, *love*.'

Hephaestus was still working, making arrows faster than Mummy and I were finishing them. Hephaestus didn't see it. He probably didn't want to, but I saw it. Mummy and Ares weren't fighting. They might have thought they were fighting, but that's because love is stupid when you're in it. It's very simple when you're out of it.

They were teasing. They were flirting. Not with intent, not with the plan of doing anything about it, not really, but they were flirting. I didn't have to shoot them, and it wouldn't have done anything even if I had. It was already there.

Mummy and Ares sitting in a tree. K-I-S-S-I-N-G.

Ares II

Told you I'd be back.

Hephaestus I

Like anything else, gods act the way that they do for a reason. By that logic, there must have been some reason my parents threw me from their home when I could not yet speak. I only ever returned to Olympus so I could ascertain what that was. That action rather spiralled out of my control.

My mother cried and begged for forgiveness without offering reason or justification. She told me that she loved me.

'How do you quantify that?' I asked her.

'I just know.'

I did not *just know*. When I looked at her, I didn't feel some emotion previously unknown to me. There was the curiosity, of course. Not only about why she did what she did or why she allowed my father to do so, but to see which parts of myself could be traced to her. I never did find them. Appearances were important to her. She spoke louder when she thought other people were listening. Her family had to be the best, even after what they did to me.

She announced to the world that her son had returned, and the family was happy. She didn't ask me what I felt. Feelings are difficult to categorise, but I would struggle by any measure to define mine as happiness. I was angry, which only grew as she offered me gifts and refused to give me *answers*.

She sent away my Cyclopes, treated me like a child. Her child. I did not feel as though I were her child. I was a stranger in a house that demanded my love.

She kept pushing. It didn't come from a place of cruelty. I know what cruelty feels like. This was desperation. She wanted forgiveness for an act *she would not describe to me*.

I said yes to Aphrodite so Hera would stop talking about a love I didn't know I could feel.

Loath as I am to admit it, my mother was right. I felt something different and completely new to me when I looked at Aphrodite. Difficult to quantify, but there.

She was kind. She looked in my eyes when she spoke to me. She did not drown me with apologies or history. She did not throw me from a mountain. And she was beautiful.

I made her jewellery. I crafted her bellflowers. I built her a house when she would not come to mine. I am not much with words, but I thought that she understood me. She did not love me, but my mother assured me that would come with time, and I chose to believe her.

We worked on it, this so-called love, through both the engagement and the wedding, but it was perpetually difficult.

That, I could not understand. She was the goddess of love. Surely, love should come naturally to her. Surely, if anyone could love me easily, it would be her. It was her job to love. Why not me?

It only became truly apparent to me how much work it was after she met my brother. The two of them spoke easily, with layers of emotions atop their words that I didn't have time to pick apart. I took to inviting Ares to our meetings so he could grease the wheels between us. It helped, but not sufficiently.

I was lonely. Desperately so. Speaking with my wife only made me aware of how many people she had in her life and how few I had in mine. I had only my loyal Cyclopes, to be truthful. They were my friends, but I knew all there was to know about them and them about me. We were bored of one another.

I found myself seeking excuses to speak to the Olympians. Ares had to test the weight of a spear. I needed Hermes to send a message. I asked Athena for advice on some new designs I was drawing up, which she happily gave, and I discovered she had excellent insight. She spoke clearly and confidently, and she had a different experience of this world to me, providing valuable perspective.

It was only natural that I should invite her around often, after that. With Athena, speaking was easy. She did not waste her words on irrelevances. I did not have to try. I did not have to be mindful of how I sounded or what feelings I might hurt by simply being myself.

After many months of our interaction, I began to wonder what life would be like if I were married to her instead. Athena. That was the maximal point of my unfaithfulness.

There is no god with the power to read the thoughts of another, but if any could possess such a thing, it would be Aphrodite. Within days of my first wondering, she had changed. She was jealous. Possessive. Angry. She seduced me as she had not done in months. She sat in my lap. She checked on my location many times in a day, even when I had not left my forges.

I no longer found myself inclined to respond. It was nice that she loved me, or that she gave the appearance of it, now, but it is not what occupied my mind.

I wanted Athena. Athena who was so intelligent. Athena who measured her thoughts and her actions. Athena who had as many plans and ideas in her head as I did in mine. Athena who was happy to sit in silence as she wove and I tinkered.

That was easy. *That* was what I wanted, and *that* was what I deserved.

I told her this one day. Directly, as she preferred.

'Athena, I believe we should be married.'

'You are already married.'

'I would leave her in an instant for you.'

Athena did not gift her smiles easily – perhaps only to those she loved – but she gifted me one then. 'Absolutely not,' she said.

'My mother will want to plan the wedding of course— Wait. What?'

'I have no desire to be married and no interest in these games of sex and relationships you are all so intent on playing.'

'You don't have to lie to me, Athena. You love me, as I love you.'

'Love is a strategic error,' Athena said. 'We will talk of this no further.'

With that, she returned to her weaving, a most accurate description of a woman's face contorted in pain as she transformed into a spider.[40] Athena's most recent enemy vanquished. I knew how the woman felt.

I had made a mistake.

My wife was soft, not stern. She laughed easily and was generous with her touches. A smile from her was not a prize to be earned; it was a beautiful thing, easily given. I loved my wife, not this harridan. I vowed then to return to her, and she would be as she had been in recent months. I wanted someone

---

[40]   Arachne. The first in a surprisingly large collection of people Athena turned into insects but, being a spider, of no further relevance. What a catch Athena is. —A

who was what I am not. Someone who could make me more than what I am.

Only when I returned to her, she too refused me. Through some intuition I will never understand, she learned of what had occurred between Athena and I. She did not take it well.

She immediately demanded a divorce. I did not grant it. She had loved me before. She would love me again.

She did not accept my decision, so we went to Zeus for deliberation. He upheld my refusal. The situation upset Athena, who did not want to become embroiled in small arguments. While I agreed with her, she distanced herself from me as a result. I was alone once more.

In her paroxysm of rage, Aphrodite had ensured that I could not have any other but her. I took that to mean she wanted me, but she did not talk to me; she no longer made her visits. She whispered about my ugliness among the gods. She questioned whether I had developed a tremor.

She was upset, I gathered, about the situation with Athena – jealous. She was acting out before she forgave me.

I did not think her so cruel as to take away the one person in this world who truly loved me and then refuse to replace him. My wife contains hidden depths.

She began an affair with my brother. Took him from me and flaunted him. She showed everyone in Olympus that she was not mine in anything but name, and in doing so destroyed my name. It should have destroyed *hers*. She was the one being unfaithful. She was cheating. She was fornicating in the thrice-damned alleys around Olympus. But she felt no shame for her actions.

When people mentioned it to her, and people did talk, she smiled. Waved. Said, *Oh it's just so difficult to keep your hands off someone when you're in love, you know?*

She did not look at me. She did not acknowledge that she was hurting me.

It cannot be all so surprising, then, that my mind turned to revenge. I wanted the world to see what she really was. Not beauty, not grace. Most certainly not love.

I was hurting. I wanted my wife to understand me.

Aphrodite XV

Look. I'm trying to let everyone have their say as the unique little fingerprints they are on this great universe, but I can't listen to another fucking word of this.

Oh, poor Hephaestus just wants Mummy and Daddy to love him. Poor Hephaestus was thrown off a mountain. Poor Hephaestus made his wife marry him and then didn't like that she was annoyed by it.

Yeah, I had an affair with Ares. I fell in love with Ares.

And yes, I did run a spirited campaign to make my husband's life so miserable he'd finally fucking leave me, because he was allowed to leave and I wasn't.

But, for once in my life, I didn't start it. *Poor Hephaestus* did.

Do you know what my oh-so-heartbroken husband did to Athena to kick all of this off? It wasn't professing his love, not unless your head is so deep in the gutter you can't think in anything but innuendo.

Hephaestus professed his love to Athena by masturbating on her.

Shockingly, my husband assaulting someone else didn't really do it for me in bed. I don't like the bitch, but Athena deserves better than an unwelcome visit from my husband's limp dick.

It wasn't bloody intuition that made me find out about it, either. They had a *child* together. Some boy Athena rustled off to Athens to be raised as a nobody because *she* didn't want the shame of it.

So, I risked everything, put every bit of power I'd ever clawed my way into on the line to try to get out of it. I had to. We all saw what happened to Hera when her husband cheated on her, saw the respect waning every day as she wasn't strong enough to hold on to him, but for me? For the goddess of love to not be enough for her husband? It would destroy me. I would be demoted and forgotten and back to the girl I'd fought so hard to leave behind before I could blink. Of course I took the other bet. I dragged him in front of Zeus and begged for a divorce.

Me: Please, Father. I know you sanctioned our marriage, but my husband loves another. Let him be free to pursue her.

Hephaestus: I do not.

Me: You got your *semen* on her.

Athena: How could you possibly know that?

Me: I'm the *goddess of love*, Athena.

Athena: That *cannot* be your answer to everything.

Zeus: Enough. Athena, you told me you had no interest in sexual relationships.

Athena: That is the case.

Zeus: Then *how* did his semen end up on your thigh?

Athena: It was an accident.

Me: A semen-based accident?

Athena: I'm led to believe that penises can erupt with minimal provocation. I would expect you to understand, Aphrodite. You have the same equipment.

Me: They're dicks, not *volcanoes*.

Athena: Actually, it is entirely possible to predict that form of eruption with the proper observation. This occasion was an accident.

Hephaestus [blushing through his beard]: There was no accident.

Me: So you did it on purpose?

Athena: It doesn't matter what happened. None of you were involved and I do not want you to be. It is up to me to defend myself and I did.

Zeus: That sounds like a resolution to me. I am not here to arbitrate your petty bickering, children. Sort it out.

Hephaestus: But what about—

Zeus: Fine. Hephaestus, if you are so unhappy, would you like to dissolve the marriage?

Hephaestus: No. I want her to love me.

Zeus: That is that then. The marriage continues. Do not bring this to me again.

Me: Aren't you going to ask me?

Zeus: No.

Can it really be a surprise to *anyone* that I stopped trying after all that shit?

He cheated first, is what I'm saying. He forced me into marriage, he was meant to love me, and he cheated first.

He risked everything I'd ever worked for.

There was no way I was carrying any part of him in me. I couldn't bear it.

The Fates I

She came to us in the middle of the night. She thought we were sleeping. **We don't sleep.** *Did she sleep, do you think?* That doesn't matter. *She thought we were sleeping.*

I – we – **right, we didn't recognise her from looks.** We could feel it. *It's not like she was one of us or anything but—* She felt like she belonged. **She acted like she belonged here.** *She knew her way around the place.*

My sister exaggerates. **There's not much place to know your way around.** *We live in a cave!*

But she did know her way around. **She went straight to the threads.** *Not the established ones that were well worn in or anything; we would have stopped her if she tried to do anything to them, right?* **Right.**

Our job isn't just to guide Fate. **It's to protect it.** *To make sure the right thing happens at the right time to the right person.*

We didn't always succeed. *Zeus?* Zeus. **The king of the gods found us.** *He told everyone they should be scared of us!* He didn't like to share his knowledge. **And he threatened us with his lightning bolts if we didn't help him change it.** *He didn't just threaten.* **No.** He burned a hole in Fate. *Just a little one!* Big enough to make sure he had a daughter with Metis instead of a son. **Big enough to make sure no one would usurp him.**

We shouldn't have helped him after that. *But we did.* **He threatened Fate itself.** *He said he was going to burn it down.* **He threatened you.** *He threatened you.* He threatened you. **So we did help.** We changed it for him. *But only once – then we started lying to him!* **Not lying.** Being selective with the truth. *We only told him the good stuff.* And it worked.

We didn't stop her though. **She felt like one of us.** She wasn't one of us. *It didn't seem like she was going to break anything.* **And she was crying.** Quietly. *Nothing else she did was quiet.* I don't know how she thought we were asleep.

When we cut people's threads, we use scissors. We make it clean. **When it's their time to go.** *She couldn't find our scissors.* I don't think that's the reason. **It wasn't the reason.**

She dug through the pile of unwoven threads. **More of a ball than anything.** *They tangled like no one's business.* **She was on her knees.** She was hurrying. *Frantic.* **She threw them all over the place.** Quite annoying, really. **They were already tangled; she didn't make it worse.** She might have made it worse.

We untangled them all together the next day, and it was a perfectly fine day, I think.

Eventually, she found what she was looking for. A single thread. *She broke it.* **She gasped when she did it.** *It sounded painful, that gasp.* **Like she couldn't believe what she had done.** *Like she didn't really believe she could.*

She broke it by pulling it tight across her palm. **It bled.** *Red, like us.*

The thread she broke was thin. *It was still a thread, still something of ours, and she broke it.* I think it was something of hers too. **It wasn't anything yet.** But it could have been. It was meant to be a baby! *Hers and Hephaestus'.* **But it wasn't. It wasn't anything yet. Does that make it different?**

She was crying. *She was.* **She was.**

But it didn't matter if she was crying or not; that thread was ours. She didn't look like she enjoyed doing it. **No, she didn't.**

She snuck out right after. **We didn't tell Zeus.** It wasn't any of his business.

Ares III

I didn't mean to go and fall in love with my brother's wife, did I? It just sort of happened that way.

It was always bloody knotty with Heph, what with him being my older brother and all, and Mum making it so clear she liked me better. He never got over that, never forgave anyone. Which I get for Mum, but he blamed *me*. I wasn't even alive yet.

Dad was always calling me detestable, but it didn't matter to Heph what Mum and Dad said to *me*, did to *me*, because they didn't throw *me* off the side of a damned mountain, so they must love me more and he'd always be the wounded one. No matter that they gave him the most beautiful – the fucking *best* person – in Olympus to marry. That didn't do shit to even up the scales.

When I met Foamy properly – only I didn't call her Foamy then; I called her Aphrodite, which was nice-sounding and all, but it just means Foamy, so when I got to know her better, I thought I'd save myself the effort and call her what she was, and when I did she always raised an eyebrow in threat of what she'd do to me later, and that was hardly a push to stop, was it? – it was right after they got married, when they were still *making an effort* – Mum's words – and even then I knew she was too much for my brother. She's loud. She talks a lot. She jumps from thought to thought. Heph hates that shit. He likes order and quiet and minimal fucking distraction.

Foamy is one giant ball of distraction if she's anything. Even that first time, she was sitting there teasing and winding me up, ready for a fight, and Heph didn't see any of it 'cause he was too busy working.

It's not like I loved her right from the off. That'd be fucking stupid. But I saw her more than Heph did, and I wanted to see more, but I didn't 'cause she was my brother's wife and I'm not a dick all the time. It was hard though, 'cause Heph kept inviting me to hang out with them to help them talk or something, and Foamy invited her son, and the two of us were there, and it was so weird I don't think we helped for shit. But, good brother and all that, I went, and I kept my hands to myself and didn't say a word about it.

She came on to me, the first time. None of that hair-twirling coy looks bullshit.

She came to my door, a spear in her hands.

'Ares, I want to fight something,' she said.

'What?'

'I don't care.'

'You can fight me if you want.'

That was all she needed. She jumped right on top of me and it was *hot*. Not normal hot, right? She fights dirty. She pulls hair and she bites, and she knows exactly how much it hurts when someone kicks you in the nuts. But she was on top of me and she was fighting with everything she had, and it meant I had to fight with everything I had, and it was just so fucking right to be like that with someone that I didn't even think about it when she grabbed my face and kissed me and held my hair tight in her hand.

I didn't think about my brother. I didn't give a shit whether she was married.

I wanted her. I wanted this. I wanted everything.

With Foamy, it was right to want.

In the middle of it, when I was half to Hades and I didn't care because she was on me like no one was ever fucking *on* me, and it was already so fucking obvious we were going to do this again, and again, and again, she came out with: 'I'm going to lie to you.'

'Huh?'

'I'm going to lie to you. I'm never going to tell you the whole truth.'

'Keep doing what you're doing and I won't fucking care.'

There was a whole lot of breathing between the words, but you get my drift.

We didn't talk about it after. Not the sex or the weird confession/promise thing. We didn't even have to fill in the time while she got dressed again because she hadn't been wearing any clothes to begin with. She smacked me on the arse and winked and walked away.

The next time was an accident.

We got called in to back-to-back meetings with Zeus. I don't know what she was in there for. For me it was so dear old Dad could tell me I wasn't going to make a single thing of myself. I'd never do anything worth doing in my life and I didn't deserve anything good that might happen to fall in my shitting path.

He didn't want me to change or nothing. He just wanted me to know what a fuck bloody disappointment I was as a son. He did this whenever he was having a crap day and wanted to shout it out. Half of Olympus would just sit there all meek and nodding, but I don't do meek, me. I shouted back. Threw things when he threw things. Bore the brunt of the pain when he threw lightning bolts and bellowed loud enough to shake foundations. Loud enough for Artemis to come complaining that there was no good hunting that day.

Foamy was waiting outside when he ran out of insults.

'Hi, Ares.'

'I need a drink.'

She found me, after she was done with my dog-faced father. I was in the far corner of the square from where Hestia sat so she couldn't give me the sad look about how I was behaving. Way I saw it, it wasn't any of her fucking business what I did with my drinks.

'I need a drink too,' Aphrodite said. She waved a jug of wine. It was bigger than her head, but she didn't spill a drop. 'Want to share?'

We didn't even have sex that night. I wanted to. Olympus, I wanted to. When she laughed and leaned forwards, I could fucking *smell* her hair. I wanted to grab her and push her up against a wall and kiss her so hard the fucking wall crumbled beneath us.

But she was married to my brother, so I bloody well didn't.

Do you know how much I want to do that I don't do, because of someone else's feelings? Nothing.

Literally nothing.

I do what I want when I want because I can.

But I didn't start sex with Foamy because it'd hurt Heph. I didn't start sex with Foamy at all. The way I see it, she started it, which meant she was the one doing the hurting, and I could say yes as much as I wanted.

She kept starting it, and we kept seeing each other. We couldn't fucking avoid each other even if we wanted to. We had to go to all these annoying family things at the same time and we talked and it was easy, and she pissed off Mum and I pissed off Dad and it was so much fun to have someone to do all that with. Heph didn't even try speaking with her. He just stared. Ragily.

After a while, I stopped stopping myself. Let us fucking do everything we wanted to do.

When I started with the whole I-love-you schtick, it wasn't all romantic. It just came out sometimes. When we were having sex. When she was beating me at games. When she jumped on my shoulders and made me carry her round. When the nymphs got all snotty with her and she used all the pretty words to explain how important she was and still one of them was shaking so hard their teeth were chattering 'cause of the sheer *force* of her.

Foamy, I fucking love you.

'About bloody time.' She laughed. She didn't swear around other people. She swore around me. 'I love you, *love*.'

She drawled it the way I did when we first met. Mocking me mocking her, but smiling. She didn't let that side of her out in front of other people, the one that was a bit mean. I hoped she liked it. I did.

And really, if Heph was so bloody annoyed about it then he could have ended the marriage and I would have happily married her instead. But he didn't. I stayed single and she stayed married, and that was that.

Mum kept trying to set me up, which was fucking embarrassing for everyone. Me because they all said no, even though I'm a bloody Olympian, them because I said no because they were boring and pale and I could crush them if I didn't pay attention, and Mum because the goddess of marriage couldn't even find her son a wife, which meant the goddess of marriage didn't have any legitimate grandkids. She hated that.

I don't know what I thought about it. Never thought much about the kid thing. Not till Foamy got pregnant.

Then I found I quite liked the idea of a kid with Foamy. A little us causing terror wherever they went.

'Oh no,' I said.

'What? Aren't you happy?'

'No. Shit. Yes. I'm so happy, Foamy. Just.'

'What?'

'We're going to have to tell Mum.'

'Oh. Fuck.'

'Yup.'

'Fuck on a fucking goose.'

'You like geese,' I said.

'They bite.'

'We can go together.'

'I'm using you as a shield.'

We went that afternoon, to get it over with. Mum did that bullshit thing when we arrived and she thought it was just Foamy there so she said she was busy and to wait a bit, until I said I was there too, and then she couldn't be through fast enough.

'I have news,' Foamy said, no fucking around. Mum wasn't even sitting down. 'I'm pregnant.'

Mum looked delighted. Happier than I'd ever seen her. 'I'm going to be a grandmother?'

Foamy smiled. Relieved. 'You're going to be a grandmother.'

'Don't mistake me here, I'm pleased, but I was under the impression you and Hephaestus were having some . . . difficulties in the marital bed.'

'Wrong son,' Foamy said.

Only then did Mum really look at me.

She shrieked and dropped her cup. It didn't smash. She looked confused. She picked it up and dropped it again. It smashed that time. She shrieked once more for luck then pretended to fucking faint. We had to send for Dad before she pretend woke up. Dad took the whole situation better, but that's 'cause he barely gave a toss about it or us.

He did glare at Foamy though. 'This is not what we discussed.'

She did this thing in front of Dad, where she scrunched up and made herself smaller, like he was the predator and she was the prey. I didn't like that. I liked her big. I liked her taking up space and being confident and proud and fierce. She wasn't prey. She was Aphrodite.

I moved in front to guard her. 'Don't you fucking touch her,' I said. I'd never threatened Dad before. I liked it.

'You have always been a disappointment, Ares. I'm sure your child will be more of the same. I can assure you, it will be of no relevance to me.'

Like *that* was going to hurt me. Do you have any bloody clue how many times he told me I was a disappointment in my life? Once more was hardly going to tip the balance. But then I looked over at Foamy, and she'd gone all pale as well as small. I tried to ask the question *are you okay?* without actually saying it out loud because Dad was still there and that's not the kind of thing you ask in front of him. Makes you look weak. She shook her head at me. Not now.

'It's a girl,' she said, abruptly.[41]

'You know that? How?'

'Feminine intuition.'[42]

---

[41] It was a girl. I checked. —A

[42] The number of times I got away with that excuse is frankly staggering. —A

'A girl,' Dad said slowly, his scowl dropping off his face. A bit. 'You're sure not a son?' As his son I could get pissed about this. What's wrong with sons?[43]

'I'm sure.'

'Well, then. Congratulations. I suppose.'

And that was that. Of course I didn't tell Heph. Why would I tell Heph? He didn't even like babies. Foamy might have thought about it, but she had her own shit going on with Heph, and I didn't want to get in the middle of it any more than I was already in the middle of it. No need to poke when the war was already well underway.

Mum told all the elder goddesses when they met up to pretend to play dice games but really just gossiped about the rest of us, and by the time night hit, every fucker on Olympus knew, and one of those fuckers told Heph.

He didn't do anything about it right away. Not that there was much to be done about it. Mum'd have his nuts if he hurt the baby. It's not like he bloody cared about Foamy anyway, I figured. But I was wrong, and he got his revenge like only he could, building one of his shitting contraptions.

Foamy and I had pissed off out of the council meeting because Dad was going on and on about our policies and our core values and some bollocks like that. I think Mum was feeding him the ideas. He kept saying we were a family, and obviously we are a bloody family, but he said it all stiff, like we weren't really a family at all; he just wanted us to think we were one. So Foamy and I pissed off and went to one of our usual spots to do something much more interesting than whatever Dad was saying.

---

[43] What's wrong with sons is that they're rumoured to have the power to overthrow you. —A

More interesting and more naked.

And BOOM. There we were. In a net.

Naked.

I gave a short, manly shout.

'Relax, dear,' Foamy said.

'Easy for you to say. I have rope-burn on my balls. How do you not have rope-burn on your balls?'

'Mine retract. And anyway, it feels like the net's made of bronze to me.'

'Then I have bronze-burn on my balls. Gonna say it's the burning that's a problem, not the material.'

'Material is always important.'

'Not as important as the *burning*.'

'Material.'

'Burning.'

'Material.'

And that by itself was enough to keep us going for a good ten minutes in the net. It must have been hung off of something, but I couldn't see what the bastard was attached to. Didn't really matter, did it? We were naked and trapped and swinging lightly in the nice spring breeze.

'Who did this? Artemis, you think? She does all that hunting stuff,' I said.

'No, Artemis likes you. This is one of my husband's contraptions, I imagine.'

I hated it when she called Heph that. I know they were married, but that didn't mean I wanted to be reminded of it. 'Why would Heph do this?'

She just looked at me.

I looked back.

She didn't blink.

I didn't blink.

She gestured to her body.

I blinked.

'Oh yeah,' I said. The affair. The baby. 'What do we do now?'

'Relax, we'll get down soon.'

'That's not very helpful.'

She stretched out. Bit like a cat, really. She stretched slow, wiggling every joint as she did it. She only looked at me once. She didn't need to do more than that. She knew the bloody effect she had on me. So even in the net I reached over and kissed her and got my hands on her and she got her hands on me, which is of course when my fucking brother arrived.

'See, fellow Olympians, what I must suffer,' he announced. He sounded like Dad. He never sounded like Dad. 'I have created this device using . . .'

Stuff. He used stuff. He used metal and cogs, and he did something clever with them, and instead of using them to make our lives easier or better or something, he used it to invite everyone to come and laugh at me and Foamy for being naked.

It was like he'd never bloody met her. Foamy loved being naked. It was her favourite thing to do. And she was right. If I looked like that, I'd never put clothes on either.

Happily for us, he started his own long, boring talk about all the stuff he did with the wire and the cogs, and everyone stopped listening. Apart from Athena, but then she looked offended by all the nakedness. More so when she caught Foamy stretching again. Don't know how she did it. She looked so comfy in there, like it was easy. My balls were still burning.

She winked at Hermes.

'C'mon, Hephaestus, you've had your fun, but don't you think it's time to let the good lady down now?' he said.

Then she winked at Poseidon.

'I wouldn't want to advertise the situation, if it were me,' he said.

Foamy beamed. Wish people did that much stuff for me just 'cause I was naked. I had to use weapons to make people do stuff for me.

'Baby brother, if you don't let us down this minute, I'm going to find whatever blade Cronus used to castrate his father then do the same to you. Capiche?'

'I think it's kind of comfy,' Foamy said. She pushed against the side so the net swung a bit. 'Wheeeeee.'

Don't know which of all those things helped. Maybe none of them. Maybe it was that no one was laughing or spitting or calling my girlfriend names. Doesn't matter. He let us down. Not gently, but I was happy enough to stand up and give my bollocks a massage till the feeling came back.

Foamy walked up to Heph. She leaned over and whispered in his ear. Don't know if anyone else heard. But I did.

'Remember, dear husband, that you have the power to leave this marriage. If you don't like the way I'm behaving as a wife then *leave*.'

She didn't actually threaten him. I'd know. Threats are kind of my thing – god of war and all – and she didn't threaten him. But she wrapped the words round her mouth like they were a threat and Heph went a bit green with all that, so there you go.

She came back to me. Put one hand on my chest.

'You take the afternoon and recover, okay? I need those bits of you.'

'The humans are having a war. I'm joining.'

'You have fun playing with them.'

'I always do.'

'Don't break them all.' She squeezed as she said it, then turned to make her exit. 'Bye, everyone, it's been a delight.'

She took three steps. Four. No one moved their eyes off of her. She whistled.

'Oi, Hermes, with me.'

He scampered behind her. Honest to fucking Olympus, he scampered. Those little wings on his shoes flapped as hard as they could, like an excited little dog, and he lifted with each step.

The two of them fucking didn't bother me. Maybe it's 'cause we started when she was already married to Heph, so I never felt like she was mine to begin with, or maybe it's 'cause I'm not thick. She'd never belong to anyone. She was going to do what she was going to do, and she didn't have an issue with my doing what I wanted to do, so we got on well enough with that.

Might have been annoyed if she'd *kept* sleeping with him, but she didn't. She slept with Hermes the once and Poseidon the once. She said it was to thank them for their support with the whole net thing, but I knew it was 'cause she wanted to punish Heph for it, remind him that if he tried to control her again then she would piss him off even more in return and, for all he was my brother, he fucking deserved it. He was so mad at Mum and Dad for what happened when he was born, for trapping him in the life he had, I don't know how he could wrap his head round doing the same thing to Foamy.

He still didn't leave her. He saved up all his rage and took it out on our daughter.

Harmonia I

Aphrodite wasn't like other mums. She didn't flutter and fuss around me like Grandma did to Dad and Uncle Hephaestus, and she didn't like telling me no. It was great. I had the run of all of Olympus, and I was the youngest so everyone talked to me and let me play, and if they ever looked at Mum, like, *should she be playing with fire?* Mum just shrugged.

'It's not like she can die, is it? Let her have her fun.'

She made sure I had weapons, though, so it was always the fun I wanted to have and not the fun other people wanted to have with me. I didn't get that when I was a kid, because everyone was so nice to me. It made more sense when I got older and I saw everything that happened to girls. Then *I* made sure I had weapons.

Dad made sure I actually knew how to use them. He said the way I held a sword was a recipe for cutting my fingers off.

'I'm immortal – wouldn't they just grow back?'

'If you want to experiment with cutting your fingers off, then you're the one telling your mother,' he said, but the next time I saw him he had a bandage wrapped up over his little finger and it looked shorter than the rest. He winked at me.

'They grow back. Slowly. And it hurts like a bastard. Don't recommend.'

I'm Harmonia, by the way, after, you know, harmony and every-thing. I'm meant to bring calm and accord everywhere I go, if you trust the name.

(It was a gift from Zeus.[44] When he said it, Mum and Dad looked at each other and snorted, apparently. I don't remember; I was just a kid then. But it's never felt quite right on me. It's not that I start fights – I'm not Dad – but I've finished a few. I'm not scared of discord.)

They were in love, my parents. Proper disgusting over-the-top can't-stop-looking-at-each-other love. Also a very we-don't-believe-in-boundaries-around-sex kind of love. Which *sucked* for me but was probably worse for my uncle Hephaestus, who was obviously, you know, married to Mum.

My family is weird. But having two Olympians for parents is great. Love that for me.

My story really began when I was a teenager, though. Mum and I were having dinner, and Dad came sauntering in. He tried to saunter. I think he was showing off for Mum, but he wasn't very good at moving smoothly so I thought it looked like he was stomping sideways, like a crab, but Mum was a fan.

'Dear, you're dripping blood on the floor,' she said.

Dad pulled his chiton off. He was wearing something under-neath, which was nice, because he wasn't always when they did this. 'Is that better?'

'Much.' Their eyes were locked on each other, like I wasn't even there.

'I'm gonna go,' I said.

---

44 She might not have been a son, but I swear this was still some weird attempt from Zeus to make sure my daughter didn't get any of her father's fighting spirit. —A

241

I was already up and out of my chair and halfway to the door by the time they managed to disentangle their eyes, and Dad held up his hand and said, 'Wait. I actually need to talk to you about something.'

'Me?'

'That's what I said.'

'Are you going to put your clothes back on?'

He looked at Mum. Mum looked at his chest. This happened a lot because the two of them were *mortifying*.

'No.'

'I'm not looking at you then.' I turned around and stood with my back to them, my arms crossed and my eyes to the wall.

'Fine. I just came to say, I've made this mortal kid my servant, so he's gonna be at my place for the next few years.'

'What?' Mum and I said together.

This was before there were heroes at all. It wasn't a *thing* for a mortal to come to Olympus, not without being made immortal first. It wasn't a *thing* to talk to one or ask them to do stuff for you. As far as I could tell, mortals mainly existed for Mum to watch when she was bored in the afternoons.

'This mortal kid killed my fucking dragon, and I am not taking the disrespect from the little sprat, so he's gonna work for me till I decide he's done.' That, I kid you not, is how the first hero came about. My dad having a strop 'cause some mortal killed his favourite dragon. 'Thought you should both know. Don't come round in your godly forms in case he catches fire.'

'That happens?' I asked.

I'd never met a mortal before. It was like, Mum's *only* rule. She said Grampa – Zeus – didn't like people messing with them, and I only had to look at Prometheus to see that, so I followed it, but it was a bit rich coming from her. She was always meddling with their love lives.

Dad shrugged. 'Maybe. Zeus seems to think so.'

'I'm coming round. I'd like to meet him,' Mum said.

'Me too,' I added.

Olympus had been fun when I was a kid, but now it got boring sometimes. I'd been to every corner of it and everyone was older than me, which would have been fine because I could hold a conversation with them, if only they'd stop telling me how they were all older than me and I was so young and sweet and innocent and I shouldn't join in with any of their debauchery yet. Calling it debauchery made them sound so old.

I was *sixteen*. Mortal girls were all married when they were my age, but gods don't have kids all that often on account of being immortal, so I was the youngest for *forever*. Apart from Eris.[45] But even she was like a decade older and her sole purpose was literally to annoy me. I'm harmony and she's discord, but people kept saying we should be BFFs because we were the only two who were even kind of the same age, but I hated her. She was always getting in my way and ruining my plans.

I wanted a real friend, not someone I had to be friends with because I didn't have any other options.

Dad kept calling this mortal *kid*. He might be my age.

'I want to go too.'

Both parents looked at me. I knew those looks. They didn't want me falling in love or getting hurt – like, hypocrisy much from the gods of love and war?

'No.'

---

[45] Goddess of discord. She *is* worth remembering. —A

'But—'

'Maybe later,' Mum said.

'I bet *Hera* would let me go.'

'If Hera ever has a daughter, then her wedding will be organised from the day she's born,[46] and she won't be allowed out, for fear of ruining her clothes,' Mum said. She scowled, then grimaced, then scowled again. 'You're staying here.'

'But—'

'Or going out on Olympus, I don't care. Anywhere but your father's house.'

'Boo.' I was basically an adult. And a goddess. She couldn't tell me what to do.

Apart from she could, because she was on the council and I was only a minor goddess of helping people get along, so I wasn't even *good* at arguing. Stupid Zeus. Stupid name.

I was just hanging out when she got back.

'What's he like?' I demanded.

'Not going to try to play it cool, are you?'

'You said playing it cool is for people who don't have anything else to offer and I have a lot else to offer, so not to bother.'

'I give great advice,' she said.

'Mum!'

'Right, sorry. You know how my head is—' Normally fine. Sometimes messy and muddled. Not with the anger that Dad gets, with something else – like she's in two places at once, like she's having another conversation at the same time. Makes her spacey. 'Cadmus—'

---

[46] I was wrong about this. When Hera did have a daughter, she was allowed to pick anyone she wanted to be her husband so promptly chose her mother's least favourite person in the entire world, but that's a story for another day. —A

'Cadmus? That's his name?'

'That's what I said.'

'Cad-mus,' I said, rolling it over my tongue. Better than Harmonia, for sure. 'What's he like?'

'He's a very angry young man.'

'Angry? Why's he angry?'

She sighed. 'It's a long story.'

'Mu-um, we're immortals. We have time.'

'You can't use that as an excuse for everything.' I could though, because we *were*.

'Zeus kidnapped his younger sister. Cadmus was sent by his parents to find her. He gathered his friends to help him look, and while they were searching, they ran into your father's dragon.'

'Did it kill all of them?'

'It did.' Urgh. That would make all of this so much harder.

'Cadmus barely survived the fight. He doesn't think it's fair that your father's acting like the hurt one.'

'And what do you think?'

She sighed. 'Harmonia, honestly, are you going to listen to a single word I say?'

'Of course!'

'Are you going to heed them?'

'Maybe.'

'Any relationship with a mortal is bound to be complicated. There will be struggles, and then they will *die*. Are you prepared for that?'

'Who said anything about a relationship?'

To that, she just smiled at me, kind of distantly, like her mind had pulled her somewhere else again.

The worst thing is she was right. She was always right about this stuff. I shouldn't have been surprised, really – she was the goddess

245

of love and all – but, like, could she stop being the goddess of love for one minute and just be my mum?

I waited until Dad was off fighting some battle and went round his house so I could introduce myself to the boy.

'I'm Harmonia.' I smiled and held a hand out to him.

'What do you want?' he growled, without even looking at me. He was my age, I thought. Just a tiny bit shorter than me. Nice shoulders. He had a big scrape down the side of his face, and there was blood in his hair. His eyes were brown. Cold, though. His eyelashes were longer than mine which was just rude.

'I came to meet you.'

'Why?'

'Because there's not a lot to do around here?'

'I'm not your entertainment.' He stomped off. I wasn't having that. It'd taken long enough to convince Mum to let me come here *and* she'd made me listen to more than one talk about sex.

(There were three: one for how to make it safe; one for how to choose a partner, which I really don't know she was qualified to talk about, given who Dad was; and one for how to have fun while you were doing it. The last one was the worst. The boy was very cute, and bits of it kept popping into my head as I talked to him.)

He tried to stride away from me, but he was all torso, so he was basically trotting and I could still keep up. It didn't work with all his grumpiness.

'I'm sorry.'

'What?' he said.

'I'm sorry. I didn't mean for it to come out that way.'

'How did you mean it to come out?'

'There's not a lot of other young gods—' I began, but I didn't get any further than that. Cadmus dove to the floor, face-down, eyes clenched shut. 'Ummm. Are you okay there?'

'I can't look at you.'

'You have my permission.'

'No. Ares said I can't look at any of the gods in their true forms, otherwise I'll explode.'

I rolled my eyes. 'He's being overdramatic. The gods don't walk around in their true forms. It'd be like if mortals walked around with no clothes on.'

'So I'd explode if I saw you naked?' he asked. He was blushing so hard I could see it on the back of his neck. Adorable.

'You'd explode if you saw me without any skin. The true form thing, it leaves you very exposed. Who wants that?.'[47]

'Then why's Ares always complaining about using his other form around me?'

'Because Dad loves to complain.'

'You're his daughter? Shit. I thought about you naked. He's going to kill me.'

And he literally ran away from me.

As it turns out, my dad, who often said he wasn't going to make any of my decisions for me and that I was a free woman with autonomy – I suspect Mum coached him – had threatened to beat the living shit out of the only person even faintly near my age on all of Olympus if he dared talk to me. But I wasn't going to let a little thing like that stop me.

I told Mum that Uncle Hephaestus had been making threatening noises and I was going to stay at Dad's until it was safer. She gave me a very knowing look.

---

[47] Fortunate for me, really. I have one form and it looks like a woman, not an amorphous blob of golden light. —A

'I hope you know what you're doing.'

I did.

I fell in love with him. Cadmus, not Uncle Hephaestus; that would be gross.

He was angry a lot, but I liked that. The world was unfair and he knew it. Sometimes we talked through all the bad stuff, and sometimes he went out and hit things until he calmed down.

He'd lost a lot of people. I tried to be sympathetic, but I didn't know any dead people. I asked Mum in case she did, but she shook her head.

'No, not anyone I know.' Her eyes still filled with tears. Weird. 'But, Harmonia, knowing you're going to lose someone, it's the hardest thing in the world. When you love them and one day they'll be gone, it means you can't make plans anymore, because they were part of every plan you had, and you can feel the space they used to take up, and it's so *loud*, echoing with everything they used to be.'

'Calm it, Mum. I didn't need a monologue.'

'I just want you to be okay, with this boy.'

'I know what I'm doing.'

I went back to Cadmus and told him about the echoes and the space and the not being able to make plans, and it seemed to help a little bit. He said he felt less alone, after, and he stopped looking at me like I was some lucky shit who'd never felt any pain. (He'd been wrong, obviously. Who hasn't felt pain?)

He fell in love with me too.

It took me a good three years before I made him laugh. Then he burst into tears because he wasn't used to the sound and he didn't think he was meant to be laughing when the world was so terrible. I told him that was stupid. He could cry as much as he wanted but he could laugh as much as he wanted too.

I didn't get to be around him all the time. He kept having to disappear off with Dad to do servanty things, which I'm pretty sure Dad made up every time he thought the two of us were getting too close, and I couldn't be having that.

'Cadmus,' I said, when he got back from one of them. 'I've decided we should get married. What do you think?'

He smiled. It still took him a moment to smile, like he had to tell himself it was okay, but that moment was getting shorter and shorter. 'Well, you know I'm into it, but I'm not the one you have to convince.'

He gestured to the statue of Ares behind us. It wasn't fun, skulking around in the literal shadow of my father. I couldn't wait until we had our own house.

'I'll handle it.'

We told my parents together. I thought Mum would have a calming, not murdery influence on Dad. And I thought Dad would have a less . . . suggestive influence on Mum, who liked dropping raunchy comments to see how red she could make Cadmus go. He was a virgin when he met me, and I was starting to worry that he would, in fact, burst into flames.

'So, I wanted to tell you both that we're in love.' I gestured to Cadmus. He was hiding behind me, a little bit. I didn't know which of my parents scared him more.

'Kid, you had one job,' Dad exploded at Cadmus. 'One. What was that job?'

'Don't fuck your daughter.' If he was a god, he would have sunk into the floor and buried himself in the stone. Better to go quickly.

Mum put a hand on Dad's shoulder. 'I think they're cute together.'

And that did all the work my arguments could not.

We were married a month later.

THE AGE OF HEROES

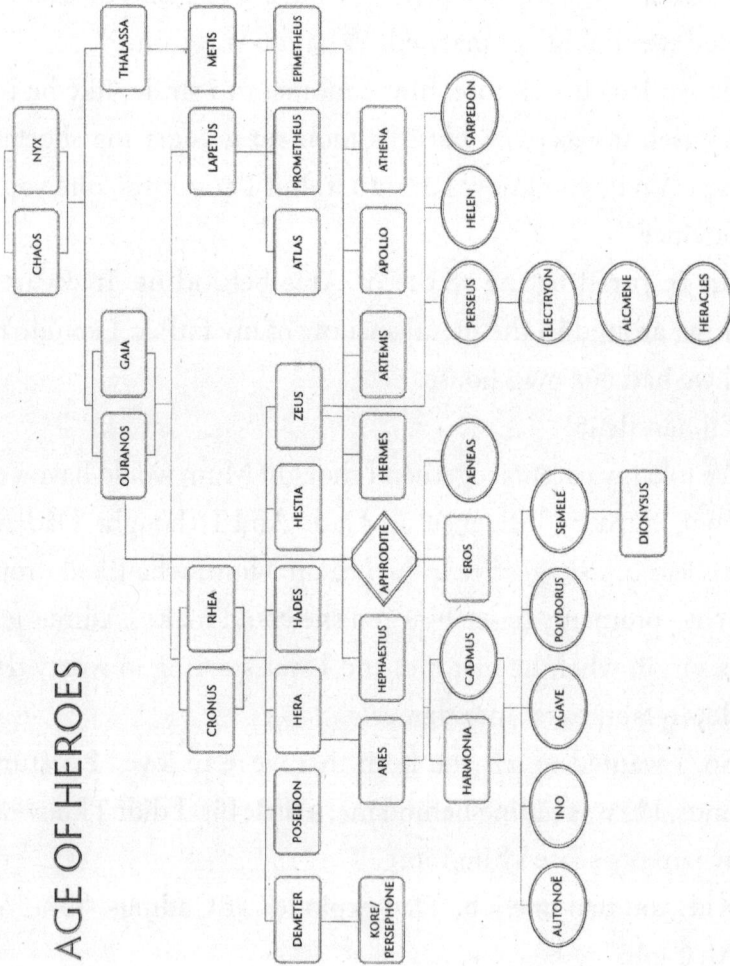

CHAOS — NYX

GAIA — OURANOS

THALASSA

METIS — IAPETUS — EPIMETHEUS — PROMETHEUS — ATLAS

ATHENA — APOLLO — ARTEMIS

ZEUS — HESTIA — HERMES

APHRODITE — EROS — AENEAS

SARPEDON — HELEN — PERSEUS — ELECTRYON — ALCMENE — HERACLES

CRONUS — RHEA — HADES — HEPHAESTUS — ARES — HERA — POSEIDON — DEMETER — KORE/PERSEPHONE

CADMUS — HARMONIA

SEMELE — DIONYSUS — POLYDORUS — AGAVE — INO — AUTONOE

Ares IV

I didn't mean to start shit, with the kid.[48] I don't always mean to start shit. Shit just starts around me. I definitely wasn't meaning to go start a new age or anything. I'd only lived in the one, and that was the Age of the Gods, and I was a god, so that seemed an all right age to me.

But he killed my dragon. I couldn't let him get away with it, could I?

I was just going to kill him, tell you the truth, but I got there and he said *do it,* and where's the fun in that? So I told him he had to be my servant instead. He was right mad about that, but that made sense to me. I get mad.

I brought the kid up to Olympus, and yeah, no one had done it before, but I didn't think anyone'd care. He was just a mortal, and I only used him for errands I didn't want to do.

None of it was heroics. Not till the kid worked out it was Zeus who nicked his sister. It might have been 'cause I told him. I figured he knew already, and it's not like Dad hid these things. It doesn't matter. What matters is the kid was so mad he went on over to the king of the gods and tried to punch him in the face.

---

[48]   Cadmus. He means Cadmus, our future son-on-law. —A

He broke his hand.

And I fucking laughed, you have no idea. Like a drain. Hestia asked what the joke was and I was howling too much to give her an answer. Then the kid was pissed at me too, but the kid was always pissed. It was kind of his thing.

Point is, it might have taken a punch to the face to get it through his thick skull, but Zeus noticed the kid after that. Decided I was onto something. Then Zeus started calling after him for favours. And the kid said no, to be fair. He didn't want to help the man who took his sister. Then Zeus threatened him with Tartarus if he didn't agree and the kid, never the sharpest spear, goes, 'I'm already living it.'

But Zeus was interested by then. He wanted my kid, and he gets what he wants. He told the kid he'd drop the sister back in mortal-ville if he helped, and the kid says, 'What do you want?'

And that's how it started. The Age of Heroes. Zeus was bored. He wanted a new toy.

He told the kid to go get something of his off a giant.[49] Understatement and a half, that. It was his lightning bolts. He'd left them in a cave while he went off seducing some nymph. Apparently the weapons were ruining the mood. Never had that issue with Foamy, myself.

Anyways. Zeus was off fucking about, and this giant found the bolts and thought ooh, this is a weapon of mass destruction. I can be using that. I dunno why Dad didn't just fight him, but he went and decided he needed my kid to be the distraction while he retrieved them, and my idiot kid said yes.

---

[49] Not a giant, technically – they were still digging their way out of the hole Zeus buried them in during the last war – but Typhus was giant-adjacent. —A

'The giant's going to splat you, kid.'

'He'll give my sister back.'

'Yeah, and you'll be splatted.'

He didn't get splatted. He sang for the giant and the giant liked the singing and Zeus got his bolts back and he was all very pleased with himself.

He went round Olympus, crowing, like, 'I have discovered a new weapon. The mortals will serve us.'

'Father, were you not recently worried about the mortals becoming too powerful if we simply gave them fire?' Athena said.

I hate agreeing with Athena.

'That was then. This is now.'

'That does not answer anything,' she muttered.

'I will call them heroes. After you, my love,' he said to Mum.

She smiled but I knew that smile. That smile said this did not make up for all the cheating.

'In thanks for his help, I shall grant this hero any bride he wishes.'

Like fuck he could. The kid was all eyes for my Harmy, and I didn't want her off with some mortal.

'Oi, he's working for me. Payback for my dragon.'

'. . . When Ares deems his penance complete.'

I kept him working for me for two years after that. Dragged things out, till Foamy got it in her head that he'd be good for our Harmy, and I'm shit at saying no to her. So I said yes, and the two of them got married, and I really thought that'd be the end of it, but Foamy said no. She wanted to be involved in their lives.

'She's our daughter. You love her. And you love Cadmus.'

'Do not.'

'What did you do when Apollo questioned his tactics?'

'Yeah but I punch people all the time.'

'I want to go see them.'

And, 'cause I'm shit at saying no to her, we went. To their house. To eat. To meet their children. To listen to Harmy complain about Eris again. To listen to Harmy say she'd made up with Eris again. To watch the kid bang his head against a wall till it dented because there were problems in the kingdom and he didn't know how to fix them.[50]

'Start a war, kid.'

'That's not a solution to famine.'

We watched them make a life and have kids, and Foamy taught them all these games and songs I never knew she knew. She liked braiding Harmy's hair, and when their daughters came along, she did theirs too. She loved the grandkids, especially. Liked giving them advice that made Harmy roll her eyes and tell her to stop being a bad influence and when she did, Foamy just said: 'Serves you right.'

'I was a great teenager.'

'You ran away with a mortal.'

'I married a mortal with your explicit blessing.'

'Same difference. Orey-gano, ore-gahno.'

I heard that argument a thousand bloody times but it never got old. Foamy laughing and joking and being like she couldn't in Olympus. Up there, she always had a face on. The right kind of smile. Her personality changed person to person, but with Harmy and Cadmus and the kids, she was always the same.

She was happy. I made her happy.

Shame it couldn't last, not with Zeus in Olympus announcing mortals were fair game now. Overnight, everyone fucking wanted one.

---

[50] We'd given them Thebes as a wedding present. Cadmus and Harmonia tried their best as rulers, but it wasn't going well. —A

Any excuse and the gods found a hero to do it. Athena taught someone how to ride a flying horse. For a bit, Apollo wouldn't even carry his own arrows. He had a boy for that. Even Foamy tore herself away from the family to get into a custody battle with Persephone over who got to keep the pretty new boy,[51] but then Persephone cheated and killed him, and Foamy, my Foamy who loved to fight so much, shrugged and said, 'No big deal.'

And she went back to our family.

She was so wrapped up with them, it was like she wasn't even a goddess anymore. She was missing everything.

And I wasn't the only one who noticed.

---

[51] Adonis. He was very pretty. —A

Eros III

Mummy wasn't like the other Olympians. They could all fly and change shape and turn the mortals into ducks if they wanted, and she couldn't. That was why she needed me. To fit in.

She was mine and I was hers. That's how it always was and it's how it was meant to be, and I didn't understand why she kept going round finding other people instead of me.

First it was Hephaestus. Then Ares. Then she got the *baby*[52] and she wasn't interested in me at all anymore.

Even when I found her the prettiest mortals – Adonis, hello! – she'd *start* listening to me tell her about them, but then the stupid baby would start crying and she'd run over to it and coo about how it was the most beautiful thing she'd ever seen.

It was a baby. I was a god. I was *her* god.

I brought her gifts I knew she'd love – beautiful trinkets and jewels, and when those didn't work, shells like the one she made me out of, to remind her that she made me. She needed me. She loved me.

'That's nice, sweetheart.'

'Just nice?'

---

[52] Harmonia. —A

'Beautiful, Eros.'

And then the baby would start walking like that was impressive when I could *fly*, but still Mummy ran after it.

I tried making other friends, like the nymphs in Mummy's retinue, but they weren't any fun at all. They were always smiling and lying around so people could admire their beauty, and they *were* pretty, but what's the point in having it if you don't do anything with it?

I still did the job Mummy gave me – even when she abandoned me because *Harmonia's a teenager now, she needs me* – and kept up with all the gossip. There was more gossip than ever since Ares had made that mortal boy his servant instead of killing him like a proper god, and everyone else decided they wanted a mortal too. They were the must-have accessory of the season, but it was so funny, because at the same time, the gods were all scared of them.

Not, like, quaking behind the furniture scared. The kind of scared that lives in whispers.

'They're living in our *houses* now?'

'What's next, they can eat our food? See our true forms?'

Everything was changing, and I didn't want everything to change. I liked it the way it was.

'Mummy,' I said. 'I have news for you, from Olympus.'

'Oh, don't worry about it, sweetness.'

I rushed to her, fluttered a couple of feet up so I could feel her forehead.

'What *are* you doing?' she said, laughing. Her laugh changed a lot. Sometimes it sounded like crying and sometimes it sounded like falling rocks, but then her laugh was so pretty. It was wind on the waves.

'Are you sick, Mummy?'

'Gods can't get sick – you know that.'

'You said the only thing worth having was being an Olympian, and now they're worried it's all going to be destroyed—'

'I was wrong, sweetness. There's so much more than that.'

And she looked through the door to the stupid baby's[53] stupid room, even though she was probably out having sex with the stupid mortal boy right at that moment.

I was meant to be enough for her.

But she wasn't interested in me anymore, so I didn't tell her everything the gods were saying, how they all thought Zeus was right for being afraid of the mortals and that Ares was impulsive and reckless for bringing this new danger to Olympus.

I could wait, I thought. Mummy would get bored of the baby eventually. Then she'd come back to me.

Only, it didn't get better. It got worse.

I fell in love. Her name was Psyche and she was a mortal and she was so beautiful people started worshipping her, and all I wanted to do was tell Mummy about it:

'Mummy, Mummy!'

'Harmonia's getting married, Eros, isn't it wonderful?' And she was smiling like it really was wonderful, even though she said marriage was the worst thing that could happen to a person.

'I want to too.'

'Sorry?'

'I want to get married.'

'One at a time, sweetness. It's Harmy's turn first.'

'But, Mummy, I've met this girl and she's said yes, and I just need your blessing—'

---

[53] By baby, Eros means my adult daughter. He never did give up the nickname. —A

'I'm a bit busy right now. Can you just make yourself useful?'

Okay. Mummy needed me again. I could be useful. I brought Psyche to visit and together we organised Mummy's pantry, but she didn't even look at it when we tried to show her.

'Hera's said she'll provide the veil but I *know* she'll put my daughter in something ugly to piss me off. What do I do? I need something perfect.'

And so it went on. *Every* time I tried to talk to her about my life.

Psyche and I did get married though! It was lovely. She was lovely. Zeus liked her so much he gave her wings to go with mine. Together we jumped out the window and twirled round into the sky, holding one another and kissing and saying how much we loved each other.

Best day of my life. Best moment. And Mummy missed all of it. Because of the stupid baby.[54]

---

[54] Eros is right. I was distracted by Harmonia. I didn't need her to help me lie. She didn't bring me power. It was simpler than that. She was my daughter, so I loved her. Around her, I could see a future where I got into, I don't know, gardening, and I exchanged recipes with Hestia, and I didn't have to scheme and manipulate to hold on to the power I had, because I had a home and they didn't care about that there. It was a dream, that's all, and a temporary one at that. —A

Hera II

Some couples cook together. Some play games. Some do not talk to each other at all. I would have taken any of them over the actual situation I found myself in with my husband.

Zeus may have loved me, but he didn't like me. He found me fussy, uptight, and unpleasant, which I may very well be. One of us had to provide the decorum for the relationship, and it wasn't going to be Zeus.

He didn't even give me the respect of hiding his infidelity.

I never followed him, because I didn't have to. My husband transmits his movements with *lightning*.

I saw them, the girls. There were boys too, but they were different. They were only going to be playthings, passing fancies. They couldn't give him what I could give him.

It was the girls I hated.

They were not women. I love women. I am the goddess of *women – but they were not women yet*. They were girls, some of them barely starting their menses. Vapid little things with heads full of romance and no idea that my husband was going to chew them up and spit them out.

They didn't have my power. They didn't have my pedigree or my strength. They didn't have our history. These girls couldn't know what it felt like to be the goddess of marriage with a husband who is chronically incapable of being faithful and still stand tall, as his *wife*, at the end of it. They didn't know what it truly meant to be with Zeus, yet they flounced around with their pretty smiles and they proclaimed themselves *in love*.

Some he saw only once, and those girls I could leave be. It's the ones he went back to that offended me.

If those girls wanted to know what it was to be with Zeus, I would make them know.

I made Semele[55] know.

Zeus was lying to her, pretending he was some mortal king who couldn't show his face for fear of retribution. I didn't understand his logic, and I don't think she did either, but she pretended to. He swept in every evening, once her parents were asleep, and he brought her bouquets of flowers and sweets from Olympus, and he told her every lovely thing his head could conjure.

'You are the spark in the cold. You are the beauty of a doe. Your arms are so long—'

This girl, this little princess, she did not immediately capitulate to my husband.[56]

When he did eventually get her clothes off – they can only ever resist for so long – and he wrapped his too-big hands around her too-small waist, I couldn't look. Even listening was too much. He growled for her in a way he'd never growled for me.

I loved him, and I hated him. I wanted him, and I never wanted to touch him again. Zeus is a complex man. The girl was not.

---

[55] Semele. Not some girl. Not just another one of Zeus' conquests. Harmonia and Cadmus' youngest child. My GRANDDAUGHTER. Hera's great-granddaughter. So much for the goddess of family. —A
[56] No one has ever chosen Zeus for his poetry. —A

She didn't deserve his attention without the suffering that went with it.

I too appeared to Semele, also as a mortal but, unlike my dear husband, I didn't appear as some bright young thing. I appeared as an old crone in need of a meal.

'You must come for dinner; my parents will be fine with it,' Semele said instantly. So trusting. So pretty. So naive.

'Let us eat here, child. The walk may finish me off.'

And off she scurried to find me berries and meats and sweets, and we sat together in the gentle sun of the evening, and she chattered and chattered and chattered away about her siblings and her parents and her cousin who was missing and how she hoped he would come back. None of it of any interest to me.

'What about you, young one? Is there anyone who has caught your fancy?'

Her eyes alighted on the horizon, where the sun was dipping below the sea.

'I must go,' she said.

'Home?'

'Yes?'

'Let me walk you. It's not safe for a girl your age to be—'

But she'd already run away, lifting her skirts higher, like a child, so she could jump over the roots and the dirt more easily.

She came back the next afternoon.

'Granny,' she said. I never invited her to call me such, but I was, in a sense, since Ares, my son, was her grandfather. I didn't see myself in her. 'I'm back! I didn't know if you needed more food, so . . .' She lifted a bag and out poured an abundant feast, even for the daughter of a king. We sat again and she told me more of her life.

So we continued, and in my own way I seduced this girl. She

might have *loved* my husband, but she trusted me. She invited me to stay at the palace, though I did not dare accept, for Aphrodite often visited the family and the gods can see through such ruses, as clear as the light of day.

Semele told me about her childhood and her city and her parents and her siblings.

Eventually, she told me about her boyfriend.

'I think he's older,' she said slowly.

'That's not so unusual.' I'm older than Zeus, after all.

'I love him, Granny, but I fear I do not know him.'

I feigned the idiot. 'You should not really *know* a man before you are married to him.'

'I didn't mean like that.' She blushed, a child too afraid to even utter the words. Too young to be doing the actions, then. 'I have not seen his face.'

'Yet you love him?' A softer phrasing than I might have chosen. *You've never seen my husband's face, but you let him fuck you anyway?*

'I do, Granny.'

'You must demand to see him in his true form.' It would kill her, of course, but that's the nature of love stories when one of the people involved is already married. They hurt.

'He said I cannot.'

'Then he's lying to you, young one. If you truly wish to spend your life with him, you must demand the truth. What if he has a secret family already? A wife?' I was beginning to like her, this stupid flimsy thing who gave her love so easily. I couldn't help myself.

'If he has a wife, then surely she doesn't deserve him, Granny. Not if she doesn't love him enough to keep him close.' She said it earnestly, without a hint of awareness of the cruelty she was spouting. This little princess who knew nothing of pain truly believed my husband hurt me because I didn't love him enough. It made things easier. She had no sympathy for me; I closed off any I might have for her.

Zeus was my king, I his queen. There was no space in that equation for his floozies.

I will give credit where it's due: the girl was tenacious, and she demanded the truth relentlessly. To begin with, Zeus said no, but she was the youngest child, and it had taught her how to annoy her elders. At each of their rendezvous, she asked, and each day my husband was forced to scrabble for some new response to pacify her. Sometimes, his excuses even worked, but then she'd come to me, her beloved granny, and I'd remind her once more that love cannot be true when it's built on lies.

She wanted to love him so very much.

My husband doesn't handle nagging well; I can tell you that from firsthand experience. After a handful of weeks, he capitulated, threw off his mortal trappings and uncovered his face so this girl could see what she claimed to love in all its glory.

She was not me, and she could not handle it.

I hoped that was the last thing she thought about as her body melted from her soul, releasing it to Hades.

I wasn't expecting her hysterical mother to come out weeping and swearing and making demands of Zeus, or that my husband would feel inclined to *follow* them. Poor, dead Semele could not be saved. But poor, *dead* Semele was pregnant, and the child my husband stuck in her was more god than not – I do not care to sit and establish the percentages – he could be saved, brought back, made one of us.

'You fucking save him Zeus. You caused this mess. You put it right,' Harmonia yelled.

Who was she to make such demands? A minor goddess at best, born from adultery and tied to a life of mortal drudgery.

'Husband, you cannot. Do you really want the mortals becoming gods?'

'I think the situation has had just about enough of your meddling, don't you?' Zeus snapped. He sounded older than I'd ever heard him.

He took the child and sewed it, still in its sac, to his thigh so that it could finish developing. He did not miss an opportunity to bemoan his pains in carrying a child to the women of Olympus, many of whom he had personally impregnated.

Aphrodite XVI

Let me tell you about my family before Zeus met Semele and blew it apart.

I was happy, not just in whatever passes as happiness for the gods; I was happy, in the way only the humans knew how to be. I had people who cared about me – *people*, plural – and I had my position on the council and I had enough power to keep my daughter safe.

I had Ares, and I made him happy and he made me happy, and I think together we made Harmonia happy, even if she did call us mortifying.

I even had *friends*. A friend, at least. I mean, the nymphs liked me well enough because I'd show up for them and not just judge them the way Hera liked to, but it never went further than that. I had Eris, because you never know when you might need the goddess of discord. We talked at my wedding – she was taking bets about what I'd done to make Zeus make me marry Hephaestus, and I was so fucking relieved that somebody *saw* – and it went from there. She reminded me a lot of Prometheus without being very much like Prometheus at all. Eris was wiry where Prometheus was solid. She made jokes where Prometheus analysed. But both of them were *thinking*. Or plotting, in Eris' case. They looked at the angles. They twisted and bent the facts to make them work in a way that would be good for them.

I had good years. So many in a row. I thought if I stayed quiet, stayed in the background, stopped fighting for more, then I'd be allowed to keep what I had.

I wanted to go back to that girl, the one who was lost and cold and alone in a cave. I wanted to find her and wave my life at her and promise, *It gets better. There's light at the end of the tunnel and the light is so fucking beautiful.*

I didn't realise there was more tunnel at the end of the light.

Harmonia and Cadmus were better parents than Ares and me. They were around more. They walked the line between too lax and too strict. They raised their kids to take over their power and happily ceded it when the time came. Even with my newfound resolution to just let things be, I wouldn't have been able to do that.

But in our world, being a good parent isn't enough. Loving and caring for your children isn't enough. Giving all your power to them in the hopes that it will keep them safe isn't enough, because one day, Zeus might just wake up and decide to fuck your granddaughter.

He told Semele he loved her, then he told the Olympians that I did it, that I took the arrows of love from my son and notched them and shot them into her. He forgot she was my fucking *granddaughter*. He forgot anyone could love someone past their eyeline. He didn't know that I couldn't make him fall in love, not with all the arrows in the world, and that my son wouldn't have done it for me, because he wasn't speaking to me. He didn't know that no one could have caused this but him, and I couldn't tell him, or the world, because to defend myself would be to give up everything I'd fought for.

Hera couldn't take her anger out on him, because he was him. So she took it out on Semele.

They fought over her, tore her apart, until she was demanding Zeus show her his true form – she just meant his face, but he didn't know that. He showed her the version of himself that's pure magic. He opened the jar.

Mortals can't see gods that way. We say it's because our glory is too much for their minds to take in, but that feels ridiculous. Zeus made them. They come from him. They should be able to withstand him, but they can't. Even then, I didn't question whether he'd done that on purpose.

He showed her and she burned to death, not in fire, but in lightning.

And I didn't see any of it. I didn't notice her falling in love with him. I didn't notice Hera involving herself in what was going on. I didn't notice any of it because I was busy having friends, a lover, a home. I was too happy to notice how fucked it all was.

So it was Hermes who found me and told me I probably wanted to be there for this, and it was my daughter who made the demand.

I took Ares' chariot – it was faster than my birds – and I made my way to Thebes without even breathing. I didn't know the details, but when something has happened to your family, and Zeus is involved, you drop everything. You go.

I could hear Harmonia shouting before I could see them, but I could smell the burning even before that.

'Save her,' my daughter yelled.

My heart dropped and my hands shook so much I could barely control the horses. Who?

'She wanted this,' Zeus said in his faux-reasonable voice.

268

'Nobody fucking wanted *this*.'

They came into my view. Semele's body lay blackened on the floor between the two of them. Cadmus paced behind her, fist crammed into his mouth. He made the occasional dive at Zeus, but Harmonia kept an arm out, blocking him every time.

No. No one wanted this.

'She begged me to show her my true form.'

'You *knew* that would kill her,' Harmonia screamed. 'You did this, Zeus. It's on you to fucking fix it.'

He stepped in towards my daughter, looming a full head and shoulders above her, until his beard brushed the top of her head. It would have been funny at any other time, almost paternal, but he was the king of the gods. Even standing was a threat, but she did not cower, step back, make room for him. I'd never been so proud of her.

'There's no point asking for impossible things, little girl.'

'Then save the baby,' Cadmus interrupted.

Both gods looked at him, both of them on the verge of their true forms, where they could truly fight and feel as gods do. He knew the outcome of seeing them, but he was too angry to be afraid.

'The baby didn't see you, did it? You can save the baby.'

Zeus sighed the sigh of a man who is constantly being met with unreasonable requests, and I kept flying. Past my daughter who needed me. Past my granddaughter dead on the floor.

I ignored all of them and flew straight on to my least favourite place in the world. I went home.

'You—'

'—should not—'

'—*be*—'

'—here.'

I ignored them too. They didn't get to make me feel like I didn't belong. I pulled the first threads out of Chaos, and I turned them into something we could understand. They might think they owned it now, but Fate was *mine* first, and I needed it back.

I threw myself into the unwoven strands, tearing them apart, flinging the useless ones away.

'Where is it?'

'What—'

   '—is—'

      '—*it?*'

'Stop,' I shouted, and I wanted it to mean more than it did. I wanted it to block everything I'd ever wanted to say no to. I wanted it to echo like Zeus' shouts, shake the ground and cast fear into all those who heard it. I wanted one word to be enough, but it's not, when you're not a real goddess.

I couldn't waste my time playing around with words that didn't work.

I went back to the threads. They still wrapped themselves around me, sometimes, when I was stressed or sad or drunk or not really paying attention. Ares noticed once and asked, and I panicked and instead of telling him the truth I said they were my veins made external, and he looked at me like I was made of magic and whispered, *You are so cool, Foamy.* I felt like shit about it, but there was nothing else to say. I was in too deep.

I tried to avoid the threads when I was in Olympus, but it was so difficult, every day, to tear them from my skin without looking, without *feeling* what they had to tell me. Every day was the temptation, the promise, the *lie*, that by looking at them I could change how things were going to go.

Today I was going to change the future.

I knew from Prometheus that I couldn't save people, but right then, I didn't care about what was true. I cared about my daughter and I'd let her down. I could take another fucking risk and do something stupid because then at least I would have done *something*.

I kept pulling at the threads, from the walls, the floor, my skin, my hair. Nothing was safe from me. My hands grabbed everything around me, feeling it, discarding it, ignoring the pictures building up in my head so big that it felt like it'd explode and we'd be left with another bloody Athena in its place.

I held on, and I found it, the child, its thread so short and already breaking.

I grabbed another thread. One as long as I could trace it, I felt it stick and cling and tear from the skin on my hands as it protested this mistreatment, and only when I was fucking bleeding red on the floor of the cave I grew up in was I satisfied.

Being a good parent isn't enough, but maybe being a Fate could be.

I took the end, the beginning, and I fused it to the baby's. The joins were knotty, bits still frayed, but the join held. Semele's child would live.

Semele wouldn't. There was nothing I could do; her thread was already gone, her future crumbled to dust. I wanted to go scrabbling in the sand, to find it, to breathe life into it like Zeus could, to put it back, but it wouldn't have done anything. She was gone.

Memory is short sometimes on Olympus. They forgot Semele was more than Harmonia's daughter. They forgot I went to eat with them at least once a month, that I'd braided my granddaughter's hair and promised her she was beautiful, promised I wouldn't let anyone hurt her. They forgot how much she liked hiding and hated being found. They never even knew how bad she was at it. They didn't know she giggled when she lied and her laughter made a beacon for finding her. They didn't know she fell asleep in her food once, or that she ate honey straight out of the bowl when no one was watching, or that everyone knew when she did it because she left grubby little fingerprints in her wake. They didn't know I loved her so very much.

I'm sorry, Semele, for what it's worth. You deserved better than you got.

'That—'

'—is—'

'—forbidden.'

'What are you going to do about it?'

There was no time to fight with my sisters about our responsibility to the future. There was only my daughter, still alive, still pleading with the king of the gods.

Ares' horses are fast, and Zeus was still deliberating when I made it back to them.

'Please, Zeus, will you save the baby?' Harmonia said, calmer now. She bowed to him, lay prostrate on the floor. A better mother than me. I wouldn't bow to him, not ever again.

'Oh, all right then.' Just like that. Maybe it was an easy choice because I had already made it for him. I hope so, but even now, I don't know how Fate works; I just break it sometimes.

Zeus took the child from Semele's stomach and sewed it to his thigh so it could finish developing.

For a moment, then, there was calm. It was over. Emotions quietened, and we stood and stared at one another, questioning how we were meant to climb down from this.

It only lasted a moment, that strange confused calm.

'You're *welcome*,' Zeus said, despite the complete lack of thanks.

'What's wrong with you?' Cadmus shouted. 'I'm not going

to thank you for killing my daughter. Fuck you and fuck the plinth you stand on.'

Zeus looked down at the complete lack of plinth beneath his feet. He was enjoying this, but Cadmus wasn't done.

'You kidnap my sister. You destroy my city. You kill my fucking daughter, and you don't care. The only thing any of you ever cared about was that fucking *dragon*. If that's what I have to be to be happy, then I wish I was one.'

Zeus grinned. He raised a finger. 'I think we can manage that.'

Cadmus' screams echoed across all the way up to Olympus as he transformed. His legs went first, before his skin, before his face morphed and cracked. But I wasn't watching him. I was watching my daughter.

As his yells grew louder, Harmonia got smaller. Smaller and smaller than she ever should have ever had to be. She was sobbing as she lost the husband she loved so much, and something broke inside her that I'd never be able to fix.

He was a dragon, and she was not quite a widow.

I was covered in thread and guilt, and I clearly had no right to be there. Any movement I made would be announcing that I was eavesdropping from the chariot in the sky. It would reveal that my blood was the wrong colour, that I wasn't one of them. It would be giving Zeus whatever ammunition he needed to remove me and replace me with one of his myriad real children. It would be a tremendous, life-altering mistake.

But my daughter was crying.

I pulled my clothes around me like a sheet, not to cover my body but to hide the damage, and crashed the chariot into the earth behind her. Ares would understand.

Zeus was gone by the time I hit the ground. Fine. I'd be back for him later. He didn't matter right now. Harmonia did.

I tried to hug her, wrap her close to me, but she wasn't having it. She kicked and flailed until I let her go. She grabbed hold of the dragon who had been her husband.

'Mummy, make me one too.'

'I don't understand.'

'I want to stay with him. Make me a dragon too.' She'd stop being a queen. She'd give up being a mother. She'd throw away her body. She'd do it all to stay with Cadmus.

I don't think I have the capacity to love anyone that much. I love so many people, so many things, that to choose one above all others is an impossible thought. Was she defective, or was it me?

'Sweetheart—'

'*Please.*'

I couldn't give it to her. The only thing she wanted in the entire world, and I couldn't give it to her because I wasn't a real goddess. It hurt so much that, for once in my life, I told the truth.

'I can't.'

'You have to.'

And then I made it into a lie. 'It would be too hard. I can't.' It wouldn't be harder than this. Nothing could be. 'I'll find someone. Just wait.'

She was holding my hand. I couldn't let go of it. I wouldn't, not when this would be the last time I ever did. I couldn't let go of her.

'*Eros,*' I whispered into a shell, just like the one I had made him with. '*My son. I need you.*'

His voice came through, loud and clear. 'Mummy, I'm busy.'

'It should only take a second. It's *love* business.'

The dragon that was Cadmus had wrapped itself around Harmonia's back, the closest facsimile of a hug it could manage, and I held her hand tight enough to remind me she wasn't going to float away. She was solid and she was here and I was here.

'I don't have time for this,' Eros said.

I looked at Harmonia and I didn't cry. I wasn't going to let go of her. I wasn't going to leave her as she whispered to please not make her do this alone. I wasn't and I couldn't.

'*Please*,' she told me.

I closed my eyes and I yelled.

It was more than my *stop*. It was more than my *no*. It was more than all my other words put together. It was Demeter looking for Persephone. It was Prometheus giving fire to mankind. It was all the love of the goddess of love condensed into a single word, and no one could doubt for a second that it was real. I shook and the world shook with me.

'ARES.'

Her father, who could make this impossible thing come true.

'He's coming. He'll help you.'

'I wish you could be braver, Mum.'

Ares came rocketing from the sky, wrapped in a ball, bouncing when he hit the floor. I'd forgotten I had his chariot, but he still came for me.

He took in the scene.

'What have you done now, kid?' He sighed and kicked at the dragon but there was no heart in it. The dragon dodged around his foot without ever breaking contact with our daughter. A fucking complicated husband, but he loved her.

'And I suppose you want to go with the idiot?'

Harmonia half-laughed and half-nodded, and some phlegm half came out of her nose. 'Please.'

Ares looked at me. I nodded. He raised his hands. And that was that.

I wish I could say that she whispered nice things as she was changing, that she managed a final cry of *I love you*, but she wasn't looking at us. Her eyes were narrowed, and she was focused on the sky above us, as her body shuddered and stretched into this new shape.

She turned back to Cadmus and booped him with her nose. He booped her back. One, two, three, before she pointed towards the sky, and the two of them flew off together, their tails wrapped around one another.

'And she called *us* disgusting,' Ares said.

'Mortifying.'

'What?'

'She called us *mortifying*.'

That was the last thing I said for a long time.

My throat was a cave-in, blocked and shuttered, but with Ares I never needed to speak. He pulled me into him and wrapped me in his arms so tight that nothing could get to me. Not Zeus. Not speech. Not even my own thoughts.

A Tragic Scene on the Side of a Mountain

[Mount Elbrus. Dusk. A man approaches, riding a white stallion. He notices Prometheus bound to the mountain with chains. Prometheus' stomach is flecked with blood, though he has no visible wound.]

Perseus: What have I found here?

Prometheus: It is impolite to enter someone's home and make demands of them without introducing yourself.

Perseus: As you wish. I am Perseus, son of Zeus—

Prometheus (softly): Of course you are.

Perseus: I am a hero. I have slain Medusa, cut off her head.

Prometheus: What did this Medusa ever do to you?

Perseus: She was a monster, with bronze talons, and tusks as on a boar, and on her head were snakes so fearsome that even now her gaze can turn a man to stone.

Prometheus: She pursued you then, this monster?

Perseus: Not as such.

Prometheus: I do not believe pursuit exists upon a spectrum; either she did, or she did not.

Perseus: I had to do it. My stepfather holds my mother captive. He will only release her in exchange for the head.

Prometheus: You pursued Medusa, then. You pursued her with the specific aim of killing her.

Perseus: She was a man-hater.

Prometheus: If you are representative of her experiences with men, I can hardly blame her.

Perseus: I acted with the support of my father and all the Olympians. Who are *you* to question *me*?

Prometheus: I am the one who brought your kind fire, and civilisation with it.

Perseus: You are Prometheus?

Prometheus: Yes.

Perseus: Titan?

Prometheus: Yes.

Perseus (hissing): *Monster.*

[Perseus reaches into his bag for the head of Medusa. Prometheus doesn't blink.]

Zeus' Announcement

Come one, come all, and rejoice, for the Titan scourge Atlas is dead. See what becomes of those who betray me? They believe themselves to be immortal. Invincible. Wrong. All that awaits traitors is pain, death, and Tartarus.

But you, my loyal subjects, have no reason to fear. Do you?

Aphrodite XVII

It wasn't Atlas. I knew that because it didn't matter how many years passed, or how much power I had, I always knew where Atlas was, just in case he decided to find me and choke me again.

I knew where Medusa lived too, and I knew where Perseus had to go to meet Andromeda[57] because I told him to, because Zeus decided the first real hero had to be his son and not some stray Ares had picked up off the street. I was still playing the part of a loyal follower then, even though I was so very angry with Zeus after Harmonia. I thought it would save me from losing anything else. I couldn't have been more wrong.

Because it wasn't fucking Atlas the hero turned to stone.

It was Prometheus.

I didn't *know* before I went to see him – I couldn't bear to check the thread – but I knew.

We don't get to keep good things, not forever. And Prometheus was my good thing. He was my first friend and my best friend and my lover and my protector, even when I didn't want him to be. He was my biggest mistake, and I couldn't regret him for a moment.

---

[57] Princess. Was briefly tied to a rock and threatened by sea monsters because her mother pissed off Poseidon. Perseus rescued her, murdered some of her countrymen, and they lived happily ever after. —A

I'd tried to be more like him. Waiting and waiting and waiting for it to be safe, for me to come back, but I'd waited and waited and waited, until he turned into stone.

I wasn't waiting any longer.

All I wanted, all I needed, was to see him, so I could know it wasn't fucking true.

Even though it was. Even though I knew it was.

My heart caught in my chest when I saw him. My breath stopped, my tongue suddenly too big in my mouth. My body didn't make sense anymore. None of it fit together right.

I didn't know how to be a person without him.

He was there. He was still *there*, tied where he had been for so long, his face twisted, as it often became when he wasn't spending all his focus on keeping it straight. But he was gone. There was no movement in him anymore. No life. Zeus hadn't lied about that bit. My Prometheus had been turned to stone.

I'd learned to live with the sight of him in pain. I'd learned to live without the sight of him at all. I'd learned to live without even mentioning his name, without thinking it too loudly because there was no acceptable reason for him to be my friend. I'd learned to live in a world where *logic* and *tactics* matter in the question of who you love. I'd learned to pretend I'd never held the thread of *his* Fate in my hands and torn it apart.

I'd learned to live with all of that, because I had to.

I hadn't learned to live with him turned into stone. I refused.

We'd barely touched in this new life of mine, not since I'd come back and started telling this world I was someone I wasn't. I touched him then, desperately. I ran my hands down his chest, counting his ribs as my fingers dragged across them. I breathed into his mouth like that would force the life back into him.

'Come on,' I whispered, but he didn't – his final rejection of me. 'Please.'

He didn't like his hair – flat on some days, messy on others – and he didn't like me noticing that he didn't like it because he didn't like caring about his hair. He thought there were so many more important things to care about than hair. But I made half my life on hair and I would have torn out all my precious hair, right then and there if I could touch his, just one more time, and have it feel like hair.

It didn't. It felt like stone.

I promised him once I'd mess it up every day. For reliability. Then he could plan for it, but he'd been petrified on a flat hair day. I couldn't mess it up now.

It was still.

He was still.

'No,' I told him. 'Absolutely not.'

I refused for him to be dead. I did not fucking allow it. Not when I hadn't seen him for so many years. Not since I'd been married and had children and grandchildren and great-grandchildren and never been able to explain that I was being fucking *watched* the whole time and I couldn't break away and come and see him, even when I wanted to.

He couldn't be dead before I could tell him all that. He couldn't be dead. He was my best friend. He was the only person who remembered who I was. He was the only person who knew what my name even meant.

He was the person I'd changed Fate for.

'So you don't make me wrong, okay? You can't make me be wrong.'

He didn't say anything back, because he was dead.

'I brought a statue to life once; I'll do it to you too. I'm warning you.'

But I hadn't. Eros had, because I asked him to.

And Eros wasn't talking to me. Eros wouldn't save my daughter, so he wouldn't save my friend. I could crumble all the apples of the Hesperides into Prometheus and it wouldn't make a jot of difference. I wasn't a goddess. I couldn't bring him back.

But I tried. I willed all the threads I could to me. I draped them over him and I tried to fuse them together, to tie them in knots and wrap them around him. I wound and I wound and I wound, because eventually one of them had to spark.

'Please,' I begged. Them and him. 'Please try.'

I didn't know if he'd want to come back, but I knew what I wanted.

I wanted him to be alive.

I wanted him to not be in pain.

'I want you to not fucking leave me, okay?'

He didn't say anything. I didn't stop shouting. Over and over again. Like it would bring him back to me. Like it would make up for all those years where he was a bit patronising so I was a bit distant because it was easier to avoid speaking to him than it was to tell the fucking truth, when he was the only person I could tell.

'I'm no one without you.' I rested my head against his legs. They were all I could reach from the floor, and I couldn't stand, not with wave after wave of this hitting me, not with the inevitable mortality of the man I'd killed. 'You can't leave me.'

I stayed there all night.

I told him about my husband. I told him about my lover. I told him I liked talking to him better than I liked touching him but I liked talking to him the most of anyone at all. I told him Pandora had died, and his brother loved her until the end. I told him my daughter was a know-it-all like he was but she was a dragon now and it was a long story he probably didn't have time for, and then I laughed like it was covering the crying.

I pretended I wanted to tell him all these things when he was alive.

I didn't. I wanted him to think I was healthy and happy. I wanted him to know that I loved him. I wanted him to know that I was thinking about him all the fucking time, that when I thought of a joke I looked over my shoulder to see if he was there because he was still the first person I wanted to share it with.

It didn't matter what I wanted him to know. He was dead and gone, gone to some other place outside of Hades specially reserved for people who got turned to stone. He wasn't ever going to know anything ever again.

I've told you about him already, but humour me.

It's easy to describe how much you love a person in lists. Prometheus was a great believer in lists. He thought they organised the mind. But the mind isn't organised and love isn't either. All the things he was to me resist such easy columnisation.

He was everything to me for so long. He was my first friend and then my only friend and then he was my secret friend and my lover and the person I hurt and the person I cursed to die. Is that a list, really? Or is it a spectrum. No two people can always love each other in exactly the same way, not unless they both turn to stone.

We were halfway to that, and it did not make him any less of those things to me.

I loved him.

He wasn't as smart as he thought he was, but he was normally the smartest person in the room. He was the first being to look at me like I was a person. He was ambitious as anything. He was a survivor. He did everything he had to do to write himself into history. He upended a civilisation to get himself there.

And Zeus was trying to write him out of it.

'Why?' I whispered. 'Why is he lying about you?'

Prometheus would know. This was exactly his kind of politics.

'Is it the torture? Does he need people to believe you're still in pain?'

I hoped he wasn't in pain anymore.

'But Atlas was being tortured too. Someone is still in pain. Is it about you tricking him? Does he want people to forget that?' But that didn't make sense either. No one had even tried since Prometheus was tied to this mountain. The punishment worked, on all of us. 'He does want people to forget, though, doesn't he?'

I looked to the statue for confirmation, and I pretended to myself that I could see it on his face.

'Okay. Okay. He wants people to forget you. Why? You helped him . . .'

In the last war, it was the three of them. Zeus and Metis and Prometheus. And now Zeus was the king and Metis was gone and Prometheus was—

It was the two of them who linked their hands together and boosted the boy king into power. It was the two of them who remembered Zeus didn't do it alone.

Prometheus was gone, and Zeus wanted him forgotten so the gods would forget that the story used to be different. He didn't want people knowing he used to need help.

'I'm not safe, am I?'

Zeus didn't remember that I'd been there too, that I was his

285

friend before I was his daughter. But he knew I was the one to tell him about the last rebellion.

One day, he'd get rid of me too.

'What do I do, Prom?'

I couldn't be too loud, too powerful, or I'd draw his attention as surely as the tallest tree draws lightning in a storm. I could try to do what my "mother" had done, withdraw myself from the world and hide in the depths and let it all pass by. I'd be safe then. Problem was, I'd done it before and it nearly killed me. I didn't know. I couldn't think.

The sun came up around me. Dawn's rosy fingers had never looked so much like blood.

And with it came an eagle.

'No,' I said. I swatted at it. Stood tall in front of Prom's body, but it was too fast, too determined. It swerved around me and nestled in what must have been its favourite spot. It had been there every day for centuries. 'Still?'

Zeus wanted Prometheus forgotten, but he still wanted to desecrate his corpse.

There was no logic to that. No explaining or understanding, just petty, ridiculous, cruelty. He wasn't some lonely child anymore, he didn't get a pass for growing up alone in a cave with a father who didn't like him. We all grew up in one war zone or another. We all suffered. We all hurt each other, but none of us like this.

That's when I decided to overthrow the king of the gods.

While Zeus was in power, none of us would be allowed to die in peace, let alone live.

Aphrodite XVIII

I had to let go of Prometheus eventually. I struggled, my fingers tensing against my will.

'I don't know what to do.'

But I could know. That was in my power. I could know what was coming, and I could twist the future to suit me.

A visit to my sisters then.

I went home first, to get changed, to wrap my wrists and my neck in jewels, to drink three cups of wine and to remind myself I wasn't that girl anymore.

I wasn't a victim or a victim-in-waiting. I was a goddess. I would destroy him. And I would live.

My sisters tried to block my way.

'You are not—'

'—supposed to—'

'—be here.'

'Yeah, you don't like me, I get it. I need to look at the threads now. Are you going to let me do that peacefully or do we have a problem?'

They took one step towards me, arms raised in threat, but their only weapons were scissors, and I'd been fighting the most powerful the world had to offer. What were they going to do to me if I disobeyed, send me to Tartarus?

I dropped my shoulder and ran, full speed, through them. I opened my arms wide and threw myself headlong into Fate.

I'd never done that before. I'd tried to control it. Tried to weave it into pretty patterns. I'd hidden from it and run from it. I'd denied its very existence and lived with my head in the sand and, the first time I'd tried bending it to my will, I'd broken it, and me, in the process.

I'd never embraced it.

I let it in then, let the threads wrap themselves around all my limbs, and, after one long breath, I opened my mouth as wide as it would go, letting them crawl so far inside me I was sure my eyes would change colour to gold.

I knew what I needed from them, and I didn't know where it was, so I took everything. Every petty squabble. Every mortal love story. Every plant and animal, past, present, and future, I let it envelop me.

Maybe I wouldn't be left by the end of it, but I'd have what I wanted. I'd have my way to overthrow Zeus. I say it was about freedom, but in that moment I just wanted revenge.

The threads called to me like sirens, promising home and comfort and safety, as long as I did what they wanted. I could be their agent, a small part of something so much bigger.

No, I shouted. Whether they could hear me, I don't know, but I shouted anyway. No. We could be partners, but I wouldn't submit.

For once, Fate listened. The threads relaxed.

They'd changed so much since I'd known them. My threads had been independent beings, intersecting sometimes, sure, but making their own way through a life that could be followed in a straight line. No longer. Each of these was bound to a thousand other things, each life sworn to so many others, wrapped up in them until the threads appeared as ribbons of tapestry, the stories so tangled together even the cleverest fingers couldn't undo them.

I found Zeus. I couldn't avoid Zeus. He was woven into every strand, every ribbon, every life. His fingers had touched everything; his whims shaped everything. Zeus was the gods and the gods were Olympus and Olympus was civilisation and civilisation was humanity, and they couldn't be pulled apart.

Was that his plan, when he made them? To build a world he couldn't be removed from, or was this his loneliness made manifest? His need to be part of everything?

It didn't matter. It took me so long to learn that. It didn't matter what he wanted, what he needed. What mattered was me. I wanted him gone, and he would not go alone.

Zeus, Olympus, the gods, the mortals. Take any of them down and the rest would follow.

A plan started to take shape in my mind. I could have more than revenge.

I would destroy this world, and make a space for myself in the ashes. There, I could create. I could weave a different pattern, where the threads didn't bear his fingerprints. They'd have mine.

My new world would be greater than this one. It would expand as long as it needed to expand, until every man, woman, and child had the freedom to be. I would not ration power, not hoard it to only my select few. I would let it loose, with no tyrant, no man-child to appease.

In my new world, everyone could be free.

I could see it all, then, my body filled with Fate and power and longing. It was clearer than the clearest waters. I could do it.

But first, I needed to destroy.

I needed a war.

And Fate was happy to give me one, offering it up like a gift.

It was great and terrible, this war, written into every strand, permeating every life as surely as Zeus did, the threads almost damp to the touch, as though they were already steeped in blood.

It pulled men from every town and country, every family. It pulled in every Olympian. It was no minor skirmish only Ares would care about. It was everything.

Where, I demanded, and the threads parted for me.

Troy.

It was always going to be Troy.

Troy was a joke, by then. Cursed for so long, but still standing, an excuse to give when you don't want to do something – I'll get round to it when Troy falls – or a way of distracting Apollo when he was being particularly annoying.

It was a pile of kindling, just waiting to be ignited.

Waiting for me.

Troy could destroy the world, the Olympians, the gods, if I played it right. The rebellion that took down Zeus would be carved from his attempts to avoid one. Prom would like the irony.

That was all I needed.

I just had to make it happen.

Fortunately, I had the god of war on my side.

Ares V

'Ares,' she shouted.

'Did you just knock down my door?'

'Might have.'

'Hot.'

She was bouncing. And holding her shoulder, because I love Foamy and she packs a punch for being tiny, but she's still tiny, and I've knocked down enough doors in my life to know I don't want other people doing the same, so I built mine proper strong.

Apart from her. She could knock it down any time. I had my hands on her before I thought about it, to be honest with you.

'No time for that,' she said.

'None at all?'

'Okay, maybe a little time for that.' She laughed. I hadn't seen her like this since before all that bullshit with Harmonia. She crawled on top of me and grabbed me, and when I was right there ready to go, she said, 'I want to start a war.'

That'll do it.

'We can do that.'

'I'm serious, Ares.'

'I'm always serious about war. Who do you want to destroy? Athens? Thebes? Athena?'

'Olympus.'

And just like that the hot was gone.

'The Olympus that we both live on, Olympus?' I wanted to support her, right? No shit I'd follow her into any fucking battle she wanted me to if there was a chance we might win, but Olympus was . . . Well, it's not a fucking starter war.

'Are there others?'

'Why?'

'I want to destroy Zeus. Zeus is Olympus. Olympus is Zeus.'

'Zeus is our father.'

'When has that ever stopped anyone?'

'Foamy, that's treason.'

'I thought you were fun.'

'I am fun. But . . . treason! It would destroy the world.'

'So we make a new world. A new nation, built on love and war.'

I liked the sound of that. But. Treason.

'You love being an Olympian.' More than anyone else. It was how she introduced herself, what she bragged about, the hammer she used to hit the nymphs when they were being snotty. 'You'd be destroying yourself.'

'I'll rebuild. I'll make myself someone I love.'

'You'd be destroying me too.'

Her voice got soft. Sad. 'Love—'

'No, no pity. I'm all for helping you start a war, but why not start with something small, a skirmish, see if you have a taste for it, rather than . . . this.'

'Because he took Harmonia, Ares. He took our daughter and I can't get her back, but I can destroy him.' [58]

---

[58] Not my finest moment, that. Don't get me wrong, I loved my daughter, and I missed her so much, but I needed Ares, and this was how I got him. —A

'So we set something he loves on fire.'

'No. We go for Troy. It's time.'

She had me there. Troy had been a thorn in my side since Apollo bloody built it. All those stupid promises about how it was going to fall – and we all knew that should be a war, not one of Poseidon's stupid earthquakes – and still it stood. Proud and strong. Mocking me.

'How? I've been trying to take Troy for years.'

'I'm going to start a war over love.'

'That's not a plan.'

'It starts with a woman.'

'Still not a plan.'

'Look, do you want to come shoot things or not?'

'What does a woman have to do with shooting things?'

Turns out Foamy didn't want an existing woman. That wouldn't be good enough for the grand plan. She wanted us to conceive a woman. Not *us* us. She wanted Zeus to sire a woman.

'Why?'

'He should engineer his own demise.'

'You know I love you, Foamy, but there's never been a war started on irony.'[59]

'This one will be.'

She took me to Sparta. I think that was a bribe. I love Sparta. Good fighters, Spartans.

She pointed at the queen, or maybe she was a princess[60] or something, I don't know. She didn't have a patch on Foamy.

'Shoot her.'

---

[59] Wrong. As much as Fate can like anything, it likes irony. —A

[60] Leda. She was the queen of Sparta. —A

'You want me to kill the queen?' Now that was a better way to start a war.

'Look at the bow, Ares.'

'This is Eros' bow.'

'Yes. It'll help with the conception.'

'If this is Eros' bow, why isn't Eros shooting it?'[61]

'Because I wanted to do this with you?'

'Why aren't you shooting it?'[62]

'I have terrible aim.'

'No you don't.' That wasn't even flattery. She had great aim. Who do you think taught Eros to begin with? 'You're being weird.'

'Please, just trust me.'

I couldn't fucking say no to her. Never could. Not when she asked me to sleep with my brother's wife. Not when she wanted me to start a war with her. I wasn't going to draw a line at a bloody arrow, was I?

It was heavy, but I'm strong. I pulled the string tight and let it fly, landing right over this girl's heart. Don't worry – it didn't bleed or nothing. Eros' arrows aren't like that.

'Well done, dear,' Foamy said. She kissed me, hard. 'Now for the other one.'

'The other one?'

'You have to shoot both parties, or the bow is useless.'

'Aphrodite, no.'

'Aphrodite, yes.'

---

[61] Because my son hates me and he wasn't going to hate me less for stealing his bow. —A

[62] Because my son's bow is a tool for a god, and I'm not one. With a thousand years, I couldn't make it work. There was only one exception to that, and it was Zeus' lightning bolts, weirdly. —A

'We're not going to shoot Zeus.'

'We're going to shoot Zeus.' She grinned. 'Don't worry, Eros has done it loads of times. It'll be fine.'

It wasn't fine.[63]

I'm the god of war, right? It imparts a whole bunch of powers but sneaky ain't one of them. We did our best though, hid in the bushes at Mum and Dad's place and waited for them to be out there and for Mum to start fussing over something in the house and let the arrow rip.

It made the faintest twang as it left the bow. I'm telling you, the thing was bloody heavy. The arrow landed square in Dad's back, and he turned, his eyes sticking right on where we were hiding.

'Shit,' I whispered. 'He saw.'

'He didn't see.'

'He saw.'

'Look, he's already going to her. He'll be too distracted by the arrow to remember anything.'

Like an idiot, I believed her.

She dragged me down to Sparta to see the results of her plan.

They say a lot of shit about me and most of it's true.

Ares is so bloodthirsty.

Ares loves war.

Ares thinks honesty is punching someone in the face.

Ares turned into a bull to fight another bull because some king said his bull couldn't be beaten.

Ares beat the bull.

Ares is stupid.

Ares is a fuck-up.

---

[63] It was not fine. —A

295

Ares fell for his brother's wife.

But you know what Ares never did?

Ares never fucked someone as a swan because Ares isn't fucking unhinged.

All my sex I did in *my* body. Don't know why Dad had to go involving everyone else in his kinky shit. It's not like the princess or queen or whatever of Sparta was a swan. She was human. She stayed human. It's only Zeus who turned into a swan and snuck up on her and— I watched it, right, and I still don't know how it worked. One minute he was following her and one minute she was patting him on the head, then the next she was laying eggs and Foamy was nodding like this was what she was imagining the whole time.

'Really?' I said.

'It's Zeus. What did you expect?' She never called him Dad. Not unless she was talking to him. 'He couldn't pull the ray of light thing again.'[64]

'He could just do sex like a normal person.'

'But then no one would talk about him.' That sounded pretty good to me. I loved it when people didn't talk about me. Meant I hadn't fucked up again.

'It's done, Ares. We did it. We're starting a war.'

Dad called us all together that night, all us Olympians. I didn't like that. It made me jumpy, knowing all us Olympians were a dying breed if Foamy got her way. When I was with her I wanted her to win, but when I was with them I wanted everything to stay the same. Y'know?

'My children,' Dad said. Never a good start. 'We're going to war.'

That was quick.

---

[64] It's how he conceived Perseus, who killed Prometheus. Heroes, like gods, can't be boring at any point in their lives. It's the cardinal sin. —A

Birth Certificate

Let this document serve as a record for a most unusual birth of four . . . children.

They appeared not as human babies but in the form of two eggs of similar size. One was brilliant white and speckled, the other a plain, matte cream. Without any signs of pregnancy, Leda – the mother on record – brought forth these eggs in her arms, claiming she had birthed them in a forest abutting the palace of Sparta. She did not wish to speak further of the experience, and grew pale and uncomfortable when the issue was forced.

Without specific experience in the matter of human eggs, these were treated under the same basis as those in a farmyard, if of a higher standard. What egg before has been swaddled in silk?

From the speckled egg came three children: a girl and two boys. The girl has been named Clytemnestra, the boys Castor and Pollux.[65] They seem happy, healthy babies, and it would be difficult to predict from their appearance anything abnormal with the circumstance of their birth.

The matte egg bore only one child: a girl who has now been named Helen. In this medical opinion, she is the loveliest babe the world has ever seen.

All are within the top ten per cent of weight for children this professional has encountered and are gaining at the appropriate speed.

---

[65] Boys irrelevant. Helen was always fond of Clytemnestra, though. —A

Aphrodite XIX

It was the wrong fucking war. The one Zeus was talking about: it was the wrong war. It wasn't Troy – Helen was going to start Troy, and she'd barely been born – it was some shit with the giants organising an uprising because Zeus had dug a big hole in the ground back when he overthrew his father, threw the giants in, covered them with dirt, and hoped for the best, and they'd finally managed to dig their way out. No wonder they were pissed.

They were my brothers, in a way. They too were born when Cronus castrated Ouranos, though they sprang from the drops of his blood as they descended upon the earth – why did everyone else get to *spring* from places when they were born? Why was I the only one to wash ashore half drowned and shivering?

The giants rose up as snakes, I hear, and that's why the lower halves of their bodies were covered in scales.

I'm not sure they were entirely *well* after they'd spent a millennium in the dark, but there you go. Once they'd broken out, they started to attack the humans, which was unacceptable to all of us. Every single person on Olympus had some mortal they were fond of – the Age of Heroes really had its grip on all of us by then – so we went to war to protect them. Yes, really.

'Could this work?' Ares said to me. 'For the scheme?'

'Obviously not.'

'Obviously?'

'There's a common enemy here. We need everyone fighting against each other.'

'I don't understand this war you're planning, Foamy.'

It wasn't going to be this one. I just knew, okay, but I couldn't tell people that, because *I just know* isn't an argument. It's superstition or it's treason, and I really wanted to keep my treason under wraps for as long as possible, thank you.

'The gods fighting together with the mortals to protect their civilization isn't going to help destroy the gods, or the mortals, or civilisation, is it?'

'You heard the prophecy then?' Ares said.

'Which one?'

'We need a mortal to help us kill the giants.' He sounded offended. Who was the oracle to tell him who he could and could not fight? Wars were his thing, and he didn't need the mortals getting involved in any relevant capacity, even if the heroes were worming their way into everything at the time. There was no escaping them. Like lice.

'Any particular mortal?'

'Doesn't seem like it.'

We had a council meeting to decide which mortal should help us. Shouting ensued.

'Stop,' Zeus yelled. Then, quieter, 'Stop. There is only one answer to this. Which living hero surpasses all others? Who is the strongest, with the most impeccable heritage?'

The sigh went round, and we answered in a single, defeated monotone.

'Heracles.'[66]

'That's right! My son will lead the charge.'

What exactly the charge would consist of caused another round of fighting, and we reached no true accord. That said, Athena can shout *very, very* loudly when she wants to, and she thought the best thing to do was to have the gods beat the shit out of the giants, then have little Heracles go round and shoot them with an arrow.

'Technically, it would fulfil the prophecy,' she said. If a being were made out of pure technicalities, it would look like Athena.

But Zeus agreed. Her plan became The Plan, and Zeus started handing out battle positions to everyone, where they would stand, who they would support, and all that, but he skipped right past me.

I get it, okay? I wasn't as strong and I wasn't as fast and I probably wasn't as immortal as the gods, but I bet I hated being ignored the most.

I decided then and there I'd show him up. Show off just how strong I can be. Get this ridiculous pre-war war over and done with so we could move on with the good stuff. Troy was waiting.

Obviously, I cheated. I found Heracles first.

'You're coming with me,' I told him.

'Okay.'

'Okay?'

'You're a goddess. You said I was coming with you. Okay.'

I found myself just a little jealous then, of *Heracles* and his blind faith in the gods. I blinked and it went away.

I snuck him into a cave around the back of Olympus and, together, we waited.

---

[66] You don't need me to tell you who Heracles is. —A

Most of the gods were lined up as Zeus had bidden them. Athena was running around like a startled chicken shouting *where's Heracles, where's Heracles?* I smirked at the image. I couldn't see Ares, but I hoped he was laughing too.

The giants reached the summit. An eagle crowed.

It was time.

Dress torn, hair loose, feet unshod, I appeared on the battlefield.

They thought I was weak? Fine. They could see me weak.

I screamed. Girlishly. Afraid.

I hooked one giant at a time, luring them my way, before I started running as fast as I could, the fear no longer entirely constructed. There's something about being chased by someone who is taller than you and faster than you that wakes up a primordial part of the mind. But this was the plan, and it was working.

I led my giants to the cave where Heracles was waiting. He did just as he was told, startling them for long enough that I could throw Hephaestus' net over them. Useful trinket, that net. They squirmed and they whined, but none of them managed to escape it, not before Heracles stabbed them and finished them off.

We worked through half a dozen of the giants that way. We'd have managed more had Athena not caught wind of the whole scheme and dragged Heracles back to work on *her* plan so she could take all the credit.

I did it, though. I fought. I helped. I proved I was worth something in a world I was already planning to destroy. Go out with a bang and all that.

Once she had him, Athena enacted The Plan with terrifying precision, marching him around the remaining giants – mostly dead – with a bow and arrow so that he could deal the final blow. By my count, the gods got one, maybe two giants each. Nothing near my numbers, but it didn't matter to them, because I didn't fight with my hands. I didn't get up close and personal with them, and the goddess of *strategy*, who claimed so boldly that she liked the clever ones, couldn't handle that. She told the rest of Olympus that I was a liar and a sneak, and she gifted me a new epithet: Aphrodite the Deceitful.

If I weren't so afraid that someone would see the truth behind the epithet, I would have enjoyed the irony of it. It's a stupid problem to have, wanting people to see and appreciate you, while knowing you're full of shit.

Zeus celebrated the vanquishing of the giants the only way he knew how: by throwing a feast. Zeus did throw a good feast. The trick, he said, was to make sure there was enough wine. He left out the part where he made sure there was something to distract his wife too so he could flirt with all the nymphs without her turning them into dancing rats or something.

Even without the recognition I deserved, I felt good. Strong. Zeus was dealt with for now. Anyone who knew about me was silent. The shattering realisation that my best friend was gone was subsiding from constant to merely frequent. I'd got rid of the giants sooner than anyone thought possible, meaning the distraction was over and I could get back to my plan. Zeus' false sense of security was falser and more secure than ever.

That night, I was a winner.

I wanted to find Ares, to celebrate the feeling with him. He liked me strong.

When I looked around, he wasn't there.

'Where's Ares?' I asked Eris. They got on quite well, as far as the goddess of discord could get on with anyone.

'Think Athena sent him out to guard the eastern front,' she said absently. She was watching the Muses' legs very closely. When I looked, I saw a very fine thread tied between them. She was just waiting for one to trip.

'The eastern front?' I confirmed.

'Yes,' she said. 'The *eastern* front. Does that mean something?'

It meant Athena was a conniving bitch, is what it meant. 'Was there someone with him?'

'Apollo to begin with. Do you want to—'

'Apollo,' I yelled. 'Get over here.'

'What's up, babe?' He called a lot of people babe. I'd heard him call horses *babe*. Heck, I'd heard him call a cup of wine *babe*.

'Were you with Ares on the battlefield?'

'Yeah.'

'He's not here now.'

'So?'

I don't think he was intentionally being petulant and unhelpful. I think he was just high. Maybe it was whatever that vapour his oracle had in her cave.

'What happened to him? Why isn't he here?'

'Calm down, babe.'

I couldn't take it anymore. I reached forwards and grabbed his ear and twisted it right the way round. 'I will be calm when you tell me where my bloody – Ares is.'

'I don't know, do I? Zeus ran out of thunderbolts and I had to go cover him.'

Oh for fuck's sake.

'And no one thought to check on him afterwards?' I asked. Politely, I thought, but I was still holding his ear and it did twist an awfully long way.

I would have kept twisting. I didn't really want to hurt Apollo.

I wanted to find Ares but, if that wasn't available, hurting Apollo felt like a pretty good substitute.

'Wahey!' Eris shouted.

One of the Muses had tripped and taken the others out with her, so they were lying on the floor in a little Muse-pile. Apollo squirmed out of my grasp to go and check on them, and I took to the party to ask around.

'Have you seen him?'

'Not since this morning.'

'Seen who?'

'Ares. Tall guy. Dripping in blood. Have you seen him?'

'Are you sure he's real?'

'Don't be a buzzkill, Gran. I'm sure Grandpa's round here somewhere.'

'I will ground you.'

'Don't worry, sweetie, he knows where his home is.'

'Then why isn't he here?'

He'll be back, they told me.

Over and over. He'll be back. He'll find his way home in his own time when he can be bothered because he's Ares and Ares is just like that and who cares if we don't see him for a while? Someone *actually* told me that.

'Who cares?'

I don't have the strength of the gods. I can't summon earth-quakes or lightning or pull the very sun out of the sky. And in that moment it didn't fucking matter because I was wrapping my hand around this Muse's hair and pulling it tight to the ground and staring right into her face with my teeth bared so much I might as well have been a wolf. She trembled.

Yeah. Fear me. Do it.

'I care. So tell me what you know.'

'I don't know anything.'

'Useless.'

I threw her down.

I talked to every fucking person in Olympus that night. Even *Demeter*, who sneered at me and muttered something about me caring about missing persons now. Even his prima dogface himself.

'Where's Ares?'

'Is that how you address the king of the gods?' Zeus crowed.

'Where's Ares?'

His eyes flashed. Dangerous. I didn't care. I was dangerous too.

'Calm there, dear,' Hera said. She patted her husband's shoulder. It wasn't good enough. None of this was good enough.

'Where is he?'

'Why would I know where he is? He's a grown-up boy.'

'He was fighting *your* war on *your* battlefield alone because *you* needed the help. *You* can fucking tell me where he is.'

'I don't know.'

'Then look.'

'You're being very disrespectful,' he said.

I'm certain it was a threat. He'd have to do better to make anything he could do to me feel worse in my head than this. Ares was mine, goddammit. He loved me. He was helping me start my war. I was *not* going to lose him. Not now.

'I don't give a shit. Find him.'

'No.'

'Find him.'

'What – are you going to make me?'

And that hurt. There was nothing I could do to physically threaten him, no matter how much I wanted to.

'It's not like you can cause a famine, can you? Or are you going to withhold *love*?'

For generations, I'd lied and stolen and hidden so I could get respect. So I could have freedom and security. And this is where it got me. Sneers of *love*.

'You,' I shouted at Hera. 'Why aren't you doing anything?'

'He'll come back in his own time.'

'He's your *son*.'

'And you see your son often?' she said. Low fucking blow. You don't talk about it. Unspoken rule. When your children leave you, people aren't allowed to bring it up.

'Fuck you. Fuck you both.'

He didn't come back. Not that night, or the night after, or the one after that, and I kept thinking that one of these days someone was going to care and they didn't. No one cared that he was gone.

I was going to make them care.

I annoyed them.

Every day I went to them and I demanded to know why they weren't looking yet. I shouted and I screamed and I did everything under the sun that could be considered ugly. I had images of him copied around Olympus, around the world, so people would remember who he was, so they would look. So they would *tell me*.

And then I went home and I screamed until my nymphs went away, and they told the others I was just grieving, which wasn't fucking true. I wasn't grieving because he wasn't dead.

I was pissed because I'm a bitch. And I wasn't enough of one.

I was fucking furious at Zeus and the Olympians – of course I was – but do you know who I really hated in that time?

Me.

I hated *me*. Every morning when I woke up to go annoy the shit out of people, I thought, *I don't have time for this*. I thought about how busy I was. I thought about how the god of war shouldn't need protecting. I thought about what would happen if I just didn't, today. If I let him go and focused on my war, my future, instead.

And then I went anyway. Not because I'm so kind. Not because I'm a hero or a martyr. I went because I was too weak to let him go. I told myself every fucking day that my power and my position and my plan were more important to me than my love, and every fucking day, I chose not to work on my plan, because I couldn't bear to let Ares go, and I didn't love him enough to be pleased about it.

I was meant to be looking after Helen. I was meant to be watching *Helen*. I was meant to be grooming her to make sure her beauty shone more brightly than a thousand suns. I was meant to be a goddess and a friend and a sister to her all at once.

But I didn't have time for Helen. Everything I wanted had to be put on hold because Ares needed me, and he loved me and I loved him, but that wasn't enough. Loving him wasn't all of me, until he disappeared, and then it was. I became the person who missed him and nothing more.

I had to carry all of that, because nobody else cared.

What do you do with that? What do you do but hate?

He wasn't in Olympus. He wasn't on Earth. His Fate held up, strong and sure. He was alive, but he was hidden from me.

He wasn't out fucking some mortal woman. He hadn't declared himself passionately in love with Athena, which I know because I broke into her house and looked for him there too.

(Athena's house is a terrifying place. It's Organised. There are weapons hanging on one wall of every room and maps stuck across the other three. Her loom is unlike anything I'd seen before, and it gives the impression that it would quite happily take apart the chaos of the threads of Fate and turn them into something more orderly and reasonable.)

I went to see Prometheus.

It didn't help. He was still stone. But I didn't know what else to do, and what I did when I didn't know what to do was see Prometheus.

The eagle was still there. The statue was missing a part, now, the area above his liver eroding more and more with every passing peck. I didn't cry. I didn't hug the eagle close to me because it was the only other thing that cared that my best friend was gone. I didn't scream because now my Ares was gone and no one cared about him either.

Because I realised there was still one person I hadn't tried.

My husband.

I didn't want to go. I went anyway.

'Hephaestus.'

'The prodigal wife returns.'

'Have you seen Ares?' I said. I didn't have time for the bickering, didn't have the energy to care whether he was the wronged party or I was the wronged party, because this whole marriage thing had been so over for me for so long it didn't matter anymore. I needed Ares back. I needed myself back. I had a plan, dammit, and it wasn't this.

'He's missing?'

'You didn't know?'

'How long?'

'A year.'

A full fucking year, and still, Zeus did not lift a finger. Still, Hera said he was out partying. Still, Demeter refused to help because I hadn't helped her.

My husband leaned back in his chair, sagging so deeply his beard near caught in the forge. A single hair singed, filling the whole space with the acrid warning, *danger*. Hephaestus blew on the fire, and with that one breath, the forge went out. It must have been connected through his palace because, in stages, everything went dark around us.

What it is to be a god.

'Ares has been gone a year, and no one told me?'

I am not a trusting person – it would be hypocritical if I was, given all the lying I do – but I believed my husband. He was positively ashen. He didn't cry, very definitely, but when he breathed, it came out ragged, as if his lungs had sprung a leak.

'My brother has been gone a year, and *you* didn't tell me?'

Accusatory, all of a sudden, the fire that was out in the room alive in his eyes. Even sitting, he managed to loom across me. He weighed more. I could run, but he was a threat.

'I thought you knew.'

'I didn't.'

'I thought you didn't care.'

'Of course I care. He's my brother.'

Is this what family is like, truly? This unending, undying obligation to one another? Nothing should be able to survive such abuse, such battering, such casual cruelty, but time and again, the Olympians forgave under the guise of *family*.

If someone hurt me the way Ares hurt Hephaestus, I would have let them rot in whatever corner of the world they were hidden in. If someone hurt me the way *I* hurt Hephaestus, I wouldn't have let them into my house. I would have shouted insults at them, poured boiling oil from the windows. What I would not accept from my friends, my lovers, I can't believe I would accept from my family, but here was Hephaestus, after all that, still loyal.

'We're going to find him, Aphrodite.'

That was the closest I ever felt to my husband, which is ridiculous and sad, but for a moment felt like a breath of fresh air, like there was progress to be had.

Hephaestus spoke to his Cyclopes who, like me, were from another time and, unlike me, had friends when they were in that other time. They spoke to people who spoke to people who couldn't tell us where he was but could tell us the last known address of every surviving giant.

'I've marked them on the map for you,' Hephaestus said. 'Hermes can scout their locations and give you the correct one.'

I was going to find him. It was happening. This would be over.

I couldn't bear to do it alone.

'Will you go with me?'

Hephaestus II

When we left for our rescue mission the next day, she looked unlike I had ever seen her before. She was wearing full armour, and seeming more beautiful than ever, but it's a fact of Aphrodite that every time you see her, she is more beautiful than the last.

'Get in the chariot, Husband. We're going to find your brother.'

She was manipulating me – I knew that – and she was not even manipulating me *well*. She was pulling the strings she thought only she could see, tugging on the binds of my affection. She misunderstood me. She did not need to manipulate. Wherever she went, I would follow, and so I got in the chariot.

'This is his,' I said.

'Borrowed it.'

'He lets you?'

'He did before,' she said.

Surprising. Let me tell you a story about my brother: he doesn't share.

'Do you not have your own?' I knew that she did. I built her a cage for the doves that pulled it, once upon a time. She called it beautiful.

'Thought he'd appreciate the familiarity.'

'Where are we going?'

'Otus and Ephialtes.'[67]

'The twins.'

'Brothers,' she said, looking over at me, her eyes so deep and encompassing I could not fathom what was inside them. I would have dived in to find out. 'Do you think he's okay?'

No. My brother had been gone for over a year. No one could keep an immortal prisoner for that long in good conditions.

'We will be there soon,' I said.

We drove east to a mountain I'd never seen before, though that was not in itself unusual. The world did not make it easy for me to see it, and I was happy with my life in the forges.

Ares' horses whinnied as Aphrodite drove them faster than they were prepared to go.

'To be honest, you guys, I don't really give a shit,' Aphrodite whispered.

She was not the woman I married. She was so much more than that.

When we were introduced, she was quiet, kind. My mother declared that she was shy and, in time, she would warm up to me. I knew this to be a lie, but I hoped differently, I hoped I could make her see me differently by proving I was not like the other men on Olympus. I would not force myself on her. I would be kind in return.

My personality grows on people. I am more fungus than rock in that regard. I do not hit, blind, or dazzle. With time, she would see that. All I ever needed was more time.

Aphrodite had none of it that day, not for me. She drove us almost into the mountain, taking the horses to the verge

---

[67] Offensively fucking irrelevant. —A

of crashing into the rocks before pulling them back so hard I thought her spine would crack. She dropped the reins and went sprinting for the door of the cave, forgetting my presence at all.

This time, however, she returned to me.

'They're in there. The giants are in there. Shit,' she said.

'You didn't plan for this?'

'I found out where he was. I got you. We came here.'

The greatest expression of confidence my wife had ever made of me. I was growing. 'Do you know their weaknesses?'

'Does it matter? I'm going to kill them anyway.'

They were immortal, like us. They had lived for longer than I had, many more spans than anyone but the divine could possibly hope to achieve, but in that moment I couldn't doubt her. Without a single soul by her side, Aphrodite would have retrieved my brother from that cave.

Ares meant a great deal to me, no matter how he behaved. I had always loved my brother, and I always would, even in the frequent times when I did not like him.

Between the two of them, I had no feasible alternative to helping.

I sighed. 'If I create a distraction, will you be able to retrieve him?'

'Yeah.' She swallowed. Twice. 'Yes. I can do that.'

I did not give her a chance to overthink, to overanalyse. She is most beautiful in her impulses.

I reached into my chair and let loose a new invention I'd been working on: an automaton. It was an early prototype, and it had many issues. It was loud, it creaked, and, occasionally, it burst into flames, but it was sturdy and, when it folded out, the faux-man of bronze was large. It would function as a distraction, at least until it was destroyed.

[Note to self: next time you go to rescue your brother with your wife, bring an automaton *for which you have created blueprints.*]

From then, the process was simple. My toy captured the attention of the giants. I pointed it in the opposite direction, and she ran in.

The giant lumbered after my bronze man in merry chase, until he walked himself directly off the edge of the cliff. As I said, an early prototype.

[Note to self: develop self-preservation protocol for automatons.]

'Aphrodite?' I called. 'You may wish to hurry. The giants will be returning now.'

'On it.' She heaved. She was out of breath, understandably, as she attempted to haul a clay jar larger than she was out of the cave. 'Let's go,' she said.

'Where's Ares?'

'In the jar.' She didn't call me an idiot, but I could feel her thinking it. How was I supposed to know my brother was in the jar? It was opaque. Once I knew, I sped in her direction to assist. The giants closed in.

'Quicker,' she said.

'Shouting that will not make us travel more quickly.'

'QUICKER, HEPHAESTUS.'

We moved more quickly. She manoeuvred the jar into my seat.

'The jar's in my seat,' I said.

'It's Ares.'

'Where am I meant to sit?'

'Is this the time to argue?' she said, spurring the horses reluctantly back into action. This time I was relieved for the force of it as the giants ran behind us, reaching greedy fingers in our direction.

'Would he not prefer to be out of the jar?'

'Not where you can see him.'

The jar wobbled with the force of the chariot. Aphrodite was not the best driver in the world. Her hands were shaking, the edges of jewellery peeking out from under her armour, though the bracelets did not clink together.

'Shall I hold it still?'

'Please.'

We drove in silence after that, all the way until the crest of Olympus appeared in front of us. It had a habit of doing that. Sneaking up on you.

'Aphrodite,' I said. 'What do you plan to tell the Olympians?'

'I found Ares.'

'Could you leave my part out of the story?'

'What?'

'I do not wish to be the person who helped my wife and my brother embarrass me.'

'You are that person, Hephaestus.'

'No. I am the person who saved my brother, who you happen to love. Please reciprocate what I did today with kindness.'

She looked torn.

'You were kind, when we met.'

'No, I was lying. But I can lie again.' There were tears running down her face. Her knuckles were tight against the reins. 'Hermes found the address from your map. I'll speak to him. Have him claim to be the rescuer.'

'Hermes does not lie.'

'Hermes has an impressive way of thinking lies into the truth. I'm sure he can work it out in his head that, by finding him, he *did* rescue Ares.'

She took me back to the forges, Ares still in the chariot. I don't believe she remembered where I lived. No one did. To them,

I existed only in my workshop, folding away neatly at night like one of my tools.

That day, she did not make me feel that way. She wrapped her arms around me, pulling me into a tight embrace, brief but true. She kissed me on the cheek.

'Thank you, Hephaestus, for everything you did today.'

'I hope we can build on this, moving for—'

'What?'

'I was going to finish if you had not interrupted me.'

'You're not going to let me go?'

'We got on well today—'

'You saw how much I love Ares and you still won't let me leave?'

'Don't you see, if we can talk again, we can grow, we can be more—'

'No. We will *never* be more. I will *never* love you, Hephaestus. Can't *you* see?'

'Give it time.'

Aphrodite XX

I could hide from him, embarrass him, try to get him kicked off the council of Olympians, and it didn't matter. Hephaestus would never let me leave. No matter how cruel I was, no matter how clear and open and honest I was – I would always be his prize, the payback for what his parents had done to him. People couldn't call him ugly or worthless when he had me as a wife.

So, no, I don't feel bad for stealing from him, though I didn't get round to it until later. First, I dropped him off at his forge, promising to come back later to talk,[68] and then I took Ares home. My place. I carried the jar into my bedroom and knocked on the top of it, gently, because I couldn't know how loud it was in there, how much of our world had made it through to him. 'It's just us now, love.'

The jar rattled.

'You can come out.'

Rattle rattle.

'Do you want me to leave you to come out on your own?'

Rattle rattle.

'Okay, I'll be back in a few hours.' I wouldn't want to be seen like that either.

---

[68] I meant steal things, but he didn't know that. —A

I went to see Hephaestus while I was waiting. More accurately, I went to see his forges, where my husband made Zeus' lightning bolts. With the war coming, I needed every weapon I could get, and they were the strongest, the only ones that could be wielded by someone other than a god. I had no plan for them, but that *was* the plan. If Ares could be kidnapped, then so could I. I needed a way to blast my way out of a bad situation.

I waited until Hephaestus was out, fetching something to drink, before I made to grab them. It should have taken only a moment, but I was transfixed by them, the energy that danced along their blades.

Beautiful.

But I didn't get long to look. Hephaestus came back, and just like that, I was out of time. I grabbed the closest bolts and stuffed them down my clothes. That would have to be enough.

I turned to him.

'Sorry, darling, I just realised I have a terrible hair emergency and I need to run home.'

'Aphrodite—'

I didn't wait to hear the end of that thought.

I counted my pilfered bolts on the way home. Three. That would have to be enough.

But I didn't spend too long thinking about them. I was distracted. I had Ares back.

He was still in the jar when I got home. I waited for him, but I didn't sit empty-handed. With his return, I got my mind back too. I could think about the plan again, starting with stealing the bolts, and moving on to making notes and diagrams, running through scenarios in my head, checking the smaller threads that followed me to see who I could pull in, who had to be there, how I could make it all bigger.

It was like he knew. As I sat and calculated our bloodshed, Ares burst out of the jar. He looked—

Thin wasn't the right word for it, but skeletal makes him sound weaker than he'd tolerate. I could see his bones jutting and pressing against his skin, but it didn't matter, because the rage in his voice still made him the most terrifying of the Olympians.

'I'm going to fucking kill him,' he said.

'Him?' I checked. It's worth doing, when you're committing treason.

'Zeus. Foamy, you and I are going to destroy the king.' He'd already agreed to help me with the war. He'd already helped me with Helen, but this was different. There was a viciousness in his eyes that even blood didn't normally spark. 'We're going to capture him and tie him to a chair and peel his skin from him, and then we're going to lock him in a fucking jar.'

Right on cue, a stretch of his skin peeled from his face. I didn't choose Ares for his imagination, but I loved this passion. I needed it. I'd been out of the game, and I wasn't sure where to go from here.

'We can do that,' I said. 'But, love?'

'Yeah?'

'How?'

'Well, first I punch him, then you punch him, then I punch him again—' What followed was an eleven-minute description of how and where Ares wanted to hit his father. He knew more about anatomy than I gave him credit for.

'It's personal now,' I said, when there was a break in violent dreams. 'That's why you're going so hard.'

'He left me alone on the battlefield so I'd get abducted. Of course it's fucking personal.'

'Wait, he left you?'

'Told you. He saw me shooting the arrow. Punishment, right?'

I hadn't considered that, and I didn't have the energy to think about it now, but it didn't matter. I had a plan.

'We have to make it personal.'

'I don't follow.'

'Leave it with me. You rest.'

'I hate resting.'

I knew he did, but I had work to do. I went to talk to the nymphs, the nereids, the naiads. I even put on a brave face and went to talk to Hestia, who knows things because she pays attention, even if she'll only tell you if you sit down and eat cake with her and pretend you want the information for the good of the family and not to start an all-consuming war.

I took my goose and my bolts – they were the most powerful weapon in my arsenal; I was never letting go of those bolts – and I went visiting. I went to Athens, Sparta, and Thebes. I followed the trails of the heroes; I checked on their children and their grand-children. I went to my cave and I let Fate wrap around me again. I followed every connection, every moment the immortal touched the mortal. I took notes. We were going to make this *personal*.

So, maybe I was gone a few days longer than I expected.

'Foamy, where were you?' Ares said, from my bed. He was look-ing better already. The family might be terrible, but being a god isn't without its perks.

'I've got it. I know how we make the war big enough.'

His eyes lit up like it was his naming day. 'Shoot.'

'So in the beginning, Apollo loved Hyacinth—'

'Who's Hyacinth?'

'Mortal boy. He doesn't matter. The important thing is Apollo loved him, but then he died so Apollo and Poseidon planned their rebellion against Zeus, and the two of them had to build Troy, which is the whole reason Troy is bound to fall in the first place—'

'Is that really why?'

'Do you seriously not remember this?'

'Was I even alive?'

I was a cradle-snatcher and my boyfriend was a child.

'Anyway, Apollo had to build Troy for Laomedon, only Apollo fell in love with Laomedon while he was doing it and kind of fell in love with Troy too, so now he loves the whole place, especially Hector, who's one of the princes, but let's be honest, Hector's The Prince, but it's not that simple because Poseidon rebelled too, and he hated Laomedon for the way he treated them, so now Poseidon hates the whole place. And Troy is allied with this guy Glaucus, right, whose cousin is Sarpedon whose father is Zeus, and Zeus inexplicably loves Sarpedon more than anyone else. He's extended his life like six times now, which only pisses Apollo off more because of, you know, not making Hyacinth immortal back in the day. Then Athena loves Odysseus because he's clever, and Hermes also loves Odysseus because he might be his grandfather, but Athena also loves Diomedes most because she used to love his father Tydeus, until Tydeus started eating people and she's not chill with that after Zeus ate her mother. And obviously we love Helen because we made Helen, and Helen loves her sister Clytemnestra but she also loves her cousin Penelope.'

'Foamy, who are these people?'

'Mortals. Heroes.'

'Why do we care?'

'Because the gods care. If we get their favourite mortals fighting, then they'll fight with them. It'll be personal.'

'Who's even fighting?'

'Everyone.'

'Foamy—'

'The Greeks and the Trojans.'

'You haven't even mentioned the Greeks. Agamemnon's the king of the Greeks.'

'Right, so we need to link all these people together with the Greeks, and the way we do that is Helen. We get all the right suitors together and make them fall in love with her, then she marries Menelaus, who Agamemnon loves because he's his brother, and Agamemnon marries Clytemnestra and the family stays close, so Agamemnon defends Menelaus' honour when Helen runs off with Paris, who's Hector's brother, but he's not allowed into Troy because there's a prophecy that he's going to destroy it, which he will—'

'This isn't war. This is gossip.'

'No, this is motivation. Agamemnon will get so up in arms about defending his brother that he'll recruit the best in the world to fight on their side, which means he'll get Achilles, who Thetis loves, even though Thetis hates Zeus for making her have Achilles, and Achilles loves Patroclus, who'll try to slow down the war so Achilles doesn't die, but Achilles does die and—'

'How does Thetis have a son already? Zeus and Poseidon were fighting over her yesterday and she didn't have one then.'

I'd spent too much time with Fate. All the edges were blurring together. Past and present and future.

'She will. I know. It's a love thing.'

'Right.'

'Don't worry about it.'

'Right.'

'Don't you see?'

'Really, no.'

'We just have to link them all up, then they'll do the rest of the work for us.'

'Are you sure I can't just punch someone?'

'We're going to send out invites. Tell the kings that little Helen's ready to get married, and she asked for them personally.'

'And that will work?'

'That will work.'

Aphrodite XXI

Helen was all grown up. It's a problem with mortals, sometimes – you blink and they've got old and died on you – but this suited my purposes so I wasn't going to complain about it. Her stepfather put out word that they were *finally* accepting bids to marry her, and it was simple enough to slip a couple of extra invitations into Hermes' bag. They were addressed to the right kings, those beloved by the gods, telling them Helen had asked for them personally. Before anyone knew it, the palace was full of suitors, crammed so tight you could lift your legs up and never hit the floor.

'What do we do?' Helen asked me.

She'd prayed to me, and I had come. I might have missed my chance to mould her into my prophet, the one who would spread the word of the great goddess to the next great civilisation, but I still needed her to love me more than any other.

I'd organised her lessons when she was a child, leaned on her parents until they allowed her to practise wrestling. If I was going to start a war over her, she deserved that at least. I talked to her, counselled her, played games with her. All of that so, when this day came, I could steer her the way Fate needed her to go.

'What do you want in a husband?'

'I want them to love me.' The romantic streak wasn't my doing. I was feeling thoroughly unromantic by that point, even with Ares back.

'They'll all love you, I promise that. What else? Would you like to be a queen?'

'Oooh, yes. We'll tell everyone but the kings to leave.'

I asked her a dozen of those questions, knowing what her answer would be, whittling away the numbers until only those suitors I needed remained.

The family organised a banquet for them all – maybe three dozen after the cull. Normally, at these things, the woman they were chasing would dance or play music or something similar to show off her gentle skills at the arts, so everyone could pretend they weren't there for appearances or power.

With Helen it was unnecessary. Everyone knew they were there for appearances and power.

The first night, the suitors just stared at her, their jaws slack, their manner placid, but as the days passed, the brotherhood soured. Fights broke out between them – little ones, all the men needling each other. That didn't work for me. I needed them fighting together at Troy, not killing each other now in some louse's brawl. I think this is where Ares got lost in the plan, so . . .

Hold.

On.

Tight.

I needed them to wait, and heroes aren't very good at that, so I'd invited a king who was. It was time for him to make himself useful.

'Odysseus,' I announced grandly.

He was walking around the palace, poking at its foundations, wine in hand.

'My darling. I heard a little rumour about you.'

'Is that so?' He was cagey. All of Athena's favourites were. Made them boring, even if her favouritism had earned him one of my special invites – it's not like Helen would marry the king of somewhere as irrelevant as Ithaca but, I needed him in the war, and I needed him now.

'You love her.' I stretched the *o* out. *Luuuuuurve*.

'Everyone loves her.'

'Not Helen. Penelope.'

'I had a donkey called Penelope.' Entry-level avoidance. Odysseus, you can do better.

'Did you love her too?'

'If I did, that would be treason.'

'No rules against loving a donkey. Otherwise Zeus would be in trouble.'

He levelled me the single most unimpressed look I've ever received from a mortal.

'What do you care?' he said. Petulant little thing.

'You seem unimpressed by the presence of the goddess of love.'

He shrugged. 'What's love got to do with anything?'

'Love has got to do with everything.' Fuck me, this shouldn't have been so difficult. I'd come down here to give him a *gift*, to point him in the right direction so that he could marry the girl he loved, and if that happened to suit my purposes too, so be it.

'We can disagree on that point.'

'I'm here to help you, Odysseus.'

'I don't need you. I have my own plan.'

'Tell me.'

He wasn't such an insolent little shit that he'd refuse a goddess. He described a plan to me. It was an overcomplicated thing,[69] involving fake vases and flowers and accidentally getting locked in a room together and ending with—

'You're still planning to marry Helen?' I demanded.

'She is the prize, is she not?'

It would be counterproductive, Aphrodite, to hold the boy up by the throat and drag him through a room of his peers to point at and laugh, so they can see him as a *prize*.

It would be counterproductive, but it would be so much fun.

'A little tip for any future marriage you have,' I said. *With Penelope.* 'Woman don't appreciate being treated as a prize.'

'You'd rather be something lesser?' He asked it earnestly, like he was going to note this down later. That was somehow worse.

'Helen isn't going to marry you.'

'I have a plan.'

'I know. You told me the plan. She's not going to marry you.' I wasn't going to let her. I needed her to start this war, not on territory, not on showing off the size of your armies or whatever it was that boys liked to fight their skirmishes over. Not even on food, like Demeter. Helen was going to start a war over *love*, and she couldn't do that if she was on bloody Ithaca. 'She loves beautiful things.'

'And?'

'You're not a beautiful thing, Odysseus, and you don't want to marry Helen.'

I would have felt bad about it if he didn't annoy me so much. Most people are interesting, and interesting is beautiful in and

---

[69] Not that I'm one to talk. —A

of itself. Ares wasn't some perfectly chiselled statue, but it didn't matter because Ares was Ares.

I won't deny that there's another kind of beauty, though, one that's exactly skin-deep. I had it. Helen had it. Even Hera had a bit of it, when she was making an effort.

Odysseus didn't. His beard made him look like he was a goat-herd. One of his eyes was a tiny bit bigger than the other. His legs were bowed. He had a *lot* of hair on his chest, and his clothes were ill-fitting enough for that to be apparent.

He was also a bit of a shit, but Helen didn't seem concerned about that.

'You love *Penelope*,' I said slowly, so he would understand. 'You want to marry *Penelope*.'

'She's not on the table.'

'Then put her there. Tyndareus[70] wants peace after this. Convince the suitors to give it to him. Have them swear it.'

'How?'

'You're meant to be all kinds of clever, aren't you? Make a plan, Odysseus.'

I turned to leave. He shouted after me, 'Why do you care?'

'I just love *love*, you know?' I giggled. The giggle sold it. It confirmed his low opinion of me, and confirmation is the easiest kind of lie to tell.

Odysseus went and made his plan, and I finished mine.

I told Helen that Menelaus was *dreamy*.

Menelaus *was* dreamy, but Menelaus also had a powerful brother who had a powerful army he'd stir up on his behalf. Who said women can't have everything?

---

[70] Helen's stepfather. Remarkably decent about the whole situation. —A

'I don't *do* younger brothers,' she said.

'Make an exception. Trust me.' I felt like I was drinking from the Phlegethon, the fire burning and ripping at my tongue, but I did what I had to. 'What's the worst that could happen?'

She told her father she was ready to make her choice – he allowed it, even though he didn't for her sister, simply telling Clytemnestra she'd be marrying Agamemnon – and he duly gathered the suitors round to hear it, dragging them from their important arguments.

I know arguments. I live on Olympus. I know pointless bickering between immortals, and I know when whatever they're arguing about isn't really the point. (Shockingly, Hera was never mad about where Zeus left his sandals and was, in fact, annoyed about where Zeus left his penis.)

When the suitors argued, it was about who ate too much at dinner. It was over lost shoes and moved bedclothes. It was over accidental spitting when speaking. And it was all very clearly over who would marry the most beautiful mortal to ever grace the Earth.

The king gulped. His face was sweating. Odysseus, never much of a runner, scurried up to him. He whispered so furiously in the king's ear I thought he might pass out, but it worked.

The king nodded. 'You may tell them,' he said.

'Right, boys,' Odysseus shouted.

They quietened a little, but they shifted on their feet. Some rolled their eyes. Just humouring him, then.

'We're all sure we're going to win this thing, aren't we?'

I looked at Helen from where I was hidden. She didn't react to being called *this thing*.

'And so, a promise. We swear on the Styx that we will defend the victor's marriage with our armies and our lives. You agree?'

No, they did not. It was a horrible deal.

'You afraid she won't pick you? This is great for you if she does,' Odysseus coaxed. He swore. He goaded. He sold, and, eventually, the men took heed. They stepped up, one by one, and every king this side of Troy swore their oaths on the Styx. If someone took Helen from her rightful husband then yes, yes, they would gather their armies and come to defend him for however long it took.

Well done, Odysseus. Just what I wanted from you.

Helen chose Menelaus, and the two of them were married in a blink.

Odysseus and Penelope too, though their wedding had less pomp to it. They chose to do it on the same day as Helen's, which can only mean that they didn't want all that.

They went to Ithaca and almost immediately settled into the kind of quiet insignificance that would slowly kill me. I think it did the same for them. Odysseus wanted to be an inventor, a hero, a trickster. Instead, he tripped and fell into the role of husband and father, but he guaranteed me my war, and that was good enough for me.

Zeus IV

It started with Perseus. My Perseus. My son. He did what I wanted. I gave him gifts. To make sure.

Didn't work. He killed Medusa. Fine. Then he killed Prometheus. Not fine. Didn't like Prometheus. Twisty bastard. But he was immortal. Nearly a god. Mortals should respect that. Know their limits.

They didn't. They refused. Kept getting stronger. Having more children. Working together. Getting bigger. More powerful. Looming. Wanting things. No one cared about me anymore. They cared about the mortals. The heroes.

Always knew I'd have to fight in one war. Fine. One war. Won that. Beat Cronus. Threw him in Tartarus. No one said there'd be more. More. More. More.

Siblings. Parents. Children. Allies. Friends. All of them wanted things from me. Didn't let me sleep. Make my favourite a god – they said that. This mortal deserves it. I love them.

Everything was about the heroes. They were meant to help us. Stay in their place. Kept getting bigger.

Tried to research them. The mortals. Started with one of my sons. Made sense. Best mortals, my sons.

This one was called Sarpedon. He was meant to be a king. His brothers fought him for it. He lost. Loser.

He didn't fight back. He let them win. He accepted.

I didn't understand. Went back to see him. Tried to understand. He didn't ask for things. Not from me. He would not attack. Uprise. Uproot.

He bowed. Cried. Honoured me. Answered my questions. I liked him. Good boy. Gave him more years. Had to go to the useless bloody Fates to do it. Had to threaten them. They remembered their place. Tied his thread to another. Gave him more life. Whenever I needed.

Six times. Six lives. One son.

Good boy. Wished the others were like him. Then they could stay.

There were thousands of them. Many thousands. So few of us. So many of them. They could hold our strength in their bodies. They just kept *breeding*.

Before. There were too many before. I flooded them. Brought them down where they could see us. Wouldn't work again. They'd dispersed. Spread thinly to refuse me.

Wanted people to be happy. Like Hestia. But less annoying. Needed them well behaved.

Needed sleep.

Didn't get to. Couldn't think. Not with people wanting things. Not all the time. Wanting and demanding. Claiming I'd said something. Didn't know what. Didn't know what they wanted from me.

Couldn't have a blurred mind. People exploit blurry minds. Lie to them.

Lied to me.

Told me they were happy. (Frowned.)

Told me they supported me. (Rioted.)

Told me they loved me. (Betrayed me.)

Told me everything I wanted to hear. They lied. They lied. They lied. Until I shouted. Told them I needed the *truth*. They shied away from me. Afraid. Not enough.

Worst was my daughter. Aphrodite. She hated me. After Ares. Wasn't about her. He shot me. With one of her arrows. Needed to get rid of him. Thought he was gone. Then she got him back.

She hid it. She liked to hide things. In her pretty hair. Her pretty smile. Her airs. Her graces. Hid so much wearing nothing at all.

Not good enough. Saw her grimace when I talked. Saw her whispering with Ares. Saw her tense as I walked past. Only do that when you have something to hide. Why was she whispering? Why did Ares have her arrows?

She did it. Only explanation. She made him shoot me. She mocked me. Turned sex against me. I gave her so much. And she betrayed me.

Not allowed. She knew how good sex was. Used it against me. But she knew.

So she could see how it felt. Suffer too.

Went to Eros. Sensible child. Separated himself from his mother's bad influence. Congratulated him on his good sense.

'Who do you need me to shoot?' he said. No preamble. Not even fake respect. Children.

'Your mother.'

'No.'

'Wasn't asking.'

'I am her attendant and her son. You must respect family, surely.'

'Of course, of course. I'm married to the goddess of family. But respect for family must come after your love for the king.' Let my lightning bolts rise to my hands. Didn't even have to try. They wanted to. They felt right there. At home. 'So you will do as I ask.'

'Okay, okay, it's no big deal,' he said. 'Who?'

'Some shepherd. I don't care.'

'Then why?' he asked. He got scared. Half-swallowed his words. Coward. Hate cowards. His mother was a coward.

'Humility is an excellent trait in others.'

Eros lifted his special bow. Shot two arrows. They disappeared over the horizon.

'Do you not need to see the targets?' I said.

'Have you seen me hovering in the distance any time you have claimed my arrows drove you to something?'

The little shit.

'I will make you pay for your insolence. I will tie you up. I will take that bow from you and I will—'

'Lose your excuse for your infidelity? I don't think so. Go home, Zeus. It is done.'

Aphrodite XXII

I didn't want to do it. Do I get to say that?

I already hated Zeus. I was putting together the war to end all wars so I could get rid of him, and he was still playing his petty little games, abusing his power just because he could. I had better things to do than this, and he took that away from me.

I didn't want to sleep with Anchises. I didn't want to seduce him. I said yes, and I didn't mean it. Somebody made me, and only one person has the power to do that.

My toerag son.

Eros' arrows bypassed all logic. They cut through your mind like a poison, cut out the thinking bit of your brain and replaced it with what I can only imagine is Zeus' brain.

I love sex. I love sex with all kinds of people. I love sex so all-encompassing I can't tell you where I am or who I'm with, only that I want more.

Which is *not* the same as waking up one day and ditching all your carefully laid plans for war, because your feet are moving without you agreeing, taking you to some shepherd's door on bloody Mount Ida because you know you'll die if you don't fuck that shepherd senseless right fucking now.

And still, a part of me fought it.

I can't change my shape as the gods do, but I've learned to disguise myself over the years. With Anchises, I didn't bother. It might not have been my thinking mind that knocked on his door, but it sure as Hades looked like me.

'Who are you?' he asked.

I said nothing. I had no answer. I had not planned a name. 'You are— You are so beautiful. You must be one of the goddesses. Artemis? Leto? Aphrodite?'

'No—'

'Themis?[71] Athena? You must be a nymph, at least.'

'I am no goddess.' The words were shit in my mouth. They were true and they were a lie all at once. I was not a goddess. He thought I was. He said my damned name in his list, but I didn't have control. He was afraid as he spoke the names of the immortals. He would not lie with them, and I *had* to. It was the only thing I was sure about in the world. 'I am a princess.'

The most power I could give myself, even then.

'From where?'

'Phrygia.'

'You speak my language well for a Phrygian.'

'I had a nurse who spoke it,' I said. Who was I? What was I doing? I lied professionally for longer than this man's *ancestors* had walked the land, and I'd forgotten all of it, lost it somewhere with my dignity, my choice. All words were punctuated with giggles and blushes and obvious fucking tells.

I fell at his knees.

I'm not embarrassed by who I have sex with, but I will never,

---

[71] Goddess of justice, seemingly didn't turn up for work in the world we were living in. —A

336

ever prostrate myself to them. I will not be a supplicant in my own fucking house.

'Please, kind Anchises—' Had he given his name? It didn't matter. He accepted the obvious lies so easily he wouldn't be tripped by this. 'I was carried here by Hermes himself, and I don't know where to go. If you marry me, I'll be the most well behaved and pleasant of wives.'

It was so obvious. But he kissed me anyway, with full force, pushing me back over my knees until I lay flat on the floor of his entryway.

'If we are to be wed, dear princess, then I cannot wait another moment to be with you.'

Nobody held me down. Anchises certainly didn't. But I didn't want this. Somebody pulled the desires from my own mind and twisted them into something that looked like they came from me, but I know they weren't mine, because it was *my* mind and I know what my thoughts look like.

Zeus better have threatened Eros into doing it. Even with all his toe-raggery and his abandonment, I couldn't believe my son would do this to me, take the thing in the world I was best at, where I was confident and beautiful, and turn it into a place where I was weak. Changing sex for me – it wasn't the intent, but it was the fucking tragedy.

The sex itself was physically fine. Anchises lay on top of me. He did not last long.

I will not play the game of who deserves their horrors. If suffering were an event in Apollo's Olympics, I wouldn't win, and I know that. I wasn't snuck up on. I wasn't tricked. I wasn't attacked. I didn't have bruises the day after.

None of that means I wanted it.

He was still inside me when my thinking mind came back, and the acid began rising in my throat as I realised what had been done.

He fell asleep on top of me.

I wasn't gentle in removing him. I threw his body from mine. I would've liked it to hit the wall, but the floor was hard enough.

I left him a note to explain the situation: we didn't make love. *We* didn't have sex. Sex occurred.

He didn't get to claim me, didn't get some badge of honour for bedding the goddess Aphrodite. He wasn't allowed to be happy it had happened. He wasn't allowed to brag.

I didn't want him. Somebody made me.

Do I get to be angry now?

Anchises Note I

Hello Anchises,

You were correct on your third guess. I am, in fact, the goddess Aphrodite. Unfortunately, this means you will not be marrying a nice princess from Phrygia. I'm sure you'll cope with the disappointment somehow. If nothing else, it will save you from telling your wife.

My true identity is to remain our secret. I mean it, Anchises. Should you break my trust, you will find yourself struck by one of Zeus' lightning bolts. I hope that's clear.

Hugs and kisses,
Aphrodite
XOXO

Aphrodite XXIII

I spent hours with my attendants afterwards, to put my face back on. I only have one, and it has to look perfect.

Then, a visit to my son. The oldest one. It wasn't the point. It wasn't the war. But you can't just do that to me and expect to get away with it.

I took him honey cakes because that felt like something mothers do.

'Eros, sweetheart!'

He paled. Good. 'Mummy. What are you doing here?'

'Can't a mother come to visit her son?'

'Zeus—' Of course it was Zeus. It's always fucking Zeus.

'Here, I brought you cake.'

'I'm not hungry.'

'It's your favourite. Eat.'

'Mummy—'

'Eat!'

And then, when he had a good amount of honey over his face and hands, I released the bees. Don't get me wrong, I wasn't trying to kill my son by setting bees on him, but I wanted him to hurt. He was meant to help me. He was meant to make it easier for me with the gods. He was supposed to love me, and he took away my favourite thing in the world.

Hence bees.

Only a couple of dozen, but that was enough. He waved his hands to get them off, and a couple duly stung him. At least *they* knew their purpose.

'Mummy, it hurts!'

'You should think about how your arrows feel, then.'

I left him to his bees. He used to be such a fan of bees.

Then I went to deal with the consequences of his actions.

I was pregnant.

I knew I was pregnant when I took the bees.

Anchises Note II

Hello Anchises,

This is our son. His name is Aeneas. I have decided he is best raised with you. You are to keep him safe, Anchises. He is to be trained in poetry and the arts. He is also to be trained in battle. He may have a specific knack with a bow and arrow – it runs in my family – but if not, do not overly concern yourself with the matter. Choose disciplines in which he excels and ensure that he remains committed to them. He will need them.

He probably won't turn into a dragon, but pray to me should that occur. It is more within my realm of parenting than yours.

I will return for him when he is fully grown to deliver him to his majestic fate. You should be proud. Our son will shape history.

Hugs and kisses,
Aphrodite
XOXO

Aphrodite XXIV

Of course I was pregnant. When Zeus makes you sleep with some-one you don't want to, it's inevitable. Your punishment for standing up and standing out cannot be so fleeting.

I could have pulled the same trick I did after I gave things up with Hephaestus. I planned to, actually, and maybe this is where I should say something about knowing that Zeus would know there was something wrong if I didn't develop an infant, but I'm not that good at thinking ahead.

I wanted it out of me. I wanted it gone.

I only changed my mind for selfish reasons.

I went back to my cave. My sisters tried to stop me, but not very hard. I think they could sense the lightning bolt I had strapped to my back. Zeus threatened them often enough that they could probably smell it.

I found the child's thread quickly – I didn't know how much grace I had with my sisters – and, as I held it in my hands, ready to snap the line and save myself, my curiosity got the better of me. I ran my fingers down his future.

A boring childhood, a kingdom, a war, all the usual for the mortal child of a god, until—

A new kingdom. A new world. A different language. *Different gods.*

My son was going to leave this place, if I let him. He was going to start somewhere new, somewhere Zeus didn't have all the power, all the choices. He'd rebalance the scales, if I let him.

Fate was telling me to dream bigger.

If I could get this child through the war, and the thread grew so thin in places that it felt far from certain, then we could create more than I could even dream right now.

'Are you rooting for me?' I whispered to the threads.

'No,' my sisters answered.

But they didn't matter. The future mattered. Fate mattered, and for the first time ever, it felt like it was on my side.

We could do this, Aeneas and I. He could be more than a punishment or an embarrassment. He could be a victory. He would spread my gospel.

I'd never cared who won the war, only that it *destroyed* this terrible world and left a space in its wake, but if I let my son survive, and I moulded him the right way, he could be my prophet. He would be in the places I could not. He'd spread my word so far I could never be erased.

He wasn't moving inside me, not yet, but I knew he was there. All I wanted was to rip him out of me, save myself the pain, the disgrace, the sign of weakness for everyone to see.

If I did that, I'd be free again – as free as I ever was. I wouldn't have to answer Hera's questions, listen to her brag about how she was better at pregnancy than me. I wouldn't have to nod when Hestia invited the infant to dinner. I wouldn't have to tolerate Athena smirking or Zeus nodding every time he saw my stomach, knowing he'd put me down once again.

I could save myself from all of it. I could win this round.

Or I could keep the baby and win the war.

I chose the war.

The circumstance of my son's conception didn't make people kinder; they didn't find an unknown well of sympathy simply because I didn't want to conceive. They laughed at me. They raised eyebrows. They judged the pregnant woman, and I couldn't say a fucking word because that would've only made me look weaker.

I told Ares the plan for the boy – only I couldn't say the boy, because there was no way of me knowing it was a boy, and I'd stretched the feminine intuition line so thin by that point it was practically transparent – and it made as much sense to him as the rest of my ideas did.

He supported me, but he didn't like looking at me. I got that – I didn't like looking at me either, not with my body stretched and bloated and feeling like it didn't belong to me – but that didn't stop it hurting.

I named the baby Aeneas because I liked the sound of it, and I didn't think his father deserved a say in the matter. He was *my* legacy, not Anchises'. He was my future, my child, and I needed him to remember that.

Which all necessitated rather more mothering than I'd anticipated.

I attempted to raise him in Olympus. Really, I did. My attendants helped, but mortal babies cry *all the time*. And when you think you're done with that, they learn to *crawl*, and then they're endlessly trying to get into places where they can die. Especially when you're sleeping with the god of war, and the baby finds its way to an axe and tries to *lick* it. Especially when you're planning a war and every minute has to be spent making sure the mortals are in the right place at the right time and checking no one else has gone and changed Fate when you're not looking.

I couldn't do it all.

I managed to get one immortal child turned into a dragon, and pissed off another so much he betrayed me. What was I meant to do with a mortal? If I kept him with me, he'd die. Threads or no threads. He'd crawl into a fireplace or eat a sword or just . . . fall off Olympus, and I didn't want to go through what Hera did.

I sent the baby back to his father. With instructions, so I knew he'd be brought up the way I needed him to be. That was better, I thought. He'd learn how to interact with other mortals, and he'd need that to be a leader.

I did visit him, though, to check he was learning the things he needed to learn, and to tell him the stories he needed to tell.

'Mummy was born at the end of one great civilisation, and at the beginning of another—' he recited, carefully.

'And there was a storm, as the kings met over the oceans, and their blades were shining as they clashed together, shining brighter than their eyes, but not as bright as—'

'You! Not as bright as you.'

'That's right, and they were distracted, the stupid kings, they didn't see the water below them, as something was rising from the sea foam—'

'How did you rise, Mummy? Was it like a wave?'

And I couldn't tell him I nearly drowned, could I? Not this child still with sticky fingers who didn't know how much pain he caused me. So I lied.

'On a shell, sweetness. I rose from the waves on a beautiful scallop shell.'

'But shells are so small, and you're so big. How did you fit? Or were there loads of shells?'

'It was one big shell.'[72]

Aeneas and I hammered out the details of my new history like this, his childish curiosity the perfect driver. I was magic in his eyes, and that was all I needed.

He grew, and the war came closer.

Everyone could feel it. They named the champions I knew they were going to name, and I only had to manipulate a couple of them into new alliances to make sure they were dragged in too. Apollo was running around trying to shore up the walls at Troy. Zeus was muttering that everyone was coming for him. It was in the air, but it was not here yet.

I grew impatient.

'Ares, everything's ready. How do we get it going?'

'It's on your girl now, Foamy.'

My girl was happy enough with her husband. She wasn't about to go waltzing into the arms of some stranger. I needed to make it happen. It had to be public. And it had to be someone else's fault.

When Zeus announced the wedding,[73] I saw my chance. It was simple enough to distract Hermes and steal Eris' invite from his bag.

The goddess of discord never did like being left out.

---

[72] I had to have so many doves to pull my chariot. They haunted me. I wasn't going to end up in the same position with shells. —A

[73] Not Helen's. That would have been too simple. It was the marriage of Peleus, a mortal who has never been relevant, and Thetis, a nereid who never would have been relevant if it weren't for the particularly awkward prophecy proclaiming her son would be greater than his father. —A

Eris I

Discord is thoroughly underrated. Sure, I'm not going to be winning any singing contests with the Muses – though wouldn't it be a laugh if I tried? – but discord, that shit's important. Every little fight about who does what and when and why, that's all discord, and we fucking need it, because without discord there's never any change and we get stuck with the same dictator for centuries.

Oh wait. That's exactly what happened.

Zeus had a big shiny lightning bolt waiting for anyone who disagreed with him, so they put on their best smiles and nodded and said yes, sir; no, sir; we agree, Mr Zeus sir; and I ended up a *dea non grata* at the big Olympic weddings because I refused to do it like everyone else.

It's funny that they think *banning* me from places is the way to stop me going to them. That's like trying to shame Aphrodite for having sex.

Even if Ares hadn't told me, it's not as if the Olympians are subtle, is it? They were all going round reading *their* invites and chattering about what gifts they were going to bring and what clothes they were going to wear and what songs the Muses were going to sing, promising to have a perfectly lovely, perfectly forgettable day out.

I tried just walking into the wedding – didn't think anyone would be monitoring the damn gate, did I? But Hera had Argus[74] stuck at the front, hundred eyes and all, and there's no way of sneaking past him. I've tried.

'Invite only.'

Bah.

I climbed a tree up and out of the way so I could get a good view. What's the point of making trouble if you don't get to see it? And I was going to make trouble. I wasn't exactly hidden, but then they were distracted "enjoying the special day" and just assumed I was following instructions. Like I've ever done that in my life.

I let them get married and all, at the wedding. From the sour-lemon look on the bride's face, I figured Thetis would provide me delicious arguments for years without me getting involved at all. No point getting in the way of that.

I don't know what Thetis' issue with Peleus was, but it was glorious. I didn't speak to him, obviously, because I was busy hiding up a tree, but she didn't either. He tried to reach out and touch her arm, and she snatched herself away. She'd been moving her chair further and further away from him until she was jammed right up next to Zeus, who was all kinds of confused about it. I think he had a bit of a hard-on, but it didn't last long. Hera hooked her ankle round the back of his seat and yanked it away. And they thought they needed little old me to cause a scene!

Peleus tried to pour some wine for his new wife. She immediately knocked it on the floor.

'Whoops.'

They grow up so fast.

It was *beautiful*. He got more and more uncomfy as the day

---

[74] Hera's best friend and bodyguard. Doesn't do anything without her say-so. —A

went on. Zeus'd told him all this guff about this prize he was getting for being such a swell guy, but it turned out his prize wanted to punch him in the face. He gave up talking and drank more wine.

Thetis grabbed a cup too, only she didn't stop pouring, not till the jug was empty and her cup overfloweth'd all over Peleus' lap. She glared at him, after, half daring him to ask if it was an accident. She clicked her fingers, and someone came running up with another jug for her.

I think they were pleased when I got involved. Took the focus off the unhappy couple.

I'd made a little tag for the apple. I was quite proud of it. I didn't bother with arts and crafts that much – it was Athena's thing, and she pretended to be all gracious about people doing it, but she'd stare over your shoulder and say all patronisingly, *That's not how I would have done it, but it's a try* – but this tag was good. I'd nicked some gold and copper from the forges and twisted them round into a lovely flower, then stuck it in the apple to hold down my note.

For the fairest.

You don't need so many words to start a fight. You want it ambiguous. Then everyone can go and fill in the cheeky gaps you left them.

I tossed the apple right at the Muses' instruments. I thought it'd make a nice dramatic thunk coming off the lyre or something, but I'm not the goddess of *throwing*, am I – that's again, somehow, Athena, with her rock-chucking habit – and I missed by a long way. It hit the bride on the forehead and landed square on the table in front of her.

Hera reached out and grabbed it, eyes daring anyone to comment. She did that all the time, making those little dares, she was always surprised when people took her up on them. Though, to be fair, it was *technically* her apple to begin with.

I'm no council member but any god can recognise the apples of the Hesperides when they see them, them being gold and immortality-granting and all.

Though they were more orange-gold than they were gold-gold, if you catch my drift. And more orange-shaped than apple-shaped, but Zeus decreed them golden apples, so there we were with our orange oranges we called golden apples.

Being in charge of the dramatic arts and all, the Muses realised something was happening and did a little roll of the notes before cutting it completely. The rest of the room stopped talking, until it was just Ares barrelling on through with his conversation. Aphrodite whispered something to him – wish I could have heard what – and he shut up too.

Hera read the tag out loud. The Olympians did that. I was *gutted* when reading in your head got all fashionable. You know how many fights people avoid by reading in their heads?

'For the fairest,' she announced.

She didn't drop her voice when she realised what she was saying. But she gripped her hand into her thigh tight enough I reckoned she'd draw blood.

Aphrodite snatched the apple, all smug, like. 'I believe that one's mine.'

'It's mine.'

'And what does the note say?' She smiled her most winning smile.

Hera did not appreciate it. 'Precisely. It is my apple.'

'The note specifies that the apple is for the fairest,' Athena said, looming behind them. 'In that case, it can only be mine.'

Aphrodite laughed. Hera laughed. In my tree, I laughed.

Athena stomped her foot. 'What's the laughter in aid of? I am the best example of fairness that we have,' she said.

No amount of planning could've made it tastier. There was no guessing the great and wise Athena didn't know there were two meanings of the word *fair*. I jammed my fist in my mouth to stop myself snorting. Like, they all knew it was me who threw the thing, but it'd be nice for my hide if they didn't think about it until this whole affair was resolved and they were mad at someone else instead.

Behind the three of them, Zeus *twinkled*. I know that look. That's my look. He stole my fucking look. The very essence of mischief, and he nicked it right off my face.

'It seems like a competition is in order,' he said. 'Do we have any more entrants? Any other lovely girls who believe themselves to be the fairest?'

Scenes broke out across the room. Tiny pockets, microcosms of relationships as they checked against the people they cared about. Me? Do I stand up? Is it worth it? Dionysus nudged Ariadne[75] and pointed up at the front, but she stuck her tongue out and nudged for him to do the same. They collapsed into giggles. I liked those two. Good energy.

'Why just women?' Apollo hollered. 'Am I not the most fair?' He was leaning on the back left leg of his chair and no other. He spread his arms lazily in front of the Muses, so they'd know to agree with him, and, well, I couldn't have that much accord going on. I breathed across my palm, carrying the air over to them, and they immediately started bickering over which of *them* was the fairest.

Apollo looked at his sister. She rolled her eyes.

---

[75] Remember Semele's child whose life I saved? That's him. Ariadne is his wife. Lovely couple. Will drink you out of house and home. —A

352

'Closing bidding in five,' Zeus said.

'Four.'

I looked around. Anyone?

'Three.'

The Muses were still arguing.

'Two.'

No one? Come on. Three might be a crowd but four's a party.

'One.'

And that was it. Competitors, take your marks.

'Who will be judging the competition?' Athena asked.

'Zeus,' Hera said.

'Your husband can't judge the contest – he'll just pick you.'

'He's *your* father,' Aphrodite said.

'And yours!'

'Yes, obviously, because my husband has excellent taste,' Hera said, demonstrating her uncanny ability to only hear what she wanted to hear. I don't think she'd ever accused her husband of good taste before.

'No.'

'What does Zeus being her husband have to do with fairness?' Athena answered.

Zeus finally took pity on her, explained that intellect and ability didn't mean shit to him and he was mostly concerned with how good his daughters look naked.

She turned bright red, but Athena's nothing if not a competitive monster, so she dug her feet into the ground and set her shoulders like she was going to throw a rock at someone and immediately started scheming.

This could not have gone any better for me.

'Does anyone know of any *just* men?' Aphrodite shouted. She *definitely* looked like she was scheming. And what do you know, who happened to pipe up but her very own boyfriend?

'There's Paris,' Ares said. He couldn't have sounded more like a plant if he'd tried, but everyone was distracted defending their honour or doing their hair, so he mostly got away with it. I knew they were cheating, but I rep cheating. All hail the cheats of the world – that's what I say.

'What do *you* know about mortals?' Athena demanded.

'I fought him, didn't I?'

'And he's still counted among the living?'

'Fuck me, Athena, that almost sounded like a compliment.'

'Purely accidental, I assure you.'

'He said he'd give a prize to any bull that could defeat his prize bull, and I was bored.'[76]

'Son,' Hera said. 'Did you find a bull to do this—'

'Not exactly.'

'You turned into a bull, because you wanted to fight a real bull, and you thought that was an honourable use of your time?' his mother said, getting judgier with every passing word. Sounded like a fun afternoon to me.

'At least I didn't fuck any swans.'[77]

Which set off its own beautiful wave of everyone fighting and shouting and pointing and playing a big game of who fucked who as which animal, and Hera disappeared off for a moment and came back with her face wiped down and redrawn and looking more competitive than Athena ever had.

---

[76] Ares didn't even question it when I asked him to do that particular favour. —A

[77] Technically, Zeus fucked someone *as* a swan, but no one was ever too concerned about that detail. —A

If you ever end up in Olympus on, I don't know, a day trip or something, and you find yourself stuck in a conversation you think might get you killed, it's a good idea to know the weak spots, you know? Tell Apollo Troy is on fire. Tell Artemis she looks sexy today. Tell Hera her husband likes fucking mortal women as a variety of wild animals. We all knew. You've just got to use them sparingly, else they'll wear out.

Ares definitely knew what he was doing, is what I'm saying. The swan thing was an easy out. I wondered what he was covering up, but all lies come out in the wash, and the longer they stew, the better they taste when they do.

'ANYWAY,' Ares shouted. 'Point is, even after he found out I was a god-bull and not a bull-bull, Paris gave me my prize.'

And because it was Ares and people don't think of Ares *lying*, they took that as that. And because they think Aphrodite's brain is in her genitals, they took her tongue going into his ear after to be a sex thing and not a reward for a job well done. It just *happened* to be the case that Paris was also a prince of Troy, the only city with more divine buy-in than Athens, and definitely bigger walls. Those two were definitely plotting, though no one else seemed to see it.

Paris was duly fetched by Hermes and spent much of his time at the wedding blinking and propping his own jaw back up.

The three competitors lined up in front of him.

If it was a *fair* competition, then Aphrodite would win and it wouldn't even be a question. She defined beauty. She stood up and pointed to herself and told the world *this*. *This is what beauty is*. And because most people are more accepting than yours truly, they believed her.

But Hera was pissed because her husband fucked a swan and

she couldn't take it out on him anymore – the last time she did, he tied her naked to a mountain for three days – but she could take it out on everyone else.

And Athena was embarrassed and competitive, which is the recipe for her to start throwing rocks.

Even without all that, they'd have cheated.

I love my family.

'Paris, you have been summoned here today due to your great reputation for fairness and kindness among your fellow men,' Zeus intoned. Paris mumbled something about it being an incredible honour and him trying his best. 'We need you to judge a contest between these lovely girls.'

He gestured at the three goddesses. Hera waved. Athena glared. Aphrodite blew a kiss.

He looked like he might throw up. Then Aphrodite waved at him. One breast escaped her clothes. Accidentally, I'm sure.

'So?' Zeus said. 'Which is the fairest?'

They took new positions. Hera mimed rocking a baby. Athena tensed her muscles. Aphrodite fluttered her eyelashes.

'They all have so many wonderful qualities,' he said slowly.

'Give us an answer, boy. We don't have all day.' Technically we had all of eternity. Yay for immortality.

He paled even further. 'It's just that, when mortals judge things for the gods, normally someone gets angry and hurts them.'

'Piffle,' Zeus said. 'Name one time.'

'Midas.[78] With the ears.'

'Hey, he looked great with those ears,' Apollo shouted from his seat. 'They suited him. Because he had the hearing of an *ass*.'

---

[78] Mortal. Judged a music contest. Decided against Apollo. Regretted it when Apollo gave him the ears of a mule. —A

Zeus conceded the point. 'The girls will promise not to hurt you. Won't you, girls?'

Athena stepped forwards. 'In addition to not hurting you, I can offer you the guidance you need to create a military and diplomatic empire, so that your legacy will be remembered around this world forever.'[79]

She stepped back. Her chiton fell off. Apropos of nothing.

Hera stepped forwards. 'In addition to guaranteeing your safety, I will ensure your family becomes happier and stronger than any other. You will grow to be an old man surrounded by people who love you and children who care for you. Your lineage will be known as the best our world has ever known.'[80]

Bribery is the easiest form of cheating. To win this, they had to go *big*.

Aphrodite had been building her bribe for two decades.

The others didn't stand a chance.

She slipped the last of her clothes off. She walked up very close to him, leaned in towards his ear, slow enough her lips could trail his neck on the way up. She was the only one of the goddesses who didn't tower over him.

'In addition to your safety, I can offer you the most beautiful woman in the world.'

He didn't even pause to consider it. It all came out in half a bloody breath.

'Aphrodite. I declare it. Aphrodite is the fairest.'

She smiled beatifically. No one clapped.

Paris turned to Zeus. 'Can I go get her *now*?'

---

[79] Sounds like it might cause a war anyway, doesn't it? –A
[80] High possibility of war from that one too. —A

News Report

WIFE OF PRINCE MISSING AFTER "FLIRTATIOUS" & "SEDUCTIVE" BEHAVIOUR

In a move that has shocked the area, the princess of Sparta has, allegedly, been kidnapped from her husband Menelaus' home in Sparta during a visit from a foreign prince now identified as Paris of Troy.

Witnesses report a previously pleasant evening in the palace. The delegation from Troy arrived and were greeted warmly. They responded in kind and were henceforth invited to take dinner and lodgings in the palace that night. It was at this dinner that affairs began to escalate.

Menelaus reports his wife's behaviour as unusual, stating that she was particularly talkative that evening, asking Paris all manner of questions, such as his name, age, and whether he could play that zither he was carrying. At this point, he was interrupted by his brother, who emphasised the flirtatious manner in which his sister-in-law spoke. 'I know now it was a seduction.'

Paris played the zither for her, whereupon she clapped and danced. It is unclear whether others joined her in this endeavour. She retired to her rooms after dinner, and her absence was only noted the next morning when her maids arrived to work on her hair.

There are reports that two figures were observed escaping the palace together that night.

It is not our place to speculate, but the correct conclusion appears obvious.[81]

---

[81] Paris joined the Trojans into the web. I'd done it. Hold on tight, kids, we're going to war. —A

THE WAR

TROY	GREECE
PARIS	MENELAUS
HELEN	AGAMEMNON
HECTOR	ACHILLES
SARPEDON	PATROCLUS
AENEAS	ODYSSEUS

Thetis I

Do I have to talk about it?

Fine.

The first prophecy came as a blessing to me, as I stood like some prize catch in the middle of a circle of Olympians. Zeus had decided he was in love with me and we should copulate. Then Poseidon remembered I lived in his realm and so technically I belonged to him and he wanted to keep me, so they competed to see who had the right to my body.

The whole thing had devolved into them shouting like gulls. Mine. Mine. Mine.

I didn't hear what Hermes said to them, but it made both kings spring away from me like I was on fire.

'That's that then,' Zeus said. 'Off you pop.'

What did those words even mean in that order?

'He's suggesting you go home,' a girl told me. She looked young but you can't know with the gods. 'The silly bear's all worried, so he won't be wanting to . . . be friends with you any longer.'

'What did Hermes say?'

They all looked away from me then, the gods. Eyes down and to the side, or up and to the side, or directly at my chest, even. Anywhere but meeting my gaze.

'No one?' I demanded.

It was Aphrodite who cracked first. 'The oracle just announced a prophecy. Your son will be greater and more powerful than his father.'

'That's it?'

I swear I saw her smile, then, but it was gone in an instant. 'That's it.'

'They'd leave all this for a prophecy?'

'Quite.'

I didn't need to be dismissed again. I swam home, thanking the oracle and the universe for my good luck. What a wonderful thing a prophecy could be.

My good mood lasted until I found out about my wedding. I was informed, along with the rest of the world, when the invites went out.

My lucky prophecy, apparently, made me too much of a loose cannon to be allowed to make my own reproductive decisions, so I came to marry Peleus, a man with the personality of a damp leaf.

He was mortal, at least. He'd die eventually and I could come home.

The wedding was the wedding. Aphrodite won the dick-swinging contest. Even though I was the bride, it became official that I wasn't the most beautiful woman there. That was accurate. My skin was dry. My scalp hurt. I didn't look like me. I should have been in the oceans with the other nereids.

I went to my new husband's home. He didn't know what to do with me, and he didn't ask. He took me on a tour of the palace, kept listing the names of all the rooms. I didn't know the difference, and I didn't care to learn.

'You won't get sand everywhere, will you?' he asked finally.

'If I get my way, never.'

Marriage wasn't optional, but cohabitation was.

The night we were married, I was drunk enough that I didn't cringe at the idea of having sex with him. I pushed him onto the bed and got it over with as fast as possible. He made a lot of noises, and I made none. I'm haunted by the sound of our skin clapping together.

It was only necessary once. Fertility runs in the family. There is a joke, on Olympus, that it's the only thing nymphs are good for.

I still didn't know if I wanted to be a mother, but the way I understood it, once I had a boy then Zeus would count the whole prophecy as fulfilled and he'd calm down about it. I could move out and go home and wait for Peleus to die and mark all of this as one blip in an otherwise happy life.

I didn't count on loving my son.

'He's perfect,' I said.

'The best of both of us,' Peleus said.

What did he think was the best of me? I wondered. But I didn't disagree. Our son was perfect; I won't begrudge the man his part in creating him.

I didn't count on his birth being met by another grand pronouncement from the oracle. He would be the greatest fighter of the Greeks, she said, but only if he was allowed to burn. His fire would be short and bright or a long, slow smoulder—

'I'm from the sea; what are you talking to me about fire for?' I snapped at Hermes. He was the messenger. He was used to being shot at.

'He will live a long and tedious life of no renown, or he will live a short life, greater and more famous than any hero thus far.'

362

'He gets a choice?'

'He gets a choice,' he said.

'Why would anyone possibly choose the second one?'

Thus began my crash course in boys, heroes, and prophecies, and my doomed attempts at avoiding all of the above. 'I'm calling him Achilles,' I told my husband.

'I thought we might name him after me. Peleus is a strong name.'

'Achilles.' It meant *pain*. A warning to our son to make good choices.

I swam down to Hades with him – all rivers are connected if you go deep enough – giving him the air from my lungs when he needed it. I took him all the way to the river Styx. If the living can withstand its current, it makes them invulnerable. After our visit, my son only needed to guard the spot on his ankle where I'd held him.

When we got home, his father proudly told me about the tutors he'd found to teach our son how to die. In return, I told him about the prophecy.

'Fantastic! Our son's going to be a hero!'

'He's going to die.'

'Everyone dies, but not everyone dies a hero.'

I never returned to the palace after that. I couldn't sit there and watch as my son was trained to die young.

His father sent Achilles to visit me, down in the water. He told me about his lessons, how much he loved his tutors, and how he thought swords were fun but running was the best. He told me when Peleus started adopting other boys.

'So I have company!'

So he'd have his own army to follow him.

He told me when a boy called Patroclus[82] came to live with them and how he was his favourite but he wasn't very good at fighting.

'Maybe you should start a farm together,' I said. 'Then he won't have to do any fighting.'

'I have to fight.'

'Why?'

'It's who I am.'

Pain. Achilles. I didn't name him wrong.

'There's a war coming!' he announced one day.

'You don't have to look so happy about it, kiddo.'

'Hey, I'm not a kid anymore.'

He couldn't grow a beard yet. He tried, but he couldn't. When he slept, he flung his arms and legs all over the place.

'You'll always be a kid to me.'

'I'm going to fight in a war.'

'You absolutely are not.'

He tried arguing, but I wouldn't have it. It was too soon. The oracle could find someone else's son to demand in the name of glory. Mine would come home and he would live a long and boring life if it was the last thing I did.

I dragged him by the ear to the husband of one of my sisters. I brought his friend Patroclus too, for company, dragging him with my other hand. My sister's husband adopted girls like Peleus did boys. He was bemused but not unwilling to hide the two of them among his charges.

'I don't want to wear girls' clothes,' Achilles pouted.

'And I don't want you to die.'

'Mum—'

---

[82] Relevant because Achilles decided he was. —A

'Please. Stay safe.'

It might have been enough, were my son not plagued by prophecies. The oracle was busy in those days, shoving out another one every time someone looked away, so often that the very timbre of them was changing. Gone was the dramatic dactylic hexameter that told me my reproductive choices were a world event: now it was a big day if the prophecy even had a meter, though the language was clearer for that, the instructions sharper.

I found I quite liked vague. Especially when the oracle turned round one day and simply told Agamemnon he wouldn't win this war without my son. Achilles wasn't even *born* when Menelaus married Helen and all the suitors made their vow, but Agamemnon wasn't worried about that. He hunted Achilles down and made a good show of "tricking" him into revealing his identity.

Truth be told, I think my son was pleased to be tricked. He boarded the boat with a smile and a wave and his best friend at his side, like this was just another adventure in the woods.

My son, off to die in the war.

The oracle said so.

Anchises Note III

Anchises, darling,

It's me once more. The goddess Aphrodite.

As you may remember, we lay together some years ago. I left you a note to explain my conditions. I must ask, can you read, Anchises? Perhaps not, in which case all of this will be nonsense to you, but on the off chance that you are stupid instead of illiterate, I will explain.

You were not to tell people that we had laid together. I know that you knew this, once upon a time, because our son reported it to me when I came to check on his progress. He asked was I not proud of him?

How dare you force me to answer that question, and how dare you fail to uphold it? I am not a drunken brag to people you don't even know. You did not earn or win me. You are an irrelevance in this story.

366

By the time this arrives, your punishment will have been meted. I hope the lightning hurts.

I trust that Aeneas' lessons continue well. I will be most displeased if he drops behind. The war is starting. Keep him out of it. He is not ready yet. I imagine you will have learned the benefits of following instructions.

Hugs and kisses,
Aphrodite
XOXO

Aphrodite XXV

To be honest, I'm surprised I got away with what I did with the oracle. I had so many overly complicated plans on the go that required exactly the right people to do exactly what I wanted them to, but the most effective thing I did was hide in a cave at Delphi and whisper some extra information when they were trying to channel the python.

It wasn't wrong information, to be clear, even if Achilles' choice was never much of a choice. I couldn't risk people doubting the oracle and losing my outlet for spreading information.

So, I turned Fate into prophecies, which was exactly the kick Agamemnon needed to circle the globe and pick up all the key players, regardless of their feelings on the matter.

Odysseus pretended to be quite mad. He ripped off his clothing and made to plough the beach at Ithaca. So determined was he that the blades sparked off the rocky shores. This was easily dealt with by Agamemnon laying Odysseus' newborn baby in front of the blades. Odysseus recoiled, refused to mulch his only child, and his ruse was revealed.

Perfect. I needed him. Athena loved him.

Achilles pretended to be a woman for about five minutes, but he too was packed up and shipped off.

It would have been easy, if I was the only one interfering, but that was never going to happen. I was building a war around the personal, which meant there were just as many people running away from the clash as towards it. Apollo, in particular, spent the days belching out prophecies, and the nights desperately fighting to prevent them.

He knew as well as I did what the destruction of Troy would bring. It was the cornerstone of our civilisation, the civilisation he embodied more than the rest of us. These people loved his arts, his sports, his sun, his oracle. He was worshipped and revered everywhere, second only to Zeus. There was no telling how much of it would carry into my new world.

Apollo's plan to avoid the war was much more simple than anything I ever managed. He waited until all the Greeks – Agamemnon's side – gathered in Mycenae, ready to make their attack, and decided he would never let them leave.

This was banned, of course. Zeus had quite clearly told everyone they weren't to interfere in the war. It was for the mortals to sort out on their own. This was met by a sea of innocent faces and a choir of, *War? What war?*

(Other than that proclamation, Zeus himself was remarkably neutral about the whole affair, which I probably should have questioned further, but, in my defence, Zeus was often an idiot.)

There are workarounds to most of Zeus' edicts, if you're willing to risk his temper at the end of it, and Apollo found one for this. He had Artemis imagine some slight against her from Agamemnon and used it as an excuse to stop the winds.[83] No wind meant no boats, which meant no soldiers, which meant no war.

---

[83]   She literally shot Zephyrus – the west wind – through the foot and stuck him to the floor. —A

Of course, it's not fair if the gods just do something to you and don't give you a way out, so Artemis did. She told Agamemnon she'd be happy to let the winds go, just as soon as he sacrificed his daughter to her.

The idea, I think, was that the bargain was so ridiculous that Agamemnon would never take it, and it worked. To begin with.

Agamemnon faltered. He wavered. He prevaricated. He told his troops there was nothing to be done. It was exactly what the twins wanted, but I'd come too far to lose now.

I waited until that evening, as the king lay in bed, on the precipice of Hypnos'[84] realm, and I appeared unto him.

'Your troops need you,' I whispered. 'You cannot let them down.'

'Iphigenia—' His daughter.

'Will die for a noble cause. Mycenae needs you.'

Agamemnon loved his daughter, don't doubt that, but he loved his country more.

That was the only lever I needed.

He told Iphigenia she'd be married to the up-and-coming hero, and he waited for her wedding day. She was primped and preened and decked in jewels, and she was walked to the altar by her beaming mother.

She said yes, yes, yes please, bless me, and, as she swore herself away, her father took a knife and drew it across her throat.

Iphigenia was dead, and Artemis had no more excuses to keep the winds still. I didn't like it, but it was done. My plan came unstuck.

The men sailed that evening.

Welcome to the Trojan War.

---

84 The god of sleep – too busy napping to do anything of relevance. Yawn. —A

The Trojan War: a Primer

In the red corner, we have ... The Trojans. They're the ones being attacked: why? Their prince, Paris, has run away with the beautiful Helen – married to another for many a year. Worse yet, for our boys in Troy, they don't have many allies. Some farms in the surrounding area, maybe, but other than that, the Trojans fight alone.

But surely, surely, you ask, they must have something going for them, and, dear punter, you're not wrong!

For one thing, their city – and its famous walls – were built by the gods! That's right – many years ago, Apollo and Poseidon came to Troy and built the city with their own hands – how's that for quality workmanship?*

*In the spirit of fairness, we must mention the prophecy that Troy will fall, but it's not come down yet, so who's to say today's the day?

So, who are our key players over in Troy? We've got:

- **Paris** – the prince who's run away with Helen.
- **Helen** – if it can be said that she is on any side at all – a woman of mystery, is Helen!
- **Hector** – the greatest fighter in Troy, and another prince to boot! If someone's going to lead these brave boys to victory, it's Hector.
- **Sarpedon** – a son of Zeus, but not much else is known about this one! It's said that he has huge experience with military campaigns, so we'll just have to wait and see what he comes up with . . .
- **Aeneas** – an outlier, but don't you go underestimating him! He does have a certain lovely lady for a mother, and we know now she's the fairest of them all.

Aaaaaaaaaaaand in the blue corner, we have . . . Greece!

It started off as the Mycenaeans, but they've done a good job on the recruitment over on this side. Couple of reluctant soldiers but they're all here now, and that's what matters! This is why you should take care when making oaths on the Styx, folks. It's serious stuff.

Why are they fighting? Because of love. Specifically, King Menelaus is missing his lady wife, Helen, and he has come to return her. Will love – and armies – truly conquer all?

They're on unfamiliar turf, but they more than make up for it in numbers!

And now, to take a look at the key players on their end:

- **Menelaus** – the spurned husband.
- **Agamemnon** – his brother, and the general in charge of recruitment. Some say the greatest of the Greeks, and that looks to be the case, until we get to . . .
- **Achilles!** – Swift in heel and fair in face, Achilles is young, yes, but already he's been making waves with his talent; beware, gentlefolks, if you go seeking his heart – he's still reeling from the death of his young bride, Iphigenia!
- **Patroclus** – a friend and fellow fighter of Achilles, he's been a great help supporting him through his grief.
- **Odysseus** – thinker and tactician; you better watch out for this one!

For now, the gods are claiming neutrality, by order of the king himself! But these viewers are interested to see how that plays out – after all, Apollo has already been sighted helping shore up the protections of his city, and can you blame anyone for wanting to protect their son?

All we can recommend now is to buckle up and enjoy the ride!

Aphrodite XXVI

We don't often speak of the first nine years of the Trojan War. This is because they were insufferably dull. It was a siege – an endless siege against a city with impenetrable walls – even if it took the men a little while to realise that.

At the beginning, for many of the mortals, this was an adventure, a chance to cast their names into the fabled cast of the heroes before them, to become the new Heracles, Theseus, or Jason. I even heard one of them mention Cadmus as someone to aspire to, despite Cadmus' hatred of both the gods and heroics, which just goes to show what happens to your legacy if you don't control it.

They took detours, stretched out the beginning. They revelled in the small glories, confident of what would come. They laughed, they drank, they told stories. Even when the portents around them shouted that this war would last ten years, their humour stayed strong.

When they did land, an excitable young man, newly married, jumped off his ship, practically sprinting to shore, so that he might claim the glory of being the first Greek in Ilium.

He was promptly shot. Fatally. His new wife traded the rest of her life for a few more hours with him – Persephone found the request romantic – and they went into the pyre together.

Which is all to say the mood dimmed after that. The adventure was gone, and the soldiers were sullen as they assembled their tents and settled in for the wait.

Nine years, they waited outside the walls of Troy. Nine years of the gods doing as they were told and not getting involved. Nine years of me running around and stoking every flame I could as they dimmed around me.

And what did the mortals do?

They played dice. A lot of dice. Achilles *always* won – a fact I attribute to his mother helping him. What she was hoping to achieve by having her son endlessly vex the rest of his army? I don't know, but every day, there would be another shout from her little darling.

'I have a four.'

'You always have a four,' the loser of the day complained.

'What do you have?'

'Nothing.'

'It looks like a two.'

'Stop looking at my dice!'

And why was I, the instigator of this whole cursed affair, watching this? Because there was nothing else to do. I'd led the horse to water and it refused to fucking drink. Not only did it refuse to drink, but as it sat in front of the water, it grew ever less interested in it, started asking questions. Was the water really so important? Maybe the water at home tastes better, actually?

Even Helen, my Helen, was doing it. Sure, she prayed, and she was all very nice about it, but when I went to check on her, on her side of the walls, she started making faces at me.

'Paris is brill and all, but is he really all that, you know?'

I raised this girl from nothing, turned her into an icon, and she was picking up slang. I blame Apollo.

'I chose him for you, remember? He's the other half of your soul, as it was in the earliest days of man.' Never said I wasn't a liar.

'You said that, but I was thinking, maybe I have two other halves, like a triangle.'

'That's not how halves work, Helen.'

'I suppose.'

'Where's this coming from?'

'There's someone else.'

How? I'd locked her in a city with impregnable walls and personally married her to one of the princes. There was a war currently being waged over her. Who else could she want?

'He's a fighter too.'

'You're a fighter.'

She grinned. 'I know, but his shoulders— My goddess, you should see his shoulders, and he's been so kind to me since I got here. He's been showing me around the palace and—'

The palace. For fuck's sake. That's who'd dare to make a move on her when she was married to a prince of Troy. The Prince of Troy.

'You're in love with Hector.' Shit. 'Okay, Helen, you stay here, and I'll fix this, okay?'

'Where else would I go?'

I could fix this and, fortunately, my solution was just down the hall.

'Paris, you get your arse out here right now,' I shouted.

'Aphrodite,' he gushed. 'It's been so long.'

'Make love to your wife, Paris.'

'Pardon?'

'Helen. Make love to her. Tell her she's beautiful. Buy her some presents. It's not fucking ship-building.'

'The war—'

'Sex, Paris! Go have sex.'

When I decided to start a war based on everyone's personal lives, it didn't occur to me that I'd have to do bloody couples' counselling.

Paris and Helen disappeared into a bedroom together and came out holding hands for long enough for everyone to see them and say aww and ahh, and remember why they were fighting this war in the first place. That sorted the Trojan side, at least.

The Greeks were more of a problem. You need two sides to make a war, and I could hardly tell Agamemnon and Achilles to get it on. I mean, I could, but it wouldn't achieve much.

'Ares, how do I make the Greeks start fighting?'

'Remind them that's the reason they're here.'

'How?'

He shrugged. 'Stir some shit up.'

I didn't know how much shit there was left to stir, and I was getting desperate. My stolen lightning bolts felt more and more like an option, but they were my prized possession and I only had two left. I didn't want to use them unless I had to. I recited all the connections in my head. Agamemnon loves Menelaus who loves Helen who loves Paris who loves Hector who loves Helen. I love Helen, and Apollo loves Hector, and Athena loves Diomedes, and Zeus loves Sarpedon. What was I missing? There was enough love there. Enough tangled stories breaking and fraying. *Who* was I missing?

I skirted the edges of the Greek encampment, eyes open, ears open, looking for my missing link, and he was generous enough to shout for me.

'A four again – I believe that makes the victory mine.'

Achilles, with his mother always standing behind him. Achilles, who was too young and too comfortable and too in love with the boy he came here with, to fight too hard in a war he had no stakes in.

That, I could fix.

I dressed up as one of the women they had serving them and held a conversation with myself outside his tent.

'Who is this Helen anyway? What must she be to be worth all of this?' I could practically hear Ares shouting in my ear that this isn't what he meant about stirring shit up, but it worked for me. 'No one can be that beautiful, right?'

It only took a couple of days of this before Thetis came scurrying up to me.

'I need a favour.'

'What favour?'

'Achilles wants to meet Helen.'

'*Why?*' I had to feign some innocence.

Thetis made a face. I knew it well. How do you explain the thoroughly unreasonable actions of someone you love and have promised to support?

'He'd like to understand how the war came to pass.'

'So what do you want from me?'

'Can you sneak Helen out of the city?'

Over the years, I've become something of an expert in sneaking people in and out of places where they're not meant to be. Young lovers, primarily, but old lovers get their share of scandal in too. It's proven very helpful in my extracurricular activities.

'Why should I?' It would be suspicious if I gave up too easily. Olympians don't do favours for nereids just because they ask nicely.

'You owe me.'

'For ruining your wedding?'

'For starting the war that will kill my son.'

People got so caught up on the *starting* the war element, when they remembered to credit me at all, that they forgot about all the hard work I put into making the war *continue*.

'Okay,' I said. 'I'll get Helen; you get Achilles.'

Despite all the actual kidnapping and running away that had happened in her past, Helen wasn't closely guarded. It was the work of moments to slip into the palace and crook a finger in her direction.

'Aphrodite!' Her face lit up.

'I have someone who wants to meet you.'

'Oooh, exciting!' She was clearly bored. She'd woven a hundred tiny plaits in her hair behind one ear, armouring that half of her head. So much for Paris' latest seduction.

Thetis had decided the meeting was best conducted in a cave only accessible by ocean – never my favourite journey to make, but I organised a boat for Helen and I – and she was waiting there with Achilles when we arrived.

We stepped inside. It felt almost like a wedding, me standing behind Helen and Thetis behind Achilles, but they shook us off quickly enough, stepped out of our shadows, close enough that they could reach one another if they held out their fingertips, but they didn't. They just looked, perfectly still, as though there was a river running between them.

Achilles coughed. 'So, you're Helen.' It was meant to sound cool, nonchalant, but he didn't pull it off.

'And you are Achilles.'

'Yes.'

'You're older than I expected,' she said.

He looked baffled by this. He'd been a boy when he came to Troy. Even after nine years, he was very much a youth. He was long, and lean, though his cheeks remained round beneath his beard. 'I am—'

'I was married before you were even born. Your parents' wedding *ended my marriage*. You're meant to be a baby. Or am I just old now?'

'You're beautiful.'

'Heard it.'

'What?' Achilles was used to a certain amount of respect. He was a prince, a demigod, a child of more prophecies than you could count. He wasn't prepared for an adult woman arching an eyebrow and questioning him. He wasn't prepared for Helen.

'I am Helen.' She waved her hands vaguely. 'Of Troy, now, I suppose. My beauty is such that it has torn the world in half. It has lasted nine years of war and counting, and kept you who have never even met me' she shuddered – '*camping*. I was kidnapped as a child for my beauty. I was born from the egg of a swan—'

'My mother is a goddess,' Achilles interrupted.

Helen flicked her eyes to Thetis, then back to her son. 'And I'm the only mortal daughter that Zeus has ever cared to recognise. I am powerful, Achilles. If you want to impress me, you have to do better.'

It was a dare, and Achilles was still young enough to know it. He dived to her, then, closing the gap between them. In the short moment between his feet moving and his mouth reaching hers, Helen let out a pealing laugh, the laugh we all knew she was capable of, the laugh that shone like the first ray of sun after a storm.

After that, neither of them made any particularly recognisable noises. Their lips did not disentangle. Their limbs did, but only for long enough to start pulling at one another's clothes. Thetis paled considerably.

I motioned for her to wait with me at the mouth of the cave. If I wanted sex, I could call Ares, or Hermes, or both. I didn't need to watch these two going at it.

'Did you know this would happen?' she asked, her eyes fixed firmly on the sea and nothing but the sea.

I should have said yes, of course, that I know all things in the realm of love, but some events are too bizarre to even claim to have predicted.

'No.'

'Why? Achilles loves that boy.' Patroclus, she meant, but she didn't like saying his name. I think she blamed him, like Peleus, and all things Trojan, for the inevitability of her son's death.

'I don't think this is about love.' I didn't say love. What I said doesn't translate. 'He's spent nine years in a tent waiting for something to happen. He got to make something happen.'

'She's twice his age.'

'What's the age difference between you and Peleus, again?'

'Zeus ordered my marriage. What's in it for Helen?'

Behind us, Helen made a very pleased noise, which should have been enough of an answer right there. I don't understand why it's acceptable to listen to music or look at art or eat good food simply because you like it, but sex has to be about something greater. You can sleep with someone because it feels good, and for no other reason.

Thetis was still looking at me expectantly.

'I expect she was bored,' I said.

'She started a war.'

'She's been locked inside a city that's not her home for a decade. Can you imagine Paris is letting her out to play?'

'She's here now.'

'Do the Greeks know Achilles is gone?'

'I don't wish to hasten his death.'

'We can agree on silence, then.'

Together we guarded the entrance of the cave, made sure that no one bore witness. The world is a very strange place to live, sometimes, and that day only served to punctuate that fact.

When they were done, Thetis whisked Achilles back to his men, and I handed Helen her cloak. I grinned at her, trying to remember what it was like to be someone's friend.

'Did you have fun?'

'He was surprised I fit together.'

'What?'

'Apparently the way they talk about me over that end, it's all my tits, my arse, my arms, and what they want to do with them. He thought I was going to be a pile of body parts on the floor.'

'I didn't know you talked that much.'

'I asked him why he kept staring at my elbows.'

I snorted.

'He said Menelaus has given up defending my honour, when they make jokes.'

I heard their jokes, when I was skulking around camp. They amounted to more violence than they managed in battle. There was no useful apology to make.

'How are things with Paris?'

'I miss my sister.'

That I couldn't help. Clytemnestra had, by then, told everyone who'd listen that Helen was a wicked woman and the thing she hated most in the world. There was no bringing her back.

Instead, I took Helen's hands in mine and looked straight in her eyes. 'For whatever you want, Helen, I will be your ally. I will take arms and fight alongside you.'

'I think there's quite enough fighting being done on my behalf.'

'I—'

'I'd like to go home now.'

I took her back to Troy, and we both pretended that's what she'd meant. In her chambers, I helped her undress and let down her hair, brushed through the curls that reached the full length of her back, and when it was done, I tucked her into bed, watching her well into the night. Helen of Troy, Sparta, and Argos. Helen who didn't know what home looked like anymore.

Thetis took her son back to camp. He gave some sort of stirring speech, I gather, about how the war was not at an end and they should not give up because they were *bored*. Clearly something in his afternoon had stirred something in him.

Hallelujah.

That evening, the Greeks went out burning and looting. It was a big night for them. They took many women, growing in confidence with each one until their egos outgrew themselves. They took the daughter of a priest.

They took someone the gods cared about.

They gave Apollo an excuse to fight.

Finally.

Apollo II

What is a man to do when his favourite city is at war with, well, the world, and everyone's believing his prophecies a tad too much and his father is telling him he can, under no circumstances, get involved?

'You'd get involved, right?'

'No,' Artemis said.

'But—'

'No.'

'Not even if—'

'No! Don't do this.'

'Okay, but it's one of my priests asking for help. I can't ignore him; he's all pious and priesty. And they took his daughter, Art. What's wrong with getting her back for him, since he's been such a good priest to me and all?'

'What's her name?' she asked sharply.

'That's not the point.'

'Brother, I think it might be the point, because the point is that you do not, in fact, want to save this woman; you just want to do this to get involved in the war our father specifically forbade you from getting involved in.'

'Chryseis. She's called Chryseis.'

'The daughter of Chryses is called Chryseis?'

'Yes.'

'And that's her only name?'

'Yes.'[85]

'Bullshit, Apollo – no one is called that. Don't get involved. Zeus said this is a mortal war, not ours.'

When did my twin get so much older than me? And so boring? Troy was falling and my priests' children were getting kidnapped and my people were splintering bit by bit, and who was I without them, but it was fine, you know? Because I was following the rules.

Fine. I would just watch. Watching isn't getting involved.

'I think so too,' Aphrodite said. Where did she come from? How did she know what I was thinking? 'You were mumbling, Apollo.'

'Ah. It's the war, you know—' I could be honest with Aphrodite – she was a fellow member of Team Troy. Maybe I should make us matching chitons. 'The Greeks have kidnapped one of mine.'

'What are you going to do about it?'

'Thank you.'

This is what I was looking for, Artemis.

Aphrodite gave a tight little smile. 'I didn't do anything but ask the question.'

'It's normal, isn't it, to want to do something?'

'When love is involved, everything is normal.'

'And it's not fair to tell us it's not our war, is it? Troy is my city – whose war could it possibly be if it's not mine?'

'Quite.'

---

[85] Her name was Astynome, for anyone more inclined than Apollo to learn it. —A

'So no one could really blame me if I did something? If I convinced the Greeks to give the girl back?'

'—'

'And if some of them happen to die in the process and give Troy a fighting chance, then so be it, right? I'm not really getting involved in the war, am I? I'm just giving my priest his daughter back.'

She took my hand in hers and leaned towards me, her face serious. 'Apollo, I promise you, if you decide to take action against the Greeks, I will be nothing but thankful.'

'Are you sure?' The last time I broke a rule like this, I had to build this beautiful, doomed city.

'Absolutely.'

'Thank you.'

I did it then and there, so my nerve wouldn't fade. I whistled, gently at first, but the tune built into something feverish, something I could tie my plague to. It rolled across dips and valleys, swelling, growing, until it swept into their camp, the miasma wrapping around the soldiers. They breathed it in, sucking their downfall deep into their lungs.

'There,' I told Aphrodite. 'It is done. I'm involved.'

'How does it feel?'

'Incredible.'

That feeling stayed with me – you have no idea what it's like, feeling so powerless for so long and then just doing it. Taking it back. Flexing everything I had for what I wanted, even if it felt like betraying my oracle.

It was the finest of my plagues, and the most toxic. It took life after life and man after man, decimating the camp and evening up the playing field. You can't cause a plague without giving them an out, so I made it clear to them: I call off the plague when

Agamemnon returns the girl. Every day, I hoped he stayed proud and stubborn and refused. Every day, I hoped for just one more day. One more day, I told myself, and Troy would have a fighting chance.

One more day, I needed, and Athena took that from me. She had her favourite go argue with the king, convince him his later victory would be greater than the chance at a second wife who was better at housework.

I looked for Aphrodite again, so she could shoot the king with one of her arrows, give him some of that all-encompassing love, the kind Paris and Helen felt for each other, the kind I felt for Troy. If Agamemnon felt that way for the girl, he'd never let her go.

I knew she'd do it – she was on my side – but she was nowhere to be found, not on the day I needed her, so I couldn't stop it. The king returned the girl and replaced her with some other woman instead, and my excuse was gone. I had to retract my plague, but I couldn't go back to just watching. I was part of this now.

My involvement broke a dam for the other gods too. Athena helped her champions win races their bandy legs shouldn't have allowed. Aphrodite watched her newly arrived son fight, yanking him from dangerous situations and, occasionally, not-that-dangerous situations. Thetis never let hers out of her sight.

Zeus couldn't punish me without taking the rest of the gods down with me, and he couldn't do that. What's a king without his supporters?

With nothing else left to lose, I armed myself and took to the field. The Greeks had no hope against me. It was no longer just the mortals.

The gods were at war.[86]

---

[86] Perfect. —A

Anchises Note IV

Anchises,

What are we going to do with you and that silly little brain of yours?

Keep him out of the war, I said. You do remember me saying that? Our son will go on to be the father of the next great nation if you can avoid the urge to get him killed first.

So what do you do? That's right. You invent some offence to do with some cattle that we both know you don't care about – king masquerading as a shepherd as you are – to convince him that not only should he go, but that honour demands he go, then you saddle up the horses that will take him to his death.

Out of interest, what idiocy do you believe our son may have inherited from you that would demand he has two horses for a siege war that he will be fighting from the inside?

It's like you don't know how to listen. I would give you more instructions, but, presumably, you would go out of your way to fail those too.

I don't know, Anchises. Maybe I'll burn your house down for the pure heck of it. You could always see what happens when you ask me not to.

Hugs and kisses,
Aphrodite
XOXO

Aphrodite XXVII

Ah yes, the cattle. Anchises' oh-so-very-special cattle that mattered to him more than his son's life and, more importantly, that mattered more to him than my son's life.

I didn't need heroics out of Aeneas. I needed him to survive, and the best way for him to survive was to stay a dull shepherd until I was ready for him. Instead, he raged about the fate of his cows – I would have bought him more cows, magic cows – and signed up to be a soldier then and there. He went to his dullard father and, rather than convincing his son not to fight in an unwinnable war, Anchises gave Aeneas two of his prize horses, which my son rode proudly as he joined the fight.

I tried to stop him, but he was only a teenager when I started the war, thus reluctant to do anything his mother asked of him, especially when I had such awful requests as *stay alive, Aeneas*.

'I want to fight,' he said.

'I know you want to fight, but I need you to stay alive.' This shouldn't have been a problem. I could see his Fate. His threads continued. I knew he'd live, but I'd *known* things before, and Zeus had changed them anyway. I needed to make sure.

'There is no greater honour than a glorious death,' he said, more seriously than someone with curls sticking up at every angle across their head should possibly be able to manage.

What fucking lies we fed to these children, we who had no possibility of death, no concept of it, telling them over and over that a glorious death meant more than a beautiful life.

'If you listen to me, you will learn otherwise, I promise.' I could have told him everything that lay in wait for him if he'd just *survive*. I could have told him he'd father more than the next great nation, he'd father the next great *civilisation*, and if he stayed present, if he stayed well, without the darkness that plagues so many soldiers, we could mould the world to our will, and our descendants would rule longer and prouder than any we'd known before.

I could have told him he'd have more fame and honour than any of the fools on that battlefield losing their lives for the pretty lies the gods had told them. I could have told him people would be free in the new world, to live their lives, to love who they wanted, to go through a day without their divine mothers yelling at them about survival.

And I nearly did. Over and over, I nearly told him the stories of the wonder and the glory that awaited him, if he'd *listen to me*, but, every time, I stopped.

Because of Zeus. Because I'd met Zeus. As a child and as an adult and for more of the in between than anyone else had known him.

The young Zeus was filled to the gills with stories, lathered in tales about his own wonder. He'd be the strongest and the bravest and everyone would support him in even his stupidest endeavours.

And look what Zeus grew up to be.

I didn't want Aeneas turned into the same. Caring for his father after my little slip of a lightning bolt – one down, two to go – made my son kinder, forced him to learn that people who are suffering are still people, which is not a lesson that should have been unique to him, but there we go. He had my blood in him. He could be something different from everything we'd seen before. He had to be.

'They killed our cattle.'

'They're *cows*, Aeneas. I'll get you some more.'

'All the other young men have gone. It's embarrassing; I look like a coward.'

'An alive coward!'

'I'm going, Mother.'

I'd kept him out of it for ten years. Ten good, long years that allowed him to grow up into someone who at least *almost* resembled a man.

'Do you know how heroes die?' I asked him.

'What?'

'The heroes you so admire, do you know how they died?' Alone. Unhappy. All of them. The heroes die, and the heroes die alone.

'Mother—'

I was boring him with my lectures, but he was mortal; I could afford to bore him. 'Bellerophon,[87] blinded by thorns and starved to death wallowing in his own misery. Jason, killed by his own patron, with his own boat. Heracles, burned to death in a shirt soaked in someone else's semen.'

'I won't be like them.'

'Why?' I shouted. 'What makes you so different? What makes you think you can possibly escape what they couldn't?'

'Because I have you for a mother.'

He said it with such easy confidence. I'd paralysed his father – he

---

[87]   Irrelevant, apart from the winged horse and the specific tragedy of his death. —A

did think Zeus did that, and I didn't disabuse him of the notion – but he trusted me to save him.

It would have been easier if he didn't have absolute faith in me. I had to live up to it.

I took him to Troy myself in the end. He was right. He was on the verge of being branded a coward, and no one would follow him if that label stuck.

I watched over him as he made his way into the camp and introduced himself to make sure they didn't think him a spy and kill him where he stood. The only thing worse than dying a hero is dying *like* a hero before you had the chance to do everything you were always meant to do.

He was excited, skipping nearly, but catching himself at the high point and realising it didn't look manly, so bringing his knee back down in the most controlled way he could, making him high-step like a horse on parade.

He found his rhythm soon enough, strapping on armour, making friends, starting fights with people who were bigger than him.

I did protect him; he was right about that.

I just didn't realise how much he would cost me.

Athena II

Father told everyone they weren't to get involved in the war, which, by my estimate, lasted negative ten years. Each and every one of us was unavoidably involved, because by the time the war commenced, the entirety of the mortal world was involved, and us gods were inextricably linked with the mortals who followed us.

When it became clear to my father that the involvement was already there, he altered his edict; he said that we were not to fight in the war *personally*. This lasted, by my estimate, nine years, in the positive this time.

Apollo was the first to falter, which should not surprise anyone. He sent a plague to tear through the Greek camp and cripple them, under the guise of returning the daughter of one of his priests, which was nearly clever of him. To claim as such was still within the limits of the complicated rules of propriety that bound us, regardless of his true and glaring motivations; he did not wish to save the girl. He wished to save the city.

To an extent, I can empathise. If someone threatened the city I fought for, the city named for me, it would hurt me. I would don armour and stand for it once more, as long as there was a positive result to be had, and the people of Athens could still take victory. I don't believe in helping those who are unable to help themselves.

I am a winner, and I refuse to apologise for that. I choose to support *winners*.

The step between sending a plague to destroy the enemy camp and fighting them hand-to-hand is a short one and, soon enough, Apollo was rampaging across the battlefield as though he had been born there.

Once Apollo had broken that barrier and taken the unacceptable risk of drawing my father's ire for doing so – which it seemingly did not, for our father was distracted by every other part of the war – fighting became an acceptable risk, and I descended to Troy. I supported the Greeks, because the Greeks were clearly going to win.

The war did not last a decade because the sides were evenly matched. It lasted a decade because Troy was a fortress. It was not a city with walls. It was walls with a city attached. It was not a matter of *if* Troy would fall, but *when*. I do not hold much stock in prophecies – I am born from a failed prophecy, after all – but I possess common sense, and that was a simple deduction.

As such, my champions fought for the Greeks, and all demonstrated the temperament and skills we should demand from our heroes. They were not my father's drunken louts or, worse, Aphrodite's poets. My champions used their minds; they considered their actions and the ramifications thereof. They won battles before they began, which made them a delight to watch; a good plan well executed is a wondrous thing.

There was Odysseus, of course. I approved his tactic to avoid the war, but I cannot claim disappointment that it failed. Such a man was wasted on Ithaca. For all of his cleverness, however, Odysseus was young still, and not yet my most valuable piece. He was no Diomedes.[88]

I had supported Diomedes' father in his day. He fought as one of the seven against Thebes, and he fought bravely, leading his men to glorious victory. When he was wounded in a later battle and it seemed he was close to death, I requested a boon from my father to make him immortal. We would benefit from more thinking immortals, and I have no children. I felt it was only my right to have my representation among the gods.

While my father granted my request, I was forced to retract the offer from Diomedes' father, for one simple reason: he attempted to *eat* the man who had wounded him.

Perhaps unsurprisingly, given the circumstances of my mother's demise, I have a particularly negative view of eating people. From that moment on, I chose to support Diomedes in lieu of his father. He had the predisposition to be an excellent hero, without having committed any atrocities thus far.

Once the war began, I supplied him with valour, the strength to continue fighting, and the wisdom to continue making excellent decisions in the face of the battle around him. In case of emergency, I also supplied an extra feature to his helmet and shield, which would unleash plumes of fire as he fought. As I said, I like to support winners.

That day, as the warriors descended to the plains that separated Troy from the sea, Diomedes cut his way through the enemies, even when they were as thick as a forest in every direction. It looked as though he could finish the war in that very moment, had he not been hit in his abdomen by an arrow, a coward's weapon.

---

[88] Fighter on the Greek side. Favourite of Athena's. Ruined my life. —A

He called for me.

'Sharp-eyed Athena, I beg of you to grant me the strength to take my own revenge.'

That battlefield was a migraine for all of the gods. Having our champions in a single locale, all of them invoking us and crying for us and, occasionally, cursing us, was more intense than any situation we had experienced prior. The demands for our time and attention were relentless, and we could not respond to them all, but, for Diomedes, I appeared.

'Athena, you honour me.'

'I do. Now, Diomedes, you must honour me. Use your skills.' I held a hand above his injury, healing it. In terms of fighting nous, he was perhaps third among the Greeks but, unlike those ranked above him, he was free of prophecies to hinder him.

'How?'

'I will grant you the ability to see the true identity of those who lie before you, be they mortal or be they god. You can strike down any mortal – I believe you have the ability – but you are to avoid the immortals; they *will* outmatch you.' I paused, for a moment. 'Apart from Aphrodite. Her, you could kill.'

I did not intend for clear sight to be the gift I gave him that day – though I had prepared it as a potential boon for my fighters[89] – but that is how it went. He surged forwards into battle once more. He cut down swathes of men around him. At that point in the war, he was said to have set a record for the damage he wrought. It was a straightforward task for him to locate the one who had injured him that morning.

Diomedes threw a spear and killed him before he could appeal

---

[89] Must be nice to be able to imbue magical abilities on your chosen mortals. —A

to any god of his choice. He was of little importance. However, that man had fought alongside Aeneas that day, and Aeneas did not need to call to the gods; his mother was following him around.

With his spear lodged deeply into Aeneas' ally, Diomedes improvised by hefting a large rock at him. I approved. It made heavy contact and smashed the bones of Aeneas' hip and knee. Unsurprisingly, being one of Aphrodite's spawn, he crumpled with no attempt at continuing. She grabbed him by the shoulders and made to escape but, remembering my words, Diomedes did not accept it. He pulled his spear from the ally's body and, without hesitation, threw it directly through Aphrodite's hand.

The bitch screamed.

It was not a scream of pain, exactly, but one of pure fear. Had she really never been in a fight before? It was her hand, not her heart, and she was an immortal. She would survive this, no matter what I wished the case to be.

Her scream pierced the field of battle, rang through the ears of everyone there, and immediately, it was joined by another shout. Ares.

'Foamy,' he cried. A ridiculous cry from a ridiculous man. He appeared in front of her, attempting to examine her hand. She had jammed the wound into her mouth and her eyes only widened as she saw him, not in love or relief but, once more, in fear.

'Aweash,' she mumbled.

'Who hurt you?' He did not wait for a response. Looking in front of him, it became obvious that Diomedes was the victor. Without pause or beat to aim, Ares threw his spear in his direction.

That wouldn't do at all. I plucked the spear from midair. It wouldn't have been so easy if Ares had ever learned to disguise his actions.

'Shave uh boy,' Aphrodite said, more urgently this time, nodding at Aeneas. He lay whimpering on the ground.

I do not choose champions who will allow their enemies time for a conversation on the battlefield. I handed Diomedes the spear and gestured towards Ares. He knew what to do.

The spear flew straight and smooth, landing perfectly in Ares' centre of mass. He could have blocked it, were he not so distracted by his emotions. He looked down, then looked at me.

'I'll get you for this.'

'You should not make promises you cannot keep.'

Aphrodite whistled, through the hand still in her mouth, and three geese appeared. She clambered on one, pulled Aeneas on another, and Ares climbed on the third. Together, the three cowards flew in the direction of Olympus, all bleeding.

I was pleased to be right about the outcome of *that* fight.

I was less pleased when the ground began to rumble. My father was summoning us to Olympus. When we got there, Zeus was not happy. Aphrodite already sat before him as he paced. Her hand was wrapped in an oversized bandage, and tears were running down her face.

'Athena, did you instruct your champion to attack Aphrodite?'

She looked at me. She did not twitch a muscle, but I knew she was taunting me in her mind.

'And me,' Ares said, lifting his clothes so everyone could see his bloody stomach, dripping ichor on the floor. He did not know how to leave well enough alone. My father recoiled from him.

'I instructed Diomedes not to attack the *gods*. He clearly disregarded my advice when it came to Ares, but he has ordered his troops to withdraw. It is done now.'

'You still—' Ares began.

'No,' Zeus said. 'She's right. What's done is done. I have more important things to do than listen to you fight.'

In days gone by, that would have been sufficient. We had our clear dismissal from Zeus. He had left the room. However, it was not days gone by, and Ares turned on me.

'I'm sick of you, always getting involved in *my* things.'

'Those are fighting words, Brother.'

'I'm the god of bloody war. All my words are fighting words.'

'Yet I only see you losing.'

He bellowed with the rage of a thousand men; I am sure those below us thought it was Zeus throwing his thunder around again. He struck me with all his might in the centre of my breast plate, my aegis, wherein I keep the head of Medusa. He might have stood a chance if he had attacked anywhere less fundamentally idiotic. As it was, his strike *bounced*.

I lifted a nearby boulder and threw it while he was recovering from his attack. It knocked him down, shredding his skin quite unattractively and trapping one of his legs. He seemed quite prepared to amputate the offending limb and make another attack, but Aphrodite held his arms down and whispered something in his ear; I can only assume an instruction to leave it.

'Listen to your whore, Ares. There's no point in us fighting. Let's be honest, I'm just better at being *you* than you are.'

I did not waste my time listening to his angry sputtering. I had a battle to return to.

Ares VI

Athena is a dick, but we knew that.

Aphrodite bleeding red. That was fucking new.

It was new, right? Someone had cursed her or something. It had to be.

I'd never seen her bleed before. Not even when we were having sex. She said she didn't like sex when she was. I knew that was bullshit. I knew she wouldn't care. We had sex in her husband's bed for fuck's sake. So what if I hadn't seen her bleed? I hadn't seen loads of people bleed. Like . . . Like . . . Hestia. I hadn't seen Hestia bleed. So it could be coincidence. It had to fucking be.

But she was looking at me and her eyes had gone wide, and she still had her hand in her mouth and a single fucking drip of blood was rolling down her chin and her neck like *look at me, look at me.*

She wouldn't be looking at me like that if this was new.

Gods bleed gold. All of us. It's what makes us different from the Titans. It's what makes us all the same. Same blood. Same family.

She wasn't a god. She couldn't be a god.

Still. I got her out of there, right? Because first thing's first when you're in the middle of a battlefield. You can deal with all the emotional shite later. Then there was the whole thing with Athena and dealing with that, then we got back to her place and *later* had arrived and I didn't want that.

Foamy kept looking at me. Not like she *looked at me* looked at me, when she wanted my clothes off right then and there. Or when she looked at me because she thought someone else was being thick and I should laugh at them with her. She didn't look at me straight on. It was out of the corner of her eyes when she thought I wasn't looking at her.

'This is new, right?'

She didn't say nothing. Hand behind her back.

'Foamy, this is new?'

Nothing. Eyes wider.

'Stop looking at me like that. You shouldn't be fucking *scared* of me,' I shouted which, right, I know isn't the best way of making someone not piss-scared of you, but I don't try and stop people being afraid of me all that much.

I tried wrapping my arm round her shoulder, to show I wasn't pissed enough to hurt her, but she flinched away. If that's how she wanted it, fine. I could be pissed instead.

'What the actual *fuck*, Aphrodite?'

Finally, she opened her fucking mouth. 'I love you.'

'What's love got to do with the colour of your fucking *blood*?'

'Why does it matter?' she shouted. That was better. Then we were both shouting and she was standing up to me, and it didn't matter how tall I was and how short she was 'cause she could be so big when she shouted like that. 'Why do you care what colour it is?'

'Because— Because you fucking know because.' Fuck I sounded thick. She made me thick. 'You lied to me.'

'I told you I would.'

She did, at that, right from the off when we were still fucking behind my brother's back and she was doing it to fuck with him. *I'm never going to tell you the whole truth,* she'd said, but she had a hand on my dick and I didn't care so I told her so.

'You told me you didn't care,' she said. 'You lied too.'

'It's not a bloody competition.'

'It never is when I'd win.'

'What does that even mean?' I said.

'You don't fucking get it.'

'Then explain.'

'I love you.'

'Yeah, you said that.'

'It's true.'

'But why lie to me about *this*? I don't care that you're married to my fucking brother – why would I give a shit about anything else?'

'Ares—'

'I didn't tell Zeus you were planning treason.'

'I was scared.'

'Don't be scared of me,' I shouted. Again.

'What was I meant to fucking do? When was I meant to tell you? In the net? When our daughter was born? The first time you ever told a person you loved them? When your father called you detestable and I was reassuring you that you're not? When was I meant to feel safe that you'd love me enough *forever* to keep my secrets?'

'I'd protect you.'

'I don't want to be *protected*. I don't want you looking at me and thinking how weak I am.'

'You could never be weak. So what, you're a nymph, a nereid, whatever. You're still you, Foamy. You're the strongest fucking person I know. I'd still bloody love you.'

'And you think that would have been the same? You think you would have let yourself be seduced for a *nymph*? You would have betrayed your brother for a *nereid*? You think you would have pissed off both your parents for a *spirit*? You really think you would have had children for anything less than the *goddess of fucking love*?'

'Obviously,' I bellowed. 'Because I fucking love you.'

'If you loved me, you wouldn't care.'

'Oh, like you fucking wouldn't? Like you didn't start all this with me because you wanted Hephaestus' brother. Like it didn't fucking matter to you *who* I am.'

'It's different.'

'Is it?'

'Yes, Ares. It is bloody different.'

'Why? If I'm so thick, then explain it to me.'

'You're strong by yourself, and I'm not. That's what's different. That's why I have to lie.'

'I'm not saying you can't lie to everyone else. But did you have to lie to me?'

Her mouth was open, but I didn't hear what she had to say. One of her nymphs came running in. The perky one. I didn't want to see her. It wasn't the time.

She looked between us and shrunk. Fuck me. I wasn't pissed at *her*. She didn't even fucking look at me. Eyes down, body turned away.

'My lady,' she said. 'I'm sorry to interrupt, but there's been a situation.'

'It's not the time, Euphrosyne.'[90]

'It's Aeneas. He's in trouble.'

Of course he fucking was. That kid got in more trouble than Cadmus did, and *he* punched Zeus in the face once. I missed Cadmus.

'Okay, I'm coming.'

'We're not done here,' I said.

'I need to go.'

'Why?'

'Aeneas can't found the next great nation if he's dead, Ares.'

'You started the war through love. You've proved your bloody worth.'

'I need to be at the beginning and the end. Creation and destruction.'

'Can't you just *be* for one fucking moment?'

'I have to go.'

She was gathering her things: her armour, her bow, her birds. Not looking at me. Like she didn't fucking hear me as I shouted her name.

Foamy.

Aphrodite.

I love you.

I'm pissed as anything.

I want to understand.

Don't go.

We're not fucking done here.

But she said we were. She showed we were. She walked out on me. She didn't want me anymore. Probably didn't ever want me.

---

[90] One of my attendants. Chirpy. —A

I spent enough time trying to convince my own bloody father that he wanted me. Never again.

'Aphrodite,' I shouted. One last time.

The stupid perky nymph came up to me. 'She's gone. Do you think maybe you should head out too?'

I didn't want her to be scared of me. Aphrodite would be raging if I made her nymphs piss themselves.

Fuck it. *I* was fucking raging. I earned it. I got one shout. We were over and it was all a fucking lie. I yelled it.

We're done.

Shouted like I could bring the walls down around me. But they held firm. Her lies were dug too deep.

Aphrodite XXVIII

I could have stayed and argued the point. I could have been honest with him and I could have seen whether that helped, whether that mattered. I could have done a lot of things for us, but I didn't, because the plan was in danger. Aeneas was in danger – Aeneas was always in danger – and I had to go and drag him out of it.

I borrowed Apollo to come cure his wounds, thinking less damage would lead to more survival, but it just made my son more brazen about starting fights he couldn't win. Ares couldn't see it, but I had to be vigilant. Everything was falling into place.

The heroes, their threads, they were all about to come loose, and I needed to be there for that.

I made my choice, and I didn't choose Ares.

I chose me.

And he chose Zeus.

Zeus V

Sons. My sons. Had to be everything. Strongest. Bravest. Best. Like me. Reflected on me. Reflected on them. Always.

First hero. Perseus. Mine.

Best hero. Heracles. Mine too. Not Hera's. Not her glory. My son. My glory.

My sons. The greatest. But couldn't forget those words. From my father. When I won.

Yours will overthrow you too.

No.

Like father, like son, eh?

No.

No. No. No. I got power. Became king. Didn't share. Quashed the uprising. No Apollo. Bad Apollo. Made him build Troy. Told him it would fall. Everything he built. To be destroyed. My power was forever. No one else's.

Then the Fates. Stupid useless Fates. Heard their words too.

Your son by Metis will usurp you.

No. Made them change it. Burned that future. Ate Metis. Liked Metis. But she knew. What my father said. What Fate said. She didn't think I was perfect. Didn't think I was strong enough. I am. I have to be. Always.

Prometheus said it too. Took him to be bound. Eaten. Destroyed. Forgotten. Still couldn't forget his words.

Those sons of yours are growing awfully strong, aren't they?

Mortals were meant to be weak. Safe. Could care about them. But they had to be strong. My sons couldn't be less. Strong and weak. Weak and strong. Too strong. Too weak.

Had to get rid of them. Change Fate. Control it. Burn it. Burn them.

But.

Met Sarpedon. My son. Not like the others. He fought. He lost. He accepted. Once. Twice. Three times. He lost. He knew how to lose. How?

Wanted to know. Wanted it to be okay.

It wasn't. He suffered. Fine. He needed more time. Gave him that. Made Fate give him that. One life. Two. Three. Four. Five. Six. Five times I made his life longer. Five times. Six lives. To show me. To prove it. To make it okay.

He had time. In this life. Didn't need more. Knew that. Checked it. Fates didn't lie. Didn't let them. His thread was long. Strong. Strong and long. I knew that.

Visited the Fates. Every day. Told the others they were cursed. Haunted. Evil. A relic from the old world. They weren't. They were new. Someone else was there before. A friend. My friend. But she was gone. And they were there. To help me. Tell me what was happening. Could control them. Control the war. The future. Make it mine. It was mine. I earned it. I deserved it. I'm the king.

Checked that day. Who would win. Lose. Die.

Not Sarpedon. He had time. Gave him time.

He died anyway.

Fought well. Not well enough. Killed a horse. What use is

a horse? Patroclus had a spear. Stabbed him. Blood everywhere. Weak blood. Red blood. Mortal blood.

Summoned my chariot. Took the reins. I could save him.

Arm blocked me.

'Husband, I implore you—' Hera. My wife. Why?

'He's my son.' Too many words. Not enough time.

'All those others dying out there, they are people's sons too.'

'Not mine.'[91]

'No, but they do belong to the gods, and you have refused them the right to save them. If you save Sarpedon, they will riot.'[92]

'So?'

'Your power, Husband. It matters more than this man.'

Let him die. Let him bleed out. Alone. To some pretender. Not Achilles. Not the strongest. Not the greatest of the Greeks. Some weakling killed my son. Made me look weak. Made me look like everyone else.

But she was right. Gods would riot. Would destroy me.

Sons always do.

Couldn't look weak. Couldn't let Sarpedon die. Just another name. A number. Someone else's kill. A sideline. My son. Lived six lives. Not enough.

They would suffer. The people who killed him. They would know the pain they caused.

I am powerful. I am the king.

I want. It happens.

My son died. The world rained blood. I made it so. Thick. Heavy. Mortal. Blood. It rained. It stuck on them. Flattened hair and covered eyes. It made quiet. Finally. Merciful. Quiet. On that

---

[91] Some of them were also his. —A

[92] I was rather banking on that. —A

field. In Troy. Everyone stopped. For Sarpedon. For my son. To know that he was lost. That I missed him.

They felt it. The mortals. They felt it.

The gods did not. Not allowed to stop. Not me. Not the king.

'Father, Father, Father.' My son. Warlike Ares. He brought this. Despicable. Immortal. Out of breath. 'We need to talk.'

'Not now.'

'Yes, now.'

Words. Too many words. One. Two. A hundred. Flooding out. No time to breathe. Shaking. Warlike Ares. Shaking. Afraid as he told me.

They were wrong. My father. The Fates. Prometheus. All wrong.

It wasn't a son who would destroy me.

It was a daughter.

Zeus' Note

Now, Aphrodite. We end this now.

− Z

Aphrodite XXIX

There are some invitations you can't say no to.

I met my "father" in a rain of blood by the base of the mountain where Prometheus had been, where his body remained.

'You look tired,' I said. I'd planned my lines, crafted them, to weed out what he knew without giving away more than I had to. It was the only control I could hold on to when my plan was stalling and the king was out for me.

The rain of blood impregnated everything, the air, the ground, my clothes, but it started with Zeus, and it covered him the most of all. His hair was matted down in gelatinous chunks that hung over his face. His beard too, dripping onto his chiton, painting a more gory image than Ares ever had. The blood had seeped into his eyes, even, staining his sclera pink.

I didn't look much better. No amount of braids or flowers can cover that much blood, but I wasn't grieving. My son was still alive.

'You should rest, Father.'

He stepped towards me. Into me. He pressed his chest against mine until I could smell the blood and the pain on him, and he bellowed, 'You are a liar, Aphrodite.'

I didn't step back. What would be the point? He would step

again, crowd me, surround me, suffocate me, no matter where I went. He was the king and I was the fraud.

'How?' Stupid question. It should have been *who*, but I knew the answer to that too. The god of war has never been very brave. We had that in common.

'Ares.'

'I thought he loved me.' I didn't plan to say that, and I already suspected it was him, but I still loved him. The confirmation hurt.

'I'm his father. His king. He loves me more.'

'He *hates* you. He's *always* hated you.'

'He hates you so much he betrayed you.'

'He panicked. He was afraid of you.'

'Good. He should be. Why aren't *you*?'

'Because I *remember* you.' As a lonely child, with the world promised to him, I remembered him. As a kid in a cave who desperately wanted a friend, I remembered him. As a new king who wanted a daughter to love him unconditionally, I remembered him, and even then, after everything he'd done to me, I wanted better from him. For him. I wanted him to be that kid I loved, not this tyrant I hated.

I let my voice drop to its natural register, to the tones I'd been holding back for so long that echoed with something primordial, the side of me that resonated with the very earth we stood on more deeply than Zeus and his magic tricks could ever hope to understand. He might have been bigger than me, and stronger, but I was older, and I understood that all worlds end, because I'd seen it happen.

'Don't you remember me?'

Ares should have been my biggest heartbreak that day. Ares, not Zeus. Not the blank expression on his face without a trace of recognition.

I really had been nothing.

Desperation hit.

'Why did you punish Atlas worse than the other Titans?' I asked. Begged him to remember.

'What?'

'After the war, why did you punish Atlas worse than the other Titans?'

'We're not talking about this *now*.'

'All the others you sent to Tartarus. But not Atlas. You wanted him in pain, on display. Why?'

'This doesn't matter.'

'Tell me.' My fingers reached for my stolen thunderbolts, hidden beneath my clothes and the blood that kept falling faster and thicker around us. It wasn't a bluff.

'He was Cronus' right-hand man—'

'You didn't punish Cronus any more than the others.'

'It set a bad precedent. Kings punishing kings.'

'Do you really expect me to believe you were worried about precedent? You, as a child, thought someone might take the world from you?'

'I don't know what you want from me.'

'Tell me the fucking truth, Zeus.'

'He hurt my friend,' he shouted. 'Okay? He hurt my friend so I hurt him.' Centuries of age peeled off his voice as he said it, and, just for a second, the younger versions of him came through. Not the tyrant stained with blood, but a kid telling me about all the good he was going to do one day, how the world would shine under his power.

But it was too late to see him like that.

We were in too deep.

I smiled at him then, broad enough to see all my teeth. 'I missed you.'

'You're Fate?'

I nodded.

'I will *destroy* you.'

Surprise was all I had, so I used it. I jumped straight up, slamming my head into his jaw, hard enough to send us both out spinning. Neither of us touched the bolts; those are a distance weapon, and this was more personal than that.

He grabbed at me, and I slid down without a measure of poise. No grip when you're standing on blood. I threw myself into him, but it did nothing. He was carved in stone, and I was so weak. He lifted his foot to press it on top of me, to crush my face down in the sludge of dirt and blood beneath us, but I didn't need to be strong to avoid that. I rolled. Maybe I cut myself. There would be bruises, but he wouldn't hold me down. Never again.

I bit his ankle, hard. Hard enough to draw ichor from it, the gold diluting and disappearing into everything else faster than I could blink. It took three bites to bring him to the ground with me.

We couldn't kill each other, so we didn't try. We were out to hurt. Our clash was all fingernails and impotent rage.

It was a stupid fight, and I lost it. He was bigger than me and stronger than me and a real god besides. I'd spent my entire life avoiding getting into fistfights for exactly this reason.

He held my face down, as he'd wanted to from the beginning, so I couldn't help but breathe in the dirt, lining the crevices of my teeth and flecking across my body.

'You're not beautiful,' he said, more wonder in his voice than I'd heard since he became the king. 'We all go around saying you're beautiful like it's a fact. The goddess of love is beautiful. But you're not. You're not even real.'

'Of course I'm real. I'm here.'

'No. Your hair's not beautiful because it's like gold. It *is* gold. Your skin *is* clay. You're not real.'

I didn't know what was happening. I'm not made of clay or gold. I'm not built like a mortal, obviously, but my skin was skin and my hair was hair.

'Your eyes are the oceans—'

As he said it, I could almost feel it coming true, that I was not a person at all, only these muddled metaphors, and I would revert to all of them under his words, split into my base materials, clay and gold and ocean under his hands, where he could form me into a shape he liked better. The power in his words . . . He could do it. I didn't know how, but he could.

'You are a lie, Aphrodite. You are *nothing*.'

I didn't need Zeus to tell me that.

'I'll make sure everyone knows it. I'll destroy everything you care about. I'll strip you bare and make everyone see what a fraud you are.'

I'd prepared for this for millennia. No one lies their way into the most powerful family in the world without a fallback.

'You loved me. Twice.'

'I know better now.'

'But do the rest of them? The gods have all used me as an excuse to get away with something at some point.'

He pushed my head down further, until I could barely open my lips, but I didn't stop.

'And you most of all. Aphrodite made me seduce that woman. Aphrodite made me steal your wife. Aphrodite. Aphrodite. Aphrodite. If I'm gone, who are you going to blame, Zeus?'

'That's ancient history.'

'Are you going to tell your wife you never really loved her? That you let me talk you into it? You think she'll support you then?'

'Shut up.'

'How about your children? If it wasn't me making you flit from woman to woman, dropping your kids the moment they were born, if it was just *you* who didn't care enough to stay, would they still support you then?'

'Shut up.'

My head couldn't go much further. The dirt and the blood were running down my throat, and it was all I could do not to choke, but I did it. I still had more to say.

'You don't have any friends, do you? It's just family. And we both know what family does when they stop loving each other.'

'Shut up. Shut Up. SHUT UP.'

'They rebel, Zeus.'

He hit me. I knew it was coming. I'd taunted him, egged him on. I braced for it, but he was the only father I'd ever known. I wasn't ready for him to hit me like that, not lying helpless on the ground when he had nothing to gain.

I blinked, because it was all I could do to compose myself.

'You need them to love you. I can help.'

'I don't have time for you right now.'

'You know I can do it. *You* loved me.'

Around us, the rain receded, and people died. We could hear them shouting. Children were killed, and couples were torn asunder. Breasts were beaten, and wails were let loose that should have had cavernous echoes but were lost in the shouts of all the people suffering in exactly the same way. But we didn't care about any of that. They were mortals, and we were gods.

'Come on,' I pleaded. 'Let me go and we can do this together.'

'No. You don't get to betray me.' He raised his hand over me again and a bolt appeared in it. This was it then. He was going to destroy me, erase me.

I braced for the pain. I thought of Prometheus.

He threw the bolt.

It didn't hit me.

There was no pain.

It crashed into the ground beside me, tearing the earth itself in half, the crack growing too fast for me to move out of its way. It pulled me in.

I scrabbled, trying to hold on to the edges, but the soil was too wet still, and I couldn't get any purchase. I managed to get one finger wedged into the dirt, all my weight hanging precariously there, but Zeus drove his heel into it, and then it wasn't enough to hold me.

'Down you go,' he said.

What the king wants, he gets.

I was falling.

Aphrodite XXX

This was not the plan.

Being kicked out of Olympus was not the plan. Zeus learning my identity was not the plan.

Falling was not the plan.

But I fell anyway. Through the ground further and deeper than I ever thought possible, through layer after layer of our world, each of them getting hotter and hotter until I thought it would peel away everything I was.

The hole Zeus had made was small enough to confine, but too big for me to catch myself. The earth rolled and closed above me, taking all of the light, all of the *air* with it. Trapping me, pushing me down.

It wasn't his first time condemning someone to Tartarus.

I had time to panic, to scream, even to hope he couldn't hear me screaming, that I hadn't granted him that extra victory, and through it all, I fell.

I fell all the way until the light came back. Only dimly at first, but even that was enough to send me blinking, my eyes tearing as they struggled to adjust. My tunnel opened up into a cavern, but still I fell, through the upper layers of Tartarus, past the mortals who had sinned so much in their tiny lives that they earned a space in the club it took me millennia to earn.

Tantalus, forbidden from eating or drinking, but haunted by fruit all the same. Ixion, strapped to a burning wheel for lusting over Hera. The Danaïdes,[93] forced to fill a bath using jugs without bottoms. There was no greater torture we could imagine for mortals than making them live out the same cycle on repeat, but in Olympus we did it for fun.

I knew their stories, but that's very different from hearing Ixion's screams and not quite knowing where you've heard them before.

My punishment awaited me at the bottom.

I was glad there was a war, then, not for any of my grand plans, not for the beautiful future that was surely crashing as fast as I was, but because it saved me from whatever suitably ironic punishment Zeus could dream up for me. It had all happened so fast, and he thought about my offer, thought about letting me go. He couldn't have prepared anything.

He could only be putting me in with the other traitors.

Let's say I stopped falling then, that I thought of my brethren and I landed. Let's say I wasn't screaming or crying or flailing as I did it. Let's say that, because who's possibly going to contradict me?

I don't remember landing, but I remember waking, thinking for one brief second that I was somewhere else, that I'd had too much to drink, and Ares and I had passed out on the streets of Olympus, until I made the horrible mistake of opening my eyes.

Nope. Still in Tartarus.

I woke alone. I could see the Titans, and they could see me,

---

[93] They were all in Tartarus. How relevant could any of them possibly be? —A

but they didn't react. If this had happened on Olympus, they'd all be crowded round, squabbling about what to do with me. Hestia would be offering me a drink, and Ares would probably be poking me with a stick.

The Titans ignored me. They sat calmly as lambs, waiting for something, someone more exciting than me.

And I remember thinking, *Is this it? Is this the great and terrible torture Zeus has been promising all these years?*

It wasn't *nice*. It was a big rock box, essentially, now that the hole I'd fallen through had closed around me. It was sealed tight, but there was enough room to walk around and talk, plenty of Titans for company. It was nowhere near what the mortals in the upper reaches were suffering. In fact, it was more like—

Asphodel, where the majority of mortal souls go. A place not of punishment but of eternal waiting. *That* was the punishment. To take those who had controlled the entire cosmos, who had made mountains and forests spring beneath their fingers, and lock them up, no better than mortals. Maybe I should have been flattered I made the list.

I didn't know how I was meant to get myself out of this, but I wasn't going to be ignored.

It's not as though I'd never done this before.

I just had to find the king. I wish I could say that I knew him across the room, that I looked upon his face and saw something of myself in him, that the kinship between us pulled on me like the threads always had. In truth, I recognised the man who's technically my father because he didn't have testicles.

I walked up to him, my back straight even though every part of me hurt from the fall. I bowed, even.

'Ouranos,' I said.

He barely looked up to acknowledge me. 'Yes?'

'I am—' I said, not really knowing how to go about the rest of this, not knowing what to say. I wasn't like the Olympians. I didn't have so much family that I could treat them like shit and know they'd come back to me. This man was all I had, and he didn't look like me at all. 'I'm Aphrodite. Your daughter.'

'I know who you are.'

We looked at each other. Both of us stopped and spent a long time looking at one another.

'Do you feel anything?' I asked.

'In general? Yes.'

'About me?'

'No.'

If anyone was going to love me, or know me, or get me, if anyone was going to stand in front of me and show where I fit into the scheme of things, it was meant to be him. I should have been able to look at him and see all these bits and pieces of myself and who I grew up to be.

With him, I was meant to be a part of something, but he felt nothing.

'I have many children,' he said, like it was meant to be some balm to all of this.

'I lied my way into Olympus.' I wanted him to see me. I wanted him to care. If I couldn't see myself in him, then I wanted him to see himself in me, to match the pieces of us together and to love me in that unconditional way I've never understood. 'I turned myself into a goddess.'

'You are no god. No child of mine is.' He wasn't trying to be cruel. He was bored and old and uninterested. I hated him for that.

'I'm one of the most important people in the world. I started a war.'

Listen to me *begging* for this person who didn't even know me to like me. Pathetic. He didn't even look up. 'I'm going to destroy Zeus.'

He still didn't look at me, but he looked around, taking in the hard stone walls around every side of us. 'I see that's going well for you.'

And then madness overtook me.

'You could help,' I said. 'We could go together. Break out of this place. Take him down—'

'You want my help?'

'Yes. I mean, no, I—'

'You think I need *your* help, then.' The way he said it, with this sneer in his voice, with this judgement like I was the least of his children, though I had done the most, lived the most. I couldn't stand it. I had to change his mind. I had to make him see how much I'd done.

'I have a plan. My son, he will—'

'So you have no intention of doing anything?'

'I *started a war.*'

'How?'

I explained about Troy, about Ares, about Helen, about the suitors and Aeneas and Anchises. I explained about Thetis and making Achilles meet Helen to get the Greeks working. I explained about Apollo and his priest and his priest's daughter. I explained about love.

'By the sounds of it, Zeus started a war, and Ares and Apollo helped, even these mortals of yours did something, and *you* did nothing.'

'I—' Lied, and I manipulated, and I left the only home I'd ever known and put everything I had on the line to make the world a better place, and I pushed and I pushed until I didn't really recognise myself anymore so I could do that.

'Not everyone can be something.'

I worked so hard for so long to become the person that I am, and I'm *proud* of it. I did this. I am my own fucking magnum opus, and he didn't see me. He didn't care to fucking know, but I didn't give up. Like a child with a toy. Like Ares with his wars or Hephaestus with his contraptions. *Daddy, Daddy, look at me. Daddy, am I doing good? Daddy, Daddy, love me!*

I'd seen it all before and I'd mocked, laughed at the stupid whims of this stupid kind of love that didn't belong to me. I thought I was above it all, and here I was.

'Together we could take over the world.'

'No, Aphrodite. *I* could take over the world.'

My temper snapped. I'd never known it to take so long. 'Clearly you fucking can't.'

'Excuse me?'

'You can judge me all you want, old man, but how many years have you been sitting here? How long have you spent waiting and dreaming about the good old days, telling yourself you're the most powerful being to have ever lived without fucking doing a *single* thing?'

'I ruled the world once.'

'And what a great job you did of it. You had, what, eighteen children before they decided to destroy you? Eighteen people in the entire world, that's all it fucking took for them to hate you, and you want to judge me?'

'I made things. *You* only exist to destroy.'

'The war's about rebuilding—'

'I am *not* talking about your idiotic war. I'm talking about *you. You* only exist to destroy. I despise *you.*'

'You don't even know me.' The words came out small, in a voice I didn't know I still had. 'How can you hate me?'

'You were born out of my destruction. What else could I do but hate you?'

He was just the same as Zeus. The way he talked about his children, his world, not like they were their own entities with their own lives, but as a subset of him. We only existed for what we could do for him.

I'd bet that I could have found Cronus down there too, and spoken to him, and got exactly the same answers.

Yesterday's tyrants were just the same as today's.

It didn't matter if I could convince him to help me, if I could rally the troops from Tartarus and break out with my own surprise rebellion, because I didn't want to. I couldn't trade this world for the one we had before, because it'd look just the same. I had to make something new, and I had to do it alone.

I had to get out of here.

How do you get out of a prison built to house the king who lived before you?

'Did you build this place?' I asked my father. He'd proved loquacious, if awful.

'With this design? No. That would be my son.' Cronus, the first king to struggle with immortal enemies.

'Is there a way out?'

'Would I still be here if there was?'

Okay, fair.

'This is a fortress built to contain Titans and gods—'

'I'm not a god,' I said.

'Are you looking for applause for stating a fact?'

'Am I a Titan?'

'Ha. The Titans were kings and leaders. They were fighters. You hardly match up.'

'They overthrew you.'

'Which requires a certain amount of power.'

What is *wrong* with the men in this family? How is that the only thing that engenders respect?

The prison was built for gods, Titans, my father – and I was none of those things. It wasn't built to contain me.

In my defence for this line of thinking, it had been a *very* long day.

So, full of unearned confidence, I walked swiftly into the walls of Tartarus and, equally swiftly, broke my nose.

'And you wonder why I'm not falling over myself to claim you,' Ouranos remarked. He was picking dirt out of his fingernails. It had to be an artifice. There was no dirt in Tartarus.

'With parenting like that, it's no wonder your children overthrew you.'

'The good ones did.'

'I *am* the good one.'

'Fortunately for you, it seems like you'll have ample opportunity to prove yourself wrong.'

I refused. The day had been so long and confusing and terrible that my mind wasn't functioning anymore. There was no space for fear or for doubt; there was only space for knowing that I could not spend an *eternity* trapped in a confined space with this arsehole.

So what if there was no clever solution to getting me out of there? No loophole for immortals who are not anything at all?

You don't need clever when you have lightning.

I stole three bolts from Hephaestus, once upon a time, and I hadn't let go of them since.

I used the first on Anchises, because I was angry, scared, and lost.

I used the second for much the same reasons, and I used it to blow my way out of Tartarus.

I didn't think; I didn't aim. I simply channelled the vast lakes of rage within me and let that bolt fly.

The wall cracked, not so dramatically or obligingly as when Zeus cast me down here in the first place, but enough for me to wiggle through before it closed again, with just enough time to smile and wave at the people behind me.

'Bye, Daddy – you must come and visit sometime!'

I am not a nice person. Maybe I got that from him.

The lightning couldn't power me back to the real world, so I took the long route through Hades, walking every step of the way. I saw the mortals in their eternal punishment in slow motion this time.

I tried walking past them – I did. I had a war to get to, and enough spite to carry me through it. I made it past the Danaïdes without problem, and Tantalus, but I got close enough to hear Ixion and my feet ground to a halt. They wouldn't move. They just wouldn't, because my brain had finally put two and two together and remembered who he reminded me of.

Prometheus. He reminded me of Prom.

'I don't have time for this,' I whispered, but I did it anyway. I patched the Danaïdes' buckets, borrowed water from Tantalus' river, let him drink while I was there, and I walked over to the man who'd been burning for centuries, and I finally put him out.

'Thank you.' Ixion tried to whisper, but his throat was ruined from the screaming and it came out dragged across rocks. 'You are truly the greatest among the gods.'

I smiled, genuinely, convinced this small act of kindness was enough to set me apart from both my fathers, from all the tyrants who came before me. I let myself revel in my own goodness. I set myself up for the fall.

I left Tartarus, and made it to Asphodel, an endless field packed tightly with the irrelevant souls, the ones who don't get their own story, whose only purpose was to die in my war.

I walked through Asphodel, and I saw the dead.

The Dead

Echepolus	Chromius	Oenomaus
Elephenor	Pandarus	Helenus
Simoeisius	Deicoon	Oresbius
Leucus	Crethon	Periphas
Democoön	Orsilochus	Acamas
Diores	Pylaemenes	Axylus
Peirous	Mydon	Calesius
Phegeus	Menesthes	Dresus
Odius	Anchialus	Opheltius
Phaestus	Amphius	Aesepus
Scamandrius	Tlepolemus	Pedasus
Phereclus	Coeranus	Astyalus
Pedaeus	Alastor	Pidytes
Hypsenor	Chromius	Aretaon
Astynous	Alcandrus	Ableros
Hypeiron	Halius	Elatus
Abas	Noemon	Phylacus
Polyidus	Prytanis	Melanthius
Xanthus	Teuthras	Adrestus
Thoon	Orestes	Menesthius
Echemmon	Trechus	Eioneus

Iphinous	Orus	Glaucus
Eniopeus	Hipponous	Alcmaon
Agelaos	Thymbraeus	Imbrius
Orsilochos	Molion	Amphimachus
Ormenus	Adrestus	Othryoneus
Ophelestes	Amphius	Asius
Daitor	Hippodamas	Hypsenor
Chromius	Hypeirochus	Alcathous
Lycophontes	Agastrophus	Oenomaus
Amopaon	Deïopites	Ascalaphus
Melanippus	Thoön	Aphareus
Gorgythion	Ennomus	Thoön
Archeptolemos	Chersidamas	Adamas
Dolon	Charops	Deïpyrus
Rhesus	Socus	Peisander
Bienor	Doryclus	Harpalion
Oileus	Pandocus	Euchenor
Isus	Lysander	Satnius
Antiphus	Pyrasus	Prothoënor
Peisander	Pylartes	Archelochus
Hippolochus	Apisaon	Promachus
Iphidamas	Damasus	Ilioneus
Coön	Pylon	Hyrtius
Asaeus	Ormenus	Morys
Autonous	Hippomachus	Hippotion
Opites	Antiphates	Prothoön
Dolops	Menon	Periphetes
Opheltius	Iamenus	Hyperenor
Agelaus	Orestes	Phalces
Aesymnus	Epicles	Mermerus

Stichius	Erylaus	Phorcys
Arcesilaus	Erymas	Leocritus
Medon	Amphoterus	Apisaon
Iasus	Epaltes	Aretus
Mecisteus	Tlepolemus	Podes
Echius	Echius	Coeranus
Clonius	Pyris	Iphition
Deïochus	Ipheus	Demoleon
Caletor	Euippus	Hippodamas
Lycophron	Polymelus	Polydorus
Cleitus	Thrasymedes	Dryops
Schedius	Sarpedon	Demouchos
Laodamas	Epeigeus	Laogonus
Otus	Sthenelaus	Dardanus
Croesmus	Bathycles	Tros
Dolops	Laogonus	Mulius
Melanippus	Adrestus	Echeclus
Periphetes	Autonous	Deucalion
Pyraechmes	Echeclus	Rhigmus
Areilycus	Perimus	Areithous
Thoas	Epistor	Lycaon
Amphiclus	Melanippus	Asteropaeus
Atymnius	Elasus	Thersilochus
Maris	Mulius	Mydon
Cleobulus	Pylartes	Astypylus
Lyco	Cebriones	Mnesus
Acamas	Patroclus	Thrasius
Erymas	Euphorbus	Aenius
Pronous	Hippothous	Ophelestes
Thestor	Schedius	Hector

Aphrodite XXXI

So many dead in the war, so many threads cut short. None of them by my hand, but all of them because of my plan. It's strange – I've never killed anyone personally, but I caused the deaths of so, so many.

And that meant I was winning.

We'd reached the critical mass in the war. Everyone, mortal and divine, had lost someone. Everyone was grieving and crying and *angry* over who they'd lost. Everyone was ready for revenge, and they didn't care who they aimed for.

Perfect.

I hid, those first few days after my return. I let Zeus tell everyone exactly what he wanted to tell them about me; I'd get my chance later.

I hid, and I watched the carnage that would destroy the gods.

It had already started.

When Patroclus killed Sarpedon . . .
Zeus tried to save his son, and Hera only stopped him so people wouldn't riot over his hypocrisy. He hated that she was right, and he started a literal rain of blood. Ares betrayed the only person he'd ever loved, which made Zeus banish his once-favourite daughter to an inescapable prison.

The gods were already fraying, but the mortals weren't done yet.

So Hector killed Patroclus

As revenge for Sarpedon, as revenge for the Trojans Patroclus took down as part of a lie, and he did it because I cleared a path for them to meet. My husband made the armour Patroclus was wearing, and I knew where its weak spots were. I'd told Hector, and when he thrust his spear, he knew exactly where to put it. Nobody saw me go down, because no one, not even Apollo, knew the palace in Troy as well as I did.

Athena panicked after Patroclus' death. She blamed my husband for shoddy workmanship – a bigger insult to him than my continued affair with his brother ever was – and he shouted back that it wasn't his fault that her fighters didn't know how to fight.

'I will show you how I fight,' she bellowed. Centuries of needling her, and I'd never seen her so out of control. She went to Odysseus, and had him stir up the Greeks. Got them fighting again. Sent for reinforcements. In case that wasn't enough, she went to Achilles, to bribe him into fighting, to promise eternal glory in her name, but she was met with sobbing through his tent.

'Leave him be,' Thetis told her. 'He's mourning.'

'He has a job to do, and I hardly think a nymph is in a position to question the will of a goddess.'

'I am a *nereid*.' The gods had forgotten how to speak. Everything came out as a yell, every voice wavered as if it could break into tears at any moment.

'Achilles,' Athena insisted. 'If you mourn this boy, show them. Make them feel the pain you feel.'

Achilles came out of the tent. He put his armour back on. And he made himself known.

So Achilles killed Hector

Because Hector killed Patroclus. Because Achilles loved Patroclus.

And Apollo lost any cool he'd ever had. Hector was Troy, and he was dead, and that wasn't enough for Achilles. He'd taken what Athena said to heart – who knew she was capable of stirring such emotions? – and tied Hector's body to the back of his chariot. He dragged it as fast as his horses would go around the city walls until the body's bones broke and the skin tore off and the blood leached out, and still, Achilles rode it further. Death alone was not enough to wipe away his suffering, and the world had to know.

Rumours of my banishment hadn't yet reached the mortals, so Helen prayed to me to retrieve the body. She called me her sister, her friend, everything I'd asked her to call me, but she told me she needed a goddess. Bad luck, Helen.

Apollo went, though, to get Hector's body. He begged his sister to help, but Artemis said no, and he retaliated by killing her best friend, her great platonic love.[94] She turned her back on him. The gods weren't just falling apart at the seams, because Apollo and Artemis weren't *seams*. They were the fabric; they were the strongest section of the tapestry, the only part of the family who loved each other unquestioningly, the only backs that always had each other, and the war was ripping them apart.

Nearly there.

Achilles returned the body, or what was left of it, but it wasn't enough. Not for Apollo, not when he was losing more than a man, when his legacy was disappearing into the sand.

The god of archery wanted payback.

---

[94] Orion. —A

So Paris killed Achilles

Because Apollo stood behind him and held his arms in exactly the right spot to shoot. He knew the weak spot in the armour too. We all knew by then, every weakness, every vulnerability. Paris, who I chose for his fairness, who openly told the world of his deficiencies on the battlefield, who was only in any of this for love, did it in the end. He killed the greatest fighter the mortals had, shot him right in the ankle, the only spot Thetis couldn't protect.

The rest of the afternoon was lost to Thetis' screaming.

She went to Olympus to protest the death she always knew was coming, the death that had come and gone. She started smashing vases, right in the middle of the council room, shouting until even Zeus had to bear witness.

'What are you doing, woman?'

'Destroying everything you love.' She said it calmly, despite smashing a vase midway through the sentence.

'What's wrong with you?'

'You did this.' She pointed down, way down, to where the battle still raged. 'You've killed him.'

Zeus looked to Hera. '*You* said they'd be angry if I saved Sarpedon. You said it'd be okay if I let him die.'

'I said it wouldn't be okay if you didn't. There's a difference. You never listen to me—'

'Maybe I would if you ever stopped bloody talking.'

Thetis smashed another vase, saving them the rest of the argument. It would come, though. Now Achilles and Hector were dead, the heads of their respective armies chopped off, the rest of the battle would fall apart. There was nothing left to fight for.

But Thetis wasn't done. Her shouts were punctuated by smashing.

'You made them think that being remembered was more important than living.'

Smash.

'You wanted the heroes you're so afraid of.'

Smash.

'You decided our children had to die with yours.'

Smash.

'You made me get married to someone I didn't love.'

Smash.

'You made me have the baby I didn't want.'

Smash.

'It's your fault I love him.'

Smash.

'And it's your fault he's gone.'

Thetis wept, for there were no more vases to smash.

'Get out of here,' Zeus said. 'And the rest of you, shut up, before I throw you in Tartarus with the rest of the traitors.'

No one shut up.

'I will do it,' Zeus said, more loudly this time. 'I've done it before.'

Still nothing, no awareness, no attention, nothing. His words were lost amidst a thousand small arguments.

'LISTEN TO ME.'

Absolutely nothing. Beautiful. The king was panicking now. You can't be a leader without followers.

'I banished Aphrodite,' he yelled. That shut them up. 'She was a fraud and a liar. She did not belong in this house. I *banished* her to Tartarus. And I could do the same to all of you.'

Finally.

He'd told them I was gone.

I could start planning my return now.

Aphrodite XXXII

'But when, Prom?'

Yes, I was talking to a statue. I didn't have a lot of other options. It was either his statue or the threads or my goose, but Zeus was always visiting the threads and I wasn't ready for him to see me yet, and my goose was in a bitey mood, so the statue it was.

'I don't want to go back there until I know what's happening. You only get to come back from the dead so many times.'

No one dramatically spat out their wine the last time I strolled into Olympus. I wanted someone to spit out their wine this time.

'And what's happening doesn't make any sense.'

The war should have been over, but the mortals just kept coming. Every day, more reinforcements arrived, ready to die for a cause they didn't believe in. First it was Neoptolemus, a surprise son of Achilles', who showed up and killed the entire Trojan royal family, bumping Aeneas up entirely too high in the chain of succession. Then it was the Amazons, who, being all women and entirely anti-marriage, had *no* stakes in the game about who would marry Helen. They arrived with, seemingly, the sole purpose of standing there ready to be killed by the prodigal son, who did so gleefully.

I was enjoying the freedom and relative invisibility of being presumed dead. It let me get into all kinds of places where I had no excuse to be. I didn't want to trade that in until it was worth it.

'What's going on? It's like Zeus doesn't want the war to end, but I started the war to get rid of him.'

The statue, of course, said nothing, but we have imaginations for a reason. I tried putting on his voice, to see if it would bring his thoughts out of me.

'Yes, well it certainly is illogical, so we must consider what forces can drive a person to the illogical.'

I hit my head against the mountain.

'Everything Zeus does is illogical, Prom. Please tell me the plan doesn't hinge on how well I know Zeus.'

The plan hinged on how well I knew Zeus.

'Fine. What do we know about Zeus, then?'

He was the god of the sky and the king of the gods. All he ever wanted was to be the king of the gods. He overthrew his father to get it. He punished his children to keep it. He didn't trust anyone because he was so scared of losing it. He threw me into Tartarus because I proved his paranoia right.

'He must be spiralling now, huh?' I said. If he couldn't trust me, his daughter who he'd loved for millennia, the one with no family other than him, who could he trust? Who could he know wasn't hiding a betrayal? 'He doesn't have anyone, does he?'

As the person who said this to an actual statue, you can trust that was an expert opinion on loneliness.

He wanted this, not because he wanted to change the world, like I did, but because he was *afraid* of it. He was scared of the race that he made, scared they were coming for him, that one day they'd take his power from him, that one day they wouldn't need us anymore. Better to destroy them and start again.

I wanted a war, but Zeus wanted a *genocide*.

We used to watch humanity together, point to our favourites, name them. They were *ours*.

I hit my head again, in case it helped.

I did this. I built the pyre, gathered the kindling, even lit the spark, fucking gift-wrapped the war Zeus wanted and handed it to him, all the while smiling at my own cleverness.

'How is he doing this? I cheated. I used *Fate*.'

There are new Fates, Prom told me, all those years ago. Zeus has been visiting them.

'He cheated too? Are you fucking kidding me?' Maybe that was more outrage than I deserved, but you know what, I am Fate. I earned it. I spent my years in the cave and the shadows. I lived in fear of the threads absorbing me if I looked too closely at them. I came by my cheating honestly, and he got to stroll in and use it? Not just to shorten lives or stretch them out or see what was coming – because this extension on the war wasn't what I'd seen – but to change it when I never could?

The king of the gods was beating me at my own game.

She who controls knowledge controls the world. Prom told me that too. And Zeus was controlling it better than me.

Well, this was one bit of power I could take away from him.

I had a fire to start.

Aphrodite XXXIII

I was going home.

Back to Cyprus, back to my cave. Still mine, after all these years.

The evidence was there. It wasn't subtle; it wasn't some nuanced lean on the threads. It was messy, ugly, almost displayed for me to see. It wasn't some mere tangle – Zeus had made a single, giant, knot, with every thread in sight wrapped into it, no matter how much my sisters fussed at its edges.

'How long?' I demanded. 'How long has Zeus been changing it?'

They looked at each other, whole conversations passing in that glance.

'Since he first found us.'

No wonder I couldn't fucking *win*. I'd seen his fingerprints in the threads before, but this ran deeper. He'd tied every life in our world to him, bound them so strictly there could be no escape from him.

Centuries I spent plotting, and there was never any hope at all.

'Can you change them like this?' I asked. Another big, complicated look. 'I can't. I could weave them, break them, join them if I really had to, but I couldn't— I couldn't do this.'

I didn't sob. I didn't throw a tantrum because the king of the gods was better than me at the only thing I was born to do. I *didn't*.

'No,' they said finally. 'It's only him. He's special.'

I think he had enough advantages.

'Sisters,' I said. 'You'll want to get out of the way.'

The threads were still tightly wound around their hands, though they were moving less frenetically than they had on my recent visits.

I was sick of it. All of it.

We didn't deserve Fate. It was meant to be a balm to the crushing uncertainty of the world, and we'd turned it into a weapon, something we tortured people with. We ignored the good and maddened ourselves with the bad. We destroyed everything around us in the vain hope that once again, we were going to change a future that had been set in thread.

A future a tyrant had been controlling all along.

No more.

Once upon a time, I had three lightning bolts.

One for Anchises, and for my pride.

One for Ouranos, and outdoing my father.

One left, for freedom.

I pulled the bolt from my back and held it in my hands. It felt unnatural – I didn't know if I should hold it like a sword or a spear, and even if I were meant to, I didn't *know* how to hold a sword or a spear. It didn't matter; just holding it was the ultimate threat. It's what they were built to be.

'Leave. Now,' I told them. I didn't want to hurt them.

'This is our home.'

'This is a fucking *cave*,' I shouted. Condensation dripped and fell into stagnant water at the back. Bugs circled around it. There were no bugs in Olympus. Nothing less than a god was allowed to survive there. Nothing but me.

One of them gripped the thread so tightly in her hand it cut through her skin, a drop of blood landing atop her foot and balancing there, precocious, precarious, prepared for any eventuality. Blood like mine. They were my family, and I *hated* them. I hated them for not seeing the poison in this place, for not seeing the pain and damage it wrought, for not seeing how it infected the mind and twisted, how it created a barrier between you and the world, stopped you ever living at all.

While they were there, I could never forget what I used to be.

'This is our home,' they repeated.

I couldn't bear to argue, and I couldn't stand to listen. 'Get out! *Please.*'

'Leave us be.'

'No,' I shouted, and it reverberated. The echo grew louder and louder, until I wondered if Echo[95] herself was there to help me. It was the sound of every *no* I should have said and all the ones I never could. It was a lifetime of lying and agreeing and cajoling. It was asking people to stare at me, because then they never looked at the real *me*.

It was all of that, and it was none of it.

I was angry. I did it because I was *angry*, so fucking furious I could barely hold still, and my hands clenched and unclenched like they were looking for something to throw. I did it because I wanted to find someone, anyone, hunt them down and yell at them until they knew what their stupid world had done. I did it because I couldn't even be the best at *this*. I did it because I needed to be free.

You don't need a thousand reasons to act a certain way. Sometimes, you only need one.

---

[95] Echo. Nice girl, bit meek. Cursed to only repeat back what she's heard – a Hera special. Otherwise irrelevant. —A

'**What are you going to do?**'.

'I'm destroying Fate.'

'*Why?*'

'So I can have a fucking life.'

That's all I ever wanted. To live. To have people who love me. To make stupid day-to-day choices and not *know,* for a fact, how they were going to work out.

'Please, go now.'

They didn't move.

I threw the bolt.

I didn't light fires often – you don't need to in Olympus where Hestia keeps the hearth roaring, and I especially didn't because I was married to the god of flame and I dated Ares, who had no specific connection to fire but did occasionally set things alight when they pissed him off – but I knew you needed fuel, and I had that in abundance.

I might have been destroying the world. Killing every mortal, every god. I didn't know, couldn't know, and that was *wonderful* and *terrifying,* but I did it anyway, because the world staying exactly as it was? That was the worst option I could imagine.

The bolt shattered into sparks when it hit the knot. They smouldered for one long moment and then dimmed. My heart stopped in my chest. I had no more bolts, no other options, and I'd staked everything on this. The fire couldn't go out.

I rushed over to that infuriating, giant, knot of Zeus', and I blew on it, as hard as I could.

And the fire came.

It leaped to life, like magic between my fingers, and I wondered wildly if this was how Prometheus felt, when he gave those flames to humanity. If this was how it felt to be a god.

The threads tried to flex away as the fire spread, but it was a cave. A limited space. And there was so much to burn.

I ran past the fire, right to the back where I'd kept *my* tapestry, everything that had been, everything I'd woven, everything I'd had to learn by myself when these three got to have each other.

It was still there. They'd kept it. Everything I did for all those years when I was alone, it was remembered. The life I'd been running from, the life I thought died with Prometheus, it was never gone at all.

I ran past the spot where Prometheus and I first had sex, the point where *I* first had sex, back when I was awkward and lanky and hopeful that just *not looking* at the future would be enough to pretend it wasn't set.

It was all bullshit.

I pulled it down. I pulled it all fucking down, from the dumpiest ends I made right at the beginning when there were so few people and I didn't know how to weave. They tickled when my fingers brushed against them, a gentle reminder of when we used to be friends. It didn't stop me throwing them into the fire.

I went to every corner of that cave and I took the threads. Every nook and cranny I remembered finding them hiding in and asking *what are you doing in there?* back when they were the only thing I could talk to.

I hated them and I loved them and they were who I always was and they were the thing that was keeping me from being anyone I wanted to be, and it was all of it. All at once.

They burned.

The flames turned gold, like ichor. Maybe this would make the gods mortal, now, without that line to hold them to life, without the certain belief that they couldn't die; maybe it would crumble around them, and they would be just like everyone else.

Maybe maybe maybe.

I didn't know. No one did. Not anymore.

What a wonderful thing it is, to not know.

I found every thread. I needed to get all of them, or they could come back, split and grow until the weight of them got so heavy I was dragged back here.

I pulled them from my wrists and my ankles. They were sticking again, wrapped all the way up to my shoulders. They covered my midriff and wound through my hair.

I pulled off my clothes, and they went into the fire too.

Everything must go.

I took the dagger that was strapped to my thigh and sliced through my hair. I scraped my scalp with the knife, getting every last bit of it into the flames.

Maybe people wouldn't think I was beautiful without it, but I didn't need that anymore.

The new Fates screamed as the fire rose, but I didn't see them while it burned. I don't know what happened to them, after. I hope they ran. I hope they chose new names and new faces and new titles, but I don't know.

I couldn't look away from the destruction.

Fate burned, and I finally learned how to breathe.

Aphrodite XXXIV

If I'd known destroying everything I'd ever known was all I needed to be free, I would have done it years ago.

My best weapon was gone, but that didn't mean I was done fighting.

I hadn't been away from Olympus long – days at the most – but it was enough for Zeus to build his own pyre. He told the gods how he'd disposed of me, deployed his ultimate threat, and banished me to a place it was impossible to escape from.

They were still living it large, the gods. I might have burned their threads, but they were too entrenched to fall apart right away. They'd have to do that to each other.

I know there was a war on, and there were other things I could have been doing, but appearances are important, so I made a diversion. I went to Lemnos and bathed in the waters there, entirely sure now of the sins I was meant to be cleansing from myself, and entirely sure the waters wouldn't work for that. I looked at the frogs, watched them argue: *brekekekex koax koax*. I anointed my skin to glisten like them.

I had no hair left to plait, but I've never needed hair to be beautiful. I wreathed myself in flowers and nothing else, letting their scents trail behind me. I didn't need jewellery or riches. I was the gem.

I let my voice drop back to its natural register. I laughed, and it was a burr in the beauty around me. It was rough and untrained, and the frogs ran from me.

Perfect.

My goose still came when I called him. He didn't give a shit whether I was a god or a mortal or something else entirely. As long as I let him *honk*, he was happy. He carried me home, my other home, the home that had known me all the years where I recognised myself.

There was no uproar as I arrived. No one, not even Hestia, was paying attention to the new arrivals. The gods fought among themselves, throwing curses and throwing rocks, their world getting smaller and smaller with every passing moment as they lost sight of everything but themselves.

It was only as I reached the inner circle that eyes landed on me.

Then I was wreathed in shock, wrapped in gasps. Wine was spat – about time – and chests clutched.

'Aphrodite,' Zeus growled. He opened his mouth to say more. He had more to say, I was sure, but the gods had gathered around us, by then. All eyes on us. Just how I liked it. 'Let's go. I need a word.'

He needs a word. He needs a word. He needs a word. It echoed behind us, that one line passed and mutated between layers and layers of onlookers.

'We can talk here.'

'Fine. Everyone else. Out.'

They didn't move.

'You know what I can do to you if you don't.'

Still, they didn't move. Another echo passed back. *She got out. She got out. She got out.*

I got out. I was free.

His bolts rose to his hands.

'Do you *want* to go to Tartarus?'

I smiled at him, at them, and the gods stayed right where they were. The king was crumbling. His words got louder and his voice less confident with every passing moment, turning back into the child he used to be.

'What do you want?' he said to me.

'Let's take a walk.'

'You *just* said you wanted to stay here.'

'I changed my mind.' It was all a power move, obviously. I wanted to show him how dangerous I was. I wanted him to think my presence was a threat. I didn't have any weapons left, but I could *bluff*.

We took off. I looped an arm through his, looking for all the world like a young couple taking a stroll.

He ripped his hand away. 'I killed you. How are you here?'

'Technically, you cast me into Tartarus.'

'A prison. I threw you into a prison that can't be escaped.'

'It seems like it *can* be escaped.'

'Impossible.'

'Are you imagining me then?' I raised an eyebrow at him. I spent *years* perfecting that eyebrow. 'What about the other gods? Are they imagining that someone could walk in and out of Tartarus at will?'

'You couldn't.'

'No?' He was right but he didn't know that. 'I suppose there's something stopping me going back then, raising the generations before you, taking the world back in their name.'

Ha. The new world would be written in my name, or none at all.

'You wouldn't.'

'Wouldn't I?' I dragged it out, I'll admit it. I enjoyed seeing him squirm in front of me.

'What do you want?'

There we were. Mission achieved. What was a king without his ultimate threat? What was someone who led by fear when you took away his weapons?

A man who'd give me everything I wanted.

'Tell the gods you lied.'

'What?'

'About me – tell them you lied. Tell them it was all an enormous joke.'

'I don't understand. What's the joke?'

You.

'It doesn't matter. Tell them I can't have been unfaithful or a traitor or any of that, because I'm your favourite. Tell them I belong here, and you never would have banished me, so it must have been a joke.'

'—'

'Make me a *god*, Zeus.'

What he said became true. I didn't like it, but it did. He could tell the world that Atlas was dead, and even if it made no sense, people would believe it. He could tell them I was made of nothing but clay, and I would melt where I stood, or he could tell them I was a goddess and immortalise me.

'Why?'

'*Or*, I could tell them I broke out of your inescapable prison, which must mean I have more power than you and they should follow me instead.'

'I hate you.'

'You're a little late to that party, honey.'

We finished our loop, returned to the waiting gods. Their whispers had grown to a roar, crushing Zeus, lifting me.

'Everyone,' he said. 'My favourite daughter has returned.'

They looked confused. They were used to inconsistency from the king, but this was another level.

'She has been doing important work on my behalf during the war. All that other stuff was just cover. To weed out the traitors among us. For only a traitor would question the love I have for Aphrodite.'

They cheered then. They cheered for *me*.

I was back, with unwavering, unremovable support behind me. It did not matter how many lies my story was built on, as long as I had the right people repeating it.

I had Zeus by the balls, and that was *so much better* than cutting them off.

I won.

As if on cue, Troy burst into flames.

Aeneas Note I

My son,

It's now. Troy falls now. Get out of there. I will provide you with a ship, with men, with everything you need to found the next great nation. It will be more than you've ever dreamed, my love; it will last longer in the hearts of men than any civilisation ever has, and our line will be at the core of it. I promise.

I've asked so much of you, but we're nearly there. Just one more day. Survive. Please.

Your mother,
Aphrodite

Aphrodite XXXV

Troy burned. Destroying Fate didn't change the fact that there was a war on; it just gave them the freedom to end it.

While both armies reeled from the loss of, well, everyone, Odysseus hatched a plan. The Greeks told the Trojans they were surrendering and here, take this *giant wooden horse* as a sign of our retreat.

Really.

A. Giant. Wooden. Horse.

They built that horse very quickly, all things considered, with the kind of teamwork neither army had demonstrated up until that point. I wondered if we'd been keeping that from them.

Regardless, the Trojans said yes, that seems like a good and unsuspicious gift. We like horses.

You fight to give the world the power of choice, of influence in their own outcomes; you destroy your own home so you can gift the world *freedom*, and they use it to build a giant wooden horse.

I'd never missed Prometheus so much as when it rolled through the gates. I had no one to laugh with.

The gods didn't interfere. They were too caught up fighting each other on Olympus.

The Trojans left the horse in the middle of the city that night, unguarded, for who would be suspicious of a giant, wooden horse?

Helen, apparently. I'd forgotten about Helen. I didn't mean to, but I made her for a purpose and she'd done it – she started my war. In retrospect, I shouldn't have been surprised when she was angry. She walked around the horse, throwing her voice, pretending to be every woman that the men inside – of course there were men inside; why else would you build a giant wooden horse? – loved and left at home, torturing them with the unlikeliness of their return.

You give the people freedom, and they get their revenge.

I didn't stay to watch. In mere moments, a hundred and nine Greek soldiers would exit the horse and murder their way out, and I needed to make sure my son wasn't one of their victims.

With so many of the royal family dead, my son had been promoted from a second cousin once removed into full princely status. He slept in the palace.

'Aeneas, get up.'

He rolled over.

'Aeneas, it is time.'

Still, he didn't wake. I grabbed him by the bedclothes and pulled him up.

'It's the middle of the night, did you ha— Mother.'

'Yes. Aeneas. We have to go. The city burns.' I could smell the smoke blowing through the streets, feel the temperature rising around us.

'I have to—'

'No, we have to go now.'

'My things—'

'I will get you new things.'

'My father—'

'Anchises is still alive?'

'I have cared for him, as a pious son does.' Someone, save me from pious sons. 'I will not leave without him.'

'Aeneas, we have a city to found, a great new civ—'

'Yes, I read your notes, Mother, it sounds lovely, but I will not leave without my father.'

I could have shouted. I could have drawn a weapon. I could have used the fact that I was immortal and he was not to cow him and bend him to my will. I could have made him afraid, and he would have run from the city faster than I could blink.

But I couldn't do any of that, because it was no longer in his Fate that he would found a city; it was no longer a given that he would spread word of me, and this world was changing. I'd seen everything that came from Zeus being at the centre of it, and I couldn't have that again. This new world would be *mine*.

Sons overthrow their fathers, but they honour their mothers.

But I needed him to love me first. I was as beholden to him as he was to me.

'Fine. We will get your father, and then we must leave.'

'Thank you, Mother.'

'Anything for my favourite son.'

He carried Anchises on his back. He didn't ask for my help with him, and I wouldn't have given it. It didn't matter how much I needed our son to love me; I'd never touch that man again.

I talked, quickly, as the city burned, rambling. There was no time. There were things he had to know.

'Do you remember when I used to visit you as a child?'

'We can talk about this later.'

'Humour me.'

'You told me stories.'

'Do you remember them?'

'Yes, Mother.'

'They're important, Aeneas. They're the truth, and you have to tell people. You have to tell them about your mother.'

'You're scaring me.'

'Don't mind that. Think of the new world. Son, it's going to be so beautiful . . .'

'I was thinking marble—'

'You have to teach them, okay? That everything is different. *They* can be different.'

'Why would they want to be different?'

'The city is on *fire*, Aeneas.'

'There is that.'

'So you go to the men I found for you, and you tell them the stories I taught you, and you make them true – do you understand? What we say now will become the truth.'

'But it is the truth?'

'That's right. Tell them that. We've fought so hard to change the world. Now is the time. *Change it.* Make space for everyone. Not just the kings. Not just the heroes.'

'Mother,' he said, breathing heavily now. 'What's happening in Olympus?'

He pointed up, far up into the sky, further than mortal eyes should have been able to see, but true enough, there it was.

'It seems to be on fire.'

Aphrodite XXXVI

I did it. Troy burned, and Olympus burned too.

No one's sure how it started, if the flames leaped up from Troy, or if the embers were caught on the wind and carried there, or if it was something less benign than that. If it was Thetis starting something because her son's anger hadn't come from nowhere, or if it was Ares in a rage, or Zeus in a panic, getting loose with his lightning bolts.

It doesn't matter how it started. No one stopped it. Only Hestia tried. The poor dear ran around with a pail of water, which may as well have had a hole in the bottom for all the good it did her.

Artemis was pulling Apollo's hair. Poseidon was flooding Athena's house. Hera was throwing Zeus' things as far as her arms could handle, and around them, Olympus burned, catching everything, until the sole spot without flames was Hestia's hearth.

The council rooms went first, our feasting tables turned to ashes. It spread outwards from there, through beautiful gardens and well-organised pathways, through spots for revelling and some of my favourite hideaways with Ares. The fire blew through to the palaces, destroying everyone else's homes as surely as I'd destroyed mine.

It took their clothes, their jewels, their trophies, their symbols.

Only then did the gods take notice.

Symbols are so important when you're a god, when you're speaking on the scale of millennia and you can change your face. They're how people remember you. They're what people use to identify you, to remind themselves of who you were.

They're what *we* used to remind ourselves of who we were. Each one was a memento of its own battle, its own victory, another spot carved out in the world that belonged to you. It wasn't a small gift when Zeus gave me two birds. It was more power, more space, a great reward for the difficult task of loving him.

Those symbols were us, and we were them.

We scrambled to save them, me included. Athena got her owl; Hera kept her peacocks; Poseidon clutched his trident like he was afraid someone would come and rip it from his hands.

We couldn't save everything.

Olympus burned, and Troy burned beneath it. The mortals didn't call out to us as their homes were destroyed. We had let them down so many times while they suffered that they didn't appeal or pray. They didn't feed us with the belief we all needed to keep going, and so, in all of that, our names burned, too.[96]

We changed, because we had to, because we'd destroyed the old world, and the old versions of ourselves couldn't exist in the new. The ground and the air around us knew it, even if the others couldn't accept it yet.

I knew.

Aphrodite was dead, and I had killed her.

I'd done what I set out to do: destroyed that terrible old routine, left room for something better to grow, and I was a part of that.

---

[96] Apart from Apollo, who had trouble letting go. —A

So, there you go. That's me. Not a goddess, not a friend, not even a lover by the end of it.

I got what I wanted. The cost was so high, and I won't know for so long if it was worth it, but it feels worth it right now, to finally be able to breathe.

I wanted a family, and I lied my way into one, but they weren't what I thought a family was supposed to be. They loved conditionally, and they hurt indiscriminately. They didn't love me the way I thought love was supposed to work.

Power, family, home, love: I got all of it, and it wasn't enough.

I did more to become the goddess of love in destroying the threads of Fate than I ever did in Olympus. I couldn't just tell people who they were going to marry anymore. They were allowed to choose.

I don't know if destroying the threads of Fate has actually freed the future and given us possibilities again, or if it only means we don't know what will come. Prometheus, I'm sure, would have said there was no difference.

It feels like there's a difference.

The threads don't grow around my wrists anymore. Maybe I've destroyed them, or maybe it was just me rejecting them, finally, turning my back on what I was, that did it.

And that feels so very lonely.

I've lied so much. I've changed and reinvented myself so many times – an advantage, right now, as all the gods try to find themselves in the ashes, and I already have a new identity prepared, a prophet ready to go – that I'm the last person alive who remembers who I used to be, the last relevant person who knows what the world looked like before the gods. I've destroyed the records and rewritten the narrative over and over until it fits the way I want it to, until even I can't remember the details of it quite right.

Is Zeus my father? Or Ouranos? Is Dione in there? Am I a Fate or a goddess or a fraud?

I don't know, and there's no one left to tell me what was real.

I'm trying something different.

My life will not be stored in the annals of the gods. The mortals can have it, protect it the best they can. Aeneas will do everything he was once upon a time fated to do. By definition, he has to be capable of it, and that's enough. I'll make it true.

He will found a city. The world we knew will never be entirely gone, but this new place will advance faster and stronger, and it will burn brighter than the old. It will take more of the good from here and less of the bad. It will be better.

He will have children, and he will tell them about his mother, the goddess, she who gave life to all of them. They will worship me because I'm family.

It won't be enough. I know that now. It won't be enough for me that it's better, because it won't be perfect – so, one day, I will destroy that new place too.

We have our cycles, boys overthrowing their fathers, rulers becoming dictators, lovers turning to enemies. Wars and famines and fights and families – all of it comes round again and again and again. This will be my cycle. We will remake and destroy every world, and it'll get better each time, until one day I can find a place that's enough.

But for now, there's a new world at my fingertips.

Time to start again.

THE TIME AFTER

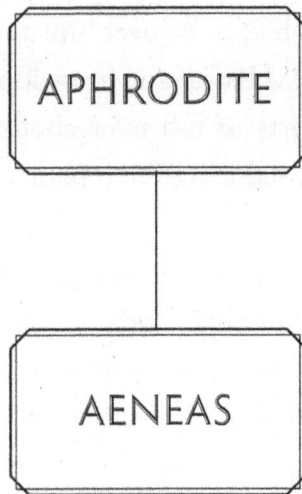

```
┌─────────────────────┐
│                     │
│     APHRODITE       │
│                     │
└─────────────────────┘
          │
          │
┌─────────────────────┐
│                     │
│      AENEAS         │
│                     │
└─────────────────────┘
```

Aeneas I

The night I realised who my mother was, my father was profoundly drunk. Some sickness had come over him and no amount of wine would slake his thirst. His tongue grew looser and looser as he told his friends all sorts of tall tales about his youth: running races, stealing horses, seducing Olympians. My mother, he said, the goddess of love.

The world, and my place in it, began to twist around me, but that only lasted a moment, before a bolt of lightning came hurtling from the sky and gave us other things to worry about.

The lightning landed square across my father's back, and he never walked again.

But I'm not here to talk about my father.

I'm here to talk about my mother.

I might not have realised the significance, but I lived with her, when I was very young, the only mortal I know of to have called Olympus *home*. I don't remember much of it – as a child, I assumed it was just another country, Phrygia, perhaps – but I remember the beautiful voices that sang to me, the stories they told.

That was all I needed to know.

After my earliest years, my mother returned me to my father, leaving my memories of her home blurry, and it was only after his lapse of the tongue that she came back to see me.

She wasn't soft, the goddess of love. She demanded the best of me, and, more than any young man I knew, I had to strive to make her believe I was giving her that.

'You must be stronger than the others, Aeneas, and you must be brave. You have to survive.'

Survive. It was the constant refrain of my youth, as though monsters were waiting behind every door for me, the ground always ready to split beneath my feet, but I never felt in any danger. I never even broke a bone, but still I was careful. I don't know who it was who paralysed my father, but just the question of it was enough to convince me I didn't want to disappoint my mother.

Besides, I loved her.

She didn't come to visit me on any particular schedule, nor did she answer my bids for attention – she was not biddable, I suppose – but she did come. If I had done well in my lessons when she visited, if I showed I was worthy of her, she would tell me stories, and I desperately needed those.

'I thought we might talk about how I was born.'

'That sounds brilliant.'

'I was born at the end of one great civilisation and the beginning of another—'

'Like me.'

'Are you in the habit of interrupting the gods, Aeneas?'

'I'm sorry, Mother, I—'

'Don't fret now, just do better and you'll make me proud one day. Now, where was I?'

'The end of a great civilisation?'

'Yes, the rule of Ouranos and Gaia, who were . . .' And so

she went, her words back and forth between stern and loving, promising and demanding.

We never fought, before the war started, but when it came, it was constant, with her demanding that I stay for longer, to only go at the very end, and my refusing. It was my responsibility to fight for my people.

'I wasn't aware that Helen was *your* wife,' my mother said.

'You love Helen. Are you not pleased that I wish to protect her?'

'You don't have to worry about any of the politics right now; you just have to survive this. When the war is over, it will be your job to—'

'Start the next great age, I know.' That *other* common refrain from my childhood.

'To tell my story, Aeneas. To make the world know your own glorious heritage.'

Eventually, the war could not be avoided. Our cattle were stolen, enough of an insult that I could hide myself away no longer.

I survived the Trojan war by dint of some excellent fortune and the graciousness of my mother. I did as she asked of me. I was strong, brave, pious, and I survived.

When the walls fell and the city burned, she came to get me. She saved me so I could carry her name.

She brought me here to speak.

'It's thanks to my mother that we're all here together, my loyal men, with the opportunity to create a better world than we have ever known. So, let me tell you about her. She is the oldest of the gods, the most beautiful and loving—'

'. . . Calm down, Oedipus.'

'But do not mistake her love for naivety, for she does not suffer fools lightly. She herself never had any opportunity for foolishness, born as she was at the end of one great civilisation and the beginning of another, battles raging on every side of her from her very first breath.

'That war – between the Titans and their parents – lasted many terrible decades, splitting the land around us and giving way to the oceans. It was violent and bloody, the passion of her ancestors growing with every passing day, until it seemed too much for this world to hold, and *that* day arrived. The day my mother was born. The day the Titans won the war.

'It was a battle between kings, and the two of them fought alone in the very eye of the storm that brewed around them, the wind and the waves growing so great not a word could be heard, not even shouted by the immortals themselves.

'They fought feverishly, exchanging blow after blow after blow. So closely were they matched that it seemed this fight could go on forever, but the king of the Titans had other ideas.

'He leaped at his father, sickle in hand, channelling all of his fear and anger and desperation into a single, perfect strike, and, with that, it was over. In just one movement, he'd castrated his father, leaving his blood to drop into the water between them.

'They thought nothing of it, those arrogant kings, but from that blood, a woman sprang to life, and she has done more with that life than either of them could have ever dreamed.

'Before she had even taken a breath, her strength and her beauty called to all the animals in the oceans. They flocked around her, lifting her, pushing her to shore atop a scallop shell. Wreathed in flowers, she rose from the sea foam, the most breathtaking creature to ever grace this Earth.

'She is the goddess Venus, the mother of Rome.'

Author's Note II

Firstly, I'd like to credit and thank Ian Johnston for his wonderfully comprehensive list[97] of all of the injuries and deaths in the Iliad, from which the chapter The Dead is drawn.

Secondly, I should talk about sources, choices, and the futile quest for accuracy. From here on out, I'm going to talk about specific details in this book, so if you're reading this before the main text, I admire your ambition, but consider yourself warned.

In Greek mythology, there are many sources, and sometimes they directly contradict each other. With Aphrodite, it starts at the very beginning. Hesiod has her born from Ouranos' testicles when they're thrown into the ocean, but Homer has her as the daughter of Zeus and Dione. It's literally impossible for both of these things to be true.

These contradictions are something I've loved playing with in *Aphrodite*. Where I could, I've blended versions together, though sometimes I have just chosen one version, either because I personally love it – looking at you, Roman fresco of Eros riding a crab – or because it makes more sense in the story I'm trying to tell.

This means that, at points, I've taken a small reference and

---

[97] Here! https://johnstoniatexts.x10host.com/homer/iliaddeaths.htm

turned it into something much bigger, like with Aphrodite being a Fate. Pausanias *did* describe an inscription at the Temple of Aphrodite where she's referred to as the oldest of the Fates, but it's not an aspect of her character that's often spoken about.

At other points, I've changed the narrative.

Most notably, I killed Prometheus. Usually, Perseus kills Atlas instead, but this has always seemed problematic to me for a few reasons.

One, Perseus is Herc's great-grandfather, and Atlas is a key part of Herc's eleventh labour (fetching one of the Apples of the Hesperides). This would have been rather more difficult for Herc if Atlas had previously been turned to stone.

Two, if Prometheus is known for any one thing, I don't think it's forethought. It's meddling. The man cannot leave humanity well enough alone, no matter the consequences. Often , Prometheus is eventually released from his torture (by Herc), and then just... fizzles into obscurity. Given how perpetually involved he was prior to the mountain-eagle-liver situation, I can't imagine him taking that kind of backseat, unless he was forced to by, say, being turned into stone.

And three, in the stories where Prometheus *is* freed, I've seen all of the horrors he experienced explained away by giving him the knowledge that he will eventually be freed. It's used to take away from the sacrifice he makes, and that's never sat right with me.

It is a big change, so I wanted to explain why I made it. If you do fancy more Prometheus content, I highly recommend Prometheus Bound by Aeschylus (maybe, there's much debate). It's my favourite of the ancient plays, and half the reason he's such a prominent character in this book.

No story is immutable. Even dinner party anecdotes get worn away and edited over time, so it's no wonder that myths, with their wonderful longevity, change with every retelling too. I hope you enjoy this version of Aphrodite, it's been a delight for me to write.